TAKING IT ALL

PART FOUR OF THE STARCHILD SERIES

BOBBIE FALIN

Taking It All

The Starchild Series, Volume 4

Bobbie Falin

Published by High Flying Press, 2025.

TAKING IT ALL

First edition. December 17, 2025.

ISBN: 978-1736642221

Written by Bobbie Falin.

Table of Contents

To my Sammy, forever

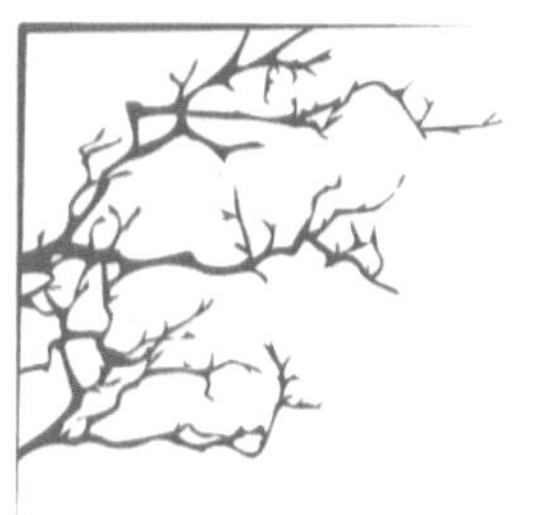

Chapter 79
Razek

RAZEK'S METAL SPUR-caps clicked against stone as he made his way along the veranda. Normally, the crisp staccato would please him greatly. Today, outrage occupied the whole of his attention.

Six more dead and a new threat emerged. All because the fool would not take his counsel. Did the imbecile think their forces were unlimited?

Since his predecessor, Clackamas, had followed Araxis' order for an ill-conceived mission of revenge two thousand years too late into the swamp and lost half their force. Their numbers were dwindling with every failed attempt to recapture the girl, their worst defeat brought about by, of all things, a forest! Imminent disaster loomed over them.

He would have begged the right to kill the Ly Kai, Araxis, to remove a major obstacle to their success, but the Master made it very clear: the small, pale one must believe he was in charge at all times. Razek bowed, put on a respectful face, and masked his frustration while he wondered what his Master planned.

Hopefully, it would include a long, excruciating end for the hated Ly Kai vermin.

Let me have my vengeance when the time comes, Razek pleaded fervently. Reward me with some time to avenge the insults and humiliation your forces have endured daily.

But even in his weakened state, the arrogant creature who thought it gave the Balandra orders could burn them all to a crisp with a simple flick of desire. Curse his power! Araxis was an inferior physical and mental specimen. The dart the Geffitz warrior delivered back at the Black Tower had rendered him even more fragile. Araxis still languished while the girl, another victim of those poison darts, had moved on with annoying health and speed. Razek knew that firsthand because he'd witnessed the whole attack last night.

His efforts had finally appeared on the brink of success. The Geffitzi warriors had left the shadows of the cursed woods and were moving down an open cliff face. With no silent, unseen deadly ally to protect them, it was only a matter of time before the Balandra struck and seized the girl.

Then things fell apart.

While his troop examined the area where their elusive targets had left the forest and descended the rock face, he flew out past the boulder, testing the treacherous air currents of the escarpment for a safe descent.

He'd seen the Ly Kai female and one of the Geffitzi appear out of nowhere, startling his troops. The girl ran for the shelter of the forest while the warrior stayed behind to defend her escape. However, before slipping into the shadows, she burned one of his troops to a cinder with her cursed Ly Kai power.

And, out of nowhere, the beast had struck.

The attack was magnificent—Razek grudgingly admitted it. The creature arrived so swiftly and unexpectedly that all he could do was watch it destroy his men with awesome, ruthless efficiency.

On the cusp of the destruction, those cursed animals from the woods had emerged to chase the beast away. They took the Geffitz warrior captive and—the ultimate humiliation—ground the remains of his troop into the mud of the cliff top.

Razek was not sentimental. He would have left the bodies of his fallen comrades without a thought. But the four-legged vipers desecrating their bodies was an insult he'd been forced to endure, unanswered, in order to bring news of another failure back to the despicable creature who thought it commanded him. News which, in further insult, had been put on hold until the Ly Kai considered the time convenient to hear it.

Convenient! There was nothing convenient about dealing with Araxis! It was just a long stream of bad temper, poor judgment, and sulks. Razek did not expect anything useful from the upcoming encounter except more rage and threats, which made him even angrier. Balandra did not live under threat. Other creatures lived in fear of them. Such was the order of the world. His world.

But this was not his world.

Razek slapped at a buzzing insect—the biting, bloodsucking things were a plague in this bog of a place—and looked about.

He hated the lush green of the living forest that pressed in around the stone structures Araxis had chosen for their refuge. Immobile things that grew from the ground were for shelter and burning, or fodder for the meat he hunted. Plants definitely should not act with considered thought.

The wood here was not the same as the thing that lay further south—the thing that had taken his forces in silent, stealthy ways over the past days—but he knew it also listened and watched.

Reaching the end of the stone veranda, he stopped before a huge set of double doors heavily carved with bas-relief images. Warriors hunted strange creatures and fought horrific battles across the bronze surface. Obviously, this place once served as some sort of temple for the savage creatures who called themselves Geffitzi. It was surprising they managed such an intricate piece of artwork, he thought critically as he raised a hand to strike the ornate surface. For inferior creatures, the door showed that at the very least they properly respected the art of death.

But then, they had learned all the requisite skills for art and death as slaves under a very discerning, demanding master.

The doors swung open at the hands of two of his troops stationed inside the building. Araxis insisted on having an armed guard within his sight at all times. Razek considered it a senseless waste of resources for a creature with the ability to slay anything around it with the blink of an eye, but it also, diabolically, worked in his favor. Feeding the Ly Kai's paranoia, making him feel under threat, made him less likely to strike out in the heat of passion against the diminishing number of Balandran warriors around him.

Could the Ly Kai worm ever appreciate the symbolic honor a Balandran armed guard represented? Razek doubted it. What sort of honor did the wretched, fragile creature command with its endless whining, petty demands, and foul temper? Given free rein, Razek would have snapped his thin neck and gone after the cursed Geffitzi warriors in an all-out attack. That plan of action was more suited to his tastes. Kill them all, take the girl, and begin the long-delayed campaign of revenge and retribution the Balandra owed this world.

Razek looked forward to that. It was a simple strategy: make the creatures of this world suffer. Make them all suffer for what their ancestors dared do to the great Balandran race two thousand years ago. It would be slow, agonizing, and pure pleasure.

As the doors thudded behind him, Razek paused, allowing his eyes to adjust to the chamber's darkness.

Araxis sat next to a window at the far end of the shadowy room.

The miserable little beast was killing whatever living creatures ventured into the area around that end of the building. Irritation curled in Razek. Charred scrub trees and undergrowth were visible beyond the opening where the Ly Kai had ignited a fire during a fit of pique the previous day. Several of his men limped from minor burns suffered while putting it out.

Razek did not care whether the creatures of this world lived or died, but the forest around them, though not as sentient as the vicious woods further south, was still awake. It might have the capacity to retaliate if it suffered damage beyond what it considered tolerable. Which was why Razek's troops took the time and effort to hunt over a wide range of territory and to kill sparingly.

While this miserable wretch sat and picked repeatedly at the same scab.

Razek advanced to stop a discreet distance from the Ly Kai and ran a narrow gray tongue over his thin lips to dampen them. Speaking the bastard's language strained his upper throat with its awkward sounds, but he had no choice. It was the only way to communicate with the Ly Kai. "The forest is alive in this area," Razek said stiffly. "We should avoid drawing its attention." He wanted to grab the Ly Kai and cuff it up beside the head. To call it the fool it was. Instead, he made a slight, conciliatory bow.

Araxis twisted to scowl at him and Razek had the satisfaction of seeing that his face was spotted with the welts of insect bites, too. "If your forces did what they were ordered to do, we would not be here, and I would not have to resort to crushing vermin for entertainment."

Indeed. Did the worm think he would be crushing Balandra instead? Or perhaps he harbored thoughts of running away from certain obligations. The Ly Kai was not as clever or subtle as he thought. Razek lowered his head, as much to hide a grim smile as to feign respect. At the end of this wretched endeavor, he would give this creature a lesson or two in inflicting pain for entertainment.

The Ly Kai swatted at an insect on its arm. "Well, report, Captain." The order rang out querulously in the high, hollow space of the stone chamber.

Araxis was on edge. Perhaps he was feeling the pressure of the situation. It also meant Razek should exercise extra caution in their encounter: it would not be good for this creature to kill him out of sheer spite.

"Lord," he dipped his head deeper to indicate greater humility and respect, "I bring news."

"But not the thing I asked you to bring." Once luxurious, now grimy fabric rustled as the Ly Kai adjusted his position forward to glare at him.

"No, Lord. New foes have entered the battle. They attacked our forces and ripped them to shreds—"

"What?" The creature surged to its feet, its pale face even whiter than usual. "What attacked them? Not her—"

Razek looked back up. "No, Lord." He wanted to lie and say she had struck out at them, to see what reaction it drew. For this Ly Kai to insist they pursue his quarry so relentlessly, he behaved as if he were terrified of her. Razek often wondered how Araxis would react if forced to confront the girl face-to-face, the way he demanded the Balandra do.

"Tell me what happened, you stupid fool!" Light reflected dully off the tarnished stars of the Ly Kai's robes as he quivered in rage.

And fear. The Ly Kai stank of it. Razek drank it up, relishing the other's distress. "We were tracking. So close. The girl and a warrior came around a boulder at the top of a cliff, fleeing a huge, clawed creature." He paused to savor Araxis' horror at the thought of a threat to the girl, knowing it would fall away with his next words. "She escaped. But after its attack, a new force of extremely dangerous animals emerged from the cursed woods to drive the creature away and capture the warrior." Razek did not care about the warrior's fate beyond that, but he did care what this new threat meant for his Balandran forces. "I fear the force that reigns in the forest has begun to implement its agenda."

"First, you say the forest protected them. Now you say it sent something to interfere with them. I am tired of excuses. I want her brought to me!"

Razek did not bother to mask the anger on his gray, wrinkled features now. "We lost more resources. This cannot continue. We must plan better."

"You must plan better, Razek. She is a useless, ignorant child. How difficult can this be?"

Obviously more difficult than the Ly Kai thought. "The situation is changing. She acted to defend last night."

"Liar! I would have felt the draw of power."

Razek paused for a moment to fight a dizzying rush of fury. "She burned one of my men to a cinder." If Araxis did not understand what they were up against, he was useless to the Master. The fool should be listening and suggesting strategies instead of dismissing new information.

"It was not starpower! One of those other vile creatures you speak of must have done something." Araxis suddenly appeared less confident than he sounded.

"I cannot say. Before my forces could react, the animals from the forest emerged to drive the clawed creature off. Then they finished crushing my warriors to shreds."

"They did not harm her—"

"She fled. They took her companion, a Geffitz, prisoner and returned to the forest."

"You are sure she came to no harm?" The Ly Kai persisted, his entire body rigid with tension.

Razek ducked his head again, this time to hide his fury. The filthy worm did not even bother to ask about the loss of his forces. "I can only say they returned to the forest."

"Where is she now?"

"The storm, coupled with these new threats... I lost them in the dark."

"I want her brought here, Captain. No more delays! Your master promised me." Araxis settled back on his stone seat, scratched at a welt, and glared.

Yes, the Master promised him. But the Ly Kai seemed to forget his half of the agreement, of the restoration of the Master's power on this world.

"She appears to be going to the city. We can lay a trap there—"

"Captain, I want her brought here, to me. I don't care where she is going or what it costs you. Bring her here!"

"Of course, milord." Razek bowed again in the face of that fury and turned to leave.

"It is impossible to get anything done with such incompetent fools," he heard the Ly Kai mutter behind him.

Razek's mouth tightened. They could not afford another quick, ill-conceived strike. The girl was growing in confidence and ability, pushed by their repeated, ineffectual tactics. The Master warned: if things continued, she would become stronger than the physical form Araxis currently occupied. It might have already happened, since the Ly Kai didn't appear to have noticed her deadly action last night.

Whatever Razek did, he must do it fast, before this Ly Kai grew totally impatient and destroyed everything. The Geffitzi warriors, away from the protection of their cursed forest, could handle. This new development, however, complicated things. Razek knew about the four-legged, poison-tailed animals from ancient times. They were deadly, cold killers like Balandra, which was why he felt such dismay at their sudden appearance.

Turning back to Araxis, he made another effort to guide him onto a more desirable, less obstructive path. "This place is unfit for habitation, milord. Let us carry you to your city. You would be more comfortable there while you wait." If they ensconced the Ly Kai in his precious, mysterious city, perhaps he would find distractions and allow Razek to act without the pressure of reporting every move.

"What do you know of the city?" Araxis bristled.

Interesting how defensive he became at any mention of the place. "I sent scouts to investigate it, in case that is her destination."

"I gave no order!'

"No, Lord, you did not." Razek managed to maintain a patient tone. "It is a necessary precaution. We must know the state of the place, so we do not walk unprepared into something hostile. The Geffitzi will move toward the city quickly if these new creatures join forces with them. We must secure the place before they arrive."

"You don't know where she is going. She's wandering like an idiot. I want her captured before she gets that far. How difficult is that? I will not walk into my city with less than my rightful power."

"We are trying, Lord."

"Well, try harder. Your incompetence is astounding. And stay away from my city!" Araxis appeared to be working himself into a fit of hysterics.

"Of course, milord." Razek lowered his head in a conciliatory gesture to hide his pleasure at the other's obvious distress. "However," he could not resist continuing, "you should know, everything appears intact and in good order." He peered from under spiky eyebrows to savor the reaction.

"You went inside?" The Ly Kai went so pale Razek thought he might pass out.

"Our Master would not be pleased if we allowed you to walk into a trap." He wondered if Araxis even noted his use of the word 'our.' He doubted the arrogant creature ever applied the term to include himself.

He should.

"You fool; you do not do anything without my order! Do you understand?" the Ly Kai shouted in rage. "I wish Clackamas was still here. He knew how to take orders."

A curl of scornful amusement burned through Razek: Araxis interacted with the Balandran captain, Clackamas, every day and did not recognize him now that he had strategically stepped back into the ranks. Hatred burned inside Razek. When the day finally came... "If you will excuse me?"

Araxis glared at him. "Where are you going?"

"To collect reports. We have observers out, assessing this change in our situation." Again, he put a slight emphasis on 'our.'

"Stop observing and get the girl, Captain." The Ly Kai turned his back, refocusing his attention on the dreary landscape outside the window in a rude gesture of dismissal.

"By your leave." Razek did not wait for a response.

The guards opened the doors onto the gray light of day. It was still raining, but the deadly lightning storm of the previous night had passed.

As soon as the captain cleared the portico, he loosened his wings and took two running steps into the yard. His leathery extensions billowed, and he caught the air in a huge down flap that lifted him speedily. He had no reason to mask his anger now as he flew over several buildings in the ancient Geffitz complex to the structure the Balandran troops were using as living quarters.

Several of his men tended their weaponry under the shelter of the porch. They scrambled to their feet and stood at stiff attention when he lit in the yard. He flicked his wings, scattering water over them as he walked past, then re-tightened his appendages onto his back. None of the Balandra made a sound or changed expression, behaving as warriors should around their superior.

The rest of his steadily dwindling force slept in the front two rooms of the building. He stalked through and shoved the heavy door to his quarters so hard it rebounded off the wall with a satisfying boom.

"Is that necessary?" a voice asked peevishly from the shadows on the far side of the chamber.

"Apologies, Master." Razek dropped comfortably into his mother tongue.

"Well?"

"He did not ask for details, and I did not offer them. He denied noticing any use of her power last night and expresses no regret at the loss of your loyal forces, Master. He will not change."

There was a rustling sound of soft, dry laughter. Balandran laughter. "That is the beauty of it, my captain. His arrogance will not allow him to consider that his choices might be in error. The power of the birthform he occupies is far below hers. It has not occurred to him that he cannot sense use above it." The other Balandra limped forward into the light. He was older than Razek and shorter, his body bent from a recent injury. Deep scars crosshatched his sinewy muscles. In form, it was the very Clackamas whose loss Araxis lamented so vocally moments before. In reality, he was something far more sinister.

"She continues to move north?" He had been apprised of the previous night's events far sooner than Araxis.

"The beasts have moved them in that direction. He continues to profess confusion over her movements."

"Because, Razek, he truly does not know." The other Balandran chuckled. "Excellent. I promise you, this new situation will work for us. Send a few of your troops out to monitor our targets but warn them: they mustn't be seen yet. The fool need not know of your activities. We will soon defang our little serpent and finish this."

Chapter 80
By the Goddess' Will

THERE WERE MORE CYRWINS this morning than there had been last night. Kaphri counted twenty in the thinning darkness. They encircled her and the warriors inside a wall of gray bodies.

When they had stopped to make camp, Tobin told them the animals would form a ring for their protection. Seeing them now, Kaphri wondered whether they were there to protect, or to hold them captive. Twenty Cyrwins were far too many to exert her will over if they should force her to act.

Memory of what she'd done last night stirred a reaction of nausea in her so strong it threatened to overwhelm and humiliate her. She was not nearly so bold in the daylight, seeing the beasts surrounding them. The stone images guarding the main gate at Caer Cadarn had proven unpleasantly accurate to the tiniest detail.

At least the threat of the tarmeuth was gone, she thought. Uri had assured them that crossing the storm-swollen river would eliminate any threat of the creature's pursuit. In Velacy's nightmare story, water had been a natural barrier to the animals, and she had definitely felt some of the tension fall away from the warriors when they reached the eastern bank of the river. Even their newfound, unpleasant four-legged allies displayed a lightening of anxiety.

Not that crossing the river had otherwise improved their situation. They were in the grasp of a new and terrible danger in the form of Tobin and his Grimmen-loyal companions. The value of the Cyrwins' aid in crossing the river, measured against the threat they presented, did not balance. Kaphri was sure that fear of another tarmeuth attack had made the encounter at the bottom of the escarpment briefer and less violent than it would have been. The real confrontation still loomed.

It was a regrettable situation. The Cyrwins seemed intelligent creatures despite their penchant for violent and petulant behavior. They would have made useful allies.

She turned back toward her companions clustered in the center of the ring of Cyrwin flesh and sighed. What a wretched sight they were in the morning light. Frax, Tobin, and Seuliac were in poor condition, and she had no idea what to do to help them.

In the Geffitzi way of thinking, this would be the ideal time to strike a weakened foe.

But the Cyrwins had not killed them, and in view of what they had just gone through, she considered them fortunate.

It had been a miserable group that emerged from the river last night. The tarmeuth, however, was not the only threat out in the stormy darkness, and the Cyrwins insisted they must keep moving. Sometime during those next miserable, wet hours, Frax had lapsed back into unconsciousness. Uri's repeated requests to stop and tend to the commander's wound had fallen on deaf ears. With no control over their mounts, they had ridden wearily onward as prisoners to their new companions.

The downpour had softened to a fine drizzle when Tobin finally ordered a halt in the darkness.

"We will stop for a few hours, then move on," he said.

Uri and Seuliac were supporting Frax's unconscious body between them after lowering him from the Cyrwin's back. The warlord staggered under the weight as Uri stopped to glare at Tobin. "We'll take as long as it requires to stabilize your brother. We will not travel again until I say so."

"You can take care of him tomorrow in the daylight."

"We'll make the time now. If you were in such a hurry, maybe you should have ordered the Cyrwins not to attack him."

Annoyance flashed across the younger Kitahn's face. "You have no idea what's at stake here."

"Then why don't you tell us, Tobin? What's so all-fired important that you can't stop to ensure your brother's life?"

Tobin had only shaken his head and refocused his attention on the Cyrwins.

They all wanted answers, but they also knew it would be a waste of time and breath to pursue the issue further.

Uri confiscated their blankets to set up a makeshift tent to tend to Frax's wound. The commander was very ill: Kaphri had felt it as if the link between them during telepathy remained slightly open. She clung to it tenaciously, alert for any changes as she watched Uri work from a distance. An air of urgency she had never sensed before hung over the Caspani warrior. At one point, he exchanged sharp words with Tobin again, but the younger warrior's posture offered no indication of repentance as he hovered, observing Uri.

Bone-weary and afraid, Kaphri huddled with the Aedecs for warmth while the wet ground soaked their clothes even deeper. They needed a fire, the one thing everyone agreed was impossible.

How much worse must Uri feel, fumbling about in the dark?

Realization broke through her weariness. She could do something to help. Her starfire, with its low draw, was so mundane it was not detectable to other Ly Kai.

Besides, after the things she'd done earlier to defend the warlord against the tarmeuth, sending out that huge blaze of power...

Out of habit, she checked for the watcher. The presence was gone, left behind, she could only presume when they passed beyond the realm of the Grimmen. It did not mean the thing's influence was no longer a shadow over them; the woods was more displeased with them now than it had ever been.

When she got up and limped over to Uri, Tobin glowered at her. *"What do you want?"*

"I can do something to help."

"What would that be?" Uri asked without looking up.

She willed her racing heart to slow down. *"I can give you some light to work by."*

"Really?" Uri glanced up. *"Light would help. How?"*

She had squatted beside him and summoned a small amount of starfire. The tiny glow of light flickered into existence a forearm's length in front of her brow. She directed it under the cover of the blanket tent to seclude and contain it.

Uri had given her a startled look. *"That does help, but should you be doing it?"*

"I fear I have emblazoned my presence on this night at least once already." She adjusted the starfire slightly brighter and directed it lower to hover above Frax's shoulder.

The sight of the angry, dark swell of the wound made her close her eyes. When she opened them again, Tobin was staring at her.

"How long have you been able to do that?"

She understood what he meant. There had been times during their journey when her starfire would have been of great help to them, but she had not offered it. *"My starfire? Since birth."* She chose to misunderstand the question rather than defend it.

Seuliac and Velacy had moved up behind her to see what she had done.

"*Light without a source.*" A glint from her starfire reflected off the white streak in the warlord's dark, soddened hair. *"Old warriors claimed they'd seen it, but I didn't believe their stories."*

"It has a source," she'd corrected him wearily. *"It comes from the stars."*

"Starfire." Uri pressed the area around the wound, squeezing a clear fluid out of the swollen flesh. *"It definitely helps. But is it wise to use it?"*

"It's a natural, inborn power all Ly Kai share. Its use is too common and weak for others to sense."

"But you can't be sure of that here, where you're the only user for leagues around, so we'll keep this short," Uri told her. *"Move the light down toward his arm a bit more."*

Kaphri closed her eyes again against what the light revealed.

"Can you make heat?" Velacy shivered.

"*I've never tried.*" She had heated water in Kryie Karth, but air was a thinner substance. "*I'm sure it would require a draw of power at a much higher level.*"

"Not air. Rocks."

His suggestion sparked Uri's interest. *"Could you heat a few large stones to help keep him warm?"* The need for her to try must have outweighed the threat of Araxis' detection, or he would not have asked. And, as she'd pointed out, she had already emblazoned her presence on this world when she attacked the Balandra at the top of the cliff. Even if Araxis noticed her use of starfire, his Balandra would still have to locate them.

Within moments, the Aedec warriors had gathered several large stones. Taking one up, she'd cautiously channeled her low-level power into the dense material. At first, there was an immense drag on her effort, like pouring water down a hole, but gradually the rock began to hold and radiate warmth. She warmed four stones, which Uri positioned in the blankets around Frax.

"That will help him immensely." Uri had smiled at her.

"I don't know how long it will last."

"It is enough. We don't want to push you too far. Thank you."

Tobin scowled but did not protest when she stayed beside Uri, offering the only support she could while he cleansed the wound with captured rainwater. He sprinkled a powder on it from his beltpouch and leaned back on his knees with a weary sigh. *"It's in the hands of the Goddess now."*

"By the Goddess' will," Seuliac had murmured as he and Velacy turned away. He meant it more fervently than he would have ever believed possible. The loss of Frax Kitahn as their leader would be a disaster for Velacy and him.

"You pray for his recovery?" Velacy erupted in tightly directed fury. *"I told you agreeing to a truce with them was a mistake. Now we're surrounded by death. We should take the girl and get out of here. This is the Goddess' land; they can't attack us now."*

"Velacy, you're a fool for even putting your thoughts into form. If you try taking that girl, you won't get ten steps. Besides, we're in this too deep."

"Because you put us here!"

"No, Velacy. Because the Goddess willed it. Otherwise, you'd be dead, and I would be in the north, fighting off an invasion and totally ignorant of all this. But we're not. We're here in the middle of it because it's where we're supposed to be. Now, let's get some sleep." If the Cyrwins killed them while they slept, he might consider it an act of mercy.

"Come, girl. You get some rest, too," the warlord ordered Kaphri.

"But you do not know—" she began to protest.

"Precisely." He, too, feared their new companions. *"But we have time to sleep. We will make use of it."*

Physical demands had finally taken their toll, and the Aedecs curled up for shared body heat on the wet leaves and fell into exhausted sleep. Kaphri wanted to curl up with them and share their warmth, but she would not let herself.

When she realized Uri and Tobin were also preparing to settle to the ground on either side of Frax, shock and disbelief sliced through her. How could they simply relinquish their control over the situation like that? Neither she nor the sleeping warriors had protection against their new, murderous allies. Someone must keep an eye on the Cyrwins' activities.

"Get some sleep, Willow," Uri had sent back in response to her sense of question.

She had ignored him.

He'd been walking for a long time. Frax paused, frowning as he tried to remember how he came to be in this gray place of drifting mist. The light was low and even, coming from everywhere except the ground. That was dark, sandy, packed earth. No plants, no debris. So, somewhere. He just didn't know where. Or how.

He tried to peer through the drifting veils of gray surrounding him. He'd been here before. He knew that much. But how? It wasn't a memory for him. It was an immediate sense of here and now, and not a why or how.

What was he missing?

His attention drifted.

The air was hot. Dry. Thirst burned his throat.

A faint roar pulled his attention. Something was approaching from above, growing louder. A sudden surge of instinct screamed for him to run, but he stayed rooted, unsure where to go. Orange light was spreading brighter above him with the rising sound. Then, a ball of fire screamed past overhead, shredding the mist. He ducked, expecting to feel the blast, but the roar continued, receding while he cringed and counted. On five, a massive explosion ripped the sky and light limned a distant line of mountain peaks.

Whatever caused the blast, that massive row of stone had protected him from an instant, scorching death.

He turned his back to the fading orange light, now a dancing glow of furious burning, and crouched, thinking. What was this place? Did he sense anything familiar?

The rising scream of more falling fire ripped the distance.

This time, minutes after it struck, hot wind, dirt, and small stones slammed him. He pitched to the ground, shielding his face while the debris scoured his back.

A faint mental call, demanding he—all of them—come to the Place of Gathering, dropped into his brain.

A part of him responded instinctively. Wild hope surged and he scrambled to his feet and turned to answer the call. But another sensation was also pulling at his attention.

Somewhere, pain and nausea whispered, rising in stridency.

Reality descended with a new, terrible wash of consciousness, pulling him away.

Sitting alone, listening to rain whisper on the leaves and sensing the hulking forms that shifted in the dark around her, time had crept past. But it had been a long day—and night. Kaphri had given in to the drowsiness of half-sleep when a weak but familiar touch brushed her mind.

In an instant, she was awake, her heart surging with relief.

Too much! Instinctive warning had flashed in her mind. Her joy must not be for Frax. Not after the things he'd done, betraying her, telling her he had made a mistake, giving her over to Seuliac's control. Bitterness tried to flow in to replace her relief, but she pushed that away, too. This was a time for reason.

Hoping Frax had not caught the leading edge of her first, unguarded reaction, she tempered her response to cool reserve. "*You're alive. Good.*" She waited, heart pounding.

"I..." A blank moment snatched his senses. *"Where are we?"*

"We have crossed into Pterfellen."

"Everyone?"

"Yes. Including Tobin and the Cyrwins."

"Ah. I feared we'd lost you and Seuliac last night. It was last night, wasn't it?"

"Only hours ago. Are you all right?"

"I was...dreaming. It's gone now. Are you sitting watch?"

"Uri says the Cyrwins will keep watch, but I don't trust them. Are you in pain? Should I wake him?"

"I can wake him if I need to." A sense of vague amusement rippled from him.

Obviously, he was feeling better if he found her concern a source of humor. So, one crisis averted. But their problems continued. She should wait until he was stronger before voicing her concerns, but she could not. Let him see how amusing their situation really was.

"Tobin is messing with the balance of things."

"Tobin is under the influence of a powerful force." His answer was cautious, as if there was a great deal more he might have said. "*But,*" he had attempted to shift to a lighter tone, *"right now even that force realizes we must rest. The Cyrwins will stand guard. You can sleep."*

"They could do us harm while we sleep."

"Priestess, if they brought us into Pterfellen, they will not harm us. I swear it."

They harmed you, she'd thought angrily. She held back the response, knowing that arguing with him would not improve his condition.

In truth, the fact that the Cyrwins had attacked him terrified her. He had made an agreement with the Grimmen at the edge of the wood before they entered it. He was Cadarn and the creatures' ancient ally, but they had ruthlessly struck him down. They might have killed him—he was still seriously ill—then where would the rest of them be? What would happen to them if Tobin and the Cyrwins took control? She still feared for Seuliac and Velacy's safety, even with Frax awake again.

And how could she go on without his overbearing, aggravating presence constantly at her back, browbeating her...?

"They want to kill Seuliac and Velacy," she had persisted.

"They won't. I have that guarantee."

If she had thought Frax was in control, she might have relaxed then. But he wasn't. Tobin was. And, she suspected, neither was Tobin to any great extent. The Grimmen had its Eldren agenda here—the same agenda Frax had warned her about in the Palenquemas.

She looked over at the sleeping Aedecs. *"No. I will sit guard."*

"Damn it, Priestess!" But after all this time, he must know it was useless to argue with her, especially if he had no immediate means of backing it up. Exhausted from the small effort to communicate with her, he broke contact, and in less than twenty breaths, he had dropped back into sleep.

How did he dare claim they were safe with these vicious creatures surrounding them? Caught between anger and a sense of betrayal, Kaphri shifted her position against the tree trunk.

The movement drew the attention of the nearest Cyrwin. An ear had flicked, a head swung slowly. Slitted serpent eyes regarded her. She'd tensed, her body responding defensively by gathering power.

The automatic reaction caught her by surprise again. Five times this night, she'd drawn starpower in preparation to use it against another creature. She'd never done anything like that before.

Yes, she had, her mind argued. She had killed Rath by drawing power and overwhelming his weaker body when he tried to stop her from leaving Kryie Karth.

She'd argued that she had not known anything of Arylla's power back then. Her control over her draw on power was better now. She'd glared at the Cyrwin, waiting. When the creature turned its attention away, she had settled back in the growing light.

Wet, cold, sore, and tired, she still found a moment of peace to let her mind drift unguarded with the sound of the rain on the leaves. The sense of being constantly observed by the watcher was gone, vanished when she slipped free of the geas, and, despite everything that had happened over the last day, she'd been in worse predicaments. In the Palenquemas, as a captive of the Wyxa, she had had every comfort she required, but she'd been in far more danger. There, she had lacked any contact with the stars...

Or Gemma. The constant sadness that ached in her heart for her lost friend swelled. Sadness, but never a sense of betrayal.

Kaphri was gripping the droplet of crystal in her fist again. Lost in thought, she had pulled it from its place beneath her shirt to clasp it and draw comfort.

The Guardian Stone. The prison that held her tiny dragon companion. The Wyxa had created it ages ago and bound Gemma inside it to stand guard in the depths of the Black Temple, to protect this world from the terrible evil they had sealed away there. But the tiny golden dragon had differed with their definition of how to protect this place, leaving the darkness and finding her way to

Kryie Karth, to comfort and guide a lonely girl. Gemma had shared Kaphri's wretched childhood. Into a sea of anger and hostility that surrounded the girl, the little serpent had brought kindness, patience, and understanding.

No matter what the Wyxa thought, Gemma had not abandoned her true task. Kaphri knew the truth: the Guardian had shifted the mission of saving this world onto her.

She didn't even belong here. The Ly Kai were invaders. Sixteen years ago, Araxis had lured a large group of their influential leaders here with the promise of a new life of wonder and adventure. She could not fault them that desire. From the crumbs of memories she had stolen from their minds in curious moments, she knew the Ly Kai Homeworld was ancient and staid. Araxis had offered adventure and new experiences beyond his wondrous gate. His followers didn't know he had driven this land's original occupants away with a terrible plague and sealed the survivors in the north with a barrier fueled by Arylla. They hadn't suspected that Araxis had ambitions to rule this new world. When he demanded their obedience, they had rebelled. He threatened to close the gate and sever them from the Homeworld, and a terrible battle had ensued.

The Ly Kai, individually, were far weaker than Araxis' Birthpower. But when they joined their starpower together, their resistance was magnified. They almost defeated him. They succeeded in destroying his physical form, but at the last moment, he struck a cruel and desperate blow, killing all the women and children, creating a distraction that broke the chain of their combined power so that his essence could escape.

Only the men and a two-year-old child, Kaphri, survived.

Of course, as the niece of the now-labeled 'evil' Araxis, all manner of suspicion centered on her. The men were anguished, angry, and confused. Why had she lived when all their wives and children were slain? Indeed, he had even killed her mother, his sister.

Only Arylla-born controlled the power to open gates, and with Araxis severed from his physical form and vanquished, there was no one among the survivors to re-activate the gate for their return to the Homeworld. They huddled around a mass grave, sure Araxis' twin, Alexar, would come and rescue them. He did not.

Eventually, bitter, angry, and fearful of Araxis' vengeance—knowing his ethereal essence still lurked in this world somewhere—they fled from the scene of betrayal, going north. They entered the lands where Araxis had driven the original inhabitants and encountered their savage hostility. Many Ly Kai men were slain before they reached the isolated refuge of the lake tower they named Kryie Karth, or Hearthstone. Cowering in the barren mountain ring, on the constant brink of starvation and with their seething hatred and resentment directed toward her, Kaphri grew up. She prayed to her Birthstar, Freya, though it never responded, and, with the men's rigid refusal to break Ly Kai tradition, they grudgingly groomed her, as the highest ranking Starborn, to become their leader when she turned eighteen.

In such bleak, bitter conditions, she might have become a wretched, twisted being—if Gemma had not found her on the lake shore one day when she was seven years old and returned with her to the tower as her companion.

It was only on the night of her eighteenth birthday, when their anger and fear finally peaked, that Kaphri discovered the truth behind her existence. The surviving men had lied. Precious, silent Freya was not her Birthstar. They had hoped she would thrive under its lower influence and protect them from Araxis' vengeance, while simultaneously fearing she would fall under Arylla's wicked influence. When she tried to warn them that an evil force had invaded Kryie Karth, they shifted the threat onto her and revealed their deception.

Terrified she was destined for evil, Kaphri had fled Kryie Karth with Gemma. Then, driven by a geas, a relentless compulsion of unknown origin, she wandered the world, steadily moving southward, until she encountered Frax, Tobin, and Uri in the shadowland of Omurda. They took her captive and planned to use her to undo the damage Araxis had wreaked upon their world—things she or the other refugees had never been aware of. She had not dared tell them about the geas at the time for fear they would kill her, only revealing its existence when they found themselves trapped at the vast, invisible barrier Araxis had created between the north and south. After the crystal and blood that had rested in the depths of the Black Temple broke the barrier long enough for them to fall through, they formed an alliance that included two new companions, Seuliac and Velacy Aedec, who were historical enemies of the other three warriors. Together, they would protect her as she followed the geas southward, and she, in turn, would find a way to remove the barrier.

During their struggle across a continent and an escape from the Palenquemas, the vast swamp home of the ancient Wyxa, she came to realize Araxis was manipulating her life as the key to regaining his power and that Gemma, as the Guardian sworn to protect this world, had sought her out and cultivated her into the defender this world would need against him.

But Frax had once warned her that the Eldren, the Wyxa and the Grimmenwood, did not view the world the same way as the Second Children of Kep, the Geffitzi. The Eldren had their own agenda. And though Kaphri had managed to free them of the Wyxa, except for precious Gemma, who they had locked back into her previous prison, the Guardian Stone, they were all at the mercy of the Grimmen and its forces now.

And that was still not the end of their trials. A heavy chill settled over Kaphri. She might defeat Araxis. But she knew nothing about this other threat—this Bithzielp the Wyxa spoke of. Even the warriors only gave her vague, horrific stories passed down through thousands of years of their history. And the Wyxa claimed Gemma was an Ancient, a Guardian committed to defending against the threat. Araxis seemed a mere ripple in a stream compared to the being who had once commanded his followers to move moons and torture the world's residents for him.

The situation was critical. Otherwise, Gemma would not have come to her side eleven years ago on the lake shore in the north. But the Wyxa had locked Gemma away again to fulfill her original purpose of guarding their world against Bithzielp's reentry, leaving Kaphri only able to draw comfort from the little dragon instead of the guidance she needed. The swamp dwellers refused to trust their Guardian's judgment on how to best confront the looming danger, prioritizing the threat of Bithzielp over Araxis. Leaving Kaphri alone in her battle to defend this world.

Kaphri had pulled upright in the darkness, ignoring the pain of protesting muscles.

Had the last thought been the natural progression of her mental process, or had something else intruded with a warning?

It was probably the simple, inevitable conclusion of her thoughts, which was the truth, after all, wasn't it? The gate where the Ly Kai had entered this world was no longer a nebulous goal on a vague horizon. Thanks to Tobin, the Cyrwins, and the Grimmen, the time to confront it was fast approaching.

As Seuliac had warned, she must prepare, which meant including Arylla as a resource.

The thought of using her Birthstar no longer stirred panic in her. She still feared Araxis would follow its trail of power back to her, but she did not fear the star. The warlord had broken her misgivings with his steady, unrelenting stream of probing questions and observations. Deep in her heart, she knew his analysis was accurate. Ly Kai somewhere had manipulated power to gain certain results: the births of Araxis, Alexar, and herself.

Weaker power manipulating stronger. It was a disturbing thought. In Kryie Karth, she would not have believed it. Now, she knew it had happened. It all came down to knowing the possibilities and how to achieve them, something Seuliac was working to achieve through her...

She had looked up at the wet canopy overhead. Despite trees or cloudy skies, she knew precisely where Arylla was at any moment. She was aware when the star cleared the horizon and when it disappeared again. It surprised her to realize that, but on thinking about it, she had subconsciously sensed those things since that first night, crouched in the cold, wet grass high on a mountainside on the southern edge of the Dark Zone, Omurda, when she'd actually laid eyes on her Birthstar for the first time.

She refused to ask for star response yet—doing so risked giving away their new location to Araxis—but perhaps it was time to begin her evening prayers to Arylla again.

Now, in the early morning light of their first day beyond the Grimmenwood, Kaphri watched Tobin leave the circle, taking one of the Cyrwins with him. He returned several hours later with a bundle of herbs, which he handed off to Uri.

Under the close observation of that particular Cyrwin, the Caspani warrior crushed a mixture of the plants and brewed them into a tea over a small, sheltered fire. She and the Aedecs, longing for the warmth of the tiny blaze but unwilling to share it so closely with a creature of the Grimmenwood, watched from a distance.

"It's no surprise the demon creatures have ways to prolong their victim's torments," Seuliac observed wryly.

Kaphri shivered. After her brief exposure to the Grimmen's huge servants, she didn't want to know more about them.

After Uri administered his brew to Frax, an air of angry disagreement rose between the big blond warrior and the Cyrwin over the remaining dregs. Uri finally shrugged and carried the cup to Seuliac.

His eyes flicked from the dried scab along the warlord's jaw to the large, darkening bruise on his forearm that was left from the encounter with Demon Tongue's tail.

"Drink it," Uri ordered.

The warlord gave him a thin smile. "Are you sure it hasn't turned to poison on your walk over here?"

"This is Pterfellen, Warlord. The Grimmen doesn't have that power here. Drink it."

Seuliac complied. He grimaced afterward at the taste.

Every few hours after that, the ritual of making the healing draught for Frax and the Cyrwin's resistance against sharing the leftovers with Kaphri, then Velacy, and back to Seuliac was repeated, until, in the late hours of the second night, the creature of the Grimmen finally gave up and ignored his actions.

Chapter 81
The Only Thing That Matters

BY LATE AFTERNOON OF the next day, Frax was moving about with as much energy as the lingering poisons in his system would allow. Their situation was far more precarious now with only the questionable protection of the Cyrwins to keep them safe from the Balandra, and they had no more time to delay on physical injuries,

The single positive thing he had noted on his first night outside the boundaries of the Grimmenwood was that the burning, obsessive thoughts which had plagued him in the woods were gone. The Grimmen's terrible influence through its proximity was broken, clearing his mind. That alone poured more strength into his recovery.

The Grimmen was not finished with him, however. He had made a pivotal decision at the bottom of the escarpment, siding with the Priestess to protect the Aedecs against Tobin and the Cyrwins. His choice had solidified the division between him and the Grimmen beyond repair. But, for now, he was simply grateful to be free from the mind-twisting influence of that force.

It was time for him to take their situation fully in hand and parse out what was going on. It was time for a bittersweet reunion of brothers.

He found Tobin outside the ring of gray bodies, staring southward.

"I don't suppose we can just thank them and they'll go away," Frax said as he stopped beside the younger warrior.

For a moment, he thought Tobin would walk away without answering, then his brother responded shortly. "No."

"You seem to be speaking for the Grimmen these days." Addressing the situation directly seemed best. "Why are the Cyrwins here? And don't tell me it's to help us. Trying to kill half the members of our party is not help."

"We're not here to help you. We are here to ensure the Ly Kai female leaves this world."

It did not sound like an answer Tobin would give, but Frax had no choice; he had to pursue the conversation. "What about what we want?" Frax could not keep the bitterness out of his question.

"She must return to her world. It is the only thing that matters."

"The barrier—"

"Has been seen to."

"What?" Frax rocked back as if he'd been struck, the movement sending a shooting pain through his back and shoulder. "The barrier is gone?"

"It will be, as soon as she leaves."

"How? The Grimmen can't remove the barrier, or it would have done it already." An ominous chill ran over him.

Tobin still had not made eye contact with him. "It will happen. After she is returned through the gate."

"Who will do it?"

"The ones responsible for its creation."

The ones? "The Ly Kai? Tobin! They can't do it. They don't have the ability. Only one of her birth can do it, and we don't even know if she can!"

"How do you know there isn't another?" Tobin finally twisted around to meet his eyes squarely, and Frax had to fight the urge to take a step back. His brother's eyes were full of gray, stormy swirls.

This was not Tobin speaking to him. This was a case of possession by the Grimmen, similar to the threat the Priestess faced from Araxis.

"I..." Frax broke off. What could he say? If the Grimmen believed it would happen, it was obviously communicating with someone, somewhere, who said it would, truth or lie. Was it possible that Alexar, Kaphri's other uncle and Araxis' twin, was alive and willing to help their world? For a moment, his heart twisted, trying to catch hope, then reason took over again. If that was true, why didn't Alexar just come forward and make things right? The Ly Kai owed their world that much! Alexar certainly couldn't use the threat Araxis presented to his personal safety as an excuse. In his present stolen form, the Evil One was no match for anyone experienced in the Power of Arylla—if what the Priestess said was true.

One thing Frax was sure of, whoever was making this offer to the Grimmen was not doing it altruistically. This situation reeked of manipulation and deceit. But on whose part? The Grimmen was Eldren, with its own, very different set of ruthless rules and agenda. Did whomever it was dealing with recognize that? The Geffitzi did. They had learned to use the greatest caution in dealing with the Eldren—especially in a situation like this—ages ago.

"Is there another one with her power?" He would not allow himself the slightest hope, regardless of the answer. He sensed treachery in the very air they breathed.

He needn't have worried. The force gripping Tobin only stared at him with a stormy, unreadable expression.

"You don't know." Bitterness welled inside Frax.

"She is to be returned to her world, unharmed, and the damage the Evil One has done here will be undone." The tone of the answer sounded rote now.

Some of those scars could never be undone! "And we have no say in this? The Wyxa don't speak for the Geffitzi, Tobin, and neither does the Grimmen."

"There are things you don't know—"

"Then tell us! Tell us, or we have to conclude they're not important to this situation."

"This is not the business of Rhynog."

"This is not about houses, Tobin. It's about our world."

"Which includes the Grimmenwood, Frax."

"And the Grimmenwood should tell us what it knows so we know what to expect moving forward."

For the first time, he thought he saw a flicker of the old Tobin in the seething eyes. "Why do you have to question everything, Frax? Why can't you just do what you're told?"

"Because I am Kitahn, Tobin. You are Kitahn. We ask the questions! We are the ones who make decisions based on the information gathered. We are not blind followers.

"A warrior does not withhold information, Tobin." In a combat situation, the selective reporting of information was punishable by death. The Grimmen, as a past ally in war, knew that.

The thing controlling Tobin relented a bit, allowing the warrior to respond. "The Grimmen's actions pre-date ours, Frax."

"That's impossible! How can they pre-date ours, Tobin? We captured her in the north, in the Shadow Zone! The Grimmen would have had to..." Realization caused him to break off. Holy Kep! "The geas?" The Priestess had never been able to identify its source. "The Grimmen claims it sent the geas to drive her southward?"

"It's the will of the Grimmen. She must leave this world. Neither you nor I have the right to interfere." The angry eyes were recognizably Tobin's now.

The Grimmen had had its claws deep into this situation for much longer than any of them had suspected. The realization left Frax staggered. Still... "Tobin! We saved her from imminent disaster half a dozen times on the other side of the barrier! The Grimmen had no control over those events. It's lying to you! She would never have gotten this far without us. It abducted you—"

"I wasn't abducted. I left after seeing something I could not abide."

The younger Kitahn had entered the guardroom and found him kissing the Priestess. A big mistake, aggravated by the machinations of the Grimmen, the Cyrwins, and the Wyxa.

Still, it was not an excuse for Frax's behavior. "I was wrong, I know. But my mistake is not the issue here." He believed he was speaking directly to Tobin now, but he didn't know how long it would last. He had to ask before his brother slipped away. "Can I reason with the Grimmen, Tobin? Is there a way—"

"The Grimmen no longer acknowledges you, Frax. Your choices have made you irrelevant." The cold fury shifted to a more personal anger in those gray eyes. "You're a fool, Frax! How could you betray Cadarn like this?"

"More than Cadarn is at stake, Tobin." Sometimes, he wondered if he was the only one who could see that.

"That way of thinking has put you where you are. The Grimmen doesn't need you, and it doesn't need the Aedecs. Come to your senses! It's not too late..."

"What? If I betray my word? If I let the Grimmen destroy the Aedecs for no other reason than its pride? I won't do it. I can't. With all the manipulation tearing at us, they must be here for a reason."

"You will never return to Cadarn." Tobin's eyes remained angry, but a tone of anguish laced his words.

"It's the only choice I've been offered, Tobin. I neither expect nor seek a change now." He glanced down for a breath to hide his pain, then he looked Tobin straight in the eye. Was it his brother looking back at him or the Eldren? He sent them both a warning.

"The Grimmen has control over one son of Cadarn. If we do not bring down the barrier, he will be the last one it controls. Ever. I hope it makes the right decision, Tobin, for the sake of Cadarn and all Geffitzi."

"Damn it, Frax! The Grimmen is giving you this one last chance!"

"It's already done, Tobin. The Grimmen set the terms, and I accepted: I gave up any ties to Cadarn at the edge of the woods. There is nothing more to discuss."

"*It is not the end of the matter.*" The Grimmen's words were an unnatural hiss of rage in his brain.

"*The bargain was made, and it will be honored: you will leave the Aedecs and the girl alone,*" Frax snapped back.

A scream of mental fury raked through his mind, causing him to gasp in pain, and then it was gone.

Tobin was staring at him, anger and frustration still in his eyes, but now they were clear of the swirling storm. "You're a fool, Frax. You think you know what's at risk here, but you don't."

Frax was sure he would find out in the most painful way possible, but neither he nor the Grimmen would bend. He could not afford to, and the Grimmen must feel the same.

Bound in hopeless bitterness, he watched his brother limp back over to the Cyrwins.

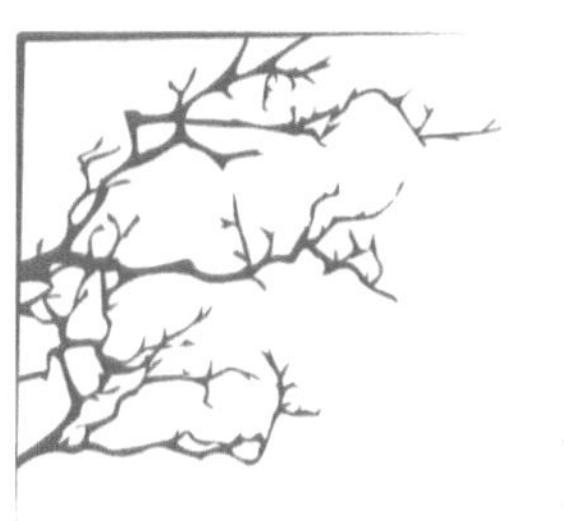

Chapter 82
Beyond the Grimmenwood

"THAT DIDN'T APPEAR to go well," Uri said

Frax grunted as he lowered himself carefully to the ground beside his cousin.

"You should take things more slowly." Uri handed him another cup of herbal mixture to drink. "Stormwraith, the lead Cyrwin, says if you drink more water, it will flush most of the poison out of your system by tomorrow morning. You'll be sore, but you'll heal without lasting effect."

"Did you thank him for me?"

"He wasn't the one who stung you." Uri's quick grin faded to a frown. "I fear Tobin is in even worse condition than you."

"They were rough on him."

"Very." Uri looked disgusted. "I suspect cracked ribs along with internal bruising."

"You don't agree with the process of selecting a Cyrwinmaster." Frax was bitterly amused.

"Fool Cadarnians! The damned Grimmen has nearly killed both of you. What kind of alliance is that?"

"One that has benefited the whole of Cadarn, Uri. If someone has to take some roughing up every once in a while to maintain those protections, it's their duty."

"Duty. Well, you've both clearly done your duty. Anymore and you might be dead."

Frax smiled wearily. If the Grimmen demanded more, he or Tobin would have no choice: they would not dishonor Cadarn with weakness or cowardice, even at the cost of their lives.

Uri shifted the subject. "What's our situation?"

"We're safe. For now." Frax went over his conversation with Tobin.

Uri stared at him, stunned. "The Grimmen claims to have sent the geas? But that would mean it's been in contact with the Ly Kai, forming its own agenda. How is that possible?"

"It would not say."

"It doesn't make sense. Who is it talking to?"

"Alexar, perhaps. Or maybe they have someone else."

"Why do they want her back so badly?"

"To keep her out of Araxis' control? To protect them from him?"

Uri shook his head. "So the plan is to take her to this gate, shove her through, then walk off? To not even think about the barrier, as if it doesn't exist?"

"Nothing is more important than removing the barrier, Uri."

"For you and me. Apparently not for the Grimmen or the Wyxa. I can't imagine—" the Caspani warrior broke off with a sudden frown.

"What?" Frax didn't like the way the other warrior paled.

"When the Wyxa held us prisoners in the Palenquemas, they didn't care about the barrier. They wanted us to replace the Guardian Stone, to stop the threat of Bithzielp's re-emergence into our world through the gate in the Black Temple. But the Balandra had already invaded through it. How does Araxis happen to command them? Did he strike a bargain to get those resources? Is he helping Bithzielp make a return? If Araxis restores his power through the girl and works with Bithzielp, what will they do to our world? We say nothing's more important than removing the barrier, but what if there is? What if the threat is so great it diminishes the priority of the barrier?"

"The Eldrens' greatest fear manifested." A chill ran over Frax. "But the Wyxan solution to remove the threat was so weak. Sending us back into the depths with the Guardian Stone, hoping we would drop it in the right place to seal the gate before we died, was ridiculous. Exiling the Priestess to their Ethereal Plain to sleep until the threat was resolved was even more absurd."

"True. But the Wyxa don't believe in killing creatures. Directly, at least," he amended. They'd had no problem sending the warriors to what would result in certain death at the hands of the Balandra.

"The Grimmenwood has no problem with killing." Frax's wound gave a twinge of pain as if to confirm it.

"True again. But it seems to have come to some agreement over removal of the barrier."

"If something goes wrong with the Grimmen's current plan, killing us all is likely its secondary plan, Uri. We can't ever forget that." Frustration roiled in him. "Why doesn't Tobin simply tell us what's going on? I'm tired of all this subterfuge. All the Eldren except the damned Guardian act as if we have no role in the protection of our world."

"Speaking of which, you said the Wyxa attacked Willow in the guard tower, trying to reassert influence over her before you could bring her into the Grimmenwood. They may come at her again now that we're out of the wood's protection."

"Another threat hanging over us. But not the only one." Frax sighed. "I wandered the gray again."

Uri gave him a sharp look. "Another dream?"

"I don't think it's a dream, Uri. It feels like someone's memory. I think it may be something I stole from the Ankar Mekt when those bastards incorporated me."

"That can't be good."

"Probably not."

"Was it the same...?"

"The first one, in the Grimmenwood, left me with only vague memories. This one I remember clearly. I was walking in smoke and ruin, with blazing lights tearing across the sky and shattering the earth. I felt immense rage, but it wasn't mine. It was as if I were an observer, feeling another being's emotions, but with no clear reason for those reactions. There was also a great sense of betrayal. And hard purpose—similar to what I experienced when the Ankar Mekt incorporated me."

Frowning, Uri rubbed the back of his neck. "We're outside the Grimmenwood. Beyond its influence. Do you think—"

"The Grimmen blocked whatever it was while we were inside its realm, and now it can't? Maybe." Or maybe it hadn't wanted anything else to detract from the torment it was inflicting on him.

"Or the Wyxa might be trying to exert their influence over you."

"Yes." Frax's expression twisted with rueful annoyance. "I may have made a mistake in taking on the Ankar Mekt in their joining, Uri. I went in wild, snatching at anything I touched."

His cousin nodded, expression grim. "I wouldn't consider a connection with the Wyxa a good thing at any time, and not right now, for sure. How do you feel?"

"Confused, but not threatened. When I'm there, I feel like I'm sharing awareness with another being who is trying to figure things out."

"The big question is: how does it affect you? Is the source trying to influence you? Are the Wyxa trying to pull you back under their influence?"

"I don't get that sense."

"Yet. Things change. Keep me advised."

“I will.”

A sudden change in the alertness of the Cyrwins stirred the air around them. The creatures were moving toward one side of the camp, churning about, snapping and snorting. A few high-pitched squeals of anger and pain rent the air.

"Well, I think our situation has at least improved on one front, Uri," Frax said after a moment.

One of the Cyrwins had returned from the hunt with a bloody kill.

To Kaphri the scene was appalling. To the warriors, it was a wonderful sight.

During their time inside the Grimmenwood, Frax had forbidden them to hunt for fear the Grimmen might conveniently choose to consider them part of the hunt in retaliation. Now, beyond its borders, the taboo was lifted.

Enthusiasm mixed with a wary concern, the warriors immediately began to talk about forming their own hunting party. But first, they took the time to question Tobin on the safety of the Rhynogians.

He shrugged. "They are as safe as any of you for now."

"For now," Seuliac repeated warily. "What does that mean?"

"This is Pterfellen. You are Geffitzi. You can go and do what you want."

"With no threat from you or them?" The warlord nodded toward the Cyrwins

"No threat."

"Why this sudden change?" Velacy demanded.

"Your safety's been bargained again, Rhynog," Tobin snapped, "at the cost of something far more valuable than yourselves. Take it and stop asking questions or I'll conveniently forget an arrangement I already don't like."

"Fine," Seuliac raised his hands, palms outward, in an exaggerated gesture to deflect Tobin's anger. "Velacy, go, kill us something to eat."

The younger Aedec gave the warlord an outraged look, which Kaphri found odd, considering his frequent complaints over the hunting ban inside the Grimmenwood.

Seuliac ignored him, and Velacy scooped up his bow and quiver and stomped off.

Kaphri waited until Tobin walked away before looking at Uri. "*Bargained? What did he mean?*" she sent.

"*I don't know, Willow, but I don't like the sound of it. You stay away from the Cyrwins. I don't trust them, no matter what Tobin says.*"

"*Best count your fingers, toes, and teeth to find out what you bargained away.*" Seuliac grimaced as he flexed his bruised arm. The mark where the Cyrwin's tail had lashed him had swelled to an ugly purple welt covering most of his forearm. "*I suspect it was something far more valuable than teeth.*"

Late in the afternoon, while Velacy's hapless kill roasted over a low fire, Frax called for an exchange of information on the events at the escarpment. He included Tobin in his request, but he would not permit the Cyrwins to participate. Ignoring the hostility his exclusion stirred in the gray circle around them, he told the rest of them he wanted short, succinct facts and observations.

Kaphri was eager to hear everything that had happened with everyone. Unfortunately, most of those details did not fall under 'succinct facts and observations.' It was disappointing to listen to what had seemed hours of terror distilled into a few short sentences. When her turn came, she relayed her experience in like manner. It dismayed her, however, to think of how much of what had happened they cut away.

Uri gently laughed at her concern. "*Willow, it's not lost. It's still in your head. And when your turn comes some night around the fire, imagine what a story you'll have to tell. I can hardly wait to hear it! But for now, it's enough to know six Balandra attacked and died. We can only hope that between you and the tarmeuth, you got them all.*"

His promise of future stories brightened her outlook, but her thoughts remained overshadowed by her uneasiness at Tobin's silence. It appeared the Grimmen was not happy with the situation and chose to exhibit its displeasure through the new Cyrwinmaster's refusal to participate. He did not even register the mildest reaction during their discussion, which was out of character for the fiery-tempered younger son of Cadarn.

No doubt, the spirit of the woods had added the exclusion of the Cyrwin to its list of their accumulating offenses. She prayed she and her companions survived its retaliation.

Meanwhile, Frax decided to continue traveling by day. The Balandra tracked best by night, and no one wanted to give them any advantage. After eating, they had several good hours of daylight left to use.

The decision seemed to mollify Tobin's hostility a little.

When they prepared to mount and ride eastward, they were surprised to discover that only six Cyrwins remained with them. All the others had silently slunk away during their meal. No one except Tobin had seen them leave, and no one asked any questions.

One of the remaining Cyrwins, Chaos-stepper, moved forward to carry Frax. Tobin designated the other, Skydevil, for Kaphri.

"No." Seuliac, Frax, and Uri all said at the same time. Placing her solely within the control of one of the Grimmen's creatures did not sit well with the warriors any more than it did with her.

"She rides with me," Seuliac declared, preempting any argument. "Caspani can see to Kitahn."

Tobin scowled but waved Skydevil away to follow.

The sullen mental presence of Demon's Tongue was easily distinguishable from the other Cyrwins. As she took a step to approach the creature, she felt a sudden, swift movement at her back.

The Cyrwins were all ahead of her, her mind flashed, so the inanimate object at her back was a threat. She reacted with a hard stab of power.

The clod of dirt exploded, spraying debris to the sides and away from her as she spun about.

Velacy's smug expression was transforming to shock.

"*Finally!*" Seuliac's slow clap jarred the silence.

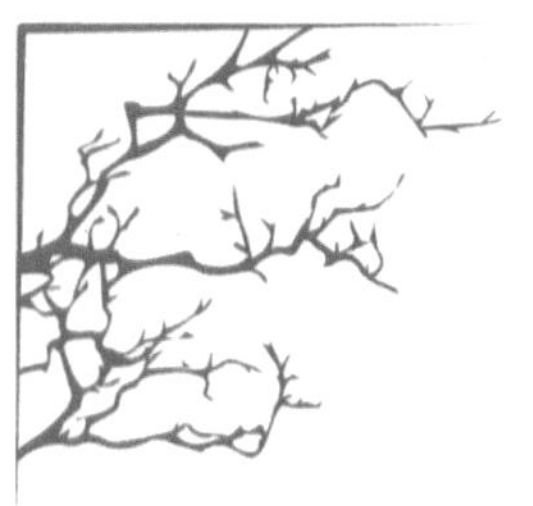

Chapter 83
Araxis

ARAXIS WOKE UP HUNGRY and focused on breaking his fast.

The wretched vegetable gruel the winged ones brewed for him should be here already. He despised the stuff and did not trust the creatures who made it, but it served its purpose.

Disgusting flesh eaters. They were hardly worth the air they breathed, thriving off other living beings like they did. He, on the other hand, could frequently find what he needed by picking through the brains of those tiny, primitive creatures outside his window who were constantly concerned with where their next meal was coming from, and then stealing from their hidden food stores.

If they wandered too close within his range, they would not need the food anyway.

He found the thought amusing. How entertaining to hold another creature's life in your hands and for them not to know. How much more satisfying, however, when they actually did know their pitiful existence was at his whim and mercy. He hadn't taken time to fully enjoy something like that in a while. His action at the barrier, when he forced the stupid runaway child to open the way for the Balandra, did not count. It had been such a tense, critical situation that he'd missed the opportunity to savor the storm of emotions in her or the Ly Kai, who had spent the last bit of their lifeforce trying to fulfill his demands.

His old associates. They had been a cringing, sniveling lot of cowards with no drive to live. All they ever wanted was a release from their lives on this world. Well, he'd given them that. Their spirits had returned to their stars, their powers put to a better use than they would have ever found if they lived another hundred years. He had used them to accomplish something.

The memory sent a tingle of heat through him. It had been a heady experience to feel their starpower coursing through him. Their combined power had not been close to the strength of his, which they had deprived him of with their rejection, but it had felt good. It was so long since he'd had access to his Birthpower; he'd almost forgotten his heritage during the time he'd hidden inside that bottom-dwelling vermin, Rath.

And this body he occupied now—how frustratingly inadequate it was. Ving, in all his arrogance and pride, had no idea what real power was. To Araxis, his occupation of this body was like being thirsty and receiving one tiny droplet of water at a time from a rushing torrent just beyond his reach. He wanted to burrow back into the torrent and bathe in it. And he would. Soon. If he could get these useless creatures to perform the simple task he asked of them.

How difficult could it be to snatch one ignorant, frightened girl, who had no idea of the power she possessed, away from a company of primitive barbarians? Such were the tools he had to work with. Incompetence surrounded him.

Araxis felt a sudden curl of mortified fury. What had he been doing a moment ago? Congratulating himself on stealing food from an animal and bemoaning the ineptitude around him? He was a gate-opener! He should be dining on the best a thousand worlds had to offer, not nibbling at leftover scraps from an animal's nest.

Someone would pay for this humiliation.

Where were the cursed Balandra? Where was the report saying the girl was cowering in some dark corner of this place, awaiting his final triumph? The being he had bargained with—the presence skulking in the vast depths of blackness below the shadow tower—had promised him these creatures would help him attain his goals if he pulled them through the crack in the gate into this world. He had brought the first ones through with the blood of small animals, then with the beings of this world whom the Balandra captured wandering too close to the shadow tower. He'd been forced to act discreetly, dividing his time between the two towers, taking years to build his force. And still, he was only marginally closer to his goal. Stupid child. Why had she run to the south? It would have been so much easier to overpower her after she fled the miserable tower, while she was weak and terrified, but no. He'd been forced to find a new form when Rath died from overreaching his paltry Birthpower. Ving's form was better but still inadequate. While during the delay—a delay she caused—she had found allies, moved into the south for some inexplicable reason, experimented with her Birthpower...and was running for the gate.

The Balandra must seize her before she got there.

They better hurry.

Hurry their own tragic destiny. How ironic. He would have no further use for them once he seized the girl's form. And the bargain he'd made with the force beyond the gate in exchange for the help of its army? He gave a mental chuckle. A force unable to help itself was no force at all. Once he secured the girl's form and restored his Birthpower, he would begin a reign of terror over this wretched place—particularly focused on those cursed warriors and their people—like they could never imagine.

He might return to the Homeworld eventually to regain adulation and glory. Perhaps he might establish his rule there, too.

Where was his food?

He refused to call out for his guards. It would have been so simple to send a summons to the stupid creatures, but the savages did not mindspeak. Small wonder their success lagged.

Araxis stormed out of his dark, stone chamber, prepared to vent his fury on the two gray creatures who always stood outside the door.

They were not there.

Minutes later, Araxis stood in the center of the ancient Geffitzi compound, looking about in rage. Every cursed one of them was gone. How dare they leave him unprotected and without resources! What did they think they were doing? Even if they brought the girl back to him in the next few breaths, he would punish them severely for this.

It was not until later in the day, when none of the Balandra had returned to the Geffitzi temple complex, that it occurred to him that he might have actually been betrayed and abandoned. His first reaction was outrage. He stormed about, setting scattered fires outside the stone buildings, which was all his current body allowed him to do, and which only infuriated him more. He slashed leaves off the surrounding trees with Ly Toma's starpower and sliced gouges into the doors of the main structure until he grew frustrated with the paltry results he produced. With Arylla's power, he could have leveled the whole area with a twitch of will.

Ving's power could still wreak terrible damage on the softer flesh of this world, however. Furious to the point where he struggled to breathe, he retreated to his chosen refuge inside the main temple to plot revenge.

Near dark, he wondered why the Balandra might have dared to ignore their master's bargain and betray him, and for whom. It could not be for Kaphri; she was too timid and ignorant to strike such a complex deal. And he would not believe it was for any force of this world. He'd heard enough cursing and whining from the Balandra to know they hated this place. They only wanted it razed of all life.

Which left the Ly Kai. The treacherous priests of the Homeworld might have found a way to strike some bargain with the winged ones. Even if the Balandra had no telepathic powers, they did speak Ly Kai.

Which was another thing that irritated him. Being forced to speak Ly Kai to those ignorant rabble was an insult beyond forgiveness. Why couldn't they mindspeak like civilized beings?

Treacherous filth. And he was very sure they were treacherous. They plotted things in his presence in their obscene tongue that sounded like a mixture of water gurgling down a hole and an injured animal crying out. Maybe they had even plotted this desertion within his earshot. He'd heard the hacking sound that passed for their laughter behind his back. They disapproved of his actions and muttered about them to each other. And that Razek. He seemed to forget who was in control here. He always thought he knew a better way. Well, they hadn't succeeded in following his orders to capture the girl yet, and she was just a stupid, ignorant child.

Now they had disappeared. The stupid creatures would never dare defy the force that had sent them here to help him. They feared and worshipped it too much. That had always been strongly apparent. They would never abandon their master.

But they had abandoned him.

A sudden, terrible thought froze him mid-step. Many days had passed since his last communication with the force beyond the gate. He'd been too preoccupied with his own plans. He'd left Balandra behind, beyond the barrier, to carry on their attacks and to grow their numbers, mostly as a diversion for their master. When he succeeded in restoring himself to a form that wielded Arylla, he would no longer have a use for any of them.

What if the force beyond the gate had begun to suspect his plan? It had once found a way to draw his attention, and it had found a way to insert Balandra back onto this world. Could it find a way to pull itself into this world without his assistance?

What would it require to manifest a presence here? Perhaps—like him—it only needed to take a body to give it a physical presence...

The next realization struck Araxis so hard that he sank to his knees.

He had never questioned it before, thinking it was a mere convenience to help further his plans.

His ugly gray servants spoke fluent Ly Kai!

Chapter 84
We Will Manage

KAPHRI WATCHED RAIN fall on flower-speckled grass. The scene reminded her of her first day lying on the blossom-covered plateau after she escaped the barren mountain ring that encircled Kryie Karth. It had been the first beautiful thing in this world she'd ever seen, and the sight of it, combined with the trauma of her escape, had held her enthralled for hours, forcing Gemma to promise her there was much more to see if she started moving again.

The tiny dragon had spoken true. The beauty of this world still amazed Kaphri. It was so different from the area around the tower, with its struggling life, where she had grown up. This world was wondrous, no matter what it threw at her. If Gemma were still with her, they might have contemplated this meadow as a place for their future home together.

Kaphri's heart twisted, making her tighten her grip on the crystal. It seemed to constantly find its way into her hand lately.

"So, you saved us all." The sending dropped into her head without warning, the same way it always did.

Was this an actual acknowledgment of her actions? From Frax?

Kaphri turned her face away to hide the rush of a sudden blush. *"I only did what had to be done."*

"You did that," he agreed, coming up to stand beside her. *"You've created quite a flurry of activity over the past several days."*

Her heart dropped as he continued. *"I can understand using your power for defense. Otherwise, you should be more circumspect."*

He meant she should not have used it to assist Uri with his medical care three nights ago. As their eyes met, frustration surged in her. *"It seemed a good idea at the time. In hindsight, you may be right; perhaps it was not."*

He gave her a hard look. *"I've told you, Priestess, stay true to your purpose. The rest of us are peripheral."*

Disposable was more the word he meant. She refused to accept that. Seuliac said martyrs were of little value in this effort. *"We are all here, and we are all alive."*

"It may have worked out well this time—we can't be sure, yet—but what about the next time? I told you: take care of yourself. Don't worry about us. We are Geffitzi. We will manage."

"Really? And where would Seuliac be right now if I hadn't acted? Tobin wanted to kill him, Frax! The Grimmen wants both the Aedecs dead. And what about you? The Cyrwins attacked you!"

"They attacked me, Priestess. They did not kill me. And as for Seuliac, of the two of you, who would be the greater loss to us? Ask him. He'll tell you the same thing I do. Without you, we have nothing. So don't expect me to thank you for putting yourself in unnecessary jeopardy."

"I kept us together, Frax. I kept people from being killed."

"You were reckless. I've told you: if anything happens to us, you have to push on. I did not say stop and rescue me or Seuliac."

She'd been expecting this encounter, but his disapproval still hurt. "*I know I made the right choices when we encountered the Cyrwins. More recently,*" with you, she wanted to say, "*yes, I may wonder.*"

"I hoped you might learn something more useful than sarcasm from the warlord."

"Seuliac has taught me to trust my instincts and to act. Which is what you want—someone to act—isn't it? I acted. I don't expect you to

be grateful or to approve. It's done, and you are alive to criticize it as you see fit." She turned to walk away.

"We are not finished, dammit!" Frax caught her forearm in a hard grasp.

Her head snapped around. Their eyes locked. *"You do not own me."*

"No, Cadarn does not."

To replace himself with Cadarn! It was as if he had slashed any link between them.

"I'm not trying to bind you to anything, so save your resentment, Priestess," Frax continued. *"When this is done, you're free to leave this world. Does that set your mind at ease?"*

It did not. She realized unhappily that she wanted him to lay some claim to her. To tell her he wanted her to stay with him. If it meant warrior claim, if that was the only way, that was all right.

"Yes," she lied.

He released his grip.

Furious, her heart twisting with pain, she stormed away.

Chapter 85
The Beginnings of Conspiracy

SIX DAYS RIDING, THEN walking in areas where the terrain grew so treacherous they could not trust the coarse ropes and bridles they twisted from grasses at night to keep their seat on the slippery hide of the Cyrwins' backs, had gotten them across the Pterfellen and north, into the foothills.

She could not have done it with the geas still gripping her.

When Frax told them the Grimmen claimed to have originated the terrible, obsessive drive that had emerged while she was wandering in the north, a flash of fury ran through her. How? How could that be true? She had been an innocent, naïve creature moving aimlessly about this world. Even Gemma had seemed surprised by the geas' emergence.

She thought the Grimmen's claim was more a desperate attempt to maintain some influence over them. But she had never been able to identify the source of the compulsion, so she could not dispute it. She only knew that on the night it released her, other things had also happened in her mind. Ly Kai things...

Besides, she had other issues to focus her attention on. Allowing the Cyrwins to assume watches and scouting duties freed Seuliac to devote more time to her lessons. They went over Ly Kai laws and endless other bits of her studies with Hyfas, picking them apart until she thought her head would reel. Then they would move on to physical activity as he attempted to coach her in Geffitzi fighting and self-defense.

There were also times, however, when the warlord was simply inclined to talk. Despite Seuliac's role as a teacher, he did not make her feel as if those random moments were part of his agenda. Their conversation drifted, seeming to take them where it would, though she knew he analyzed her every word later. The exchanges were a welcome diversion from the fear and pain that ate at her every time she tried to envision the future.

She understood the warlord's constant pressure to explore her abilities. His descriptions of the things he'd seen the Ly Kai do as they fled north away from the site of betrayal, of actions made to defend against attacks from angry Geffitzi, had moved her out of her ignorance. The child's blocks implanted in her mind had burned away when Seuliac's descriptions forced her to accept the reality of Ly Kai power. She had walked a different, tortured Paths of Power the night the geas released her, motivated by, of all things, a Geffitz warrior, and her new sense of Arylla's full power made her shudder.

Since she had not walked the traditional Paths of Power, guided by a Ly Kai master, there was a chance some of the blocks restricting her abilities still lurked inside her. Fear of making an unfortunate discovery at a time when she might need her starpower the most kept her awake at night, and she and the warlord continued to push the exploration of her abilities, even though fear of drawing Araxis' attention by her use of Arylla made it difficult and frustrating.

They continued the journey toward the Ly Kai gate now because the Grimmen demanded it. As long as the Cyrwins agreed not to harm the Aedecs, she supposed she should be grateful for their help getting her there. What would happen after they arrived, however, concerned her more.

It concerned Frax, too. She sensed the disquiet in his thoughts during silent moments like this, even though she sought to avoid it. She hated the link that invaded and revealed those hidden parts of them equally. Curse the Wyxa! It fueled her resentment toward them, even though she knew it was not their doing. The link had taken hold long before either of them had encountered the swamp dwellers, though how much earlier, she couldn't say. Was it before Windmer? Before the Black Tower? Perhaps it had started on their first encounter in Omurda, when he was intimidating and tormenting her for his entertainment—in which case, he deserved the annoyance of it. She, however, did not. Still, whatever caused the link, it worked both ways, and though they never spoke of it, he was as unhappy with it as she was.

He certainly had more to hide, she thought resentfully.

Across the grassy slope, Frax glanced over his shoulder at her with a frown, and she instinctively tightened her mindshields. Had he caught her last thought? She must be more careful to keep her musings private.

"*What's stolen your thoughts, Willow?*"

She gratefully shifted her attention to Uri. "*That.*" She pointed across the amazing vista of the Pterfellen toward the north. "*Omurda,*" she named the dark shadow, like a heavy mist, stretching across the horizon in the distance.

"Ah. I hadn't realized it was visible from here on the mountainside. I guess we're so used to seeing it."

"You know it exists in the same manner that I know Arylla is above us."

"Well...maybe. It doesn't do us any good to know it's there."

"But a sky without it would be strange to you."

"Yes. Why? Are you taking it away?" He grinned at her.

"No," she answered solemnly. *"I just think the Ly Kai should have noticed it, too."*

"I would think so."

"But somehow they kept it out of their thoughts, along with the barrier's existence." And marginalized their encounters with the hostile Geffitzi to a minor instance she had barely noticed.

"You said this was a new world for them; maybe they simply accepted it as part of this place. Or maybe you didn't recognize it when you encountered it in their minds."

Or maybe they agreed not to deal with it and pushed it out of their collective mind like they had done so many other things. She had certainly done that often enough, shoving things tightly away and refusing to deal with them until a later time. Some of those issues had come roaring back to the surface, emerging at inopportune times, while others still lurked, unresolved, which was an inadequate solution. She would have to confront all those painful revelations and emotions eventually. She needed to resolve them in small background bits before life forced her to confront them head-on. Regardless, she would never know why the Ly Kai had not exhibited the slightest awareness of the massive, shadowed area, Omurda, or the barrier. They were all dead except Ving—and she certainly wasn't able to question him.

"That's not what's bothering you."

"No." She sighed. *"Uri, I don't understand how I forgot Gemma while the Wyxa held us prisoners. She's the most important person in my life! And don't tell me it's because she's a Guardian and is manipulating me! Gemma cares for me."*

"You don't think the Wyxa blocked your memory?"

"No."

"Then perhaps the Guardian did it. To protect you."

"Or," and this was the thing really haunting her, *"perhaps Gemma did it to protect herself."* After the Wyxa had attempted to join her in Ankar Mekt and failed, they had tried to lock her away on their Ethereal Plain to isolate her from this world and her companions. In her fear, she had called out for Gemma, enabling the Wyxa to

recapture the tiny dragon that they called the Guardian, and to trap her back inside the crystal Kaphri was holding so tightly in her hand.

A sob caught in her throat. *"They used me to lock Gemma back into the Guardian Stone. I called her to me. I helped them..."*

She had betrayed Gemma and didn't deserve to mourn her loss. But relaxing her fingers away was like prying them from a friend's hand as they slipped beneath the surface of a lake.

"Did you put her in there?"

"No. But I was selfish and weak. I called her..."

"You reacted the way they anticipated. Manipulation is not a new theme here, Willow."

Frax had said the same thing many times.

"If you had anticipated their trap and refused to call for help," Uri continued, *"where would you be now?"*

Trapped on another plain of existence, sleeping and unaware while the warriors lay dead in the darkness beneath the Black Tower.

The truth settled over her: with the Wyxa blocking her access to Arylla, she could not have acted otherwise.

"So, let the Guardian fulfill her role without your angst and lament."

"I will find a way to free her."

"There may only be one way to do that."

Follow this path to its inevitable conclusion while conquering everything thrown at her.

The odds were not on her side. *"I might not succeed,"* she whispered. She might never see Gemma again.

She met the warrior's eyes, and the truth ran through her: they already knew that. They took their chances every day, knowing they might never again see the people they cared about on the other side of Araxis' barrier. They moved forward with the belief she, or they, would find a way to fix things. She might never see Gemma again. But like the families that the warriors had left behind, the little dragon was still inside her heart and inside her head.

Their situation held no easy answers, no clear path forward. Only allies with a common cause.

Allies not always in agreement on the way forward. Sometimes not even in agreement on what the end solution should be.

"Uri, the Grimmen insists we go to the city. But what about the barrier? I agreed to try to remove it. You all expect me to, and rightly so. I'm the reason you're trapped down here. But I don't know what will happen at the city. What if... I could be gone, " she blinked twice, hard, for emphasis, *"just like that. I would never choose it, but it is a possibility."*

Uri smiled ruefully. "*We know. It doesn't look as if we have much choice with our new friends watching our every move. I'm not much help if you're looking for new answers.*"

It was time to bring up the thought that had been gnawing at the back of her mind. She no longer feared her starpower. Perhaps it was time to put it to use.

The problem was how to present it. She believed Uri's blood chant, that blood spilled in the Grimmenwood once was obliged; twice, tied; thrice, applied. Meaning the Grimmen could eavesdrop on one's thoughts at the first drop of blood shed inside its realm, seek one outside its domain with the second incidence, or—if one's blood was shed three times—manipulate the victim's thoughts and actions.

Other things the warriors believed had proven to have basis in truth, and she did not doubt the Grimmen currently had several ways of knowing what they might plan.

Who did the Eldren of the Woods have its tentacles into the deepest? Frax? She firmly believed so. Seuliac? The warlord had shed blood more than once before they escaped the Grimmenwood on that last stormy night. So, yes, they were at least under some influence. Tobin was beyond question, and she would never trust

Velacy. That left Uri. The Grimmen had treated him as if it recognized his ties to Cadarn. He had not shed blood within its confines—that she was aware. He was the only candidate of the five with whom she dared discuss this.

But she had to approach it carefully. "*Uri, perhaps we can do more.*"

"*You have an idea?*"

She picked up a short stick and held it up. "See," she told him, speaking aloud in her limited Geffitzi vocabulary. "Do not send."

On the flat stone surface between them, she traced a small, invisible cross mark. "Us." She drew a circle a short distance away from it. "City." A long line north of the two marks. "Obstacle." She avoided the word for barrier in case the Cyrwins around them might cue in on certain words. When Uri grunted understanding, she drew a series of chevrons, representing trees, around the cross mark. "Listener." Abruptly, she cut a diagonal line across the symbols for the trees. She looked up at Uri, and then slowly pressed the stick onto the area of the cross. "Us." She lifted it and set it down on the line she had named obstacle.

She might be able to teleport them back to the barrier, out of the influence of the Grimmen.

He mulled what she had done for a long moment, his eyes narrow. "Can you?"

Now that she was free of the geas? She nodded. "Trees." The way she said the word imbued a deeper meaning. Danger. Mistrust. The Grimmen.

Uri looked at her, understanding but troubled. The question in his eyes was clear: could she move them such a great distance?

There were risks, yes, but letting the Grimmen force them forward on its agenda was worse.

Thinking about it would make her doubt her decision, and doubt would make it impossible to act. She would make the shift now if she thought she could pull the others with her without their close proximity. Scattered over the mountainside and without a shared, specific focus, she didn't think she would succeed. "We eat together at end of this day. Eat well. It may turn into a long night."

"Who?" Uri asked.

She held up five fingers on one hand and the forefinger on the other. She folded it down. Tobin. Including him was too great a risk. The thought of leaving him behind did not make her happy, but she did not believe the Grimmen would harm him. He'd be angry but safe. And she would not leave Seuliac and Velacy, even if the warriors believed all Geffitzi were safe from the Grimmen in Pterfellen.

"Where?"

"Outside Windmer's main gate." Using that location had failed on the night they fled the Palenquemas. She would change it at the last moment, taking them directly to the barrier where she had broken through Arylla's power with the help of the crystal, but she did not have to tell him that now.

"Are you sure?"

No, she was not sure. This was a dangerous undertaking, especially if the Grimmen's influence extended that far. She was now convinced the Grimmen had interfered with their jump out of the Palenquemas, pulling them to Cadarn. They could accept its control until their time ran out, or act before it could stop them. She nodded. "No more talk. Tonight."

Uri looked grim as he sighed.

Kaphri glanced around. The Cyrwins had been feeding on the lush grass while they rested. Now, they were drifting toward a mountain stream beyond the crest of the hillside. *"Our break is ending. We should prepare to move on."*

Frax spun about to find Tobin standing a step behind him.

Well, the outer shell was Tobin. The gray eyes seethed with something else.

"She plots." The words were flat, emotionless.

He stared at his brother, or whatever held him, warily. "How?"

"She schemes to counteract the Grimmen's will. Stop her or others will die. The Grimmen will not be thwarted in this."

"The Priestess is plotting something?" He had to say the words out loud from sheer incredulity. What? Certainly not an escape to the Homeworld; the Grimmen was already pushing them to that. What else could she think of?

The barrier. He knew it still troubled her. Kep, it troubled them all. But was she involving others at the risk of the Grimmen's wrath?

Who, knowing their immediate situation and Uri's explanation of the blood tie, would be stupid enough to think the entity in the woods would not know what they did? Seuliac had come back to them a bloody mess after the Cyrwins captured him. True, not much of the blood ended up being his after the rain washed him clean, but there had been the slice on his jaw from the edge of a Cyrwin's tail. The warlord must be bound in the second phase of blood tie to the Grimmenwood, if not the third—if one believed such things—and, after everything else he'd seen before leaving the forest trail, he grudgingly did. Like it or not, the Grimmen had a mindlink with the Rhynogian warlord, and nothing he thought slipped past it.

Seuliac would know that.

Kaphri had to be aware of it, too, his mind argued back. Besides, the warlord was a cautious, long-term schemer. Even if he was dubious of the blood tie, he would not test it unless he grew desperate. Since Tobin had backed off his dour threats, Frax couldn't believe Seuliac felt endangered enough to take the risk. Besides, no threat to Seuliac or Velacy would ever fire the tiny flicker of distress he thought he detected in his brother's eyes.

"She's putting Uri in jeopardy?"

The muscles in Tobin's face tightened slightly as if he were fighting to resist an expression. Of what? Relief? "The Grimmen will not be thwarted in this."

And I'm supposed to stop them? He wondered fleetingly if he should. She had to be thinking about the barrier. That was the way she was: she had given her word. She might even have a chance at success now, with the additional time she'd had to get comfortable with her power.

If the Grimmen didn't take away the opportunity for her to act by shoving her off this world...

Pain stabbed his upper arm. He looked down to find Tobin's hand gripping him above the elbow. His brother's fingers were white from the pressure they exerted. Tobin's face was equally pale. Something fought for expression behind those storm-swirled gray eyes.

Curse the Grimmenwood! Frax felt a wash of bitter frustration and anger as he watched his brother struggle to put something of himself forward. How many times had he asked— begged— the Grimmen to release Tobin? Still, it kept its talons embedded in him.

"Stop her, or the Grimmen will," Tobin managed to send before the struggle faded from his eyes. He released Frax's arm and abruptly turned away, stalking toward the Cyrwins as they crested the slope and disappeared beyond to the rushing stream on the other side. He did not look back.

Kep! Frax cursed. The little fool was putting them all in grave danger.

He stalked up the hillside to where Uri and Kaphri sat.

Chapter 86
No Room For Emotion

"AND YOU THOUGHT YOU could do what? Just jump out of here? Were you even planning to tell me, or were you just going to go?"

Kaphri paled. *"We were only talking. I didn't think—"*

"That's the problem: you weren't thinking!"

"There was no plan—"

"Frax—"

"We'll talk in a minute." Frax shot his cousin a glare before turning his attention back to the Priestess. *"You can say anything you want to us. We understand. It's the Grimmen you have to worry about."*

"I was only talking to Uri!" Kaphri protested. *"Besides, he didn't—"*

"He didn't what? Give blood to the Grimmenwood? Do you know why? Think, Priestess! He's my cousin. He has Cadarnian blood. That's why it didn't come after him with the rest of you at the edge of the Ilex. Anything you say to him goes right to the Grimmen. Not by his intention. He can't stop it. The Grimmen is always listening!" Frax rubbed his forehead with hard fingers. *"Did you forget that you shared blood there, too?"*

The Grimmen would have suffocated her if Frax hadn't sliced her wrist. "*It did not accept my blood. You said—"*

"The Grimmen didn't accept your blood because it doesn't intend for you to stay on this world. It doesn't want a connection with you. That doesn't mean it doesn't have one. Cadarn doesn't know the extent of its powers, and we've shared a link with it for thousands of years. Now the

Grimmen thinks you're trying to circumvent its plans, and it will stop you however it deems necessary."

She had put Uri's safety in jeopardy. The realization shook Kaphri. Now, the threat from the Grimmenwood lay more heavily over them than before.

But why? What did the Grimmen want from them that they didn't want for themselves? She was only trying to set things right for this world. "*I'm just trying to help!*"

"*Don't help! I've told you: do what you're told to do when you're told to do it!*"

"*Like some spoil of war that you order about?*"

"*That is not the point—*"

"*It is precisely the point! I agreed to do something, and I'm trying to keep my end of the bargain. You don't know what will happen when we get to the city. I might simply disappear. What will happen then? If I let the Grimmen have its way, it might strand you here to die in the south. The Grimmen won't care.*"

"*We don't need you to make things more complicated.*"

"*Then what, exactly, do you want from me?*"

"*I want you to stop! You're going to get people killed, including yourself.*"

"*Or I just might succeed.*"

"*Or you just might die,*" he snarled.

Angry frustration swirled through her. "*You want the barrier down. I am trying to find a way to do that first, before some stupid forest spirit falls prey to a lie and whisks me away. Maybe you could do something to help me instead of criticizing and giving in to everything the Grimmen demands. I haven't seen you do anything to help.*"

Time seemed to freeze as Frax stared at her. Oh, Hredroth, she thought, I have gone too far.

"*No, Priestess,*" he finally sent coldly. "*I'm not contributing anything at all. Just dead weight. Sorry.*" Abruptly, he turned and walked away.

Kaphri stared at his retreating back with sickened dismay. Oh, Hredroth! What had she done? After everything they had gone through together...

She had made a monstrous mistake, and he would never forgive her.

Uri knew when it was best to shield from a conversation and walk away. Besides, Frax would find time to express his displeasure with him soon enough.

"*Uri...*"

He paused in his retreat. Open. Waiting. But he didn't turn back toward her.

"*I said something terrible to him! It was wrong and unjust, but I wanted to make him feel the same way I do every time he's angry with me. I've made him hate me.*" The last was a young maiden's cry of despair.

He should keep walking, he told himself. The big warrior sighed as he turned back to her. Such a small bundle of misery and despair! Hadn't they all felt the same at least once in their youth? "*Emotions are running rampant inside all of us right now, Willow. Frax may be very angry with you, but he doesn't hate you.*"

"*Why must it—he—be so difficult?*" Pained frustration shifted to frustrated anger.

There were times when it was best not to pursue a subject, and he was a fool for not backing away this time, but Frax had asked him to help her stay emotionally balanced through this mess. As powerful as she might be, she was still a child in a world-shattering situation. Besides, he genuinely liked her.

But Frax would owe him big for this one. "*Interactions between people are never simple, Willow. Sometimes, it's as if there's a price in misery that must be paid.*"

"*And then, when this price is paid, it becomes less painful?*"

He caught a sense of irony in her question. She knew the answer but was hoping for something better. Did she want him to lie? He didn't think so.

Uri smiled wearily. "*It is never smooth between a man and a woman. I would be lying if I said it was. Or perhaps it is just us Geffitzi.*"

She gave a soft, bitter mental laugh. "*I don't know, Uri, but I doubt it's only with your people.*" She looked up at him now, her eyes clear but sad. *"Why can't things be different between us? I want them to be different."*

"*Willow, I think sometimes we choose our own lives, and sometimes the times choose them for us. I believe this is one of the situations when it is chosen for us.*"

"*Can you accept what these times bring you?*"

An image of his beloved Ladrienca, laughing up at him as she waded in a sun-dappled brook, came into his mind. It made him sad to think she might never know what had happened to him. It didn't matter whether he accepted it, however. He only needed to know he had done his utmost to keep her safe.

"*It's in Geffitzi nature to question, to fight, to reject what we feel we have not chosen freely. We have an ancient tale of a man who throws away a precious stone merely because someone gives it to him. He did not pick it up himself. In the story, the Goddess grants him a long life of wretched poverty so that he might regret his action every day. A newer version adds a line that says he never even gave it another thought.*"

Kaphri gave a short, hard laugh. "*Did a Guardian give the precious stone?*"

"*In this story, yes, it was a Guardian.*"

"*Do they interfere in your history frequently?*"

Interfere? He blinked at her choice of words. "*Well, yes, they probably do. But Geffitz lore generally paints them as positive in their influence.*" He did not sense a positive feeling from her.

"*Frax does not believe so.*"

"*No. Perhaps there's another story there.*"

"*I pity the poor Guardian who might try to give him a precious stone. I know everything I do is wrong.*"

Uri sighed. "*Frax feels a great deal of responsibility for this situation—*"

"*Why? Because he thinks he stopped Tobin from killing me?*"

"*Well...*"

"*But you stopped Frax, Uri. You saw Gemma first and called his attention to her.*"

"*So, I did.*" Uri looked surprised at the recollection.

"*Which means he can stop blaming himself, Tobin, or you for all this.*"

"*Willow! He doesn't blame—*"

"*Yes, he does, Uri. I wish you had not seen Gemma. I wish Tobin had not stopped...*"

"*Willow, you don't mean that. You're upset. And that's all right. But please stop trying to shoulder the blame for everything. Between you and Frax, you would think no one else was involved! Thousands of years of history intersect here. You didn't cause this situation—*"

"*Then why—*" she broke off with a deep gasp to prevent dissolving into tears. "*Why do we always end up arguing?*"

This "we" did not include him. "*What can I tell you, Willow? Sometimes two people look at each other for the first time and it just happens as if it was destined from birth. You can't stop it no matter what you do. And conversely, if it isn't meant to be, there is nothing—nothing—you can do to make it happen. No amount of trying, crying, and begging will change it. It's simply the nature of things. Sometimes it takes years—a lifetime—for people to work through their problems with one another."*

"Years?" She stared at him with horror.

"I know. You don't have years. We don't have years." There was a time for kindness and a time for harsh reality. *"We work with what we're given, Willow. It's all we have."*

Years.

She looked away, down into the woods where Frax had disappeared, pained but knowing everything Uri said was true.

Seuliac was correct, too. There was no room for her emotions here. The distraction risked getting them killed. The bitter truth burned anything else she wanted to say, any protests, away.

She feared Uri would leave her then. He did not. She was grateful as they stood in silence.

His mind seething with bitter anger, Frax stormed down the slope to the lower tree line.

The Priestess was right about one thing: he wanted her to remove the barrier as much as any of them did. He'd fought and maneuvered to bring them this far. But, at no cost to him? She had no idea...! The loss of Tobin to the Grimmen, alone, was a high enough price to pay! Kep, hadn't every Geffitz over the last twenty-five years lost enough to the Ly Kai?

He desperately wanted the barrier gone, but how could they succeed with the Grimmen making its ruthless demands upon them? It was tearing apart everything they had worked for, grinding them beneath its will with careless disregard. And there was nothing he could do about it. The Grimmenwood claimed it had manipulated the Priestess into their grasp, then manipulated them all to Cadarn. It had stolen and bent Tobin to its will, and it punished him for refusing to abandon the Aedecs to its deadly whim by denying him any return, ever, to Cadarn. All to push her off this world while it allied with some other force, already proven treacherous, to remove the barrier.

He could only hope, unbelievable as it seemed, that the other force would come through and the Geffitz people could return to their homes.

Anger and frustration swirled inside him. He shared the Priestess' fear that if she went to the city, if the Ly Kai took her away, the barrier would never fall, and the Geffitzi would never return to their lands. The Grimmen was deceived if it thought whoever it bargained with could be trusted to remove it.

After all these years, what did the Grimmen have to lose if it allowed them to deviate in their plan a bit? Once she removed the barrier, she could still go to the city and make her exit. After all their destruction, the cursed Ly Kai could wait a bit longer, dammit!

Frax stopped in his tracks. What, indeed, did the Grimmen have to lose if it was willing to sacrifice the return of the whole of the Geffitz race to the south? It said it had placed the geas on her, forcing her to come southward into their hands. But, until she found the crystal in the Black Temple, she never could have passed the barrier. Their fall through it had been a monumental accident. The Grimmen could never have anticipated it. So, what had it planned to do with her after it placed her within their reach? What had been the next, unfulfilled step in its grand scheme?

His answering thought sent slivers of ice through his veins. Had the Grimmen planned to turn her over to Araxis in the north at the Maugrock to get the barrier removed? The Evil One already had his Balandran minions invading the north. Was the Grimmen willing to allow Araxis to regain a form capable of wielding starpower? To let him renew his reign on this world with the singular hope that Araxis would only enslave the Geffitzi and not destroy them, believing, sooner or later, the Children of Kep would throw off the Evil One's shackles once again and Cadarn—a broken, weakened Cadarn—would eventually rise?

The immensity of that sacrifice was too much to consider.

A small stream cut through the trees to his right. He stalked toward it, needing a splash of cold water on his face to clear his mind and ease his sudden nausea.

A shadowed movement jerked him to attention. He looked up, stunned, at the shape looming above him.

Razek gave him a razor-toothed smile.

Other shadows were dropping silently out of the trees around him. Before Frax could react, hands seized his arms, and a cloth with an overwhelmingly bitter smell clamped over his face.

Their attack had been efficient: they had not given the Geffitz warrior the opportunity to react and had not lost any of their forces. With dwindling numbers, Razek appreciated that. It made his next action the more regrettable.

Taking his short knife in hand, he stepped up behind the nearest of his men. Throwing his arm around the Balandran's neck, he jerked him backward, driving the weapon into his body just so: not deep enough to kill immediately, but enough to kill eventually. The warrior would not live more than a thousand breaths. Long enough to do what Razek needed him to do.

The Balandran went stiff with shock. "Listen to me," Razek hissed against his ear while the rest of his force continued to secure the Geffitz for transport. "You will tell them exactly this, then you may die..."

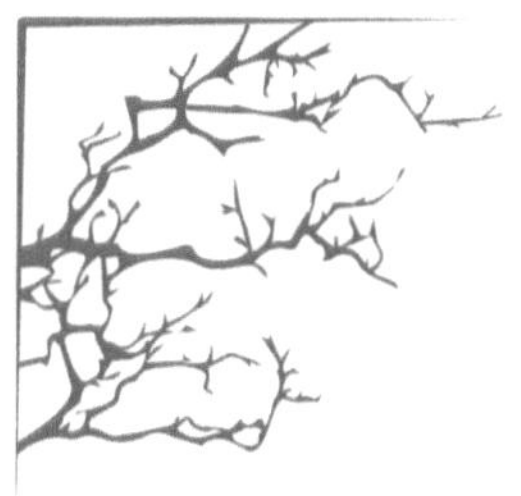

Chapter 87 Aftermath

EIGHT DAYS AND NO SIGN of the Balandra. Seuliac frowned.

Velacy had asked him if he thought the six gray warriors the Cyrwins had killed on the escarpment might have been the last of the gray men's forces and Seuliac had said no. He'd seen the black dots flying in the west, hovering above the distant trailhead that would have been their path out of the forest if the fresh pile of bones in the center of the trail had not alerted them to the lurking threat. There were at least three times that number swirling in wait, and it would not have been the total number of their enemy.

No. Instinct told him the threat of an attack from the Balandra grew stronger and more inevitable with every passing moment.

From his position in the shadow of a large boulder, Seuliac kept watch over the mountainside. Their short break was over, and they should be moving on. Instead, the Cyrwins had disappeared over the edge of the slope, and some sort of high drama was playing out between the girl and Kitahn. Despite the distance and the girl's natural lack of expression, he could see it was a heated discussion.

He watched Kitahn turn and storm toward the tree line below.

The brothers had had their heads together a few minutes earlier. What sort of trouble were baby Kitahn and the cursed woods stirring up?

When the girl turned her attention to Uri, he decided it was time to intervene. Every hard knock life dealt her could not be softened by Caspani. Not now, not in the future. Feeling a mixture of intrigue and irritation, he strode down the slope.

He was within two steps of joining them when the four Balandra rose out of the forest below. He could have sworn they looked directly at him, their expressions twisted into evil smirks, before they turned northward, wings pumping as they towed a bundle suspended on ropes between them.

"*Kitahn,*" He snarled at the girl. She'd seen the Balandra, too. "*Do you feel him?*"

"*No.*" Rising panic edged her sending.

He cursed. A disaster had just befallen them, and this was not the time for her to add to the problem with a reckless action. Before she could react further, he swung out his arm, catching her across the chest and knocking her to the ground. "*Keep her there,*" he hissed at a stunned Caspani. "*I don't care what you have to do short of killing her; don't let her do anything until I tell you!*"

Giving a shout for Velacy, he ran toward the place where Frax Kitahn had disappeared into the trees only moments before.

The Geffitz commander was gone, his mental presence extinguished like a candle flame pinched out.

Not dead. Gone.

"I've got one!" Velacy's triumphant hoot shattered the woods' silence. "The bastard's down, but it's still alive."

A Balandran? "Don't kill it!" Seuliac ran.

Velacy was squatted beside the fallen creature, his knife poised for a killing thrust. The leaves and ground around the area had been churned up as if there'd been a scuffle. The downed creature looked barely alive.

"I said, don't kill it!"

"Why not? I'm only finishing what Kitahn failed to do." The younger Geffitz was aching to strike a killing blow.

"We need to question it." And this young fool thought he had the instincts to rule Rhynog. Idiot! "Did you fight with it?"

"No." Velacy gave the creature a look of angry disgust and stood up. "It was already down."

The warlord quickly looked over the area. Whatever had happened to Kitahn had played out here. It hadn't involved much of a fight, but the disturbed area was large.

He shouldered Velacy aside and kicked an ugly spear beyond the reach of a gray, bony hand. Too bad, the thought flashed in his head, if the creature had used it on Velacy, it would have solved one of his more delicate problems.

Dropping to his knees beside the fallen Balandra, Seuliac ran his hands over its body, tossing away any item he remotely suspected could be used as a weapon. Then he looked for wounds. There were none on its front side. Rolling the creature half over, he examined its back. It took a close search to find the small puncture in the black leather jerkin. Beneath was a small stain of blood on discolored flesh; the wound had already sealed off. It was deep and deadly, expertly delivered with a specific purpose in mind. He lowered the creature down onto its back. "Kitahn didn't do this. This creature is only intended to live long enough to deliver us a message.

"Where is the Geffitz warrior?" he snapped at the creature. "Why did you take him?"

The creature made a few harsh sounds in its native tongue.

Velacy snorted derisively. "How are we supposed to understand that?"

Memory flashed. Kaphri had expressed shock at how the creatures spoke her native tongue of Ly Kai. "We need the girl."

The distance would make a sending from a Rhynogian Geffitz difficult. He had to reach Uri, and it had to work the first time.

Urgency strengthened his effort. "*Windmer! Bring her down here. Fast!*"

The effort left him feeling as if hands had grasped his brain and stretched it.

Not a good feeling. But there was a faint brush of a response from upslope.

Tobin joined them. "So, it's only intended to live long enough to deliver a message." He stared at the fallen creature dispassionately.

The younger Kitahn seemed remarkably calm for someone whose kin had just been snatched by a bunch of flesh-eating devils.

"Where were the Cyrwins when this happened, Kitahn? I thought they were supposed to be guarding against this."

Tobin flicked him a cold look. "They were on guard."

Really? Seuliac bit back his anger. They had enough of a problem on their hands without the distraction of an argument over the Cyrwins. There would be time to delve into their strange lapse in protection later.

"Keep a close watch overhead for an attack," he snarled at Velacy. Best not to put their faith in an ally that had already, quite obviously and for whatever reason, failed them. If this was a trap, he didn't want an accusation of negligence laid at his feet.

He didn't think it was a trap; however, Araxis had played this one out very successfully.

He scowled at the Balandran on the ground, torn between caution and the need to know what message the thing carried. Should they jeopardize the Priestess's safety long enough for her to speak to it?

They had to. There was an obvious message here, and they needed to know what it was.

The girl arrived with Uri. Seuliac raised a hand, stopping them several paces away from the Balandran. Kaphri's face was pale, but she held her composure.

"Where's Frax? What the hell happened here?" Uri kept his tone carefully controlled.

"Gone." Seuliac looked at Kaphri. *"Speak to this thing quickly, girl. Ask why they did this."*

From the moment she'd come within view, the creature's eyes had never left her. Fearing it might explode to life with a hidden knife thrust at her, he squatted behind it to pin the thing's shoulders to the ground. *"Ask it!"* he ordered.

She was obviously uncomfortable speaking to the creature in her own tongue. The warlord caught the Ly Kai word for 'why.'

The creature's response was short.

Kaphri said something in a surprised, defensive tone, and the Balandran responded again. To Seuliac's ears, the answer did not vary, as if it repeated the same phrase.

She looked at Seuliac. He could feel frustration in her mind, but calm overlaid it. *"It just keeps saying I must go to the city."*

"Why? What's there?"

The creature spat more words. Kaphri shook her head. *"No delays, it says. They took Frax there. If we want him back, unharmed, I must go there quickly. I am only allowed four days before they will kill him."*

The Balandran's strength beneath his hands was beginning to fail.

"Why?" Seuliac demanded. *"Ask him what they want!"*

Kaphri fired off the question, but the knife thrust, so expertly administered, was taking its final, intended toll. The creature managed a twist of a mocking smile at her question before it went limp.

"*Damn!*" Seuliac shoved the body away in disgust and climbed to his feet. "*What did it say, Girl?*"

"It said go to the city. No delays. The Geffitz warrior is held there." Her composure finally cracked, distress seeping into her sending. *"I don't understand. They took him to make us go to the city? Why? We're already going there."*

Tobin flashed her a disdainful look. *"You were plotting other strategies."*

"Not 'plotting,'" Kaphri's shock was wearing off, her outrage beginning to rise. *"We were considering other options—"*

"Apparently, that doesn't matter, does it, Kitahn?" Prepared for any reaction, Seuliac studied Tobin intently. *"Did you know the Grimmen was selling your brother out today?"*

Tobin paled but his expression did not change. *"She must leave this world,"* he repeated the mantra of the Grimmenwood once again.

"What if we, as Geffitzi, disagree with that, Tobin?" Uri stared at his cousin in disbelief.

"Then you're the next in a long line of casualties because of her, right behind Frax Kitahn."

He called his brother Frax Kitahn? And he called them 'casualties!' Seuliac blinked.

Uri's expression went aghast. "Did the Grimmen let this happen?"

Tobin met his cousin's eyes coldly. "You were warned."

"Warned—!" The flash of fury that ran through the mild-natured warrior scorched them all. Seuliac stepped forward, thrusting a shoulder into Uri's chest to block him as he surged toward Tobin.

"You knew? You knew this was going to happen?" Uri shouted as the warlord strained to hold him back.

The thing that held Tobin Kitahn in its thrall regarded him impassively.

"It doesn't matter," Uri said bitterly. He abruptly relaxed his attempt to get at Tobin and pushed Seuliac away. "We're committed to going there now." He glared at his younger cousin in disgust. *"How could you betray him like this?"*

The younger Kitahn swayed slightly as if he'd been struck, but his expression remained stubbornly unreactive. *"The Grimmen has found a way for him to be of use."*

The outrage that exploded in Kaphri's mind made her dizzy. The Grimmen had just rendered everything Frax had worked for, everything she had heartlessly accused him of failing to do only moments ago, useless with one cold stroke of betrayal. *"If you allow Frax to come to harm..."* Hredroth! The thought seared like a knife thrust to her heart.

Tobin's expression twisted in disdain. *"What do you care about what happens to him? He bargained everything away for you, and you plotted behind his back. He's alive for now. If you want him to stay that way, you'll do as you're told!"*

"Frax would not agree to this, Tobin— "

Tobin shot Uri a warning look. *"He will agree to whatever he's told to do. And so will you."*

Or what? Kaphri bit back her challenge. They all could see how far the wood was willing to go to force their cooperation. Emotion drained away, leaving her cold and empty. Frax was gone and it was her fault. Her careless actions had put him in peril.

She looked at Tobin. The younger Kitahn looked near to collapse, yet his posture conveyed absolute defiance. Had he really known what was going to happen here? Had he remained silent by choice, or was he forced to put a face on the incident for the

Grimmen while suppressing what he felt? No matter what he had recently done, she refused to believe he would willingly put Frax into this danger. Her, yes. Frax, no. Which confirmed that the Grimmen had such deep control over him that he could not reveal or protest its actions.

Aware of her regard, he looked over at her. *"What?"* He snarled.

"The Grimmen wants me gone so badly it will give up any hope of removing the barrier?"

"There are others who will do it."

Others? Plural now?

"Who?" Seuliac broke in.

The being who possessed Tobin twisted the scout's face into a feral snarl that Kaphri would not have believed possible. *"You! Be silent!"* it hissed at the warlord.

"The question is important!" she snapped. *"Who?"* Hredroth, the implications of more Arylla-born with access to this world set her heart pounding harder.

Tobin's eyes flicked between her and the warlord. The creature inside remained stubbornly silent.

"Is it the brother to the Evil One...?"

"Him?" There was a snort of dismissal. *"He is a victim of his blind trust. There are others. Cubs with skill."*

Cubs. Others of her Birthstar? On the Homeworld?

Seuliac had untangled the manipulation of the High Sabbat easily enough. All Ly Kai men and women went on separate, simultaneous journeys to massive temples dedicated to their Birthstar during that holiday—a holiday cleverly machinated by Hredroth to prevent the conception of an Arylla-born child during the star's rising influence.

For the first time, she wondered where the people responsible for her and her uncles' births were. Had they come to this world and subsequently died, or had they remained behind, manipulating power and creating more like her—any of which would be far more knowledgeable in their starpower than she was.

The implication sent a cold chill running down her spine.

"How many? I don't have to remind you of the damage a gate-opener can do." It was not a threat from her specifically; she made sure it understood that.

"More than one," the Grimmen responded sullenly.

Uri, Seuliac, and Kaphri exchanged glances.

"This is bad," Uri said.

"Why do they want me returned to the Homeworld?"

"That is the price for removing the cursed barrier."

Or Araxis' manipulation to regain a physical form

Either way, she had no choice. *"I'll go to the city, but the Grimmen better be sure nothing happens to Frax."*

"Willow," Uri broke in. *"Let's take a moment to consider—"*

"There is no considering, Uri. I have no choice." She locked eyes with the gray swirls in Tobin's face. *"My only stipulation is you do not harm any of these warriors. Frax, Uri, Seuliac, Velacy, and Tobin: all five must be released, unharmed, from your influence. They will not be pursued, harassed, or harmed by you or any of your minions for the rest of their natural days."*

"You are in no position to name terms—"

"Actually," she held the seething gray gaze without blinking, *"I am. Accept my terms or leave us alone."*

"This one doesn't need you to protect—" the being binding Tobin spat.

"Tobin does! Probably more than any of us. If he didn't, you would not have to suppress his reactions so relentlessly!" She softened her tone. *"You could have approached me at any time with honest civility and reason,"* she told the Grimmen quietly. *"I would have tried to work with you."*

"I do not want another ally! I want you and your kind gone!" the thing snarled.

"Fine." She looked around at the warriors. *"We—"*

"*You do not speak for Geffitz warriors,*" the thing snapped.

"*A Geffitz warrior's choice is his own. I, however, am going to the city, regardless."* She felt her resolve slip with fear, but it was not fear for herself. Thought of the cruelty Araxis might inflict upon Frax during any delay made her deathly afraid for him.

"We're going," Uri announced aloud as well as sending. "How much time do we have?"

"It said we have five days," Kaphri replied. Her skin itched with desperation.

"*The Cyrwins will continue to carry you to the city.*"

"After what just happened?" Velacy exclaimed. "We don't want your help—"

"You don't give the orders here, either, Aedec!"

"No, he doesn't," Seuliac agreed evenly. He looked at Uri. *"Which is something we should establish right now. Command of our group reverts to you as Kitahn's second. I can accept that. But I will not accept him."* He nodded toward Tobin. *"He wants to kill all things Aedec. You may share his sentiments, but you're far more capable of self-restraint than he is."* He gave a flick of mocking smile at Uri's exasperated expression.

"You really go out of your way to irritate people, don't you, Seuliac?" Uri growled, seizing the opportunity to focus his fury away from his cousin. The warlord, by all reputation, had some of the best diplomatic skills of any Geffitz alive, though sometimes it was hard to appreciate them in use.

"Under current circumstances, when I look at you, I don't see sky blue; I see the red and green of Cadarn. I do not presume forbearance."

"I think you presume too much forbearance. A little less abrasiveness would go a long way toward assuaging some people's hostility toward you."

The warlord shot him a look of mock shock. *"Where would the fun be in that?"*

"Go to hell, Seuliac." Uri's expression was disgusted, but inside, he felt a wash of relief. The warlord had diffused a dangerous situation by redirecting the topic onto another critical subject and resolved both without argument. He looked around at the others. *"Everyone get moving. We will continue to use the Cyrwins for their speed."*

Velacy muttered a curse as he stormed back up the slope.

Before she could move, Uri slid a hand beneath her elbow and held her back. *"Priestess, we need to talk."*

"I said I agreed," she said defensively.

"Is it telling the truth?"

"What?" She looked toward Tobin, but he was already retreating uphill to the circle of Cyrwins, who were openly emitting an air of hostility. Curse the Grimmen! *"I don't know. I need more information."*

"We don't need a further confrontation with the Grimmen." Seuliac interrupted. *"Reacting emotionally to this situation is dangerous. It's what Araxis wants you to do. You must stay calm so we can formulate a plan of action."*

"The plan is clear: I'll go to the city. What else can I do?"

"For now, you don't do anything," Uri ordered. *"Do you understand me?"*

She looked at the two warriors, despair exploding inside of her. *"Why did you stop me? I could have stopped them—"*

"Think, Girl." Seuliac snapped. *"The Balandra came at us indirectly because they can't handle a direct confrontation with you. Now they have something you want. You have to face them on their terms. If I hadn't stopped you, they might have panicked. If they dropped*

Kitahn the fall might have killed him. Then how do you think you would feel?"

"He's right," Uri agreed. *"We can't pick up and mindlessly tear after them. That's exactly what Araxis wants. We—and it is we, whether you like it or not—will ride toward the city until dark—"*

"I will not ride one of those treacherous—" Her anger surged again.

"They know the way. We will ride. For speed."

Bitter as she felt, she could not argue with their reasoning. *"Fine. We will ride these damn Cyrwins nonstop until full dark."*

A small price in discomfort for the creatures to pay for their treachery. Uri smiled. *"Then we stop and build the biggest damn fire you've ever seen. Stealth doesn't matter anymore. We cook something, work on the details to our approach, and get some sleep. We get up tomorrow with a plan and we will do the same thing all over again."*

Uri motioned the warlord aside while the Cyrwins, reflecting the Grimmen's anger, sullenly assembled. "If you had let her act, she might have done something to prevent this."

"And brought a fight with the Grimmen down upon us for which we are unprepared? She already slipped control of the geas it claims to have laid on her, and she can exert her power over the Cyrwins."

"It feels threatened," the fair-haired warrior sighed. "We suspected it might react. Who could have foreseen this alliance, though?"

The warlord's eyes went to where Kaphri stood staring in the direction the Balandra had disappeared. "They knew exactly what they were doing. They took him because they think he's the key to controlling her. But now we know the Grimmen is working overtly against us, and the rest of us are still intact to move forward."

Uri drew a slight breath as if he were on the verge of a denial, then let it go. "It's that obvious?"

"Caspani, I've been trying to break that infatuation since the day I took over her training. It will doom us all."

Uri suspected the warlord's attempts to break what he termed as her "infatuation" partly centered on what might be better described as the best interests of Rhynog, but he found no reason to disagree. "Setting the obvious aside then, does any of this make sense to you? The Grimmen claims it laid the geas on her to bring her here. It insists she go to this Ly Kai city and leave our world. The Balandra serve Araxis. He wants to steal her form to restore his power and savage our world. To remain here. He doesn't need her to be at any particular location to do that. He tried to snatch her at the edge of the Palenquemas. If she makes one mistake, like lusting for power, she says he can steal her away."

"True. So, why this strange tactic?"

"I admit she and I probably stirred this mess a bit by considering a jump to the barrier, but they didn't miraculously show up. They were already here. Why is the Grimmen suddenly working with the Balandra to force her to this so-called gate? It could have let them snatch her in the heart of the Grimmenwood. Instead, it butchered them."

"And the Cyrwins slaughtered the Balandra at the top of the escarpment." The warlord frowned. "Something has changed."

"Based on a greater mutual need?" Uri suggested.

"Against a greater threat...?"

"Bithzielp," they both exclaimed.

"How? How can he re-establish his filthy, evil grip over our world?" Seuliac was not one to give in to emotional reaction, but the thought of the Geffitzi's ancient tormentor actually returning sent cold blades of anger and aggression driving into his flesh.

"Maybe the Wyxa were right to fear his return after the Priestess removed the Guardian Stone."

"It wasn't working." Seuliac shot him an angry glare. "The Balandra were already re-invading our world."

"I'm not saying their solution was right." The Wyxa had tried to send the warriors back into the Black Temple to return the stone to its place as a seal on the gate, disregarding the fact they would meet their deaths in the heart of the invaders' stronghold. The Priestess had thwarted the plan by snatching the Guardian Stone and teleporting them out of the Palenquemas. "I'm saying they believe he can return from exile."

"It's been over two thousand years."

"The Balandra are here."

"And under the command of the Evil One..." Seuliac's eyes narrowed with thought. "A nightmare alliance for our world."

"Perhaps their alliance has gone wrong?" Uri said.

"Ly Kai deceiving someone? Imagine that!" Araxis was the catalyst for this whole situation. "But the girl. Why doesn't the Grimmen destroy her instead of trying to control her actions and push her off our world?" Seuliac asked. "We all know her very existence is a threat to us. For that matter, why haven't we done it?"

"Because we think she can do something for us..."

The warlord gave Uri a hard smile. "Are we insane? Should we follow the Grimmen's agenda, or should we slit her throat, call it done, and go our separate ways?" He had argued for that as the simplest solution in the past.

Uri sighed. "The Grimmen will likely kill us if we try. If we're dead, our people will have no say in the final outcome of this mess, and that does not sit well with me."

There was a cold glint of appreciation in Seuliac's eyes. "My thoughts, as well." He paused. "And your cousin?"

Uri shook his head. He wasn't sure whether he was furious with Tobin or sympathetic. "I refuse to believe Tobin would ever willfully betray Frax."

"And yet, he did."

Uri sighed. "Yes. Best to get moving. It's the only way we can get answers to our questions."

Kaphri caught up with Tobin as he prepared to mount Stormwraith. *"What did you mean when you said Frax bargained everything?"*

The younger Kitahn gave her a cold stare. *"Bringing those Aedec bastards into the woods cost him his ties to Cadarn; the Grimmenwood completely surrounds the caer and he can never pass through it again. When he backed you in refusing to leave the Aedecs behind at the bottom of the escarpment, it took Azay Rhiad, too. They, and you, have cost him everything."*

"No." She was firm in her sending. *"The Grimmen took everything from him with its stubborn refusal to bend. For what? It abandoned him."* She turned away before he could see her utter despair. Frax had bargained away everything in his life to get her this far and it had not been enough.

She had accused him of doing nothing! Anger and sorrow made her want to scream aloud. Curse the Grimmen! Curse the Ly Kai, Araxis, and the Homeworld! Curse this world, the Geffitzi, and everything in it for making her feel this pain!

Curse her for being an incompetent fool and for caring!

A tear slipped from her eye. She dashed it away, refusing to let her companions see any sign of her inner turmoil.

Her boot skidded on a clump of grass, causing her to jerk the necklace chain and abrade the back of her neck.

Gemma.

The wave of bitter frustration the memory brought broke against a contrasting flood of warm comfort.

Kaphri stopped, confused. Gemma? A quick probe drew no response, but the thought of her tiny companion pushed back her despair. Determination swirled in to replace it.

You will do this. You will save the things you love.

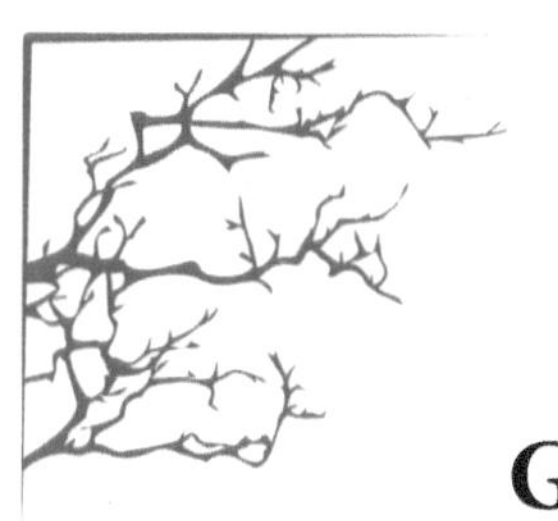

Chapter 88
Garden Prison

HOT, SALTY WATER SPATTERED Frax's face and chest, jerking him awake.

"Son of a—!" he surged to his feet and took a swing at the Balandran warrior standing over him. It danced out of his reach with a dry rustle of laughter.

The rattling sound of movement around him brought Frax up short. He blinked to clear his vision of urine and saw the tips of familiar spears leveled on him from all sides.

Kep! Even the murky light couldn't mask the Balandra's ugly faces as they glared at him from behind their weapons.

A harsh string of sounds rang out from beyond the circle of his captors. The echo told him they were in a large, enclosed place. His eyes flicked upward. A very large space. He could see the dim shapes of graceful, sweeping beams. They were not any style of Geffitzi architecture he recognized.

Which left only one place where he could be: the city of the Ly Kai.

Why bring him here? Did they have the Priestess?

Kep. His head hurt from whatever they'd used to knock him out.

"Anyone here?" he called out mentally.

No response.

That didn't mean they weren't out there somewhere: his range was not as sweeping as Kaphri's. Or maybe the others had fended off the attack. With the help of Cyrwins, they could do that. He would not allow himself to consider any other alternative.

The circle of Balandra separated. Frax squinted to focus his still-blurred vision in the dim light. Another Balandra was standing about twenty feet in front of him. Sometime in the recent past, the creature had suffered a terrible wound that twisted and compressed one side of its body so that it was awkwardly hunched forward. It spoke again, the same sounds ringing out.

Before Frax could shake his head to deny comprehension, fingers knotted in his hair from behind and shoved him to his knees.

Damn! That hurt! He slammed his elbow backward, into a metal leg brace. It stung, but he felt the metal connect with the leg beneath it. The answering grunt of pain accompanied his gasp as the tips of eight spears jabbed into the flesh on his back and sides.

Another staccato of harsh Balandran sound. The hand released his hair and the spears withdrew, leaving him to shiver with stinging pain.

Warm blood trickled from the shallow wounds, and now his elbow hurt, too. Bastards! He tossed his head, flicking urine over the creatures around him. There were angry hisses, but the spears did not return.

He gave a hiss of his own; the movement hadn't helped his pounding head.

The circle of spear tips moved closer to Frax as the scarred creature limped forward to stop a few paces in front of him. It repeated the sound.

Did the stupid thing think repetition would make him comprehend its language? Wary of how the circle around him might react to any movement with their leader so close, Frax stared up at it.

The creature repeated the sounds more slowly, and Frax realized some of them were vaguely familiar. Was it speaking a form of ancient Geffitzi? Perhaps an ancient patois evolved between master and slave? Anger shot through him. Whatever it spoke, it was not the language of his people. He scowled, his facial expression the only action he dared make.

The creature shook its head in obvious disgust and fired off another rapid chain of sound.

Stars exploded as the butt of a Balandran spear met the back of Frax's head.

Balandra. A vast, echoing interior. Balandra. Pain... His head felt as if it would burst. Frax held his body still, letting the details of his surroundings come to him.

The air that blew gently across his face smelled clean—fragrant, actually—and it was cool, bordering on cold. Outside? There were no sounds of insects or bird calls, but the steady, quiet splash of water behind him had the contained sound of a fountain.

Most likely he was still in the Ly Kai city.

He was lying on his left side, the slightly uneven surface, probably stone, pressing against his skin. His wrists were bound together in front of him. He mentally checked his extremities. Except for aches and soreness, he seemed fine.

Nothing broken, then. He opened his left eye a slit.

A clean stone walkway stretched in front of him. Grass, backed by bushes, formed a border. The shrubs were tidy and laden with blotches of color.

A chill ran down his spine. If this was the Ly Kai city, did someone remain here as caretaker?

No ugly gray Balandran feet blocked his line of sight, so he opened his right eye. Blue sky glowed through leafy branches above.

He closed his eyes and rolled onto his back with a moan. Kep, his body was sore!

The memory of Balandran spears slicing into his skin brought him upright. Bastards!

He'd been stripped down to his leather breeches, everything else, weapons, boots—even the tie that held back his long hair—gone.

In contrast, he sat on an elaborate mosaic walk in the middle of a small, lush garden. The wall surrounding it was high, its stone face softened by vines and dense, bloom-laden bushes. In one direction, past a gate made of delicate, white, spiral shapes, he could see a paved surface, like a street, then more plants. Behind him lay a rectangular pool. Spouts of water splashed soothingly from its corners. The metal cuffs that bound his hands were tethered to the side of the colorfully patterned pool wall by a light chain. Past it stood a portico of white stone columns, fronting some type of building.

He wound the chain around his hands and tugged. The base was firmly anchored. He tried to spread his wrists apart. The metal bit into his flesh, but the chain linking the cuffs showed no sign of stress. Given time, he would find out which was stronger, his will or his bonds. First, however, he needed to relieve himself and slake his thirst. The chain allowed him enough range to get over to the perfectly maintained bushes but not to the manicured bit of turf between the pool and the columned portico at the back of the garden. He offered no apologies to whatever gardener kept the place as he made use of what was available.

Afterward, he went to the pool, dipped cupped hands into the clear water and sniffed it. No odor. Most likely the clean source of water was why they had imprisoned him here. He splashed several handfuls on his face, letting it drip into the grass, then bent to drink directly from the pool. Then he settled on its generous edge to think.

He had water but no obvious food source.

He could worry about that later. It was time to inspect and tend to the damage the Balandran spears had done.

The blood from the gashes had dried where it ran down his back and sides. His chief concern was infection from a filthy speartip. None of the cuts felt feverish or swollen, however, so he washed away as much blood and urine as he could, scooping the water out and letting it fall on the walk to avoid contaminating his drinking source. When he finished, he sat down in the middle of the walk.

Where were the rest of his people located in this beautiful prison?

Perhaps there were no others here. The cost of capturing them all would have been high. For the thousandth time, he wished he had Kaphri's mental range to search out other minds.

His head still ached, partly from whatever they had used to knock him out when they snatched him and partly from the nasty lump he had on the back of his skull now. When he moved, every muscle in his body shrieked protest.

The sun, however, was warm, and the sights and sounds around him were soothing. He'd been a prisoner before. Rest and recovery would benefit him more than anything else.

Curling up on the warm stone with the pool at his back, he dropped into exhausted sleep.

A shout woke him.

Frax jerked upright. The sun was low, casting the garden into evening shadows.

The call came again from behind him, and he twisted around.

A Balandran perched on one of the crossbeams of the portico bared its teeth in what Frax hoped was a grin. It spoke in rapid staccato, a stream of nonsense for all Frax comprehended. They knew he couldn't understand their gibberish, so why bother?

The creature repeated its sounds, this time brandishing something in its left hand. It looked like the hind leg of a small bush hopper. The creature repeated its words, the horrible grin on its face widening.

Kep! Frax blinked in disbelief. Was the damned thing actually playing a game of "say please"?

No matter. He was hungry. He listened carefully as the creature repeated the sounds and parroted them back as best he could.

With a bark of what must have been laughter, the Balandran flung the meat at him and, with a mighty sweep of dark wings, lifted and flew away.

It was a portion of a fresh kill. If they were feeding him, they must plan to keep him around for a while.

He stripped the furry hide back and bit into the muscle, ignoring the reflexive twitch of uneasiness from his stomach. Raw meat had kept him alive more than once, and he planned to stay alive this time, too. Besides, it wasn't the worst thing he'd ever sunken teeth into.

He chewed the flesh and sucked the marrow from the bones before he buried the leftovers in the dirt beneath the bushes. Afterward, he washed his hands, got another drink of water, and, feeling better, set about trying to wear down the chain that held him to the stone of the pool, grinding until his wrists and fingers were raw.

"A*raxis must feel very confident he has things under control."*

Uri's comment pulled Kaphri out of her heavy thoughts. She'd been silent, mulling, most of the day. Now she shivered despite the heat of the fire blazing on her face.

"Maybe he thinks he's found a temporarily more suitable form," Seuliac added grimly.

"*Frax?*" The Wyxan wafer tasted even drier than usual in her mouth.

"He presents a better form than the Balandra. At least he has mindspeech."

The idea horrified her. *"Frax would never—"*

"He wouldn't have any more choice than you, would he?" Seuliac's sending was hard.

If anything, he would have less.

They were trying to warn her. To prepare her for what she might face when she confronted Araxis.

Frax had bargained with her to protect and aid her when the geas drove her deeper into the south. In exchange, she would use any knowledge of power she gained to remove the barrier. What would stop him from making a necessary bargain with another source of that power to achieve his goal?

If it helped the Geffitz people, he would have to do it.

He wouldn't do it, her heart whispered.

He could not hesitate, her brain told her.

Was Araxis lying to the Grimmen, promising to leave this world if it helped him attain a physical form, while plotting to stay and resume his tyranny?

Or did he expect the Ly Kai to welcome him back to the Homeworld? She did not think they would. There would be too many questions about the loss of all the people who had followed him here. All those murders...

But, if he opened the gate under the guise of a lost child returning home, the Ly Kai might never know what they welcomed back into their midst.

For a moment it was difficult for her to breathe. The trap was growing tighter. If she resisted, Araxis would kill Frax and find another way to force her to his will. If she went along with it, everything might be set aright on this world. Perhaps the Ly Kai would remove the barrier and the Grimmen would be satisfied, though they could never bring back everything Araxis had taken. The question for her in this moment: should she endanger the lives of these four warriors in the last step of the journey?

If only she could talk to Gemma, she might reason this all out. Her tiny friend would not tell her what she should do; that was not a Guardian's role. But Gemma would answer her questions, and having Gemma close would give Kaphri the much-needed strength to do what she must do.

The tiny bit of crystal felt hard in her fist.

She looked at Uri and Seuliac sitting on each side of her. *"If you know I have made the move to leave this world and you see me again afterward, you must kill this body before Araxis can turn on you and take vengeance."*

"That's reasonable. But what if it really is you? What if you come back for more delicious Wyxan brittle paste?" Seuliac asked gravely

She stifled a manic giggle despite the seriousness of the conversation. *"I will ask you if the stars shine...on..."* What? Something only their small group would recognize... *"Lady Ladrienca."*

They gave her the respect of a silent nod.

This wasn't natural fog. Smoke burned his nostrils and throat dry, and dirt seemed to find its way onto his tongue. His eyes stung, defensive tears accumulating in the corners from the parching wind. Orange lights sparked, glowed, and sliced the thickness above. The trembling earth beneath his feet occasionally lurched more violently with the sound of distant explosions. Rutted, hardened mud made his steps treacherous beneath his long clawed and scaled feet. He was thirsty, so thirsty, but the water was gone. He must find the others or their world would die. They must assemble in order to push the destruction back. He could not do it alone.

Bitter emotion twisted his nervous system, causing his body to vibrate.

Bithzielp, his mind whispered, your vanity has destroyed us.

Locked in dream memory, Frax searched on.

The new day began with a Balandra throwing him another chunk of raw meat in pre-dawn light.

Though it would sustain him for a while, his system couldn't survive on that diet forever. His body required more, but he didn't dare eat anything growing in the garden around him. Kep only knew what horrific poisons might lurk in the lavish Ly Kai flora.

Isolated in a garden fit for any high hold on his world, his mind burned with questions. The dreams were a mystery, confusing, and painful while he slept, but they were not new, and though they seemed to be increasing in clarity, they presented no threat after he woke up. He could push them aside and focus on the more immediate peril.

What did the Balandra want from him? Where was the Priestess? Had they captured the others—or had his companions successfully fought them off? And why was he still alive?

He tried to communicate with the Balandran who delivered the meat, first with words and motions, then by shouting, but the creature only gave him a menacing, toothy grin before flying off. So, he paced. The past few months of constant upheaval on this journey, coupled with the stress of dealing with his family's deadly ancient ally and their Rhynogian enemies, had been hell, but this silent inactivity was far worse. He'd been held captive before, but during those times, he had known something about the situation. He'd always held out some hope for escape. This time, things were different. He'd tried everything at hand to break his bonds. His wrists were bloody and raw, and the edge of the pool bore a groove where he had tried to weaken the chain by sawing it against the stone. So far, the chain and cuffs remained unmarred. Time was the enemy here and he had no idea how much he had left.

The morning sun was spreading its warmth over the garden when a sound brought him sharply about. Two Balandra were pulling open the fanciful gate. They moved quickly and nervously, scurrying out of sight beyond the wall before the gate stopped moving.

Curious behavior.

In the next second, all the air went out of his lungs in an exhale of horror as, out on the paved way, a tarmeuth slunk into view.

It walked through the opened gate.

Chapter 89
Foundations Shift

TARMEUTH! ALL OTHER threats snapped to insignificance in the face of the huge cat padding toward him.

Useless to call for help. Even if they wanted to, his captors could never respond fast enough to stop the beast from killing him. The chain tethered to his wrist made him a bait animal awaiting slaughter.

He backed over the edge of the pool, sloshing into the shin-deep water. It was a remote hope, but if he could get enough slack in the chain, he might wrap it around the creature's neck to strangle or drown it. No doubt, the cat would rip him to shreds in the process, but he refused to stand helplessly and not defend himself.

His eyes locked on the beast as his hands slid along the chain, looping it loosely in front of him.

"You can relax, Geffitz. This is not your day to die."

Telepathy? From a tarmeuth? Shock rolled over Frax.

"You cannot imagine how it feels to use mindspeech after so many years of mental deafness." The animal paused midway up the walk between him and the gate to stretch luxuriously. *"I should have possessed one of these creatures long ago."* It came up out of the stretch to regard him with golden eyes. *"Do you have any idea how the scent of your flesh stirs this creature?"*

A telepath was controlling the tarmeuth?

A Ly Kai, his mind flashed.

What had the creature said? Years of mental deafness? He and Kaphri's encounter with Araxis, as Ving, had been less than eight weeks ago in the Maugrock. "*You're not Araxis.*"

"That craven fool?" The animal's mouth drew back from its teeth in an expression that conveyed the same scorn as the sending.

But this being commanded Balandran forces... *"Are you Alexar?"*

There was a flash of cold humor. *"I will answer your questions in good time if this conversation goes well."* The cat settled to its haunches. *"First, we talk about what you will do for me. Come out of the pool."*

"What do you want?"

"Warrior, please. Relax."

Relax? The damned thing must be joking. It was almost impossible to keep his mind focused on this exchange while his primal instincts screamed for him to run away. Did the being controlling the tarmeuth read his distress in the same way as a normal telepath? Communicating with it took none of the edge off what his eyes told him sat three body-lengths away.

"What do you want?"

"For the moment, conversation. I do enjoy my bloodthirsty servants. They are delightfully focused on death and the best way to achieve it. But they have no capacity for mindspeech, and they butcher the spoken language. I want to savor this recovered ability.

"So," the other continued brightly, *"seeing as you have nothing to do but await my pleasure, I thought we might talk. Unless,"* there was a flash of false concern, *"you prefer pain? My Balandran captain is very curious about the pain threshold of your legendary warriors. You are a Geffitz warrior, are you not?"*

"I'll take the conversation." Fighting the near-impossible urge to run, Frax stepped out of the pool and settled uneasily on its edge.

"I thought you might." Silence drew out between them. *"Do you like your prison cell?"*

"What?"

"This garden."

"Where am I?"

"Right where I need you to be. Aren't you going to ask why my servants abducted you?"

"It crossed my mind. I'm just not sure what the rules are."

"Rules?" There was a mental tut-tut of reproach. *"You think I would put restrictions on this exchange? Never! How can we become friends if I restrict our conversation?"*

"How, indeed?" Frax sent dryly. He held out his shackled wrists.

"Oh, we are not friends yet, so I must insist the shackles remain for now. It will take your companions several more days to get here. Plenty of time for us to get to know each other. Then we'll see."

Several days. So, definitely still on his world. They must be on the plateau of the High Sentinel's Watch. His people had neglected the area in their respectful worship of Kep—which had helped create this situation. *"Did you bring these with you?"*

"The chains and shackles?" The other's sending carried a light sense of mocking despair. *"In a sense. One simply has to know where the tools are stored."*

The cuffs were not of Geffitzi make, and it knew this place, meaning, as he suspected, this was a Ly Kai space. *"Would your basic Ly Kai know they existed?"*

"Why should they? Their participation in the real governance of their society has never been required. Or encouraged. Why do you care?" The last question carried a note of rising annoyance.

"I don't. Why did you have the Balandra snatch me?"

"I want to send her a message."

"Tell me what you want to say. I'll carry your message back to her."

"You misunderstand. You are the message. If she wants to keep you alive, she will do what I tell her to do."

"She won't come here for me. The moment she feels threatened, she runs. She runs from everything." Dare he say it? *"That's why you've had to bargain with the forces of my world."*

"She does that," the other agreed thoughtfully. *"But she'll come for you."*

Not after their last encounter. Not after she had accused him of being useless. She would come because, with the Grimmen at her back, she had no choice. She would come, but not as the desperate, cringing, innocent that Frax wanted to encourage this manipulating bastard to expect. If he could stay alive, he might strike a blow from the inside when the real confrontation came. *"What do you want from her?"*

"That doesn't concern you. You should be more worried about your own status. You have four days. If she doesn't come for you in time..." there was a mental shrug, *"you die, and I take another one of your number to persuade her."*

"There are still forces on this world that will stop you."

"You think I accomplished this without help from those forces? You feed my vanity. Granted, some deception has been necessary to obtain their cooperation, but trust me, your Eldren want me gone. You are simply the means to an end. I have you; the girl will do what I demand in exchange for your life."

Eldren. The Grimmen. Did that also include the Wyxa?

"My people will kill her before they let you steal her physical form."

"You think I want her form? Don't be ridiculous."

"What do you want then?"

"What can you, a primitive, comprehend of what I want?"

"Try me."

The cat got up and walked over to thrust its face close to his.

Kep! He never, ever wanted to be this close to a tarmeuth!

Fighting an overwhelming impulse to cringe away, Frax held his position and stared into the orange-gold eyes of the deadly beast.

Hot air brushed his skin as the creature exhaled with an impatient gust. *"I want vengeance. I want blood. I want others to feel the same—no, more!—more pain than I have felt. I want satisfaction. Can you understand that?"*

Who was this? Asking again, however, might close the exchange, so... *"You'll never find it."*

The tarmeuth drew back slightly, eyes narrowing. Its lips curled, exposing teeth longer than his fingers.

"Nothing you do will ever be enough to give you the satisfaction you crave."

The creature stared at him for a long, frozen moment. *"No,"* the being inside its mind abruptly agreed. *"You're right. It will never be enough."* The tarmeuth turned and strolled back to its original spot to settle on its haunches again. *"Perhaps I have misjudged you. You seem...capable...of some thought and understanding equivalent to that of your ancestors. Interesting."*

Frax's mouth felt as if it was suddenly filled with ashes. *"What can you possibly know of my ancestors?"*

"Can't you guess, clever one?" A speculative light burned in the cat's eyes. *"You intrigue me. It has been a long time since I've had a challenging conversation. I think I should like to prolong this contact."*

Prolong. Not the word he wanted to hear, but it would keep him alive. *"Tell me what you know about the Geffitzi and how you know it."*

"Later, perhaps. I have more immediate interests at the moment. The girl—" The cat paused to lick at its shoulder rigorously, the rasp of the rough tongue on its fur loud. *"I want her to perform a simple task."*

"You want her to open the Ly Kai gate so you can pass through to her Homeworld. You're Ly Kai, but you're not Araxis." He had to put the thoughts into form to make them real.

The cat blinked once in silent acknowledgment.

Was this some other Ly Kai left over from Araxis' betrayal, stranded here for over twenty years? If the Evil One had survived, bodiless, why not others? "*Since you've requisitioned"*—stolen seemed too aggressive a term—*"the tarmeuth's form, it must mean you don't have your original body, either.*"

The cat appeared to bristle in irritation. *"You should concentrate on your own original form. I want the girl to open the gate. The price for her to do this is your continued existence."*

"And what will you do after that?"

"Not your concern. You will live, and you can have the girl to do with as you see fit. I don't care."

Not the answer he expected, and most likely a lie. *"And Araxis?"*

"Pfft. She could defeat him right now if she turned to face him. As things are, she's far more powerful."

Of course. As an Arylla-born she was more powerful than Araxis' present form of the unfortunate, lesser birth-starred Ving. But she was also woefully inadequate in knowledge of her power despite Seuliac's work with her. Their only hope was that learning to think like a Geffitz warrior might imbue her with some unique and unexpected actions.

Which was a supremely dangerous arrogance on their part that he must play down.

His heart raced; the Priestess had told them once that it was impossible for Ly Kai to lie while using mindspeak. Though none of the warriors had admitted it, the rule did not seem to apply to Geffitzi. Many holds mistrusted mindspeech for that reason.

Neither did it fully apply to Ly Kai, he suspected. This was not the time to risk finding out, however. Perhaps a half-truth... *"She's inexperienced. She has no one to teach her about this starpower of hers."*

"Nothing is perfect. I will help her remedy the problem."

"By invading her mind? No."

There was a sense of amusement. *"You are right. The Ly Kai fools in the north tower rendered her useless to my needs. Through careful planning, I have better options in place."*

"I don't care about your plans for the Ly Kai Homeworld. Whatever happens, they deserve it. Just get off my world and take Araxis with you."

"Alas, I cannot. He will not approach the gate for fear of Ly Kai retribution. He did great harm to many powerful families, and the form he currently possesses is fourth from the highest starpower in the Hierarchy. There are many who would quickly overpower and confine him. Their desire for revenge, however, is merely a thumb prick in comparison to mine. The arrogance! He has long planned to betray me. He thinks he can steal the girl's form, restore his starpower, and run away to avoid a reckoning on his deception."

A wave of lightheadedness rushed over Frax. Who was this being? *"You've let him believe he can use her to escape you."*

"Sometimes it's useful to let a fool think they are clever. They work so much harder when they believe they are attaining their goal."

Was that what this being was doing to him? A chill ran down Frax's spine. *"You've let him kill Geffitzi and Wyxa. He commands the Balandra..."*

"It has kept all of you so wonderfully occupied, has it not?"

"This is a diversion?"

"Some things take time and require the assistance of people who would not cooperate if they knew the truth."

Frax's chest felt so tight he could barely breathe. *"Who are you?"*

"Alas, my current form is growing more excited by the scent of your flesh. I must remove it from temptation, or I may not be able to contain it. Which would be most tragic." There was amusement in the sending. *"We will talk again."*

The tarmeuth rose to its feet and padded out the garden gate.

Kaphri held her silence for the rest of that night and the next morning while her thoughts shifted between waves of panic, frustration, and a desperate search for a solution to their situation. One thing she was sure of: Frax was in danger because of her, and she didn't want any of the others to come to harm.

The warriors couldn't help her with this, anyway.

Now, standing in the warm rays of the noonday sun, she found the crystal in her hand again. How many times today? Every time her mind pulled her into the miasma of her emotions, she found it in her grip.

She faltered, awash with fear and indecision, then pulled her thoughts together. The crystal was a link to Gemma, but, like in the Palenquemas, when Frax lay at her feet with his blood soaking into the mud of the swamp, she had to act on her own.

Seuliac and Velacy were in the woods below, hunting or gathering wood, and Uri's attention was focused on building up a fire. As for Tobin, who knew?

He would not object to what she was about to do.

The Cyrwin watched her approach without a twitch of muscle. She stopped a few feet in front of it. The thick ridge of scarring on its shoulder identified it as Chaos-stepper, the animal that had carried Frax. It remained with them despite the fact it no longer had a rider.

She did not find anything redeeming in that. *"You betrayed Frax Kitahn."*

"You will leave this world."

She'd prepared to argue against the Cyrwin's denial or defense. Its response saved them both precious time. She drew a deep breath to steady her nerves. *"You know the city?"*

"I have seen it."

An image flicked in her mind, of an immense, translucent white wall capped in a delicate filigree of stone and metalwork, with a graceful tower of similar material rising behind it. The thing was not like the images of star temples she had gleaned from the memories of the Twenty-six, but she recognized the style if not the place. The surviving men had never seemed anxious to recall the details of the scene of Araxis' betrayal and the mass murder of their loved ones. She was not looking forward to seeing it, either. All that mattered was if she could use the image to make a jump—if she chose to trust this creature.

"We will speak. You, me, and the Grimmen." She must do this before the warriors interfered.

"Speak."

"I will leave this place under my previously stated conditions."

"There will be no conditions."

"Again, I am in a position to name conditions. I want a solemn oath that the Grimmen will honor them: a straightforward agreement with no twisting of words or meanings."

"Speak."

"The Geffitz warriors, including the Aedecs, are free to go immediately, with no threat of harm or retaliation for who they are or what they have done. The Grimmen will not harm them or allow them to be harmed by its inaction. They will be free to go anywhere they desire."

"They will be free to go, unharmed and unthreatened."

"And Frax Kitahn must be free to go where he pleases, also."

That brought a gap of silence. The Cyrwin gave a sweep of its snaky tail. *"He can never return to the Grimmenwood: he made the blood bargain, and you cannot dissolve it. However, the Grimmen gives its word; he will be released, unharmed, when you leave this world."*

"Restore his access to Cadarn and his claim to Azay Rhiad."

"You overreach."

"You betrayed him. He did not betray you. I will give you what you want; this is what I want."

"It is restored."

"With no retaliation for his efforts in any of this."

"That was agreed!"

"The barrier—"

"Is no longer your concern."

She was pushing things, but there would never be another opportunity like this one. *"The warriors bargained in good faith with me. I have to know."*

"Its removal is the price of your return to the Ly Kai Homeworld."

Her return to the Homeworld. Was that the lie Araxis was using to manipulate the Grimmen into handing her over to him? There would be no return to the Homeworld for her. At least she had warned Seuliac and Uri to slay her if they saw her once she'd been removed from their sight for any length of time. Araxis would not expect that reaction from them.

Who told the Grimmen they were able to remove the barrier? Was it possible, after all these years, Alexar was really alive? Why had he never stepped in to rescue the Ly Kai when his twin, Araxis, abandoned them here? While possessing Ving's weaker form, Araxis was no threat to him. Perhaps it was why Araxis was so desperate to steal her body—so he could fend off a challenge from his twin.

A sudden ripple of fear ran through her. "*Why are you so anxious to force my return to the Ly Kai*?"

"Ly Kai do not belong here. As long as you all leave our world, we do not care what happens beyond it."

Succeed or die. It was on her shoulders. "*We are agreed, then?*"

"*We are agreed.*"

"*Give me the image.*" Sadly, there could be no farewells.

Chapter 90
Creeping in the Woods

VELACY SHOOK A TWIG out of his right boot. The leather on the side near his big toe had worn through, letting in debris. He looked at the hole in disgust. They had been good boots. Expensive boots. But nothing lasted forever, especially if you walked across half a continent. The aggravating part was he had no idea when he might have access to another set of quality boots again. Seuliac said he could leave with his life if he helped them save their world. Very generous of the warlord, making him a ghost to his own people. Still, a live ghost was better than a dead one. Dead was dead with the Geffitzi. They didn't come back like those bastard Wyxa and the Ly Kai! At least this way, he had some hope of recovering his rightful claim to the title of Holderlord after he killed Hraben and his father, the heir apparent. Maybe he should have targeted Hraben instead of going for his father on the first attempt. Maybe Hraben would have actually appreciated his ruthless ambition a bit more if it had been directed at him personally. Seuliac said all his co-conspirators were dead and that Hraben had ordered his execution, to be completed conveniently out of sight while on their trek to the Maugrock.

Well, thanks to the Balandra, the execution order had gone awry, with the warlord forced to decide he was more useful to him alive. Perhaps Velacy would take the time to thank the next winged demon he came across before he ran a knife into its heart.

Then again, maybe not. He might have survived the order to eliminate him, but it wasn't due to his cleverness. If he'd been that smart, he'd still be in the north.

He could take off right now and leave all this behind. He didn't owe anyone here anything. He could go to the real Rhynog, sit in the Holderlord's chair, write out death warrants by the hundreds for people he knew would oppose him if he became Holderlord. It wouldn't amount to anything.

He deserved better. He deserved to rule! If it hadn't been for all these other distractions, he might already be Holderlord of Rhynog. And the first person he would order to kiss his boots would be the Warlord of Rhynog, Seuliac Aedec. And the first Geffitz to die by his assassination order would be Tobin Kitahn. Kep! The thoughts sent a thrill of satisfaction through him. Here he was, struggling in the dirt with the others, worrying about what came next. He had forgotten his ambitions!

Let everyone else worry about bringing this plot down. Let them worry about surviving. Let the others break themselves on this disaster. He had bigger plans. He would stand back—they didn't really expect much from him anyway—and he would walk away alive. He would return a hero, and Lord Hraben would have to accept him back into the Caer. He would have no choice when his grandson brought back all the glory to Rhynog. It might even appeal to the old bastard.

Perhaps he would ask for Seuliac's job. A warlord commanded the family's ground forces. If they were loyal to him when he made his move to take over, nothing would stop him. Seuliac had that power, and he wasted it on loyalty. But not loyalty to Hraben. Velacy was sure Seuliac despised Hraben and what the holderlord had done to force his loyalty when he was a child. No, Seuliac foolishly squandered his loyalty on Rhynog.

Well, if he loved the hold as much as he professed, why didn't he push to assert Rhynog's rightful place as the ultimate seat of power for the Geffitz Clans? Even treacherous Hraben would back that. But no, Seuliac Aedec pursued a higher calling, to keep Rhynog a leader among equals when Rhynog had no equals!

A movement on the slope below caught his eye. The warlord slipped between the trees, tracking some prey. Careless of him to expose himself to the upslope. If Velacy happened to hit him with an arrow, who could say he hadn't mistaken him for a Balandran? One more obstacle removed...

His hand did not go to his weapon, however. The risk was too great. If he failed to make the kill on the first shot, there'd be hell to pay.

Velacy straightened, frowning. Had there been a flicker of movement between the trees, headed toward the warlord?

A growl of anticipation rumbled in his throat as he pushed to his feet.

Hunting was never one of his strengths. He usually had enough warriors under his command to take care of such mundane necessities. But sometimes it was good to get away from everything and walk. Besides, Velacy was hunting up the slope and pride would not permit the younger Aedec to return to camp empty-handed with Tobin Kitahn around, so Seuliac needn't worry about his personal success at killing anything. He mostly wanted to take advantage of a rare situation. As holy ground, Pterfellen was off limits to ordinary Geffitzi, so he might never have the chance to see this land again once they regained the south.

Seuliac leaned against a large tree and took a deep breath of sweet, clean air. It was hard to grasp the idea that there was not one Geffitz body between him and Omurda. That was hundreds of leagues of unpolluted land!

Unpolluted. Hardly a proper term for the warlord of the world's most powerful clan to apply to Geffitzi land. Still, he couldn't help but appreciate the situation. So much land and so few occupants! With a few fine Geffitz girls and some of his best warriors, he could create a clan down here, away from the politics and treachery of competing houses. The girls didn't even have to be Rhynogian—he'd seen several from other holds that suited his tastes most delightfully—but the warriors definitely had to be. With his best men, he could build a new world.

Except some of his best warriors were dead, their bones gray and covered in hoarfrost somewhere in the shadows of Omurda.

Seuliac sobered, pulling back to the present as a squirrel scrambled into view. It froze in place for a heartbeat when it saw him, then scurried on. Odd, it hadn't scolded him; the cursed things were a bane to warrior stealth at the absolute worst times. But then, it hadn't seen many Geffitzi creeping about its territory lately, had it?

Another of the creatures ran past, this time without even pausing. Maybe he should shoot one of the damned things since he already held his bow notched and ready. It would be better than returning empty-handed, though the creatures were hardly a mouthful.

The snap of a twig brought him cautiously away from the tree. His fingers tightened on the arrow, and he silently drew the bowstring taut.

It had to be Velacy thrashing about. How easily explained would a hunting accident be in this place, where Kep-knew-what might be skulking? It presented another in a long list of opportunities he had already passed on. For now, he agreed with Kitahn: they needed every warrior they had. Velacy Aedec owed him his life. Again.

A figure stumbled around the trunk of the tree, nearly impaling its thin body on the point of his arrow. It stopped, eyes widening with terror when it saw him. It made several gasping grunts, then burst into tears.

A wave of panic and confusion slammed the warlord's mind. Kep! He threw up his mindshields and leveled the arrow at the Ly Kai's heart, ready to release it if his blocks failed.

The mental assault broke off, and the creature crumpled to the ground.

"Consider any debt I owe you for sparing my life paid, Warlord." Velacy stepped into view from around the tree. Dropping a short, heavy branch, he brushed the dirt from his hands with exaggerated care.

Seuliac gave a hard blink to clear the webs of alien assault from his brain. The sticky sensations of terror and desperation clung, reluctant to release their grip.

"I saw it stalking you from upslope." Velacy nudged the limp form with his foot. "It must've seen a chance to steal a new form and decided to take it."

"Perhaps." The creature had not acted as if it was stalking him. Its mental reaction had been more one of helpless terror. Stealing a Geffitz body would put it in the perfect position to get next to the Priestess, but it obviously wasn't a skilled hunter.

The encounter didn't make sense. What in Kep's name was this Ly Kai doing here? Why wasn't it at the city with the Balandra and Kitahn?

Sudden suspicion ran over him. Were there more of these creatures in the south than the Priestess had told them? Had she lied?

Seuliac knelt down beside the Ly Kai. It was filthy and ragged, the skin covered with scabs and insect bites as if it had been wandering around in the woods of Pterfellen for days. He turned the bald head so he could see the wound on the back where Velacy had struck it. It was bleeding, but the injury didn't appear life-threatening. He took in the dirt-smudged skin and the ragged edges of the blue and silver robe. The creature loosely matched the shared image from the tower at the edge of Omurda that he'd received from Kitahn and the Priestess. The being was thin—thinner than the girl—but that was probably the result of relying on the Balandra to scavenge for the special diet they required.

This must be the stolen form of Araxis—Ving, she called it. But, if Araxis was here in this condition, who held Frax at the city? Had the creature's Balandran forces gone rogue?

Or was this a bizarre trap to weaken their forces further? The warlord's gaze flicked upward, his eyes searching the treetops around them. With the Balandra already having snatched Frax, he and Velacy were careless to wander about alone. They could die as the penalty for their lapse in vigilance.

Mercifully, there were no Balandra.

What had changed in this creature's situation?

So many new questions! Most importantly, how would they handle the creature once it regained consciousness? Kep! How were they supposed to contain a Ly Kai?

Velacy dropped to his knees, straddling the body, and drew his knife.

"What are you doing?"

"Killing his bug-eaten ass. He looks like every insect between here and Cadarn has taken a piece of him. We can't let him wake up!"

The younger warrior was right. Still—the opportunity for information this presented... "No."

"We should kill it!" Velacy persisted.

Single-minded. So like Tobin Kitahn. Small wonder they didn't get along. "Put the knife away. I have a better idea."

"Are you insane—?"

"It's bleeding. If I can get the Priestess to send the image of its sign, we can lock its powers away the same way the Balandra did to her in the Black Tower."

"No!" Horror ran over Velacy's face. "This thing is dangerous, Warlord. We should kill it.

"No! We can finally get some answers. Stay here and guard it while I get her help." The Priestess could send the image to him, and he could secure the situation before she got down here, saving them precious time. But he had to move within sending range first. "I'll be right back."

"Make it fast, or I will kill him," Velacy warned sourly.

"Don't!"

Chapter 91
Truth Closing In

SHE FACED A LY KAI male, younger than her—but the sense of starpower he exuded... Recognition of her Birthstar drove a shaft of confusion through her.

His cold eyes bored into her, appraising her as if she were merely some insect from the Palenquemas. Then she saw the shift, the rise of hunger in his eyes, and realized that despite the sense of power he exuded, he was an empty vessel. He had a massive capacity for Arylla to pour power into him, but he did not command it. Was that what she had felt like to the others, to the Twenty-six? Like a coal that glowed in red fury but gave off no heat?

Perhaps in the lonely northern tower, but not now. She had touched Arylla. Araxis had forced her to draw its power in order to crack open his barrier on the southern edge of Omurda so he could bring his gray, winged forces through to the south with him. Even if she declined to use it, the star's power resided inside her now. This other one recognized its presence in her, and he lusted for it in a way she had never done, even when, misled, she sought Freya's star response.

Three things she knew: this youth wanted power, he would wield it without mercy whether for good or bad, and that Araxis had made a mistake when he let her flee Kryie Karth. Back then, she had nothing except Gemma's friendship, and she had viewed starpower only through her selfish, childish need. Falling prisoner to the Geffitz warriors had opened a whole world for her to care about.

To fight for.

The air rippled with mental activity, and she was suddenly aware of other Ly Kai clustered around him. She sensed their uneasiness, as if they feared the youth, but she also felt their rigidity of purpose. They were prepared to carry out his every order.

Kaphri abruptly realized her own mindset was as hard and unyielding as the boy's. She was reacting to something he'd said, something of which she had no memory. "You will not—"

Starpower blazed in a surge of overwhelming evil. "Just die with your worthless friends," the boy said, gesturing behind her.

She twisted to see a glowing white stone floor, smeared with blood.

"No," she screamed in horror.

Everything abruptly shifted, and she was standing on a grassy plain, staring at a distant pale wall that curved away from sight on both sides as if it were circular. It shimmered softly, swells and swoops of denser white scrolling along the top.

Air ripped and heaved from her lungs. Her legs trembled, but she managed to stay upright. All the light, hostility, and anger that had pounded her were gone, replaced by the sounds of birds calling in a chilly afternoon breeze.

What had just happened? She had jumped. The image before her was the same one the Cyrwin had given her, except for more clarity in detail.

The Ly Kai youth...

What had just happened?

Memories flashed in her head: other jumps and the disorienting moments immediately after. Of rain and Cyrwins attacking in the dark. Of running in the woods. All so real at the time. All coming to life later in exactly the same way she had seen them.

She stared at the wall in horrified realization. She was catching glimpses of the future! Her future.

No, no, no; the protest ripped through her head. It couldn't be true.

Realization flashed, overriding her shock: dark forms were rising above the beautifully carved rim of the wall. Balandra. She must flee before they captured her.

Before what she'd seen became real.

The crystal was still in her hand. Panicked, she tried to visualize Uri and the rolling hillside she'd left only heartbeats ago.

A sudden sense of warning seized her. She should not use the crystal out here in the open, where the Balandra would see her disappear. They would tell Araxis.

The forest was only a few steps behind her. The Cyrwin, Chaos Stepper, had not moved far from the shelter of the trees when it had viewed the Ly Kai structure that intruded upon its world.

She turned and ran.

Velacy waited for Seuliac to disappear from view before he turned his attention back to the Ly Kai. He leaned forward to study it. Jerked back when the creature heaved a gasp and opened its eyes.

It looked about wildly, vision unfocused, until it found him.

The Geffitz warrior felt a strange sensation inside his mind. After a moment of confusion, he realized the Ly Kai was attempting to send to him.

"You have the girl..." it gave a mental whisper.

"Not your concern," he responded instinctively.

"Tell her..." Images blurred inside Velacy's head as the creature struggled to send a clear thought.

"What?"

"Tell her..." The creature heaved a breath.

Velacy drew his blade from its sheath, then sent a blast of fear out over the mountainside to mask his action as he drove it deep into the Ly Kai's eye.

"I don't think so," he said.

"*What in Kep's holy name were you thinking?"* Uri gripped her shoulders, his expression a mixture of fury and alarm.

She wanted to answer, but she was crying too hard. Oddly, she didn't remember when she had started.

He shook her, hard. *"Why would you do something so stupid?"*

"I—"

"Willow!" Uri looked over at her, startled. *"I didn't hear you."*

She stared at him, her expression flashing from relief to horror. "*Uri! Oh, Uri, I—*"

"*What's the matter?*" He surged across the space between them, catching her by the shoulders as her legs gave way beneath her. Horror replaced confusion. "*You jumped. You jumped to the city!*"

The emotions she fought to hold back broke in a deluge of tears.

"*What in Kep's holy name were you thinking?*" Uri's hands tightened on her shoulders, his thoughts a mix of outrage and concern. She wanted to answer, but she was crying too hard. He shook her. "*Why would you do something so stupid?*"

"*I—*" She had just seen this! She had seen this future, in the same way she had glimpsed the future in front of the gates to the Ly Kai city.

Realization only made things worse.

"*Willow—*"

"*Damn it, Priestess, answer me when I call you!*" Seuliac's furious sending cut across the chaos of her mind.

Hredroth! The warlord would not tolerate her current emotional state, regardless of what had occurred. The thought of his harsh reaction cut off her emotions with a painful twist.

Feeling the abrupt change, Uri released her shoulders. She regained her feet, straightening and hastily brushing away her tears. *"I am here,"* she answered, leaving Uri inside their contact loop.

"*We have a situation.*" The warlord appeared at the edge of the trees down the slope to glare up at them. "*What is the Ly Kai power symbol for Araxis' current form?*"

The question took her by surprise. *"Why?"*

"We've found something."

"I'll be—"

"No! Send the image I need. Now!"

She sent a simple shape into his mind and watched with rising apprehension as he dropped to his knees and traced it on the ground.

"What are you doing? What have you found?" Fearing a sudden threat, she mentally reached out, searching. What she found took her breath away.

The warlord leapt to his feet, disappearing back into the trees.

"Oh, Hredroth, Uri! He's here!"

"Who?"

A sudden blast of terrible fear rushed over them and was gone.

Uri caught her by the arm as her face went white. *"What? Kep! What is it?"*

"Velacy just killed Ving," she answered hollowly. *"By the Stars, Uri, I really must sit down."*

Chapter 92
Unraveling threads

"DAMN IT, VELACY! HE could've been useful to us!" Seuliac cursed as he stared down at the lifeless Ly Kai body.

He should have followed Lord Hraben's orders and eliminated this fool weeks ago.

Velacy glared at him. "No he wouldn't. He only wanted access to the girl so he could steal her form. He woke up and tried to snatch my mind. I killed him. Araxis is gone. She belongs to us. She owes us! With him gone, the barrier is ended, and we can go home."

"We stay with the current plan."

"We don't need Frax Kitahn! If he's gone, she'll come with us, back to Rhynog."

"Not 'us', Velacy. I told you, you can walk away, but you will not return to Rhynog."

"I deserve some credit here, Seuliac! I killed the Evil One! I should be able to walk back into Rhynog as the hero."

"I'm not sure what you did, Velacy, but no. We're going to the Ly Kai city."

"Oh, come on, Warlord! We can return in triumph. I know you've considered the advantage having her as an ally would give Rhynog. Admit it."

"Velacy—"

"Don't deny what we're all thinking. Kitahn and Caspani have thought about it. The clan that secures her abilities will hold all the influence. No one will dare go against it. Only you and the rest of these self-righteous fools would give up that kind of power!"

"Velacy, you heard her warning. Don't—"

"I'm bound by your oath to do whatever you and Kitahn say, Seuliac, but you don't get to control my thoughts."

"Damn you, Velacy! You put us all at risk."

"I don't have to desire power, Warlord. I am Aedec. I am power! And I know what to do with it. So, stay out of my face!" Scowling, Velacy took a step back.

"Velacy, she warned us—"

"Oh, yes, she warned us about desiring power. The big, bad ghost will get us! Well, Araxis is dead. I killed him. He's not a threat anymore. We can admit what we both know; with her as an ally, Rhynog could rule this world."

"That's not going to happen. She has to leave this world."

"Says who?"

"Says the Grimmen and its four-legged enforcers." Maybe the cursed Eldren were right after all. The girl, in the wrong hands, could be a disaster for everyone.

"The Cyrwins? She can handle them. You saw that firsthand. She could make Rhynog undefeatable.

"It's what Hraben would expect, Warlord," he continued. "You really should return your focus to your position and your obligations to our clan. You've had every opportunity to steal her away from Cadarn, and you haven't even tried!"

It was true. Lord Hraben would expect that sort of self-serving mindset—Rhynog first and foremost. But the Holderlord would also recognize there were times to conspire and times to cooperate, a thing Velacy never seemed to learn. Which was why he was already dead in Rhynog's eyes. Besides, there were less obvious ways to secure someone's allegiance. "You'll do what I tell you, Velacy, or we'll move forward without your company."

Velacy lifted his hands and smiled mockingly. "As always, I'm your loyal soldier, Warlord."

"Just focus on the task at hand and forget the empire-building. You heard the girl's warning: lust for power, and you could lose yourself to that bodiless demon."

"He's dead, Warlord. I killed him."

"The body is dead, fool. That's all we know. Nothing else has changed."

"I faced a Ly Kai boy—younger than me—but so powerful! His eyes were cold and hard, as if he cared for nothing. There were priests around him." Uri had insisted she explain what she had done and her resulting claims before they addressed anything else. *"They behaved as if determined to carry out his every order, but they also seemed wary, as if things weren't going the way they expected."*

"Imagine that," Seuliac muttered.

Uri shot him a frown. *"What else?"*

"He was born to Arylla, but he felt so empty! Which I don't understand. He knew so much more about the star than I ever learned..."

"What do you think the vision meant?" Uri persisted.

"It was not a vision, Uri!" His question pulled her back into focus. *"It was a flash forward. I saw the future."*

"How? How do you know you saw the future?"

Four pairs of doubting gray eyes regarded her. Behind one of those sets, another was listening and considering what an extension of her life was worth after her broken agreement. Tobin watched her as intently as any of the others. Had the Grimmen known this would happen?

Of course they didn't believe her. She hardly believed what she was saying. But she'd mulled the strange flashes of disorientation, the last of which had occurred at the top of the escarpment, for days now, and it suddenly made sense. *"Because it has happened to me twice before. When we leaped from the Palenquemas to Cadarn I saw the Cyrwin attacking me in the first moments after we arrived. It happened again in the woods above the escarpment: I saw myself running through the woods right after we jumped to escape the tarmeuth. Within minutes, I was running!"* Thoughts of the most recent flash made her want to claw her arms in despair she felt so helpless, but she had to make them understand. *"It is true."*

"Why didn't you say something before?"

"At Cadarn? In all the confusion after making that leap? I had no idea what I had done, much less what any side effect it might have. And when Seuliac and I made the leap up the cliff, we found ourselves facing the Balandra and a night of disaster, so I had no time to dwell on it. This time I know for sure: when I use the crystal to jump over a distance, I catch a glimpse of the future. It's as if it pushes me forward the same amount of time it would have taken me to normally cover the distance. I see a brief flash of what will happen at that point in the future before it inserts me back into real time."

"Sort of a displaced view forward," Seuliac suggested.

"Yes." Exactly.

"You saw Ly Kai when you jumped to the city. Were they on this world? What were they doing?" Concern tightened Uri's sending.

"It was a strange place, the boy and some priests were facing me. I was angry, but I can't tell you what I experienced before that moment. I know we were in disagreement."

"You opened the gate?" Seuliac asked sharply.

"I don't know. I think I must have."

Uri nodded. *"Did they threaten you?"*

"I felt a huge lust for power in them. Then he told me to die with my worthless friends, and I turned and saw blood. So much blood! And," her throat tightened so much she thought she would choke, *"I abruptly found myself on a plateau in front of the place in the Cyrwin's image, here on this world. I got scared and confused. I didn't know what to do, so I ran into the woods and jumped back."*

"And then?"

"There was a flash of you, scolding me. Only a few words, then I was here again, and you reacted and were scolding me again. The same words, as if I came back to the exact time where I belonged."

"I can see some potential use for this," Velacy said.

"She can't go leaping around places just to see the future," Uri snapped at him.

"Why not? You said we need every advantage we can get."

"Because nothing is free, Velacy. Who knows how her use of this is affecting some other aspect of her life. Or our world. What if it has a limited number of uses?"

The thought of not being able to return from one of those jumps drove a chill of horror into her.

"How do you know it was the future?" Uri returned to his previous line of questioning.

"Because three out of four times, when the seemingly correct amount of time passed, it happened exactly the way I envisioned it!" And the fourth time still lay ahead in their bleak future. Kaphri felt a rising panic. *"I can't do this. I can't face this one—"*

"Pull yourself together." This time, Uri nodded in agreement at Seuliac's harsh tone. *"It is not the same. The other times, you kept walking directly forward into it. This time, you didn't. This time, you came back after you saw it. It might have changed things."*

She started to disagree, then stopped as she recalled Frax's story in the Palenquemas about seeing a Guardian and being forced to have second thoughts on one's actions. Hope tried to well inside her, but she suppressed it. Hredroth, she wanted to believe the future could change, but... "*Do you really think it might have?*"

"*Kep only knows. Things have changed already since you made the jump.*"

"*Yes,*" Velacy spoke up. "*I killed Araxis.*"

His smug expression made her want to lash out at him. To scream that it wasn't that easy. It would never be that easy. She was the one who would have to face Araxis.

She refused to display emotional weakness in front of Uri and Seuliac again. "*The being you killed was not Araxis, Velacy. It was Ving.*" When she put it into words, she was sure it was true. "*For some reason, Araxis abandoned Ving's form.*"

There was a long moment of dismayed silence as the warriors considered her words. They wanted to believe Velacy had killed Araxis—she did too—but they all knew she was right.

"*What are your thoughts now?*" Seuliac asked.

Her thoughts. They were willing to listen. That did not mean they would agree and let her carry them out without their input. "*If Araxis abandoned Ving, he must have gone to the city. Everything remains the same. I won't abandon Frax. It's my fault the Balandra have him.*"

Uri's expression said he disagreed with her last statement, but he didn't comment.

"*There is a way to check out this future thing,*" Seuliac said. "*Make another jump. See if it's changed the future. Of course, the mere action might change things, again.*"

"*No.*" Uri shook his head firmly. "*Every action has a cost. We don't know what this might be doing to her.*"

"*We can worry about that later.*"

"*Unless the next jump kills her, Warlord.*"

"*You can't be suggesting we pass on this strategic advantage! When did Windmer become so cautious?*"

"When this started slipping out of our control and into a realm of farseeing and chance."

Seuliac gave a bark of humorless laughter. *"It's always been out of our control, Caspani! We've just been too vain to admit it."*

Uri relented with a sigh. *"I know. But we wouldn't have made it this far if we didn't believe this problem was ours to solve. It's too risky to experiment with her. She said the Balandra spotted her. They'll be searching the area for her now."*

"True," the warlord conceded. *"Perhaps she should wait until more time has elapsed before taking another action. When we get a bit closer..."*

"Gather your gear," Tobin spoke for the first time since she had returned. *"We still have hours of good daylight left."*

"First, I will bury Ving." Kaphri took a step back out of their circle.

"No!" Seuliac, Tobin, and Uri exclaimed simultaneously. *"It's too dangerous."*

She agreed. But— *"Twenty-three bodies lie on a mountainside beyond the barrier."* She couldn't even think about what the Balandra who remained on that side might have done to their remains. *"No one will ever tend to them. Ving is a victim of Araxis, like thousands of others who have died in this world. You will bury your dead when you come home. I will bury Ving before I go."* Even though Araxis had claimed Ving lusted for her, she had never established a mental link with him that would make her feel the agonizing Ly Kai sense of lost contact in her brain. But she had felt him die, another in a long list of sacrifices to Araxis' ambition.

Uri gave a nod. *"We'll help you."*

There was nothing left of Ving's remarkable beauty in the haggard, scabbed body that Kaphri performed the Ly Kai burial ritual over. Her solemn actions were part of the role she would have fulfilled if she had remained in Kryie Karth, if a terrible evil had not tried to lure her into its power. If, when she tried to warn the Ly Kai men of its invading presence, their hatred had not exposed the lie that their fears of Arylla had let them perpetrate upon her.

Her heart ached at the irony. If they had not sought to deceive her, telling her she was born of Freya instead of the Great Star, she might have brought them home. But they had fallen victim to Araxis a second time when Rath, under his influence, had persuaded them to lie to her.

Now she was burying the last of them on this alien world.

All the anger and resentment that had burned between her and the proud man was gone as she traced the symbol for Ly Toma in the air above his lifeless form, drawing full power from his star down to accept his essence back into its glory.

When she stepped back, the warriors hurriedly piled stones over Ving's body where it lay beneath the tree, giving him a grave of sorts on the mountainside. They did not mark it, which made Kaphri sad, but many more Ly Kai were buried in unmarked graves on this world, killed on the refugees' journey north. There were also marked graves at the foot of Kryie Karth, and, as she understood it, mass graves lay outside the city.

All of the deaths linked back to Araxis.

Velacy came up alongside her halfway back to the waiting Cyrwins. *"It must feel good to finally be able to do what you want without fear."*

His sending stunned her. *"What?"*

"You're safe now. You can return to the barrier and figure out how to take it down for us."

"No, Velacy, I am not safe. Araxis is not dead."

"Of course he's dead. I killed him."

"You killed Ving." Saying it sent a surge of anger through her. Despite her dislike for the man, Ving should not have had to die. If Velacy had waited for Seuliac to get the symbol from her, there might have been a way for him to walk through the gate, back to the Homeworld he'd missed so much. But there was also no way Velacy could know if the threat of Ving's presence had been reduced there in the woods. Araxis was such a constant, looming danger... *"He was weak and confused after being held in thrall for so long. Araxis abandoned him."*

"I think someone might be a little jealous." The younger Aedec gave her a smug, derisive look and strode on past her.

"You did not honor your word."

Kaphri looked at Chaos-stepper, standing on the slope a short distance away.

Red eyes gleamed with hostility.

This situation must be resolved. Now. She walked over to stand before the Cyrwin. Although fear tried to lock her breath inside her lungs, she met its eyes. *"It was an unexpected situation, and retreating was the best I could do. Warriors scout and analyze situations before they act. This bears no exception: I may have to back away again before I succeed. That's all that's important to you—me leaving—right? I will not betray my word."* Or Frax.

The glossy black scales on the Cyrwin's shoulders twitched. The long, muscular tail flicked but did not rise.

"Reasonable." She knew it was the Grimmen who replied. *"The next time you back away, you will die. So, succeed."*

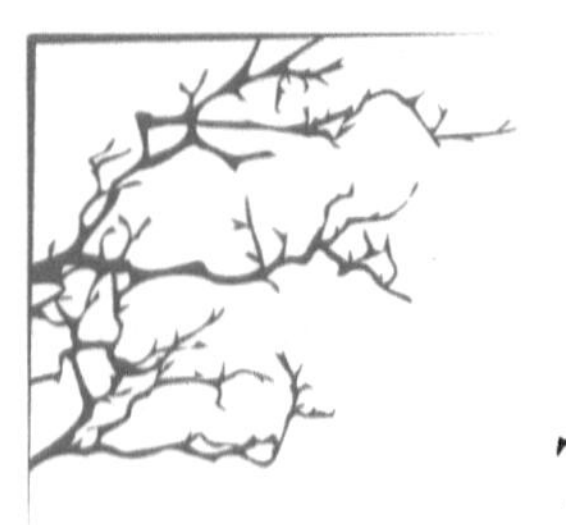

Chapter 93 Thought and Understanding

"MY WARRIORS REPORT seeing the girl outside the gate. She appeared out of nowhere. How does she do that—move over large distances?"

Frax looked up from sawing the tether of chain against the edge of the pool, his heart racing. *"What are you talking about?"*

The tarmeuth chose a sunny spot on the walk and settled gracefully. *"Don't play with your life, Geffitz. I don't have to return you in the same condition as you arrived. And stop doing that. You deface the pool for no reason. The chain will not break."*

"I still don't know what you're talking about."

"She appeared outside the gate of this compound a few moments ago. It's barely been a day since my warriors snatched you. She could not walk or run that distance. How does she do it?"

Damn the Priestess for acting rashly and giving away one of her advantages. Who let her use the crystal? Then again, could he have stopped her from making the jump if he had been in charge? And how did she know where to jump? Who gave her the image of this place?

It had to be the Cyrwins or the Grimmen. The Cyrwins had been starkly missing when the Balandra attacked him, which meant the Grimmen, in all its determination to have its way, had betrayed him. He could only hope the others were aware of the massive treachery surrounding them.

Frax straightened, letting the chain fall. There was a glaring gap in their timeline of which this being might be aware, so it was useless to feign ignorance. He didn't dare risk an outright lie, but he could twist the truth. *"The Wyxa used some trick to move us out of the swamp to safety when your forces attacked them."*

Safety. What a bitter irony.

"Do they still assist her?"

Interesting that it asked. After the Balandran attack on the Palenquemas, however, he would be dangerously naïve to believe the thought of Wyxan support would scare this creature, and if it thought she wielded a weapon or response beyond Ly Kai power, it could lose them a valuable advantage. It was best to guide it toward expecting a relatively helpless girl to arrive here—and pray to Kep it was a ruse and not his misguided expectations. *"The Wyxa are the Wyxa. They serve their own purpose."*

The being behind the cat's eyes stared at him as if weighing his response.

A bit of truth might be in order, especially if it reaffirmed what this being already knew. *"She's scared of using this starpower for fear it will draw Araxis' attention."*

"She is wise."

"And you are the preferable alternative?"

"I told you, I only want her to open the gate to the Ly Kai Homeworld so I can claim what is mine."

"Her physical form. But it's not yours."

"Again, I have no need for her form."

"If you speak true, swear you will not steal her form. Swear by whatever is holiest to you."

"Really? Swear an oath to a Geffitz? How amusing. Very well, I swear by Arylla: I neither require nor want her physical form beyond her opening the gate."

By Arylla? Frax's brain burned with the new bit of information. *"You are Alexar."*

"The stars forbid!" The creature managed to imbue the words with immense scorn.

"Then your oath is meaningless. There are only three Ly Kai who can honestly swear by that star."

"*What does a savage Geffitz know of the Ly Kai and our Hierarch of Stars?*" The question was a mixture of amusement and disdain.

Our. So, this creature was Ly Kai. "*Enough. There are only three Arylla-born. If you are not Kaphri, Alexar, or Araxis...*" Sudden caution tightened its grip on him. *"There was only one other, from two thousand years ago. The one she calls Hredroth."*

"That arrogant slime is long dead! She mentioned no others?"

All Frax could do was stare at the creature in silence.

"She did not tell you about our history? About the Great Reckoning?"

"She mentioned it." Seuliac had passed the conversation on to him. *"She didn't know what it was."*

"Curse Hredroth and his pious interference!" The being's attention slid away from Frax, the huge, tawny body shifting position with fury. *"The fool has erased our greatness."* Yellow tarmeuth eyes locked back on him. *"He has reduced us to nothing."*

Frax's throat tightened. How to keep this being talking and not die? *"Perhaps that is justice."*

"Don't be obnoxious, warrior. The girl must realize many more Arylla-born once existed—before Hredroth's interference. We were destined to become the rulers of the universe!" The cat's claws extended, gouging the stone walk.

Cold fear flashed through Frax. If this being's recollections proved too distressing, it might lose his hold over the tarmeuth. He had to stay engaged with it. *"I don't know—"*

"Of course, you don't know! Your lot was long gone before it happened."

Frax thought his heart would stop beating. *"What—?"*

"Silence!"

The being who held the tarmeuth in its control sat in tense silence, the tip of the animal's tail flicking back and forth as if it was preparing to spring on some oblivious prey.

Frax dared not breathe or think.

After a long pause, yellow eyes locked on him again. *"The Ly Kai are the rightful masters of this universe. Listen and learn and I might spare your life so you can educate your people to their place in the order of things. What I am about to reveal is knowledge none of your kind was ever allowed access to before."*

Kep!

"You are familiar with the existence of the gates from your contact with the girl, but neither of you knows anything beyond the simple concept of their existence."

Frax was unsure if the being expected him to acknowledge or deny the statement, so he stayed silent, locked in dread and fascination.

"You obviously know only an Arylla-born can open them. But, the same way the gate from the Homeworld gives access to your planet, so does another gate give access to an infinite number of worlds if one knows of its existence. True mastery of the gates lies in access to the Corridor of the Worlds."

"That doesn't exist!" It was a myth among Geffitzi he'd even referenced on occasion, but no one believed the thing was real.

"Of course, it exists." The creature paused to glare at him, and Frax feared it would stop sharing information if he continued to express his disbelief.

"All those lights you see in your night sky? Those are stars, surrounded by planets. Worlds. Some are similar to yours, adequate

to support life. Others are different beyond your imagination. Some are places from hell, while the dwellers of others create and command things that almost seem like magic to me. The Arylla-born of the Ly Kai accessed them freely by using the Corridor and the power of their Birthstar, conquering populations and bringing them to heel. Some of those worlds, however, generate their own starborn, from stars outside the Ly Kai Hierarch. Which allows them to hold an exclusive dominance in their realms. Sometimes those starborn fought us for control of their domains. The battles were glorious!"

"You stole worlds from other peoples..."

"We took what we wanted, and we did not apologize to the weak. But inevitably, some Ly Kai overreached in their ambition. Some of those otherworld starborn were immensely powerful and did not share our sanguine appreciation for battle. They followed Arylla's power back to the Ly Kai Homeworld and counseled with Hredroth, who was the Ly Kai High One at the time. They threatened to join forces to conquer and punish our Homeworld. Of course, they could not have succeeded." The tarmeuth flicked an ear. *"But they might have done some damage to our ancient home. Our weaker starborn cried out in fear, and Hredroth, being a coward, caved to their demands. He ordered all Arylla-born gate-openers to return home and gave them an ultimatum: remain on the Homeworld to live out their days or go out the gates to their fate and never return. The Homeworld would deny any responsibility for their actions, leaving them alone to face the consequences of their future behavior. They would be forever banished.*

"We—the ones who ruled the gates—were Gods! We had whole worlds at our bidding! Hredroth wanted us—me!—to give up everything! To surrender it all for the Ly Kai Homeworld's peace of mind. I subjugated worlds. Why would I go back to living as one among many, to return to an excruciatingly boring life where we had eliminated all strife ages ago?" The immense sense of scorn and disgust

from the other sizzled through Frax's brain. *"Of course, we refused to give up our empires!"*

"But that is not the end of the story for you." A sick sensation tightened Frax's stomach.

"It is not." Hot irritation and pride laced the other's sending. *"Younger Arylla-born, not yet gate-openers, entreated me to parley with Hredroth and ask him not to sever them from their birthright. I persuaded him to allow my return to the Homeworld. To talk."*

Frax recognized the underlying treachery in the term. *"You tried to kill him."*

The cat's golden eyes locked on him. *"Clever creature. Of course I did. But,"* the tarmeuth's tail flicked in irritation, *"I—we—miscalculated. One does not expect a fanatical purist to react so strongly on something outside their belief system. He destroyed the young ones with a simple blow of power. Then he turned his fury on me.*

"Because of its proximity to the Homeworld, I had previously considered your world for a project. My need for a swift refuge brought me back here before I had thoroughly investigated it. Because of their reclusiveness, I overlooked the existence of a powerful civilization that had the ability to block our stars. I also failed to note that the multiple other gates leading off this world were all bitter gates—meaning they led to pocket worlds. Miserable dead ends. I became trapped here when Hredroth closed gate access back to the Homeworld in the Great Reckoning and eliminated the possibility of more births to the Great Star by masking the secret of their conception in the ritual of the High Sabbat. After all that, he had the audacity to gut Arylla's temple and secret away all its collected knowledge of the Great Star's power to prevent any chance of another Arylla-born attaining full skill. He erased our history, deprived us of our legacy, and shoved its empty bones here to taunt me! And that, simple creature, was the Great Reckoning.

"But it was not the end of things. I immediately set out to reclaim the Homeworld by fortifying this one and building an army with the

paltry resources available to me. In my obsession for vengeance, I became careless. I met resistance to my plan for glory and conquest and paid an excruciating price. The swamp dwellers cursed my armies and pushed us through one of the bitter gates onto a barren pocket world, leaving me to languish and die. But greatness learns from its mistakes. I did not die, and I have fought my way back."

The horrified realization that had been building in Frax finally broke free. "No!" The conclusion sounded too familiar.

The other paused, as if surprised, then chuckled. *"Ah, I have fallen prey to my vanity. I thought you would recognize who I was, especially since I've had the greatest influence over the Geffitzi of any single creature in the last two thousand years of your existence."*

Hardly daring to breathe, Frax stared at the tarmeuth. Two thousand years. Two thousand years and more. It could not be true. *"He was not Ly Kai."*

"And you were doing so well."

"The Ly Kai have nothing to do with my world's past—"

"The Ly Kai have everything to do with your world's past, stupid creature."

"You lie!" Frax's lungs felt as if they would collapse inside of him as he fought for a breath.

The cat rose and turned to walk away. *"You are obviously afraid of the truth."*

If the creature left, he might not ever hear the rest of its story, truth or lie. *"I want to know the truth."*

It turned back to regard him with baleful eyes. *"Then show me you are ready to accept it. Who am I?"*

Frax looked away, fury, disbelief, and despair choking him. It was all he could muster to say the hated name. *"Bithzielp."*

"Very good." The tarmeuth returned to its place. *"There is so much more I can tell you. Are you ready to listen?"*

Frax fought the urge to spit. *"Yes."*

The tarmeuth settled back to the walk. *"A gate is part of an unimaginably vast system. Once opened, it never completely seals again. I niggled my way through infinitesimal crevices and unimaginable distances to find and commune with Ly Kai shadow born—the Shades, those whose births between the transitions of stars will never let them access real power and who take up the priesthood to the trueborn to feed their pathetic need to be near pure starpower. Hredroth, in all his vile efforts, could not prevent their births, and they harbor a deep, frustrated need for purpose. I found them, and through those wretched, tiny cracks between worlds, I showed them how to break the trickery of the High Sabbat."*

"You created Araxis, Alexar, and Kaphri." Two thousand years passed in Geffitzi history, and this thing still persisted in its fight for power over other beings...

"Not the girl child. Araxis, calculating viper that he is, did that. He even succeeded in hiding her existence from me for a time. But his treachery also laid bare his secret ambitions. He wanted to build his own puny empire and, aware of the risks, he plotted a backup plan with her birth. He thinks he can outwit me. He thinks he can regain his power through the girl, using my Balandran forces against me, and escape this world. He is wrong.

"Now," a dizzying sense of triumph ran through the sending, *"I am on the verge of recovering everything I lost and so much more. Others will soon pay for the things they have done to thwart me."*

"You chose—"

"I did not choose this!" Temper blazed. *"I did not choose to be trapped in a twisted, crippled Balandran form. Locked away on a hellish world, fighting for a scrap of food, a lungful of air for thousands of years! I did not choose that!"* The creature inside the tarmeuth raged while the animal's brain struggled to express things it was never meant to articulate.

Frax watched in horrified fascination, afraid the other might lose what looked to be a precarious hold while the cat's muscles spasmed and quivered.

After a moment, his captor remastered the tarmeuth's physical reactions.

"You've lived for thousands of years?" Frax's heart continued to race.

"Those who command power have ways."

"Stealing bodies." It seemed a common theme among the Ly Kai.

"I liked my birth form! I was admired for my beauty on a score of worlds." The fury transitioned to burning resentment. *"Until the creatures of this world forced me onto a world where it could not survive."*

"You use a Balandran form now." The Wyxa claimed they had cursed Bithzielp's followers after their ambitions destroyed Kep's Second Daughter, the small moon, Twyfel, and nearly ended the world. They had twisted Balandran beauty to reflect the hideousness of their actions and drove them through a gate in the Black Temple. The history he had questioned in his youth as overblown by the telling and the passage of time was opening its dark maw to engulf his world again.

He could not let that happen.

Fool, his mind whispered, you will only delay it. Delay and time were the only weapons he had available. But time offered a chance...

The cat licked at a forepaw. *"Of all the slaves I have had, your people were truly my favorite. You exhibited such cleverness and innovation. If only I could have cut the stubborn pride out of you, I would have had armies capable of conquering infinite worlds."*

"You did not conquer this one."

"No, I did not." A dangerous, steely quality laced the sending as the tarmeuth lowered its front paw and regarded him. *"This time it will be different."*

This creature thought it could re-establish its hold here? Cold rippled across Frax's skin. *"The Geffitzi bow to no one."*

"Still such tedious creatures. We shall see. Perhaps you are clever enough to prevent me from asserting a claim on this cursed world. Are you, warrior? Are you capable of mastering your savage instincts if it means the future of your world?"

The refrains of his argument in the Palenquemas, when he stood before Klandar Bayne, rippled across his mind. Did he have the control to do what must be done? It depended on the task. Frax swallowed hard. *"Speak. I will listen."*

"I want the girl to open the gate." Frax did not miss the slow slide of cunning that infiltrated the sending. *"But the Geffitzi want something from her too. Tell me what it is."*

"I want the return of my people's lands."

"You want that extravagant wall of power removed. Quite an amazing and deliciously treacherous feat, that. You do realize you are on the verge of losing her, and not from me. Araxis wants her form so he can escape my vengeance, and the Ly Kai desperately want her returned to the Homeworld. They think she can protect them from a looming threat they sense. The threat is me. They are wrong, of course. They have bargained with a force on your world for her immediate return. It is a bold deception. They could not have contacted the force that rules the woods if I had not established a link for them and led them to it by their noses. I admit there were difficulties along the way. After discovering her existence, I had to lure your Grimmen to assert its geas in the north to give me time to ensnare her. But Araxis, surprisingly, betrayed me by severing her link to Arylla with an inspired trick of reversing Arylla's sign to seal her power inside her." Frax felt the sting of Bithzielp's bitter amusement. *"I could feel something beyond the gate in the Black Temple, but I could not distinguish what it was. Who would believe a foolish Geffitz warrior would free me by positioning her to remove the Guardian Stone? Where is the thing, by the way?"*

"I don't know." It was not a lie.

"You know it blocks me from sensing her location."

"We know it blocked Araxis."

"I cannot sense where she is right now."

Frax met golden eyes. *"Neither can I."*

"She still has it, then. No matter. Because of the things Araxis did, bringing her here and keeping her ignorant, she will never be able to counter my power, and she will die if she attempts to intervene in my plans. Such a senseless waste of your efforts and an annoying inconvenience for me." The creature paused a moment as if to let its words sink in. *"So, it appears you have a decision to make. You can watch her die and suffer the consequences of me remaining on this world, or you can cooperate with me and persuade her to help me reclaim my Homeworld."*

The cursed creature said Kaphri could stay here and remove the barrier if she opened the gate for him. It was a lie. Bithzielp would never dare turn his back on her.

Meanwhile, she was rushing here to save him, an innocent to the slaughter...

He had to warn her. To warn her, he had to stay alive. *"I appear to have no choice. She must open the gate so you can leave my world."*

The cat stared at him as if it would strip him down to his soul. *"I like you, Geffitz. When I leave, I think I will take you with me."*

"No."

"I'm sorry; did you think I was asking?"

Frax ground his teeth.

"Good. The best of you always learned so quickly. I remember now why I kept a select few as pets."

"You're insane." Frax made no effort to mask his fury and revulsion.

"Again, perhaps. If you live as long as I have, you might be, too. If you manage to survive the next few days, you can consider your own sanity and immortality."

"I'd rather die."

"Yes," Bithzielp cocked his head to one side, examining him critically. *"Perhaps you will. It seems the ones worthy of my interest usually do."* The tarmeuth rose to its feet. *"It is a trait that quickly grows wearisome."*

Chapter 94
Betrayal Under a Cold Moon

THE DUST BENEATH HIS gnarled, scaled feet stank of dead animal flesh, and the thick ruts of hardened dirt, reinforced with shriveled, rotted plants, made walking treacherous and painful. Thirst burned his long throat and unrelenting hunger gnawed his gut. The dry air blurred his vision, but he was almost there. The mental call from the others as they gathered was increasing in number and strength. Desire for revenge raked the edges of his brain, while a desperate appeal for retreat to a safer plain of existence slid through his mind like cool mud.

Differing factions were seeking majority control.

For him, retreat was not the solution.

Their previous warnings had not been enough. They had tried. Now everything was at risk. It was time to take action. To do something that required great sacrifice.

Regret and massive fury swirled inside him.

Too much! Frax jerked upright, his body quivering in the grip of emotions that had no place inside of him.

What the hell?

Movement caught his attention: the shadowed hulk of the tarmeuth was settling to the walk in the bright moonlight.

Despite the hot blast of breath from the horror, he could not shake the dregs of the dream. His heart raced with the question. Had Bithzielp...? But no. The rage and sense of loss had come from another place entirely.

Cold realization flooded over Frax. He'd made a mistake. A huge mistake. Now he understood. When the Ankar Mekt had engulfed him, he had wrenched at Wyxan ancestral memory, snatching randomly and wildly. He could have stolen any memory from their endless centuries of stored experience. But he had not. These were Wyxan memories of the destruction this being, who was seeking a return to power, had wrought on this world. The dreams carried a specific message: Geffitzi had sought to take on this battle, and this was what they confronted. This was the strength of Bithzielp. This was what he had done. This was what he could do again. Perhaps the memories that Frax had snatched were not as random as he had thought... He could not lose this battle.

His merciless captor was staring at him with a killer's golden eyes.

"What do you want?"

"You lack proper respect, Geffitz," the being controlling the animal fumed. *"I have worked on this project for ages, before Geffitzi were barely aware of their existence."* Frax caught an image of the Ly Kai refuge in the north that he had never seen before. Three elegant towers graced a blue lake inside a verdant mountain ring that teemed with life. *"My towers! My beautiful Geron Maed that the cursed Swamp dwellers routed and rendered a wasteland."*

It didn't look like Kaphri's shared images of the place she called Kryie Karth. *"Things long passed."* Frax shrugged, rejecting more memories that were not his.

"Foolish Geffitz, what do you know of the past? You, who have no idea of your people's history." The cold scorn stung like a lash.

"And you do." Frax's heart beat harder as he climbed to his feet and settled on the edge of the pool.

"Yes. I said I would tell you about your people's past. I am bored with all this waiting." The impatience slid to a cold, slicing sense of anticipation. *"But there is always a price for knowledge. Are you willing to pay it?"*

"What price?"

"Oh, I do not set this price. The burden of truth will be yours to bear."

A fair warning: either way, he would regret his choice for the rest of his days.

Obscured in a haze of horror and misery, Geffitzi history only extended back to the ancient time when this being had enslaved and tormented them. The age of their holds and their culture, however, belied that. There had to be more. They recognized it, but no one had ever found anything to shed light on their deeper past.

He would rather regret the knowing than be devoured by regret at what he had declined to learn. *"You destroyed our history."*

"I did not. Your people made their choice ages ago."

"Will you tell me the truth?"

"I have no reason to lie. I will warn you: I am the last person alive who knows the full story of Geffitzi origins. You have this one opportunity. Decide."

A glimpse back to the dust of ancient times, thousands of years ago? The price of the knowledge would likely be his death.

He was doomed, anyway. *"Tell me."*

"Very well. Your people do not belong to this world. They were forcibly removed from the Ly Kai Homeworld, driven through this very gate ages ago."

"No." Frax's body was paralyzed by a sudden dread.

"Do you want to know your true origins or not, Geffitz?"

Waves of cold were washing over his skin. Shock. But he had to listen and remember. He had to know. "Tell me." He whispered the words aloud, not even realizing.

"You were always a difficult lot. Full of ambition. Aspiring, and... brilliant. But endless trouble. There were Ly Kai who were fascinated with you, working beside, loving, and even sharing your beds. Contaminating our bloodline..." Bithzielp's contempt was nearly overwhelming. *"Always drawing Ly Kai into your endless bickering and fighting. Into your battles. It was ripping both our civilizations apart. The Ly Kai Governing Council finally had enough."* Bithzielp's resentment and anger burned through Frax's numb disbelief. *"This world is not your home; it's your planet of exile. As a small child, I watched every last one of your forefathers—every creature contaminated with your blood—march through this gate to thrive or die on this world. That is how I knew of its existence. Mercifully for you, a powerful being from this world was enamored with you. It conspired with your ancestors to obscure your true origins and ease your pain of loss."*

Kep's Second Children. The words tumbled like blazing embers in his mind. The Geffitzi called themselves Kep's Second Children...

"The force that conspired..." he had to put it into words, *"It was the Grimmen."*

"And now it lives in constant fear of losing you."

Frax crumpled off the pool edge to his knees as an alien outrage ripped through his brain.

"Oh, is it reacting to my revelation?" Bithzielp laughed. *"It has jealously guarded the secret of your origins for ages, fearing your people might desire a return to the Homeworld if you knew your truth. It does not want to lose you. The spirit in the woods is so desperate to keep your people shielded from the truth that it stayed silent, willing to sacrifice a portion of you when I came here. It even allowed Araxis to drive the*

Geffitzi north rather than see you completely slaughtered by the plague he brought down on you. But it won't let you live to tell the story."

The scale of the Grimmen's exposed betrayal was too immense for Frax to immediately comprehend, which brought him to one clear truth. *"It already plans to kill me,"* he snarled in floundering defense.

"Oh, it does not plan to kill just you," came the silky reply. *"It will not let your companions live, either. It cannot risk this story getting to your people. I warned you there was a price for the knowledge. The moment I revealed the truth about your origins, I broke the ancient pact between us, and it acted. Your friends are gone. Its barb-tailed minions will bring the girl here to me—it has no choice if it wants me to leave. She will do what I demand in the hope she can keep you alive, but alas, I fear you, especially, are doomed."*

And so was the Priestess. This evil creature would never risk leaving her alive at its back.

"I'm afraid there will never be a return of the Geffitz clans to this land now. Such a waste, but you did ask for the truth. Now you have a choice to make: you can come with me, or you can die at the hands of your Eldren protector. At least you have the consolation of knowing no one will ever know what the price of your knowledge cost the Geffitzi except you. And me."

"The Little Sister will be bright tonight," Uri said.

Seuliac glanced at the sky. Kep's remaining daughter, Pona, was cresting the mountain behind them. *"Too bad she can't give us some heat."*

"Yeah. That's a fierce cold wind sweeping up out of the gorge," Velacy added, shivering.

Giving in to the need for speed, they had ridden relentlessly through the day, the Cyrwins moving above the tree line where the ground was clearer and the travel faster. It also put them closer to the melting snow line, colder air, and boggy ground. They were all spattered with mud and chilled to the bone when a natural obstacle of a deep gash in the bare granite of the mountain, filled with rushing, icy water from late spring runoff, ended their day's travel. The Cyrwins had moved them down a steep slope speckled with jutting rocks and clumps of low-growing briars to a place along the lip of the gorge.

"It's a damned wretched spot," the warlord continued the complaint. *"You could have found a better place to camp, Kitahn."* The meltwater from the granite channel behind them poured off the rocks in a crashing waterfall. The catch basin, to their right and at least forty feet below their place on the cliff, threw up a cold mist that drifted over them. It was windy, wet, and noisy, a terrible location for a camp. Their protests against it had drawn no sympathy from their mounts. The creatures simply waited for them to dismount, then moved off into the twilight.

Tobin looked up from spreading his blanket next to a briar clump and shrugged. *"I didn't pick it."* It was easier for them to send than to shout over the noise of the water. *"You want to complain, take it up with them."* He jerked his head in the direction of the dense darkness marking a line of trees in the distance.

"I will if I see one of them." Seuliac stared into the darkness, searching for the single guard the creatures habitually posted. Not a glint of light off a cursed black scale out there. *"Something is going on with those treacherous snakes."*

"You noticed, too?" Uri frowned.

"It seemed to start shortly before we stopped for the day."

Both warriors locked their attention on Tobin.

The younger warrior shrugged. *"The Grimmen does not share its reasoning with me."*

From her place between Seuliac and Uri, Kaphri thought she saw Tobin's mouth tighten at the corners, as if he, too, had noticed a change but was refusing to acknowledge it.

Finished with their sparse meal of brittle paste and dried meat, the others put down blankets as far from the lip of the ravine as the briar clumps would allow while still staying close together, but the edge was only a few steps away.

"So, what's our next move?" Velacy asked as he settled to the ground.

"*We're going after Frax,*" Uri snapped. "*Why the hell do you even ask?*"

Kaphri pulled her blanket tighter against the chill and waited for the younger Aedec to respond. Beyond Uri, the warlord was a dark profile as he leaned forward to blow on his cupped hands.

"Because things have changed. I killed Araxis," Velacy responded.

"You keep saying that!" Kaphri exploded. Why did he keep saying that? *"I told you that was not Araxis. It was Ving."* The more she said it, the more she was sure it was true. *"Why do you keep saying that?"*

"Because now that the Evil One is gone, we don't have to go to this city of yours. We can go north to the barrier. You can remove it, like you promised."

"I will not abandon Frax!"

"Really? What's to stop you from running off and abandoning all of us once you get to your gate?"

"Let it go, Velacy," Uri warned.

"No. If she goes to the city, she'll be gone. That's the end of it. She should go north like she promised and take down the damned wall. Use her precious power for something useful! We need that done, and we don't need Frax Kitahn for her to do it—"

"Stop talking!" Kaphri scrambled to her feet. *"Stop talking now!"* She was shaking from anger and fear.

"Why are you being so stupid about this?" the younger Aedec demanded.

"You don't know what you're saying!"

"Willow, calm down," Uri said uneasily. *"Velacy's being a fool—"*

"Stop. All of you." Tobin shot to his feet. *"Something is wrong."*

"What is it...?" The vibration she felt in her feet was more than the stress of their conversation. She searched out mentally.

A dark wave seemed to be racing across the slope toward them.

Uri was up. *"On your feet! On your feet!"*

Shadows surged, and then the Cyrwins were upon them, teeth and hooves slashing.

Seuliac twisted beneath the fangs aimed at his shoulder but was not so lucky at avoiding the rest of the creature's body. The Cyrwin's shoulder struck him a glancing blow to the hip, knocking him backward.

"The hell! What—?" Tobin ducked the sweeping stroke of a bony tail.

Another thick coil sliced the air, slamming Velacy across the back and knocking him to the ground.

"*Get over the edge!*" Tobin made a flying dive past Uri and Seuliac. He caught Kaphri about the waist, carrying her to the grass, and rolled, taking them both off the edge of the ravine.

Uri grabbed Velacy by the back of the shirt, dodged slashing teeth, and followed Tobin with Seuliac close behind.

Chapter 95
If We Stay, We Die

"YOU BASTARD! YOU SHOULD have stayed up there with your scaly friends." Seuliac shoved Kaphri behind him as he squared off against Tobin in the heavy, clumped grass of the bank where they'd come to rest. Water rushed over the large rocks a few feet below them.

"They're not my friends, Aedec! I'm down here with the rest of you."

"You snatched her—"

"To keep them from killing her! Something changed with the Grimmen. It moved to kill all of us."

Starfire flared, and the warriors threw up their hands to keep from being momentarily blinded.

"Look at me, Tobin," Kaphri ordered. *"Look me in the eyes."*

Blinking, Tobin lowered his hand and stared at her.

The scout's eyes were as clear gray as any of the other warriors.

"It's true, Warlord. I've seen his eyes when the Grimmen is working inside him."

"The Grimmen is gone." Tobin snapped.

"Why?" Seuliac lowered his knife, but he did not sheath it. *"What changed?"*

"I don't know." Tobin's mouth tightened. *"It was like having a fist slammed into the side of my head. The Grimmen blasted surprise and outrage, then it released me, and the Cyrwins charged us."*

What would make the Grimmen change its whole purpose so abruptly? Kaphri felt a rush of deeper fear. It must be something of major impact. Had something happened to Frax...?

"You're sure it's gone out of him, Priestess? Priestess!"

Seuliac's anger pulled her back into focus. *"Yes. It is for now."*

"He still bears watching." With a glare at Tobin, Seuliac shoved the blade into its cover. *"Kill the light, and let's get out of here."*

"Velacy and Uri—" Kaphri protested.

"They'll catch up."

"They might be injured."

"They are Geffitzi." Seuliac sent her a sizzling sensation that questioned her reasoning.

Yes, but they were also flesh and bone. *"We find them first."*

"No. We get out of here before the Cyrwins locate us again."

"They are coming for us," Tobin agreed. *"But they can't risk descending this slope; it's too steep. They'll go farther down the mountain to access the gorge."*

"Cutting off our escape route." Kaphri's heart raced harder. The warriors would find a way out of this trap. *"Velacy is in the brush, up there."* She pointed off to her left, back up the slope. *"He is injured."*

"We should leave him."

"No." She sent the Warlord hard rejection.

"He's probably the cause of this, you know, with all his mouthing off."

"Frax said we needed every warrior we had," Tobin reminded them firmly.

"That's a new song for you," Seuliac snarled. *"How long can we expect you to remember it?"* He stormed off to find Velacy.

Heat from Tobin's anger flashed, but he didn't object to the warlord's comment. How could he?

The younger Kitahn looked at her. *"The past is not open to change. I couldn't stop the Grimmen from abandoning Frax. Now it has abandoned the rest of us, including you."*

"Do you know why it changed?"

Abruptly, all the pent-up anger and hostility drained out of the young warrior. *"Something happened after we settled in. Something huge. The Grimmen registered a sense of immense betrayal and it turned on us."* He paused for a heartbeat, then asked quietly. *"Is my brother dead?"*

"No." The tenuous link between her and Frax was still active, even over what must be an intimidating distance. It did not annoy her now.

"Good." Visible relief ran through him. For the first time since their arrival at Cadarn, Tobin actually looked like the warrior she'd encountered in Omurda. Still prickly, but taking fire with his youthful emotions now rather than the immense and ponderous weight of vengeful intent that motivated the Grimmen.

She had to ask. *"Do you think the Grimmen shifted its alliance because of Velacy and his stupid claims?"*

"No. It didn't like what he said. It wanted to kill him despite its agreement with Frax, but he isn't what caused this. It felt as if the Grimmen suddenly experienced something terrible. It went into an explosion of fury and decided to kill us all. That's all I know: it has severed ties with me."

Was the younger Kitahn truly no longer a puppet of the Grimmen, or could that change again at the worst possible moment?

Tobin caught her by the arm. *"I don't want Frax to die. I never did. The Grimmen held me in such a thrall I couldn't speak or act against its will. I don't know how long this will last, but while I'm out of its control, I want you to know: I don't want our world to suffer anymore, either. Do you understand?"*

"We do what we must do, Tobin."

The Geffitzi warrior code.

"*Yes.*" He hurried to follow Seuliac up the bank.

Uri erupted from the water with an explosive gasp. "Son of a bitch!"

He'd jumped, the addition of Velacy's weight pulling him off balance so that when his feet hit the slope, he'd fallen into a tangle with the younger Aedec.

They'd tumbled, separating at some point, with Uri finding himself alone against a clump of brush. Then he'd moved, the brush gave way under his weight, and he plunged off another bank.

Luckily, the basin below the waterfall was broad and deep.

"Son of a bitch," he exclaimed again, his teeth beginning to chatter.

The icy water left him clearheaded, and numbed any injuries he had, but it would also quickly suck the life out of him. He struck out, swimming away from the roar of the pounding water until his feet touched stone; then, he pulled himself out of the rocky shallows and got to his feet.

Bent and gasping from the cold, he ran a quick check of his body, flexing arms, hands, legs, and neck against the ice crystals beginning to stiffen his clothes. Nothing broken—or maybe so cold that it simply didn't hurt.

The bank from which he'd jumped hung darkly over the pool to his left, the walls of the ravine towering and steep. The place was a pit with only one way out—down the rushing stream leading away from the fall.

The air in the gorge was freezing, and his wet clothes were sucking away his body heat. If he didn't get warm quickly, he would die.

"U*ri!"* Kaphri sensed rather than saw the warrior stumbling toward her. *"Hredroth! Are you all right?"*

"Freezing and soaked, but intact." He loomed, nearly upon her before she could see him in the shadows of the gorge.

"Come. Sit." She caught his arm and tugged him over to the bank. *"Take this."* She pressed a fist-sized stone into his hands.

"Heat? Kep, Willow, that feels so good. But should you do it?"

"Given the alternative of letting you freeze? Yes." She put her hands on his arm and channeled a small amount of heat into the cloth and leather. The cold breeze tore away the curls of steam that swirled into the air..

"Are you alone? I saw Tobin grab you."

"He went to help Seuliac bring Velacy down."

"How do you know they won't kill each other in the dark?"

"Because they know we need each other."

"The Cyrwins really tried to kill us?"

"Even Tobin. Apparently, he's no longer of use to the Grimmen."

"We should get out of here."

"Tobin says the Cyrwins will find a place to enter the gorge and come upstream for us." She took the cooling stone and gave him a warm one. When the back of her hand brushed his cuff, she felt the stiffness of its frozen edge. For the first time, she noticed that her feet were numb.

"We have to find another way out."

She put her hands on his chest and sent warmth across the leather and cloth. "*We have one. We must act quickly when the others get back here.*"

"*A jump.*" She felt wary displeasure in his sending.

"*We have no choice, Uri. If we stay here, we'll die.*"

"*Willow— The Wyxa.*"

"*I don't want this either. I am afraid. But the dying Balandran said we have five days. If the Cyrwins were really taking us to the city, it can't be more than two more days of riding.*"

"*To the city.*" Uri emphasized 'city.'

"*We all know Velacy is right about us needing to return to the north, but I will not let Frax die. I'm sorry, Uri.*"

"*Then we better get it right.*" Uri had stopped shivering.

Kaphri picked up another stone to warm. Paused, her heart beating like thunder in her chest. "*Yes.*"

A slide of gravel and dirt announced the return of Seuliac and Tobin, half-dragging Velacy between them. They dropped him to the ground beside Uri.

"*He says his arm is injured,*" Seuliac announced.

"*Cousin.*" Tobin nodded stiffly at Uri. A quick sense of a private exchange flashed between the two in the darkness.

"*Which arm?*" Placing a weak bit of starfire between them, Kaphri turned her attention to Velacy.

He extended his right forearm to reveal a rip in the dirt-caked sleeve. The fabric was wet with blood.

"*Uri...*" Injury of this type was beyond her.

The big warrior handed off the warm stone to Seuliac and bent to tug the tear wider. "*It's not serious,*" he declared. "*Splash some water on it so the cold will slow the bleeding. We've no time for more right now. Douse your light, Willow. Quickly, everyone, an inventory of weapons and supplies."*

"I have my knives, nothing more," Tobin replied.

"Same here," Seuliac answered. *"Blankets, bow, arrows, all left up above."*

"I have nothing but a knife," Kaphri said. Even the dwindling store of brittle paste was gone.

"Knives," Velacy forced his sending over the discomfort of the gorge's cold air.

"Food for the Priestess will quickly become a problem," Uri warned. *"I still have my belt pack, so we have some medical supplies if they aren't ruined by water, and I have a few other small items."*

"Can we climb back up and get our things?"

"Going to the top of this gorge in the dark is too dangerous. You can be sure a Cyrwin's waiting in case we try. And, no, she can't jump and grab our stuff. We lose her now, and this is all over."

"We should go," Kaphri told them. Further discussion was useless. With the roar of water in this place, the Cyrwins could come up on them at any moment, and they would never hear their approach.

She felt the warriors' uneasiness as they shifted their attention to her.

"Where? Backwards? Forwards?"

"To the barrier," Velacy said. *"That's where she will be best used."*

"Used?" Tobin challenged. *"We have no guarantee she can do anything to help us back there."*

"There never was," Seuliac agreed.

"To the woods outside the city. Anywhere else is a delay we cannot afford," Uri said.

"You expect Geffitz warriors to go without weapons?" Velacy's annoyance exceeded the sense of his pain.

"We'll acquire new weapons when we get there."

Kaphri might not see the cold anticipation in Seuliac's smile, but she could feel it in his sending.

Uri gave a low laugh, and Tobin sent hard agreement.

"I'm telling you, we should go north, to the barrier," Velacy protested. *"If she doesn't take it down now, it will never happen! Kitahn is as good as dead; you all know that. We have to move on."*

"No, Velacy, we don't know that," Kaphri responded sharply. *"He will be, though, if I don't go to the city. There is no safe place on this world for me to run from Araxis. It's time. You come with us, or you stay here. Those are your choices. If you are coming, grip arms with the others and clear your mind."*

"You are all fools," the younger Aedec ranted as he grasped Seuliac and Uri's arms.

"Kep." Tobin muttered as he took his position between her and Seuliac, "I hadn't planned on doing this again."

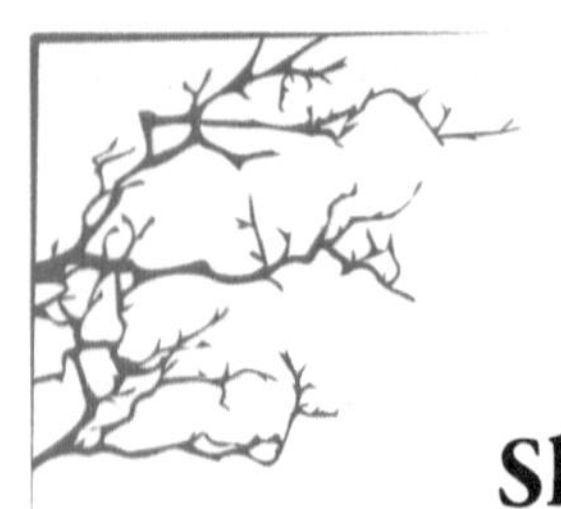

Chapter 96
She Is a Warrior

"STARCHILD."

"Swampfather! No!" Horror rolled through her.

"Wait..."

"Do not interfere!" She couldn't locate him in the swirling gray around her.

"We cannot. This is outside our domain. But we can block the power of your stars."

"No, don't!" If the Wyxa denied her access to Arylla, she couldn't open the gate and they would all die.

"You and the Blood Warrior must defend our world. If you fail, we must ensure no one else can restore their power through you."

Blood Warrior? No matter. The warning: the Wyxa would kill her. Not new information. *"If we fail, then do what you must."* She did not want to be the continued source of this world's pain.

"We will attempt to save your companions."

"Frax—"

"The Wyxa will owe you eternally for your sacrifice."

Then he was gone.

Everything vanished.

No sound. No trees or structures or people.

Just stars. Stars everywhere. And a horrible, suffocating sense of loss... Frax—! Sorrow and pain twisted inside her as the memory of a hulking animal flashed across her mind. Then the raw power of Arylla hit her, shredding everything else with its immense impact.

"Willow! Are you good?"

Thousands of stars and the vastness of space locked her mind.

"Willow?" An echoing whisper, Uri calling aloud from a distance. He was taking no chance of being immersed in the mental shock of her jump.

The press of silence around her was so isolating. It was a pain like nothing she'd ever experienced before. She was nothing and it was devouring her.

She needed something physical to pull her out of the void...

She latched onto Uri mentally and physically.

"Stop!" The warrior had her forearms in his grasp and was forcing her to her knees. "Stop, Willow! Now!"

Uri's face, furrowed with concern and anger, came into focus as he bent over her,

She must not put anything about Frax into thought or words. *"The Wyxa... Klandar Bayne..."* Shuddering, she fought free of his grasp and got to her feet. *"I can't jump again..."*

"So be it." The big warrior nodded.

The dry leaves of the forest floor crunched beneath her wet boots. The other warriors were silently clustered around her, trees looming behind them.

She had made the return leap back to the forest across the plain from the city.

"What did you experience?" Seuliac demanded.

"I... don't know." How to put what she'd experienced into words? It didn't make sense. She shared a brief image of stars, along with the sensation of silence and cold.

"That's useless," Velacy declared tightly above the others' puzzlement. *"You have no idea what it means or when it will happen."*

Knowing he was right sent an edge of panic coursing through her. Seuliac might have been correct when he suggested her return leap to the mountainside had changed the future. If so, it was even more terrifying.

Better to worry about the present. Had their jump alerted Araxis? Were the Grimmen and the Wyxa able to track them to this destination? The Balandra might not be immediately aware.

Uri sensed her concern. *"Balandran patrols have excellent night vision. We have to find cover for you while we scout things out and form a plan. Did you notice any details about this area during your earlier jump?"*

"No. I just ran into the woods to hide my return." With trees obscuring the barely risen moon, the forest was almost as dark as the mountain ravine. Despite that, she was aware of exactly which direction the Ly Kai structure lay.

At least the air was warmer here than in the ravine.

"Thank Kep," someone muttered aloud at the thought.

"Does Araxis know we are here?" Uri asked.

"It's possible. The Grimmen might even alert him after the Cyrwins' failed attack." Death was death, regardless of who administered it. *"We may have another problem. The Wyxa were waiting for me this time. They know where we are."*

Dismay rippled around her.

"Did they try to interact or interfere with you?" Seuliac asked.

"The Swampfather spoke my name. He did not try to detain me, but he warned they could block starpower."

"Was it a threat?"

"I sensed some hostility in the background, but not from the Swampfather." She desperately wished the Wyxa had revealed something of the approaching confrontation. *"They are aware of*

what is coming." The warriors should know so they didn't mistake delayed Wyxan action for Wyxan indifference.

"They'll never let this go unaddressed," Tobin said. *"They want to control everything."*

"I wonder who'll arrive here first," said Seuliac, *"The Cyrwins or the Wyxa? And whether we'll have to fight them both."*

"Without weapons? Tobin exclaimed. *"Unless one of us is particularly good at words, we'll lose those battles."*

"I'm afraid the one of us who's good at battling with words is missing," Uri said.

Frax.

Grim chuckles sounded around her in the darkness.

"Then we should make every effort to recover him quickly. First, let's find some cover and have a look around," Seuliac said.

Tobin located a hollow space beneath a bank in a dry streambed. It was similar to other places where they had sheltered during their time in the Grimmenwood. It smelled musty, but it was dry.

Despite the slight rise in temperature, Uri's clothes were still wet. The warriors agreed he would be best left behind with Velacy to guard her.

"What do you have in your pouch?" Seuliac asked Uri.

"Flints. Small hooks. A whetstone. Spare gut for stringing bows. Cord." Uri emptied the contents of his beltpouch on the forest floor in front of him. *"We can use it to make spears and a sling or two."*

"Velacy can gather stones for a sling while you wait for us to scout this place. We'll find some straight poles for the spears."

Uri sighed as he pulled his blade and sliced through the seam of his leather pant leg. *"These were good breeches."*

"A bit aged and rank for social interaction." Tobin grimaced. *"You'll have fair maids bearing the best of everything the holds can supply when we're done."*

"Yeah." Uri smiled wryly. *"I only need one fair maid. I'd like to see her at least once more before I die."*

The younger scout's humor vanished. *"You will grow old with Ladrienca, cousin. I swear it."*

Tobin had no control over the upcoming events, but Kaphri knew his display of determination was a strong boost for the Caspani heir.

The younger Kitahn rose to his feet. *"Stay alert for our return,"* he told Kaphri. *"We might need you to defend our backs."*

"*Yes,*" she agreed quietly. It was the first time he'd ever indicated he might use her help. *"The woods end at the edge of a broad field in front of the city, so please be careful."*

"W*illow, how are you holding up?"*

Kaphri was channeling warmth across Uri's back, trying to dry his clothing as he cut lengths of cord. *"I..."* she paused. This was Uri. She could talk about what was really bothering her. *"Seuliac said caring for any of you gives my enemy a tool to use against me. But fear for Frax's safety consumes my thoughts. Uri, I don't want to live in a world without him."* It was not what a Geffitz warrior would want to hear, but she had to say it, once, to someone. She broke off her sending, humiliated by her admission.

"The warlord is right. You can't become distracted from your purpose; that's what the enemy wants."

She sighed. *"I know you all better than my own people. You've taught me how to live, how to laugh, how to—"* she broke off, unwilling to put the last bit into words. She remained their enemy, no matter how she felt about them. Nothing would erase that. *"I am a fool."*

"You're not a fool. You are no more or less than any Geffitz warrior. Why do you think Seuliac warned you of those traps? The most dangerous warrior to fight is the one with no attachments. He acts without fear because he has nothing to lose. Everything you fear losing becomes another cord to bind your hands."

"Uri, I cannot abandon him—"

"Frax is not where your battle lies." Uri's sending was gentle but firm. *"You're the only one who can get Araxis off our world. You have starpower. He doesn't. That's how you fight him."*

True. But the barrier... She wanted to scream her frustration.

He moved around to face her. *"This is our time to act, too. We will not accept pain and upheaval for our people ever again if even one of us can stop it. That is how I feel. That is how Frax feels. If it means dying for it, then it is a good death."*

"I wish we were able to go back to...anywhere over the past few weeks." Even the worst of those times was preferable to what lay ahead. She sighed. *"I have to become another person now."* Her hand closed about the crystal. She had already lost Gemma to it. Now, she had to put away everything else she had learned to care for. She had to become the warrior with nothing to lose.

He nodded solemn agreement, and she swallowed hard. This time, when she faced her foe, she would not expose her throat to the knife and wish for death. This time, she had a purpose. *"I don't know what will happen to me, but I swear to you: I will do everything I can to remove the Ly Kai threat from this world forever."* Her heart ached. She would miss them all so much. *"I will not fail you."*

"We know." Uri was undoing one of his braids, pulling the beads out of it. *"Come here."*

He positioned her facing him, his fingers gently lifting the hair along the left side of her temple.

"I—?"

He caught her chin and tilted it down. *"It's time for you to display the warrior that you are to this world."*

Her mind flashed to the night after they had left Windmer, when she had watched him work with the other warriors, inserting beads, feathers, and twisting braids into their hair, making them look fierce and bold. They had taken some of that essence internally, giving them more intensity and purpose afterwards.

This was a good thing. The right thing.

Velacy hissed a warning before leaves rattled on the bank above them. There was a swift sense of mental exchange, and a dark form plummeted down, followed by a second.

"Here," Seuliac quietly laid several stout poles on the ground. *"Caspani, let's have that cord so we can attach our spare knives to make spears. Quickly, everyone."*

Kaphri only had one knife. She would not sacrifice it for a spear.

Seuliac nudged one of the poles toward her with a boot. *"It will still make a good weapon, even with the blunt point."*

"We're at the Lone Sentinel's Watch, as we suspected," Tobin told them as they hurriedly snatched up cords and set about notching staffs to affix blades to poles. *"You wouldn't believe the view out over the northern lands from the plateau's edge. But there's also something up here that's not from our world. A walled structure. Its edge sits so close to the cliff on the west and north that they don't even have to post a guard on those walls, but we did spot a few Balandra sparsely scattered along the south and east."*

So, they were actually on the plateau that had caught her attention when she viewed Tobin's mental map after falling through the barrier. Araxis had chosen a place where the Geffitzi's respect for their Goddess' solitude made them blind to his invasion.

Tobin's images flashed in their minds, and Kaphri drew a sharp breath. A smooth, high wall glowed like a broad line in the moonlight. Across its softly illuminated surface, shadowed shapes writhed and twisted, creating intricate patterns that glided along its length. It looked like a piece of elaborate, seething sculpture set on the blackness of the plain.

"Strange, hunh?" Tobin sounded intrigued.

Velacy blew a hard sigh but stayed silent.

"What are those things moving across it?" Uri asked.

Kaphri studied the drifting forms. *"Starsigns. Some... Others, art, I think."*

"Well, they are immense. The size of that thing is deceptive from a distance. And the weird thing is, bright as it looks, you can barely see your hand in its light when you stand beside it."

"You went that close to it?" Uri asked.

The scout shrugged. *"They couldn't see me. The moon's not up yet here."* He gave her a sudden sharp look, his eyes flicking to her hair.

He nodded approval, and she felt a squeeze of happiness. Although she couldn't see what Uri had done, what it represented made her feel stronger and more confident. She was a part of the battle for this world.

"She is not Geffitzi," Velacy protested.

"She is a warrior who will stand beside you in battle," Tobin told him. *"Give her respect."*

The younger Aedec warrior gave a surly grunt.

"How far away is that thing?"

"A quarter-hour at a good pace. The illumination makes perceived distance deceptive. The thing is big. And the odd thing," the young warrior looked over at her again, *"It just sits on the grass like the*

bastard dropped it there today. We only located one opening. A huge, arched way with no gate and no road leading in or out. Any ideas?"

"The first time I ever saw this place was when I jumped here in the daylight. The wall looked the same as I would expect to see encircling buildings on this world. When the Balandra rose up off it, I ran into the woods and returned to our camp."

"Are any weapons stored inside that place?" Tobin sounded hopeful.

"The Ly Kai in Kryie Karth were very averse to physical aggression."

Tobin gave a derisive snort.

"Yes, I know what they did when they fled north, and I am sorry." There was no value in arguing that the Ly Kai had been fighting the Geffitzi for their lives. *"But I never encountered a memory of violence except against Araxis, and that was a mental attack."* The night the others revealed her true Birthstar, pushing and shouting were on wide display, but neither time involved the kind of physical weapons Tobin wanted.

"We are not facing those Ly Kai," Uri reminded them as he gave his spear a short, one-handed slice to his right. *"Something else is forcing this situation. Something with very strong aggression and ill intent."* He looked at Seuliac. *"How do you suggest we do this?"*

"Fog is rolling down from the western heights. We can use it for cover on our approach to the wall. Once there, things will be up to her."

Fog? Kaphri's mouth went dry. The Wyxa? She looked up to meet Uri's intense stare.

"Is it...?"

"I don't know." It was a bad time to realize she had never actually tried to sense the physical or mental presence of the Wyxa at work.

The warlord shrugged. *"Maybe it's natural. Maybe it's a timely event. But it's dense and it's moving fast, so we go now if we plan to use it to our benefit."*

Tobin suddenly frowned. *"A group of Cyrwins has arrived at the eastern edge of the plateau. They are beginning to search the woods."*

So quickly! *"How did they get here so fast?"* Her fingers found the tiny crystal beneath her shirt.

"Our destination has never been a secret, but these Cyrwins are not members of our troop. They do, however, share the same murderous intent."

Strange to think of any of those murderous beasts as "ours."

"You're still connected to them?" Uri asked, surprised.

"It appears so."

Velacy gave Tobin a sidelong look.

"Hey. They tried to kill me, too," the scout snapped at the younger Aedec.

"Have you determined any reason for the Grimmen's sudden change toward us?" Uri's question pulled his attention back.

"No. But it's really angry. It intends to stop our approach to the gate. I can lure the Cyrwins away from the rest of you..."

"No." Uri shook his head. *"We need you with us. This is a dangerous tactic, but I need you to continue monitoring your connection with it, in case it has another change of heart. How close are the Cyrwins?"*

"We can finish our plans as we move." Seuliac gathered up his spear and gestured for them to start moving.

"When we get inside, Seuliac and Tobin can peel off to locate Frax and get him out," Uri said as he got to his feet. *"Velacy and I will stay with Willow."*

"It won't work! We should—"

"No, Velacy!" Kaphri cut him short.

The younger Aedec gave her a glare.

"Sounds easy to me." Seuliac shrugged. *"Inadequately armed, blindly walking into a place teeming with Balandra. What could go wrong?"*

"Our people have done it before and triumphed," Tobin told him.

"Indeed, we have." Seuliac smiled in cold anticipation.

They were picking over events in their people's past. She knew it was a long, highly convoluted path to go down. Had earlier triumphs been with so few warriors?

"We will have new stories to tell," Uri said. He caught Kaphri's arm and drew her forward as he picked up his pace to follow Seuliac between the trees.

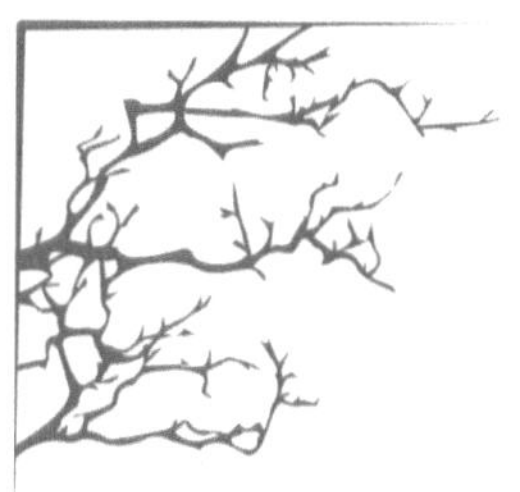

Chapter 97
It Begins

SILENT BILLOWS ROLLED down the ridge to the west, engulfing the forest and roiling in a slow advance over the grassy plain. On the heights the intruding mist glowed, but Pona had not yet risen high enough to illuminate the plain where they stood.

"Kep! The magnitude of this intrusion never occurred to me before!" Uri stared at the distant wall of light.

It had never occurred to Kaphri, either. She rummaged through her memory for the images gleaned from the Ly Kai men's minds over her years in Kryie Karth, comparing them to this place. Ly Kai cities were built up around a walled section at their centers which housed the most ancient and sacred of their structures, the Temples of the Hierarchal Stars. Most of the living areas would have sprawled far beyond those confines in nature parks and homes. None of their memories, striking as they were, looked as beautiful as this, with its translucent, pale walls capped with elaborate carvings.

They were similar enough.

This was a temple. A major one.

Her forays into the unguarded thoughts of the Ly Kai survivors had revealed images of all the Hierarchal Temples except one.

"Araxis didn't build this." She'd been in too much distress to notice the first time—if she had even looked at all. A shiver of awe ran over her. *"This is not a Ly Kai city. This is the temple complex of Arylla."*

"How is that possible?" Uri's question was as strained by disbelief as her own realization. *"Why is it here on our world?"*

"I don't know."

"You can't compete with the power that moved that!" Velacy put her doubts into form. *"This is folly."*

What had the Ly Kai, including her parents, thought when they emerged on this world? Had the presence of Arylla's temple on the plateau been one of the several shocks they experienced that fateful day, as thousands of hope-filled Ly Kai citizens gathered here? Had they known what they were doing—stealing a world—when they stepped off the gate?

A sad, bitter thought ran across her mind: had her parents arrived with the hope of securing a glamorous life of adventure for their two-year-old daughter? The memory of her father, Ebel's cold remoteness toward her in the tower of Kryie Karth squeezed her stomach. Had he blamed her for everything he'd lost?

Uri gave her a mental nudge. *"Here is not the spot to stop and consider your place in this world."*

True. But speculation on the massive effort required to summon this structure into creation here, whether it was built or transported, held her frozen.

Araxis had also used that power to create a barrier to divide this world, doubt whispered in her mind. How could she defeat someone with such immense ability? She knew nothing—nothing!—about how to use power in comparison to him.

"So, this thing is here. How does it change anything in this moment?" Seuliac's question sliced her self-doubt.

It didn't.

The warlord started forward along the edge of the cold mist. *"We have to stay ahead of this mess. Link up so we don't get separated and pick up the pace. Once Pona tops the ridge we'll lose the cover of the shadows."*

Jogging forward, Kaphri kept her eyes carefully riveted on the light ahead while fog swirled in more heavily.

"Every bit of knowledge about Arylla might be stored inside that place," she said.

"Here, out of their reach?" Tobin asked. *"How is that bad? If the bastards can't get to it, they can't do more damage."*

"People don't easily give up powerful things like that, Tobin," Uri warned.

Especially not people like Araxis.

"It doesn't matter whether they want to give it up. It's here. The fight is already over," Velacy declared.

"No," Seuliac said. *"As Caspani says, no one gives up that kind of power without a fight. My question is, do they expect you to return a massive building back to their world? I haven't seen you do anything to make me believe you're capable of that. It took you days to figure out how to shatter a clump of dirt."*

The statement was bitterly amusing and true. His question, however, raised a more dangerous possibility. Was the place anchored solely to this world, or did it exist simultaneously on the Homeworld? Were Ly Kai inside the place? Even some of the lesser starborn would be far more skilled than she was.

If there were any Arylla-born...

But the Grimmen claimed it had bargained for the removal of the barrier in exchange for her return to the Homeworld. If the Ly Kai had skilled Arylla-born, why would they want her?

"There is another possibility," Uri said grimly.

"You mean tricking her into opening the gate so they can come here? No. The Grimmen will not allow it," Tobin said.

"It couldn't stop the first event, which put the thing here. Our best solution might be if she can destroy the damnable obscenity. Maybe that would ensure they never grow a new crop of power-hungry despots."

"The Cyrwins have paused at the eastern edge of the plateau," Tobin announced.

It was impossible to see anything in the distance across the plain.

"Are they aware of our location?" Uri asked.

"You mean, do they intend to kill us," Seuliac corrected.

"They're hostile. But the Grimmen seems suddenly conflicted about their next action."

"We're not waiting to find out what it decides. Run," Uri ordered. *"Run!"*

"T*he Cyrwins are moving."* At least a dozen large bodies were approaching at a run, angling to cut them off from the gate.

Why? Kaphri's mind screamed. What had changed about the situation to make the Grimmen want to kill them?

A breath later, Tobin announced that a second group of Cyrwins had emerged from the woods to the south, at a greater distance from them, and was running hard, minds blazing with the intent to trample them.

"The first ones are gaining ground," he said. "*Should we defend*?"

They were all breathing heavily. Even she knew their makeshift weapons had no chance against the huge creatures. She had to do something to stop them, or she and the warriors would never reach the gate.

Seuliac would approve of killing their attackers in defense. Tobin and Uri, less so. But what could she do? A wall of fire would make a quick barrier, but the grass and weeds on the plain were too green and wet with early dew; she did not have the skill to compensate for anything beyond the materials at hand. Other actions that had once seemed outrageous when the warlord put them into her head now rushed through her mind. If she tore up clumps of grass, creating pits in the ground, the risk of breaking a leg would slow the Cyrwins down.

She stopped running.

They would lose their precious element of surprise—if they still had it—but they might live to reach the gate.

The warriors skidded to a halt, mental questions, then curses, flaring as she spun about to face the Cyrwins.

Kaphri gathered starpower. Don't pull mindlessly, she warned herself. She must think. Calculate. If Arylla had the power to move a massive Ly Kai temple, it could, if uncontrolled, destroy even more.

She carefully shaped the force in a wide front and rammed it at the nearest attackers.

The invisible wave of power struck the three lead Cyrwins, pitching them sideways and slamming them into the animals behind them, while the runners in the rear crashed forward. Squeals of rage and frustration wafted across the field to Kaphri and the warriors. Two of the Cyrwins, the ones on the opposite edges of the group, managed to avoid the floundering mass. They recovered with a shake of their heads and continued their charge, with others recovering to stumble after them.

She sent a blast of hot air rushing toward them. The mists on the plateau between the Cyrwins and her companions vanished, and the creatures swerved, forced to cut around the edge of the cleared patch of heat to continue forward.

Tobin crowed with exhilaration.

"*Enough!*" Uri sounded horrified and furious. "*We can't stop moving.*" The edge of the fog was folding around their feet.

But they would never reach the gate if she did not stop the Grimmen force's advance.

Kaphri drew power and formed it into a massive blade of invisible energy, which she drove out into the ground of the plateau ahead of the creatures. She raked it from west to east across the space between them, erupting grass, roots, dirt, and stones into the air.

"Holy Kep!" one of the warriors exclaimed in awe.

Dirt particles hazed the air, but all the larger material thudded back to the earth. It was not enough.

The Cyrwins had slowed with the eruption of debris, but now they continued forward again, regaining speed.

"*You need wind,*" Seuliac told her. "*More debris and wind to throw it around.*"

He was right. But trying to exert power over the thin element of air was too demanding at this moment. She needed a more substantial element. She sliced the blade of power again, throwing up sheared grass, dirt, and stones, then followed it with a controlled gust of power to catch the debris and spray it up in a thick wall.

"*They'll come through,*" Tobin said.

Then she needed to do something to discourage them. She drove Arylla's power into the broken earth, lifting the displaced soil and stones into the air and sent the larger pieces randomly zinging about, making a churning barrier between them and the creatures. The Cyrwins would go around the edges, but it would give her and the warriors enough time to get to their destination.

Tobin caught her as she crumpled and swept her forward at a run.

"That's how you use power." Seuliac's sending was hard with approval. *"Well done."*

An Arylla-born flinging dirt and stones at her opponents? Hredroth! What had she become?

She drew power from Arylla in a small sip to give her strength, pulled away from Tobin, and stumbled on as the mist rolled at their heels.

A sudden downdraft of air pressure and the dry rustle of folding wings announced the arrival of three Balandra. A clawed hand dragged Frax roughly to his feet while a second gray man stood guard, spear ready, and the third freed his wrist from their cuffs.

Frax remained silent as they briskly shoved him out the garden gate and down a long, paved avenue toward an elaborate doorway that led inside an immense, palely glowing white structure.

"Ah, Geffitz." His brain burned back to life as the hated voice chuckled in his head. *"The time has arrived to determine the fate of your world."*

The tarmeuth emerged from the doorway. The Balandra took panicked flight as the cat sprang for him, its broad paw striking him low along his left ribs and back. The hard pads knocked the air out of him and sent him tumbling. Before he could catch his breath, the cat crouched over him, pinning him with its weight. Its face hovered above his. *"Just in case you had other ideas, your role is to remain silent and survive. Test me and I will butcher you where you kneel. Now come. It is time for me to reclaim what is owed me."* It lifted away, ignoring the blood that streamed from his ribs as it turned and continued forward.

The Balandra dropped back to the ground but kept their distance, leaving him to walk behind the animal as they passed through the door and deeper along the hallway.

A darkening in the eerily glowing wall. An arch.

Kaphri sensed out ahead and behind them as they dove inside the huge opening.

Boots ground rawly on smooth stone, and heavy breathing whispered off the strangely illuminated, seamless walls. Light from outside did not extend into the space, making them moving silhouettes on the pale surfaces.

The shift left her momentarily stunned. Perhaps it was different for the warriors, but for Kaphri, the step from the plateau of the Geffitzi world to the interior of the Ly Kai structure was an abrupt transition from panic and chaos into eerie calm. Still, she avoided physical contact with the wall.

"No inner gates," Uri observed tersely as he continued inward along a wide passage perhaps ten steps deep.

"They have other security measures," Seuliac growled as he followed.

The warlord was right; starborn did not have access to places above the level of their Birthstar unless explicitly permitted. Was an Arylla-born who had not walked the Paths of Power allowed to enter this place?

"Pursuit has paused." Tobin hovered at the outer opening.

A swift sensing back in that direction let Kaphri feel the fury radiating from the clump of bodies milling where the two Cyrwin groups had joined up along the thickening edge of fog outside.

On the opposite end of the passage, Seuliac peered past the moonlit edge of the inner opening. *"This is a bad time to ask, but can Geffitzi enter this place?"*

"Good question," Uri responded grimly. *"The fog does not appear to have access. Here's another one: Tobin, can the Cyrwins enter this place?"*

"They aren't responding to me right now."

Did anything of this world, even a bird, dare to intrude on the starpower radiating beyond the arched entrance?

"I've seen Balandra on the wall in the daylight." She should have asked more questions of Chaos-stepper, Kaphri thought.

"There could be traps..."

Velacy's warning went ignored as Seuliac waved the point of his spear inside the space, testing for reaction. *"I don't see any sign of life. Priestess?"*

The massive, moonlit plaza before them was free of fog. And life. *"I don't find anything—but remember, I cannot sense Balandra."*

"Is Kitahn here?"

"Yes." She'd sensed his presence the moment they emerged from the jump, and his general direction even before that.

"Anything else?" Ahead of her, Uri was a black shape against the white plaza beyond him.

Arylla's power emanated quietly from a massive, elegantly ornate structure across the space. Was Araxis inside there, waiting, burning with furious hunger and desire to recover Arylla's lost power?

She did not want it. She never had. But she needed it.

How was she supposed to do this? She had no idea what he really wanted: the gate to the Homeworld opened, like the Grimmen claimed? Or to steal her form and restore his power? She and Seuliac had discussed dozens of possible scenarios in the days since the Balandra had taken Frax, even asking the others for their ideas. Most of the speculation had seemed ridiculously unlikely, but the warlord had pointed out that at least those would not catch her by surprise. The fact that they couldn't cover every possibility haunted them both.

She didn't know what would happen, but she did know she must not fail. She would remove Araxis from this world. If it included her death, it was the necessary cost.

We do what we must do.

"I'll focus on Araxis' demands." Despair tried to force a knot in her throat. *"You rescue Frax."*

"Seuliac and I will step out there first, then Willow. Tobin, you and Velacy follow," Uri ordered. *"If anything happens, Tobin will get her back out and up along the wall to the west. The Swamp dwellers are our most likely allies if this fails."*

As much as Tobin hated the Wyxa, he did not argue.

"No more delay then." Uri and Seuliac stepped out, the cresting moonlight glazing them, and Kaphri followed.

Chapter 98
The Darkness Will Rise Again

THE SENSATION OF SPECIFIC power, as if anything other than Arylla was forbidden in this place, hung in the air, yet Kaphri sensed something lurking in the background. Something immensely powerful but barred to her access. It made her hesitate in confusion. What could be greater than the Ly Kai Hierarch of Stars and Arylla?

The power of the Goddess Kep?

No. Though it might cling along the outer edges, it did not enter this place.

"*The beings of this world have no power here,*" she told the warriors as they stepped forward. "*This is a place of the stars.*"

"*Arrows and blades still kill,*" Tobin said behind her.

"*Do you sense where Kitahn is?*"

"*Only inside the place.*" She could not discern his physical status but knew he was alive.

Uri glanced upward. "*It's good the fog does not intrude over the wall.*" Framed in its eerie glow, the sky above them glittered with stars.

"*You should not have come here!*" Velacy hissed behind her. "*We should leave now! We should go where she would serve us best.*"

The warlord spun to glare at the younger Aedec. "*Then stay here. Your choice, the same as everyone else. But it's time to get things moving.*"

"No." Velacy surged forward to catch Kaphri's arm. He jerked her against him and stumbled back a step toward the outer opening. *"This is as far as we go."*

Outrage shot through Kaphri when she felt the familiar cold burn of a geffitzi knife blade against her neck.

"You!" Velacy snarled at Tobin. *"Get over with them!"*

Tobin snorted in disdain. He took a step back, away from the older warriors.

Velacy twisted to keep her between himself and the others. *"I tried to do this the easy way. I tried to reason with you, but you wouldn't listen. Now we do it my way."*

His way? Her mind twisted frantically, searching for a solution. Could she use her power to freeze him into immobility or stun him with a wave of pain?

Uri took a step towards her.

"No!" Seuliac caught his arm. *"This is no longer Velacy, is it, Evil One?"* Kaphri's knees almost folded with the warlord's calm sending. *"We lost him days ago, on the hillside where he killed the Ly Kai."*

"You should have killed this form then if you knew," the being inside the younger Aedec warrior hissed at the warlord.

"And lose track of where you were?" Seuliac smiled coldly. *"You underestimate us. You have attempted to take control of a Geffitz warrior."*

"This insect?" Disdain sizzled. *"I know about your scorn for him and your Holderlord's order to execute him—how you attempted to secure his cooperation with a pitiful offer of exile. You stupidly fail to appreciate his devious nature. When this is over, I may free him to wreak the chaos he so much desires to exert on your precious Rhynog. In the meantime, I have what I need and the rest of you can rot in misery and decay!"* He shuffled toward the opening, dragging Kaphri with him.

Despite his bold words, Seuliac hovered on the verge of panic. He sorted through his rushing thoughts, seeking a reasoned response to the situation. One thing for sure—the one thing he counted on—was, despite his shortcomings, Velacy was as proud a Geffitz as any who ever existed. Seuliac had no idea how deeply Araxis had buried the Rhynogian heir's essence inside him, but Velacy would be fighting possession. And the girl's attachment to Kitahn ensured she would not simply jump out of this place to escape this threat. Her reluctance would give them a few valuable seconds to react to this disastrous twist. He only hoped the younger Aedec still had the ability to recognize what he must do if his words could reach him.

"You're not so clever, Geffitz, or I wouldn't have her." Araxis continued to drag Kaphri with him toward the mouth of the opening.

"You have her. Careful you don't hurt her. You need her," Seuliac warned. If the idiot stepped outside the gate onto the plateau, the Cyrwins or Balandra might kill them both.

"Of course I need her. I engineered her birth just in case I might require her." Wariness crept into the sending, as if the being who possessed Velacy realized that if the warlord moved to kill Kaphri, the dynamics of power would shift drastically. He continued to shuffle back, taking her out of range of direct attack. *"If you stupid creatures had listened to me, all this would be unnecessary. I tried to persuade you to return to the barrier so I could seize her when she tried to remove it. But, no, you wouldn't listen! You had to desecrate this place with your stinking savage presence. So now you can die here and those filthy Balandran traitors can suck the marrow from your bones."*

Tobin Kitahn had been off to the right and half a step behind Velacy when Araxis made his move. Now, the warrior was inching toward the hapless Aedec warrior.

Seuliac kept his eyes locked on Velacy. *"Take us out of here with you,"* he urged.

"We won't fight you. Remove your barrier from our world and you can have her," Uri added, speaking aloud. Velacy would understand what he said, but the force that possessed the Aedec heir might have to think in order to convert the spoken words.

"Your world? After what I have endured here? It's mine!"

"This will never be your world." Seuliac straightened, crossing his arms with an exaggerated movement.

Angry gray eyes flicked between the warlord and Uri. *"I don't have time for this. Make the jump!"* Araxis gave Kaphri a hard squeeze, driving a gasp from her. *"Now!"*

"Look at me, girl," Seuliac commanded. He locked eyes with hers. *"Don't do it! He won't kill you. He can't."*

He had never seen the Priestess display any physical emotion, even in the horrifying confrontation with the Cyrwins at the bottom of the escarpment. Reliably, her delicate features remained placid now, despite the firestorm he knew must be raging inside her. In contrast, Araxis seemed to convey all his emotions through Velacy as he flinched and twisted to keep her between him and the warriors.

She had told them the Ly Kai demanded deep control of their emotional reactions. So, why was this creature's behavior so volatile? Was he trying to misdirect them? Or was he so damned arrogant he didn't care? After all, the girl said he had been the charismatic one, the one who won everything he wanted, while his brother hung back as a dark and brooding shadow in the background.

Araxis had never had an equal. He would face one here, even if it took all their combined effort. The demon had dared to manipulate a Geffitz warrior. Death—whether he was insane or arrogant—was too good for the miserable creature.

How much of Velacy survived?

The warlord carefully kept his attention away from Tobin. *"So. Araxis."* He let cold humor seep into his sending. *"Stealing the body of a highborn Aedec is a crime of the highest order on this world, akin to murder—though at least you aspire to quality."* He tilted his head and gave a mocking smile as the scout crept into position behind Velacy.

A dark form plummeted to the ground, shoving Tobin violently aside.

Before any of them could react, Razek rammed an ugly, thin blade into the base of Velacy's skull.

Velacy went rigid, his eyes widening.

Razek slapped the inside of the warrior's forearm down, knocking the hand away from Kaphri's neck and sending the blade spinning to clatter on the surface.

As the younger Aedec sagged, the gray man jerked his blade out and let the body fall.

"Wretched scum." The Balandran spat on the body. His thin gray lips twisted with a smile of satisfaction, and his red eyes swept the rest of them. "That was long overdue," he continued in rough Geffitzi. "The interruption is ended. My master demands your full attention."

"Dammit," Tobin roared as he surged to his feet. "I was going to do that!"

Chapter 99
To Spread On Swift, Dark Wings of Night

"IS HE DEAD?" SEULIAC stared dispassionately at the body lying between them.

"What do you think?" Tobin snapped.

The warlord swept him with an impatient glare. "Not Velacy. The Evil One. Did Velacy bind the Evil One and take him into death?"

Kaphri scrambled away from the fallen body. *"I felt his death."* Her sending was numb with shock and wonder. *"Araxis is... gone..."*

"Of course he is," an unknown source snapped peevishly in their heads. *"Razek would not fail in his long-anticipated vengeance."* Harsh mental laughter crackled. *"Well done, rabble! You have succeeded in helping rid the universe of a pitiable, incompetent, but dangerous force. I did not anticipate any of you being so cognizant as to see the obvious solution."*

"Another Aedec warrior you owe us vengeance for," Seuliac said.

The voice took on a mocking tone. *"Another in a long line. Perhaps the girl will convince me to spare the rest of you by doing what I require."*

"Who is this being?" The warlord twisted to look at Kaphri.

"I don't know," she stammered. What she sensed...

But— That...was...impossible.

A hand slid under her elbow. Uri, stepping in to give support. In the same instant, Seuliac gave her a mental sting of impatience: this was no time to display weakness.

She wrested her thoughts into focus. *"Who are you, and what do you want?"*

"An Arylla-born with a legacy beyond your imagining," came the reply. *"I want what is owed me. You will make it happen."*

Hredroth! Who? *"But— How...?"*

"Razek will bring you to me."

The Balandran dipped its head in acknowledgement when she looked over at it. "Greetings, Great One."

The words struck her like a slap. In Kryie Karth Rath had gone to great lengths to address her by the title of a Ly Kai Council Leader. Unbeknownst to her at the time, Araxis had controlled Rath. But this...

"Are you Alexar?"

"Must the creator only be known through his creations?" Mock despair burned in her mind.

Before she recovered enough to ask another question, the Balandran looked at her with shrewd red eyes. "I am Razek, commander of my lord's forces. I will take you to him now."

Kaphri stiffened at the sight of the narrow ridge of scar tissue that sliced down the Balandran's left cheek and pulled the left corner of its mouth into a permanent sneer. In the Black Tower, this one had sliced her arm and painted her starsign in reverse on her forehead with her blood to seal her starpower inside of her.

In the Maugrock, he had commanded hundreds of the winged men. How many of those beings were in this place?

"Priestess?" Uri asked uneasily.

"We have come for the Geffitz warrior you took," she told Razek in Ly Kai. She kept the warriors inside her mental loop, as they had done so many times during their journey.

"In time. Now, this rabble is dismissed."

The warriors? Panic fluttered at the edge of her thoughts. Kaphri did not have to mentally touch the black arrow tips scattered along the wall to know they were trained on her companions. They would come under attack as soon as she stepped away, and she could not afford to be distracted by trying to defend them.

She truly wanted to send the warriors out of danger. Removing Velacy's body was a sound reason, but, as Tobin had once said, she did not command Geffitzi warriors. Even though her mind screamed agonized protest, she had no right to choose between their survival and their actions.

We do what we must do.

Masking her emotions, she sent the warriors a false mental shrug. *"Balandran weapons are trained on us. Stay or come with me with no fault placed upon you for what your heart tells you to do."*

The warriors stared back at her in stony silence.

"They come with me," she told Razek.

He flicked a dismissive glance at Velacy's body and shrugged. "Then they will join this one on the garbage heap." He lifted an arm above his head as if to signal his forces.

"You will not touch him!" Kaphri ordered.

The Balandran looked at her sharply.

"The warriors will carry him away when they leave," she said.

"This will be their only opportunity to walk away." Razek smiled mockingly at her.

Was facing what gathered outside the wall any less threatening than what waited inside? "We shall see. I am here. Take us to the Geffitz warrior and your master."

"Geffitz trash," the Balandran said disdainfully. He waved his arm in a brusque gesture, then turned and walked across the broad plaza.

"It doesn't consider us a threat," Tobin fumed.

"Which is something to consider carefully," Seuliac cautioned. *"We must stay alive if we want to correct his error."*

Araxis was dead. The threat that had driven her across half a world was...gone.

The realization left her numb. Only a flicker of the mental pain Ly Kai suffered with death's severing of their telepathic links touched her, meaning his mental contact with her had been minimal.

A relief.

But the physical reality of the massive wall and courtyard surrounding them had not flickered with the slightest loss of starpower at his death. This place was not created or influenced by Araxis.

She faced a new and greater threat of which she knew nothing.

Gather information: it was a thread of reason to focus on. A way to get her mind working and to aid her companions.

Kaphri shivered in the cold night air. Araxis was dead. And he had taken another Geffitz warrior with him. Some of her anger filtered back in. Velacy had been annoying. Arrogant and obnoxious. Dangerous, even. But he was their companion. Theirs!

The warriors' loss went far deeper than hers. And their anger. They had a right—and a need—to know everything possible in order to determine their next actions.

"How did you know Araxis possessed the warrior?" she asked the Balandran, Razek. She continued to share a link with the warriors.

He stopped and turned to her. "My master knew. The aspiring fool has been his tool since his birth."

"Your master—"

"His name is Bithzielp."

She and the warriors froze in their steps. "No!" Horrified denials erupted around her.

But—this mysterious being claimed it was Arylla-born—! Everything inside her shrieked in horrified dismay. Beyond her mind, she felt the churn of the warriors' stunned reactions. Did it extend even further? Did the Wyxa and Grimmen...?

She had believed the carnage started here, with the deaths of Ly Kai women and children, and extended north with battles between the Ly Kai and Geffitzi as the refugees fled to Kryie Karth. Many more graves, created from illness and starvation, lay around the tower and on the mountainside beyond the barrier.

Those numbers were nothing in the Geffitzi accounting of Bithzielp's reign over this world.

Kaphri fought an urge to grasp the crystal as cold realization settled over her. Everyone on this world had as much at stake in the outcome of this encounter as she did.

This was no place for personal reaction, Seuliac's training asserted in her head. It was a time for listening. Evaluating. Sharing information. Were the beings outside the wall listening? The Grimmen was. It had placed a link inside this place with Tobin's presence. And the Wyxa? Did they have their link through the crystal? Through Gemma?

She must focus on what was happening around her now or anything else would fail to matter. "This being, Bithzielp..."

Massive disdain for her anticipated question twisted gray, wrinkled features.

"He is Ly Kai?" Stories of the devastation, the torment this world and its people had endured, flooded her mind. She fought to keep the tremor out of her voice. "How?"

"It is not within my authority to explain." Razek turned and resumed the walk across the silent plaza toward the temple. "Now, follow me."

"One down and more to go," Tobin muttered furiously.

"Enemy count on wall?" Seuliac hand-signed, redirecting the fiery scout's attention to their current situation when the Balandran turned away. It was safer to assume the new intrusive force monitored their telepathy, and hand signs were a common means of communication among warriors in the field—though it had taken a bit of effort over the last weeks to coordinate the differences between their clans.

"Not see," Tobin replied in kind.

"Stay plan," the warlord ordered.

They had run through multiple strategies during their hours in the woods, but this horrendous opponent had not been a consideration. Araxis had acted in desperation and lost, they could not afford to make the same mistake.

A Ly Kai enemy, terrible as it might be, was the Priestess' problem. Their adversaries remained the same: Balandra. From this moment forward, everyone had a role to focus on, with Velacy's loss leaving Uri to act alone. Allowing a distraction might doom someone else.

And, if anyone else was listening, Tobin's statement was as clear a declaration of war as they could make.

The warlord smiled.

The temple of Arylla was as pristine white as the star's power would project if she traced its symbol in the air.

A shiver ran over her. When she lived in Kryie Karth and believed Freya was her Birthstar, she prayed and traced its sign in pale blue light every day. But she had only manipulated Arylla's power a few times under duress, the largest effort when Araxis forced her to break the barrier and allow the Balandra to invade the south, and moments ago, when she had wielded power on the plain in front of this place. Anything else had been a child's experiment in comparison.

One thing she knew: Arylla did not belong here.

Her footsteps, grinding in the accumulated grit of this world, became a steady drum of horror in her head. Bithzielp. Bithzielp. Bithzielp. She had traded the vaguely familiar threat of Araxis for a terrible unknown. She knew nothing of this ancient being. She knew nothing—

Stop. Her brain ordered her to sanity. She was panicking. Painting an overwhelming threat onto this being.

Her eyes went to the night sky, tracing out now-familiar Geffitzi constellations. A few Ly Kai stars were scattered wide and far beyond what would be their locations in the Homeworld sky. Burning brighter than all the others was the Geffitzi Even' Star, her Birthstar, Arylla, as it held fierce reign above this place.

Tonight, she must be Arylla-born.

Her right forefinger twitched. A sudden desire to trace her starsign fluttered. Not yet, her mind whispered. She had already given away some advantage outside this place, drawing power to defend them.

She returned her attention to the temple before her. Were other temples on the Homeworld built with materials matching their star's drawn power? She had never noticed a distinction of color in the memories purloined from the old men, but then, how could she have known to look? They would have been furious if she'd asked, and this was her first direct experience with a Ly Kai structure. She had no desire to pull up those images right now.

Delicate minarets, fragile in their height, gleamed against a black sky filled with stars on the northern side of the plaza. It appeared as if the entire structure had been shaped from a single block of material, with massive columns seamlessly supporting an elaborately carved cornice.

Kaphri drew a sharp breath at the sight of the triangle shape dominating the crest of the frieze. Framed inside white stone borders, the stars of the Ly Kai Hierarch actually glittered against the background. Arylla blazed at the crest, with Freya and the other stars descending in their perfect order.

It definitely was not the pattern of stars she saw in the sky over this world.

She must not let this place become a distraction; her mind created her own version of Seuliac's rebuke, even when he did not send it. A bitter prick of protest fought back: this was her history, of which she had been deprived.

A trivial point which did not matter. Not here. Not now.

She tore her attention away before an overwhelming urge to mentally reach out and touch the twinkling lights of the frieze overcame her.

Still, there were so many otherworldly wonders to see. In this brief moment, before her life might be snatched away, she wanted to fill her mind with everything around her.

Immense carvings of Ly Kai people, their identities unknown to her, stood in niches along the base of the portico. She was sure she should recognize the figures as part of Arylla's history, but the dull books on Ly Kai law that Hyfas had forced her to pore over had not given her the correct education.

A flash of frustration dissolved with swift reason; nothing could change the past—hers or these warriors.

Or their worlds'.

She suddenly noticed that while the plaza they were crossing looked level from their far position at the outer gate, they were approaching a point where a section of the stone sloped downward. The base of the temple sat even with the surface, but a massive gash lay beneath it, as if the temple had settled, pressing its lower levels down through the plateau, gouging into this world's skin. A portion of the white plain sloped flawlessly to crush the earth beneath, leading to a yawning horizontal slot that ran the length of the temple portico above. The way down remained perfectly smooth despite the distortion, and the walls of the opening looked as clean and as beautifully ornate as the structure.

Cautiously, she sensed out, searching for any trace of starpower that might seep from it.

The way lay quiet.

But there was something more. Frax was here.

How to convey it to the warriors? Anything she said might put him and his rescuers in further jeopardy.

"Stop," she ordered. "Not another step until you tell us where you're taking us."

"To the gate," Razek explained in a reasonable tone. He gestured down the incline. "My master awaits you there."

"I want to see the warrior."

"Certainly. When we get there. I'm sure he'll be equally pleased to see you."

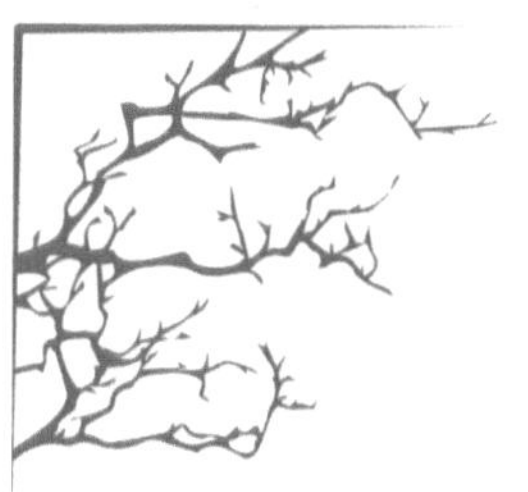

Chapter 100
Then...

THE SCALE OF THIS PLACE was immense. Illusion? Seuliac would not rule it out. Whatever the reality, it did not belong on his world.

The walk down the incline drew out to several chilled minutes before they paused in front of the massive horizontal slot. Six times wider than it was high, the opening was taller than three Geffitz warriors standing shoulder on shoulder. It stretched almost half the whole width of the white temple that towered above them.

Indifferent to their presence, silent, cold air flowed out over them as they followed the Balandran inside. The smooth white slope leveled into a vast, empty room. Light from an undetectable source illuminated it, revealing smooth walls and a ceiling decorated with delicate vaults, arches, and carvings. The Balandran led them across to a smaller, but still broad opening where the floor continued its long, gentle downward incline. A lower ceiling paralleled the floor as they moved deeper.

Minor side passages occasionally broke the smooth walls, but they remained dark and void of movement.

Footprints leading in or out of the place muddled the layer of dust covering the slope. Most were Balandran, long, skinny, with dotted impressions of their vicious claws at the tips. A few tracks led into the side passages. Their edges were sharp, marking their freshness. Interesting, since the winged men mostly flew. Over along the wall to Seuliac's right, however, the dust looked more heavily disturbed. He drifted as far over as he dared go without drawing Razek's attention.

Dismay slid through him. Another creature had passed there. Though more recent Balandran scuffs made it difficult to clearly distinguish the tracks, the rounded impressions reminded him of paw prints. A large animal had entered this place.

Stalking the gray ones? Had it found another way out, or had the gray men killed it?

Impressive, if they had.

He looked over at Tobin. Signed. The scout scanned the narrower surface on his side of the passage and signed back. Nothing odd over there.

The warlord returned to his position.

Two openings later, well above where a brighter light indicated the corridor's end, a cluster of Balandran footprints churned the dust in front of a lefthand passage. He and Tobin silently slipped inside it.

Uri and Kaphri stopped beneath the edge of the sloped ceiling at the bottom of the ramp.

A huge, circular arena lay before them, its smooth walls broken with regularly spaced, wide openings. Above it rose levels of balconies, extending up to a circle of night sky. Like the building outside, the details of the temple surfaces were beautifully worked.

Kep's Daughter, Pona, had cleared the southern rim above them, while the Even' Star, Arylla, blazed off to the western side.

Here on this world, her star would never perfectly dominate the center of that opening the way it would on the Homeworld.

"This is an insult embedded in the flesh of our world," Uri growled as he looked around. It was on him to hold their enemies' focus with his comments and actions, but his outrage was not forced.

The floor was as white as the stone of the incline on which they stood. It was also covered in a layer of fine dust, the debris of this world encroaching on its intruder. Living power radiated from beneath it.

"Oh, Hredroth," Kaphri breathed. She'd felt something like this before, back when her only illumination was the blue glow of the canna disk she'd swung to fight back creeping darkness while she crossed a floor strewn with shards of razor-sharp black stone. *"It's so like—and unlike—the Black Temple."*

Beneath the tower of the Maugrock, her starsign, painted in reverse with her blood to lock her starpower inside her, had severed her presence from that gate's recognition. Memory of the evil force curling around her, trying to lure her to look upon its symbols, made her shudder.

She did not detect a sense of evil from this gate, however, and trying to unravel what lay in the Geffitz world's past was a waste of precious time.

The Balandran, Razek, had continued forward, dust puffing beneath his feet. He stopped and turned, motioning them to advance. "We seem to have lost two of your number." He gave them a razor-toothed, knowing smile as he spread his wings with a soft poof of sound. "They will make for an entertaining hunt." His red eyes locked on Kaphri. "I leave you to my master's tender mercies."

Launching into the air, he flew off to take a position somewhere in the levels above. Scattered movements in the shadows of the galleries warned of other Balandra posted there. Their weapons likely tracked every movement she and Uri made.

Were the winged ones already searching for Tobin and Seuliac? She had not been aware that her two companions had slipped away.

She suppressed a flutter of panic. Their fate was beyond her influence.

"*Welcome, lost child of Arylla.*" The sending that fell so softly into her brain nearly undid her.

A flicker of movement in a direct line beyond where Razek had walked out locked her attention. Across the space, Frax knelt, his head lowered. He was disheveled and dirty, but she did not see blood.

Uri caught her arm to stop her moving toward the other warrior.

"Ah, an intrepid Geffitzi warrior." Bithzielp gave a mental chuckle. *"As you can see, I have one of my own."*

"Are you injured?" she asked Frax tightly.

He did not respond.

A shape moved behind Frax, rising in a slow swell of fur and flesh, and Kaphri's mind went blank with horror.

"*A tarmeuth? Isn't that a bit excessive?*" Uri's sarcasm carried a solid command for her to steady herself. She would not save anyone if she lost her head.

She must speak very carefully. Where was the originator of the greeting? She needed to locate the source. Pulling away from Uri, Kaphri drew her body up as tall as she could muster. *"I am here. Let the warrior go."* If she gained Frax's freedom, she might still get the warriors out unharmed.

"You do not make the rules here. If you want him to live, you will do as you are told." The tarmeuth took a sinuous step forward, yellow eyes locked on hers across the distance, and a jolt of raw terror ran through her.

Seuliac's repeated warning flashed in her mind: anything perceived of value to you becomes a weapon to use against you.

No value. Frax must have no value to her. *"I am here. What do you want?"*

"I require something from you."

Frax did not matter. *"Remove the tarmeuth, then we will talk."*

"I prefer its continued presence. It adds a certain immediacy to the situation."

Nothing mattered. *"Tell me what you want."*

"First, infant, I want the respect due me!" The tarmeuth lashed out, claws glinting as they caught Frax and slammed him to the surface.

"Do not react," Uri ordered.

Blood trickled from Frax's shoulder as he struggled back onto his knees. Still, he did not look at her.

Not long ago she would have surrendered at this point—if she had even been brave enough to come here at all. Her time with the warriors and her experiences had changed her. This time, when she slid into the cold detachment and isolation that had been her shield against the anger and resentment in Kryie Karth, she did not retreat into lonely isolation. She went with calculation and purpose.

The cat's action had revealed something; it had acted too swiftly.

In her numerous interactions, pleasant or unpleasant, with the animals of this world, Kaphri had learned wild creatures did not respond quickly to any external mental suggestion she tried to plant in their brain. Something in their instinctual reflexes resisted and delayed their response to her intrusion.

This was more than a wild creature of the woods.

She sent out a discreet tendril of seeking.

As she suspected, the being who controlled this situation occupied the animal's mind.

"Did you know tarmeuths have a form of mindspeak?" She asked Uri.

She heard the warrior shift slightly behind her. "Damn," he muttered. "Is Bithzielp...?"

Controlling the animal? "Yes."

"That explains how Frax is bleeding yet remains alive. It must take immense discipline for Bithzielp to exert that level of control over the animal."

That discipline would not be infinite. She must be careful not to jeopardize Frax by distracting from it.

Seuliac and Tobin's activity only added to the danger. "Can you warn them?" she asked.

"No," he responded.

They were all on their own.

No more delay. *"My sincere apologies,"* she sent. *"How may I address you?"*

"Ancient One will do." The sending took on a querulous tone. *"And let me dispel any illusion that you can act against me: there is no negotiation between us. I cannot wield the power of Arylla in my current state, but neither will it affect me. If I abandon this form, you, along with your warriors, will die. A setback to my plans, but one I can eventually overcome. Meanwhile, I will find new forms with which to wreak havoc, and this world will never know another moment of peace. No further elaboration is required. Activate the gate to the Homeworld and await my instructions."*

"I—"

"Do it."

Panic slid over her. Where were the Eldren of this world? They had been willing enough to act against her, and she was nothing! This was Bithzielp, the ancient threat who had come close to destroying their world and was now threatening to terrorize it again. If any one of them stepped forward, they might swiftly end this.

If that were true, they would have already done it.

This was her fight.

Acceptance pushed away doubt and brought cold focus. Did he plan to steal her form? Geffitzi reason inserted itself: fighting her was too risky at this point. He would either strike after she opened the portal across the gate or he would flee, leaving the tarmeuth to slaughter every living thing he left behind.

A rising heat burned the skin over her breastbone.

The crystal! Gemma was pledged to the protection of this world.

Despite her long silence, the tiny dragon must have some purpose here, even—a painful thought—if it was only to return to the original role of Guardian, to lie eternally in a pool of Kaphri's blood at the center of this gate.

Realization rolled over Kaphri. The Guardian was not locked away or unwilling. Gemma was waiting. There had only ever been one goal in all of this: to remove the Ly Kai threat from this world. When the tarmeuth killed her, she must make sure her blood and the Guardian Stone took their place on this gate to seal it.

She was mentally prepared to do that. But the issue of the barrier remained unresolved. And warriors did not give up so easily.

She looked across the space, and calm seeped over her. Frax had returned his stare into space, his face pale, expression resolute. Was he aware of the exchange between her and the evil force that held ultimate power over his world? Of course, he was. Bithzielp would relish tormenting him with every detail of his helpless state. With a telepath controlling the animal beside him, Frax could not send without risking his life. He had to trust her to make the right choices. But he was also waiting. If he saw an advantage, she knew he would die to give her the chance to act.

She had been so stupid and ungrateful for all his sacrifices to get her to this point.

Every one of the warriors had come here, willing to die to ensure she fulfilled her role in ridding this world of Bithzielp. She could not fail them.

Still... This next admission might kill them all. *"I don't know how to open the gate."*

The hostility in the other being's sending actually eased slightly. *"An Arylla-born who passes through a world gate is forever imprinted with the ability to manipulate it. Despite the ignorance those lesser Ly Kai fools sought to impress upon you, you have lived and breathed the proximity of this place since the day you arrived here. Walk the gate. Command the power of each star. When you draw Arylla, you will know what must be done."*

Of course. She'd glimpsed the rune-etched floor between the massive, shattered columns in the Black Temple. Felt the subconscious pull of its power even while the blood sign painted on her brow shielded her from its recognition. This gate lay silent and hidden beneath a layer of dust, but if she opened her senses and allowed it, she would find a massive presence ready to answer her command.

This starpower was far beyond the barrier dividing the north and south, or the gate locked in the darkness beneath the Maugrock. This was the power she had touched on the tower heights of Kryie Karth in what seemed ages ago.

Because it was Arylla.

The mechanism activated by her Birthstar was only steps away, waiting for her to act.

She had not opened to the starpower inside this place for fear it would overwhelm and destroy her resistance to another user's will. She did not know what would happen, but the time for the inevitable had arrived. It was time for her to claim her birthright.

Chapter 101
Out of the North

KEP DAMN THE TARMEUTH and Bithzielp!

Frax clenched his teeth and tried to focus on the external world to divert his attention away from his body's screaming physical pain. Anything else, even the slightest movement, risked destroying them all.

It was the most excruciating thing he had ever done. And yet, even in the darkest moment, his brain found hope. Bithzielp, for all his power, had an insurmountable flaw in his strategy as vast as the Great Water. Using the tarmeuth's form cut off all contact with the creatures he commanded. The Balandra did not have telepathic power. This evil Ly Kai could only gather information on what was happening around them by feeding on Kaphri and the Geffitzi warriors' awareness. And his captor was cruel and stupid enough to force Frax into that stream of awareness, allowing the Geffitz limited access to the situation. Frax knew from the sparse information that filtered through to him that the others were aware of the threat around them. Their silence spoke volumes. He had to stay on the edge, waiting and ready for what might happen next. He pushed down pain, focused on the tiny bits of awareness that flicked his way, and waited while his blood began to drip onto the floor.

She could draw on the lowest starpower to clear the dust from the gate, but—a mundane question—where to dispose of it? Aiming at the tarmeuth crossed her mind. Frax, however, would have no protection against the flying debris, and the tarmeuth might kill him in a fit of pique.

Mercifully, the recent encounter with the Cyrwins on the plateau outside had taught her something about controlling power. She drew lightly on Callis, as she had done multiple times before, but this time, she shaped it to her will and sent a spiraling blast of air to whip the debris up along the wall. Then she moved it inward and lifted the mass, drawing it into a tight swirl above, and shot a stronger blast of power through the center to spray the dirt out into the balcony levels above.

Scattered movement revealed lurking Balandra as they scurried out of the settling grit.

"Not amusing," the being who controlled the cat snapped. *"Stay focused, or your pet behind you will suffer."*

Uri. She refused to look back at him, focusing instead on what her blast of power had revealed.

Starsigns. A spiral of symbols, their translucent, sweeping shapes barely discernable against the more solid white background, lay before Kaphri. She was standing at the leading edge of the Ly Kai gate to the Homeworld.

A quick flash of concern, then relief. The tarmeuth and Frax were still on the far opposite edge, close to but outside the gate.

Thousands of Ly Kai had passed through this thing, only to die on this world. What would happen when she stepped onto it? In the Black Temple, all starpower had been blocked to her by Araxis' deviousness, but the sense of lurking evil had still been paralyzing. Here, she felt nothing.

Because the gate was not active.

Of course! The Balandra had been sacrificing residents of this world to pull their warriors through the gate in the Black Temple. Sudden fear seized her. This gate would not require something so horrific, but... *"They said Araxis broke this gate..."*

There was a dry chuckle. *"Those who hold knowledge can tell lesser beings anything, and they must believe it. The gate is intact. The fools trapped themselves here by denying your birthright. Get on with it."*

The revelation twisted inside her gut. If the refugees had not lied to her about her Birthstar, she might have found a way to return them home.

As she stared at the wide, slightly more transparent lines of the first shape, they scintillated. Her vision blurred, and disorientation tugged at her brain.

Was she too weak and ignorant to look upon the lowest symbol of the Ly Kai Hierarch? She was not! She walked out to its edge and, closing her eyes, bent to place the tip of a forefinger on the sign. Tracing a short line on the stone, she cautiously channeled starpower from its star. The warm, gentle flow of Callis rose to meet her flesh, and she trembled. It was so much more powerful in this place than anything she had drawn before. And it was the lowest star in the Hierarch.

Callis' power did not threaten. Rather, it hung ready, waiting, and as she made herself relax in permission, it settled through her body. She opened her eyes. The lines of the first starsign had illuminated with a pale green glow.

How ridiculous she must appear. Like a young child encountering a gate for the first time. She wanted to step back and consider what she had experienced.

Such a delay was not an option.

"You display a disgusting lack of hunger and ambition." The observation was harsh with impatience.

Beyond Callis's glow, the next two spaces had begun to take on luminescence. Though the strength of their light tapered off as it extended deeper into the gate, she could see the faint border of the three-ring spiral leading to Arylla's symbol at the gate's center. Eleven spaces flowed inward to the center circle, each containing a graceful, looping shape with which she was very familiar. Eleven signs, eleven individual colors...

"Remember, you command the Even' Star," Uri's said behind her, using the Geffitzi name for Arylla. His message: her experience enabled her to think and act differently than other Ly Kai.

"In more violent ways," she whispered sadly.

"Get on with it!" Bithzielp ordered.

When she stepped forward onto the gate, she might forever leave this world. She looked back at Uri. "I... I'm sorry..." She pushed down her sorrow.

Uri nodded. "It's not over yet, Willow."

Darkness eliminated the use of hand signals, but the passage was silent and the ceiling too low for Balandra to fly, limiting the risk of a surprise attack by the gray men.

When Tobin encountered a gap in the wall to his right, he put a hand back to stop the warlord. "Do we want to move inward or continue on?" he whispered.

"We need to see what we're up against."

"Inward, then." The side corridor would lead toward the center of this place. "I'll take the far wall." He darted across the opening while Seuliac slid around its corner. They crept forward.

Within a few steps, they encountered a blank wall.

Seuliac ran a hand lightly over the surface. "Why bother to cut such a shallow notch?" His fingertips brushed a vertical slot near the right corner.

"I don't—"

The space around them went unstable.

"What the hell was that?" Tobin gasped a heartbeat later when they regained their balance.

The warlord cautiously stepped back into the corridor, spear held at ready and sniffed. "Air is cooler. Smells of night and Balandra stench. So, a type of lift, I think." Some of the Caers had mechanical ways to move people from level to level without climbing stairs. "Considering Ly Kai trickery, let us hope we only changed levels and not locations."

Muttering a vehement curse of agreement, Tobin followed him out of the niche. "The corridor is wider here." It took him two additional steps, arm outstretched, to locate the opposite wall of the passage.

"An upper hallway," Seuliac said. "There's an opening on the right up ahead."

Before they could move, a shadow rippled across the thin light, and a snuffling sound broke the silence.

The warriors instantly molded their bodies to opposing walls as a dark shape emerged from the side passage. The Balandran moved its head to both sides as it sniffed again. Darkness was no shield against that nose. Stories about the cruel creatures' ability to hunt Geffitzi still brought a chill to a warrior's skin around a campfire at night.

But the creature would also carry weapons...

Tobin moved with a slight creak of leather. The Balandran's head snapped in their direction. The creature paused for a second, as if trying to see the warrior in the dark, then stepped fully into the passage to face toward them. With its wings half-opened, it came close to filling the space.

Bad for them if this was the point man in a patrol. Silently cursing Kitahn's bloodthirsty enthusiasm, Seuliac dropped into a crouch, his spear grasped ready, and watched for any shadow movements behind the creature.

A sense of wicked anticipation filtered from the younger Geffitz as Tobin scraped a fingernail down the wall to draw the creature's attention toward him.

The Balandran lunged.

"Gah!" Seuliac hissed a moment later as he jerked his spear tip from the gray man's neck, and blood gushed over his hand. "Damn you, Kitahn. I didn't need to get soaked in stinking blood!"

"You'll make for conflicting scents now." Tobin wrested a longbow off the creature's back. "Not the best combination for sneaking around this place, though. Can you get the quiver?"

Seuliac worked a strap off a bony shoulder and handed the arrow case across in the darkness.

"Got its knife." The body twitched against Tobin's shin as Seuliac rammed the blade into the lifeless form's neck. "Let's see if we can sow a little discord with this thing. Drag it into that porting notch. Maybe it will move the evidence to a different location." Blood would still be in this hall, but the lack of a body might make for confusion.

They stuffed the body into the space as best they could, though it was impossible to completely compress the wings.

"We can't activate the lift thing without entering it," Tobin hissed.

"Too risky." They might not emerge in the same area as before, and separation was not an option. "Let's see where that light is coming from."

"I'll take the lead. They'll smell you coming."

Much to their relief, the side passage extended several lengths before opening onto an upper gallery of what they hoped was the same temple structure they had entered. Pona's light, just cresting the opening above, revealed seven more Balandra lurking in scattered positions around the huge circular space. Two similar levels of decorated galleries rose above them.

"Too many." Tobin's fingers flashed in the dim light.

"Agreed. Enemy focus, action below."

"Go look." Tobin was gone before Seuliac could protest.

Keeping low in the shadows, the scout slithered to the outer balustrade and peered down between the posts.

Two levels below, a quarter of the way around the arena, Uri stood a few steps behind Kaphri, near the outer edge of the space. Only at the last moment, as dust began to swirl off the surface, did the younger Kitahn notice the other figures across the space. He scurried back into the side passage to take shelter from pelting grit.

"It's bad," he told Seuliac.

A tingle ran through her as she eased a toe across the pale green line of light on the floor. True to Bithzielp's claim, this gate was not dead. She paused, sensing for malevolent links as the purity of Callis' power flowed through her.

This star, the lowest in the Ly Kai Hierarch of Power, was the first one she had drawn at the barrier while trying to escape Frax and his impossible plan to force her back north to be questioned by the Geffitzi Inner Circle. If he had succeeded, the geas would have immobilized and possibly driven her insane. Luckily—in a twisted way—the appearance of Balandra pursuing Seuliac and Velacy across the mountainside had stopped him. Instead, a brush from the blood that, unbeknownst to her, held the crystal plastered to her clothing, had temporarily broken the barrier open, and they had all fallen through.

On that mountainside, gripped with fear and desperation, she had cautiously pushed her power, drawing up from the weakest star in the Hierarch to the strongest. But she had hesitated to fully command Arylla's power at the last second and failed to push through the barrier.

It had been a fortunate failure back then: she could not have survived the geas-driven journey across the south by herself. But here, failure to control her power was not an option.

She slid her foot deeper into the space, and the gentle green glow of Callis rose, spreading upward and outward as the outlines of the gate took on its light.

"What in the...?"

She twisted around at Uri's whisper, her eyes following his upward.

The sky had changed, replaced with an unfamiliar, star-pattern. At its center sat Callis, gleaming peacefully. Meanwhile, the arena floor inside the gate's circle had risen to a pale white glow. Forward and to her left, a dark clump that was Frax and the tarmeuth sat outside the light.

Fighting the urge to retreat, Kaphri stepped forward into Callis's space.

Chapter 102
The Warriors Will Come

"HOW IS IT POSSIBLE?" Seuliac murmured, half to himself, as they hunkered in the darkness. "How is it possible the damned beast hasn't ripped your brother to shreds? He's bleeding, for Kep's sake!"

"Something has to be controlling it."

"Bithzielp!" They both whispered at the same time.

"Once he gets what he wants, he'll abandon the tarmeuth, and Kitahn is dead."

"I'll eliminate that problem." Tobin shifted the bow.

Kill the beast? "No. If Bithzielp escapes, we won't have any idea who he will possess next." Damned Ly Kai! He may as well plunge headlong into this insanity. "We know how that Balandran killed Araxis. We can do it, too, but it must be carefully timed. We have to move back down to the floor level."

"Then we have to do it fast. Before he gets what he wants."

The cat could kill them all. Or, if they succeeded, they would win back their world. If Bithzielp succeeded, their world might even be safe for a while. But he would return. Somchow, he would find a way to return and torment their people. They could not let that happen.

Once the tarmeuth was freed, they were all dead anyway. "Let's find a way down to that opening behind them."

The surface blurred, then came back into focus.

The gate and the arena floor had extended to become an immense, borderless plain.

She froze at the sudden vastness of the space Callis' symbol occupied in front of her and to her left and right. Frax and the tarmeuth were tiny in the distance. She twisted to look back at Uri, who was still only a few steps behind her.

"Willow?"

"You don't see it?"

"See what?" The warrior's concern quickened. "Do you need help?" He started forward.

"No!" If he did not see the change in the gate, the shift in dimensions was exclusive to her. To a Ly Kai. To a gate-opener? She gestured him back to his original position, to where she had stood beside him only seconds before. Then she understood. Of course, Callis's space on the gate would be huge to a starborn walking the path! Not only was it the lowest star in the Ly Kai Hierarch, but it was also the one that encompassed the majority of the Homeworld's population.

Callis burned in the center of the sky above her.

But she had ten more starsigns to draw on and pass through, and this first space was immense. The thought of the time required to cross it made her falter.

The green light around her dimmed with her doubt, a reminder she must not lose control of even the weakest star's power, or it would destroy her. She must cross on to Rasef.

She walked forward.

The light around her transitioned to yellow green. She looked down to discover that with only a few steps, she had advanced to the edge of the symbol for the eleventh star.

So vast a move. Was it an illusion? She twisted to look back. This time, Uri was a distant blur.

Had her desire to move carried her forward to Rasef's edge? She drew its power, stepped into the space, and looked up. The star, Rasef, had joined Callis, and now it occupied the central position above her. Pain twisted her heart. Truly, she was not on the Geffitzi world any longer.

This star's space was nearly as large as the one she had left behind. She walked forward again, a strange, swift step to the edge of Doeis' starsign. The yellow light of the tenth star in the Hierarch bloomed warm around her.

Her body began to prickle with the rising, pure starpower.

Control, she told herself. Told it. She had so much further to go.

If she lived, then, maybe. Maybe she would release its power . But not now. The thought brought back her purpose. Frax. Bithzielp. The Gate.

She took her time, carefully drawing on each star as she moved forward. Orange, fierce Jaro, then red orange Sois, and red Leox. She took everything each star had to offer with the greatest care and respect before she moved on.

As she progressed forward, the light rising off the gate intensified, but the glow also tamed, dropping lower with each progressive starsign so that by the time she had mastered red violet Tier, the light was mid-thigh. With the haunting indigo of Ly Toma, Ving's star, it dropped to her knee level. The sky followed the light down, erasing the temple walls, while the stars of the Hierarch populated and shifted above. The areas on the gate were smaller now as she approached the center, and she could see the color transitions along the border of the starsign ahead of her.

With Ce's violet glowing before her, Kaphri snatched a moment to look about and steady her resolution.

The next star she would draw on beyond Ce was Freya, deceptively assigned as her Birthstar by the survivors of Araxis' betrayal. Though it had never answered her prayers for star response, it had been the Birthstar she had claimed for sixteen years.

She fought off distracting sadness with a more urgent thought. Where were Frax and the tarmeuth? Bithzielp had been silent for what seemed ages. Was she too late?

His sudden lash of irritation at her delay was sharp. She hardened herself for the next step.

As Kaphri drew its power and walked into the pure blue illumination of Freya's sign, the recognition she had craved all her young life swept over her, tearing a gasp of joy from her.

The joy was short-lived, however. She had reached the edge of the last starsign.

Though she had drawn on its power, she had never fully claimed the Great Star as a true Arylla-born.

The rune before her burned white. Waiting.

Bithzielp must be raging for her to take the last step. Kaphri searched her mind for some instinctual guidance.

Making an error risked too much.

Delay also risked too much. She stepped onto the rune at the center of the gate, and Arylla's light enveloped her.

Her elation surged. This! This was what she had been denied all those lonely years in the tower of Kryie Karth. The subconscious hunger she had endured since birth, the hollow core that had lain cold inside her, was filling with warm and glorious light. When she exhaled, she experienced her breath as the slow flow of life force moving out of her physical form, while an intake of breath pulled new life back inside her. Arylla recognized her! She was becoming whole.

Then, once again, she was on the edge of a precipice, blinded by the darkness engulfing her, silence pressing in as the universe waited for her response. This time, she did not hesitate. This time, she took the final step forward, embracing her Birthstar and letting it claim her.

Cold and silence engulfed her.

She opened her eyes to find herself floating in a sea of stars, hard points of gold, white, blue, and orange light blazing at her feet, her head. Everywhere around her. So many stars. Billions. But her eyes sought only one. Arylla blazed white in the distance and her whole being reached out for it.

Starfire flowed through her, gliding along her bones, her nerves, her tissue. Her nails and hair tingled. It was the same light she'd felt twice before, once on the heights of Kryie Karth, where she had rejected it in fear, and once on the mountainside on the border of Omurda, when she had fought to break its power.

Again, the intuitive command: Take control or die! And, just like at the barrier, she sank into the power. But this time, she did not struggle to control it. She absorbed and took possession. As it burned over and through her, she gathered it in, reveling in its strength and response.

Her Birthstar had finally acknowledged her.

The heady sensation could easily go wrong. Someone might become intoxicated with it and desire more...

"Why are you standing there! Get on with it!" Bithzielp's anger jerked her back to reality. A wave of terrible hunger singed through her. Bithzielp. His claim on Arylla was the same as hers, but on a much vaster scale. His need shook her to the core. He was so much more than she was. Massive on a scale she had never imagined. But though he could bask in the star's glory, like Araxis, he could not wield its power without a physical body born of Arylla.

He desperately wanted to restore his physical existence, and trying to wrest possession of her form would waste time. He wanted to swiftly pass back onto the Ly Kai Homeworld, undetected, while she and the warriors died.

Kaphri curled her fingers at her sides. Oh, her death would not be wasted.

There might be Ly Kai on the Homeworld ambitious enough to aid Bithzielp. There might even be Arylla-born, dangerously eager and unsuspecting in their vanity.

Was there a way to warn the Ly Kai? Would they listen? Did it matter, as long as he left this world? Where did her duty lie?

Her doubt was weakening her control over the power coursing through her body. If she did not regain focus, it would devour her.

Kaphri shut away her doubts and took back her thoughts.

All the starsigns on the gate fell to an even white glow.

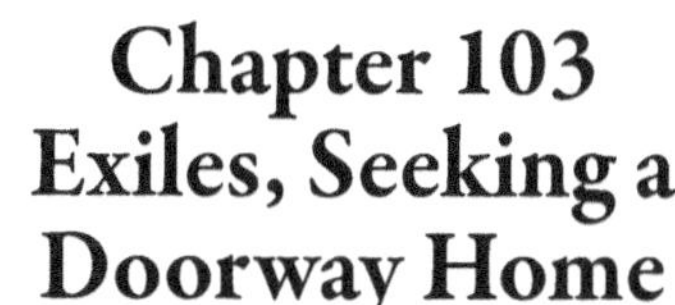

Chapter 103
Exiles, Seeking a Doorway Home

"DAMNED HAZE IS BEGINNING to drift down," Tobin fumed as he peered out into the arena. They had finally located a ramp leading to the lower level and were paused in the shadows of an opening. "Between it and the light from that cursed thing out there, we'll barely be able to see." The glowing circle Kaphri was moving across was steadily rising in brightness and color.

"At least it will also obstruct the Balandra's view," Seuliac said. The creatures were sensitive to bright light. "That haze," uneasiness tightened his voice, "could be Wyxan fog, infiltrating the place."

Tobin shot him a fierce scowl. "No!"

"They might be trying to help us."

"Or attempting to sabotage our efforts!"

"Consider this, Kitahn: they're here, and they've made no effort to stop us."

"True," Tobin conceded grudgingly. "They are a long way from their damned swamp. But we can't trust their motives."

The slow, thin drifts above the arena were beginning to ripple with the colors from the Ly Kai gate. "Working against us does not make sense at this point."

"We're probably a convenient sacrifice. But it doesn't matter what their motive is; how do we use it to our advantage?"

"It does help obscure our movements from Balandra in the upper levels." Seuliac stared at the horror crouched in the arena. "Kep.

Bithzielp must be exerting tremendous effort to harness a tarmeuth's natural instincts. I've seen firsthand how fast one of those things can move. It can leap..." the warlord paused for a moment, the memory of the tarmeuth's deadly movements on the clifftop tightening his chest. "The Balandra won't want to be out there if he loses control of it."

"You think they might withhold their attack on us?"

"None of us want to distract his hold on that creature." Seuliac suppressed a shudder. "It would stalk and kill us all—and we would still have to deal with Bithzielp. If we mount an attack on the tarmeuth from behind, before he releases it, we might trap Bithzielp inside and finish this. But we have to get over there fast."

"There are two of us: One to attack and one to guard the other's back. You take the bow." Tobin shoved the weapon at Seuliac. "I need the largest, sharpest blade we have. Your spare?"

Seuliac drew his second knife from his belt and offered it for examination.

Tobin grunted approval. "Better suited for this task than mine." They exchanged blades, and Seuliac shouldered the quiver.

"The animal has blazing speed," the warlord warned again.

"Yes. But if I time it right, I will succeed." The younger warrior gave Seuliac a sudden, penetrating glare.

"Do you think I'm foolish enough to sabotage this?" the warlord snapped.

"A warrior must consider all possibilities."

"Reasonable." As a leader of warriors, he would not fault one for rational caution. "I will defend this action with my life." He glanced at the gently thickening haze in the opening high above the arena, then gave Tobin a sidelong glance. "Besides, it will be good to have Cadarn in my debt."

"Rhynog will always be welcome to ask Cadarn to rescue their warlord."

Seuliac gave a soft huff of humor. "Well met, Tobin Kitahn. Now I must keep you alive, in case I'm ever caught in that situation."

Her heart thudding, Kaphri stared down at the starsign etched into the white stone. What would happen when she drew on the power represented by those lines?

Would she find crowds of hostile faces glaring anger and resentment at her? Blaming her for all the dead who would never follow her back through the gate? Or would she discover relief and happiness?

"Activate the gate but do not open it."

"Send the tarmeuth away. Place the need to return to its den in it and I will surrender—"

"Activate it!" Bithzielp demanded with ravaging fury.

"Trust." A whisper swirled in the back of her mind.

She twitched, instantly recognizing the source was not one of her Geffitz companions. But she didn't dare think about the other possibility for fear Bithzielp had invaded her thoughts and might recognize it.

Trust. Some things were simply beyond her control. They required a measure of strength and knowledge she did not have. Kaphri drove her fingernails into the flesh of her clenched hand to keep from reaching for the crystal and focused on the rising sense of urgency inside her. The symbol at the heart of the gate was demanding her full attention.

As she looked at Arylla's sign her starpower ramped in intensity. Perhaps Araxis or Bithzielp, who had used it before, knew how to contain or partition that force, but she was not skilled enough. The star demanded use. It demanded she open the gate at the center of this star path.

Pure white light sheeted up around her, the heat searing through her body in the same way that it had when Araxis forced her to create a breach in the barrier for his Balandran forces to pass through.

An image of the Ly Kai men, surrounded by the gray-winged warriors, fearful and demanding that she act to save them, flashed before her eyes. Breaking the barrier had not saved them. She fought to push away the memory of Balandra savagely cutting them down while she stood helplessly pinioned by the power of Arylla and the rest of Araxis' evil forces rushed into the south through the gap she had torn.

She had not loved them, but she had not wanted the Ly Kai men to die.

She cared about the Geffitz warriors. They would not die here if she could do anything in her power—Arylla's power—to save them.

"Control it!" Bithzielp roared in fury.

Of course. She must control Arylla's power or the star would burn through her and this world would be lost to his evil.

Every one of her predecessors had done this. They all had to open their first gate. Recentered, she gathered Arylla's burning power and focused it into one seething stream. Then she extended a hand, her forefinger pointing to a place in the air before her that was commanding her attention. Gentle pressure met her flesh and she released the flow.

The light around the circle streamed forward, physically tugging at her as it rushed to her fingertip, the colors of the stars weaving into strands that twined to form a growing cable of interconnected light. It expanded, lifting up and out to bow over the gate. As the streams glided forward, Arylla's white light burst upward to solidify into a blazing arch that spanned the diameter of the gate. The colors continued to flow forward, resolving into detail as an image formed before her.

As the last color settled into place, the white arch gave a hard pulse, as if connecting all its components into a whole.

"Hredroth!" she breathed.

A shaft of light ahead warned they were approaching another opening onto the arena.

Seuliac stopped to take a deep breath. This was a fool's errand! Rhynog needed him far more than Cadarn did. They were enemies, for Kep's sake! The fate of their world depended on a silly Ly Kai girl, and this would all come to a disastrous end, regardless of whether Frax Kitahn lived or died. There was no good outcome for their world, no matter how he twisted or turned the players or the situation.

Ahead, silhouetted against the light, Tobin peered around the corner. He raised a hand and signed before sliding across the shadows of the back wall and up the other side of the opening.

They were behind Frax and the tarmeuth.

Having taken the much-needed moment to unleash, confront, and purge his doubts on their current course of action, the warlord exhaled and moved forward again. Cadarn was going to seriously owe Rhynog for this.

Seuliac paralleled Tobin up the short stone channel to a position near the mouth. Their target was thirty steps out in the arena, facing inward. Frax was on its left.

The Kitahn commander crouched, head down, unmoving. His skin was mottled with either dirt or dark bruises. There were streams of drying blood along his ribcage and the glint of bright red on his back and shoulder, where the beast had raked him with its claws. Tobin would have to be careful not to intrude on his brother's peripheral vision as he approached so that Frax did not react and give his presence away. Meanwhile, the tarmeuth's attention was riveted on the girl.

Seuliac's stomach muscles tightened. One burst of speed—a heartbeat to them—and the damned thing would have her in its teeth. Getting people out of this place alive was going to be very difficult when all hell broke loose.

Tobin signaled again, this time with his hand close to his side to avoid any flicker of movement that might draw attention in the galleries. He was waiting for the right moment to move out into the arena.

Seuliac silently notched an arrow and waited while the scout, crouching low, eased to the edge of the opening and positioned himself so his shadow fell back into the darkness of the space.

Light from the Ly Kai gate illuminated the whole circle of the arena walls outside in shifting colors.

Was there a twitch of movement in the balcony across from them? Seuliac's lips separated in a slow snarl as he narrowed his eyes. Were the Balandra just now recognizing this major weakness in their security—that they should have posted a guard here?

A chill crept down his back. It was a flaw that the winged demons would not take long to remedy. He would soon be dodging the jab of spears from the passage behind him.

But, with the risk of setting loose a rampaging tarmeuth, who would be stupid enough to volunteer for the task?

Only some desperate Geffitz warriors...

The Balandra would have to be extremely cautious in their attack. At the moment, the tarmeuth sat rock-still. Bithzielp exerted total control over it—an amazing feat which the slightest distraction might shatter. Any distraction...

It all came down to timing. They had no way of knowing how their actions affected Kaphri or her power over the gate. He and Tobin agreed that duplicating Araxis' manner of death was highly unlikely, but they had to try. If that failed, it all came down to a successful strike on the tarmeuth at that split second after Bithzielp abandoned it, when it was, hopefully, dazed, and before it could recover its senses to attack Frax—or the rest of them.

A drop of sweat trickled down the side of Seuliac's forehead and a twisted shot of amusement ran through his mind. When was the last time he'd sweated over anything beyond a hot day?

He could not remember.

Chapter 104
The Children of Kep

ACROSS THE OTHER HALF of the gate beyond the burning arch gleamed a pristine white floor and a massive slot, twin to the one behind her where they had entered. Instead of an enclosed hallway, however, she saw a street, trees, and walkways beyond that entrance's mouth.

She was staring at the purloined memories of the Twenty-six come to life!

"Stop," Bithzielp ordered. *"I will tell you when to act."*

The half-circle of gate around Kaphri glowed with light, while the stone in front of her was plain white and unmarked, as if it had been scourged of starsigns. Still, a sense of starpower lurked beneath its surface. Waiting...

Her stomach tightened. At the far edge of what would have been the gate's border, on a simple stone bench, sat an elderly man. He looked across at her, blinked, then hurriedly pushed to his feet. *"At last, Child, you are returning home!"* He scrambled forward, a hand extended, but he stopped well before the demarcation between the gate halves. *"Come to us. Hurry!"*

Fear laced his sending.

"Remain where you are." Bithzielp's order cut across her mind.

She could feel it now, like the distant monstrosity that divided the Geffitzi world, a barrier of power that stood between her and the Homeworld. She stared at the old man, unable to decide if she felt fear or relief, and unwilling to make mental contact. Past experience with the Ly Kai had never been pleasant and usually treacherous—like her present situation.

The prospect of facing a world full of them terrified her.

But her terror was buffered by the view of the world beyond the gate. Through the slot behind the man, sunlight blazed on a bustling space. She saw Ly Kai, in colorful clothing, rushing past it without a glance in her direction. A sense of wonder crept over her at the sight of women, their brilliant red hair twisted up with sparkling stones and strips of brightly colored cloth, and men with smooth heads, some wearing small, elaborately decorated accessories on their scalps.

No, her mind shot quick warning. These were not her people. She knew nothing of the beings who were beginning to pause in their activities to stare at her.

The call of a small child rang out, and more moving figures slowed, looking about, finding the child at the same moment as Kaphri.

The little one was pointing at her.

Immediately, the stir of Ly Kai mental communication rippled across the gate. One or two adults walked through the far opening, their eyes locked on her. A man caught the child's hand and drew it out of sight. More people came into view, staring, the crowd eerily silent as they pressed forward. But, unlike the old man, these people kept a cautious distance, stopping at the gate's outer rim. Behind them, two people ran away.

The old man seemed to recover from his initial startled reaction. He bowed, his eyes flicking over her. "Greetings, Lost Daughter. I am First Sentinel, assigned by the High Council to monitor the gate. To alert them to a return—to your appearance. But..." He twisted to peer past her. "Where are the others? Do they forget us in the pleasures of their new world? Are you come to open the way so the rest of us might indulge, too?"

Pleasures? Indulge? The words drove arrows of bitter sorrow and anger into her heart.

There were no expressions on the faces watching her, but she was sure hope raced in some of their hearts. Araxis had lured away a thousand people, but they were from the ranks of the highest born. Now the rest of the Ly Kai were waiting for her response.

She saw no benefit in prolonging their hope, and Bithzielp had not ordered her to be silent. "They are all returned to their stars," Kaphri told them softly.

Wails of sorrow rose up from several people in the crowd. The sound swelled as her reply spread further, and Kaphri felt her throat tighten. How many of them had held out hope for a reunion with lost family members after all these years?

"Come to us. Hurry!" The First Sentinel did not ask what had happened to the others as he gestured for her to step through the gate onto the Homeworld. The man seemed on the verge of panic again. "Come to us!"

She would have to draw on Arylla to break the membrane separating the worlds. Why was Bithzielp suddenly silent after raging for her to act only seconds ago?

An intrusive sense of cunning crept across her thoughts: he was waiting for something more.

A disturbance at the back of the crowd drew the old man's attention. "Come to us," he repeated urgently when he returned focus to her. "Come to us. We need you here."

"That old fool." She felt a singe of amused scorn. *"Stay as you are."*

As long as Bithzielp waited for his moment, Frax remained unharmed, and Seuliac and Tobin had a better chance of rescuing him. "I have questions," she told the old man.

"They will all be answered. The Homeworld needs you. Come."

And risk putting herself into another battle for power? "Where is Alexar?"

"We... you..." The old one pulled his body more erect. "We expected you to tell us..."

"He was never on this world."

The old one stared at her as if she were something he had never seen before. "Impossible! Alexar went with Araxis to help prepare the way. He did not return. Come to us now. Please." He gestured her forward. "Come, now, and close the gate."

That was an abrupt shift in attitude!

The disturbance was growing closer behind him.

"Come." The elder gestured. But Kaphri's attention had shifted. There was something in the people's posture. A rising sense of something in the air... Tension. Fear. And it was not directed toward her.

These Ly Kai feared something among their own numbers.

"Arylla-born child, come to us!"

"Not yet."

How large was the remaining Balandran force they would have to fight? He'd spotted a few dark blotches scattered in the upper area across from him, but more would be posted outside, guarding the wall.

Seuliac pressed patience over his racing thoughts as Tobin edged out toward the tarmeuth.

What was happening at the gate? The younger warrior was better positioned to see that, but he had other concerns. They were taking a huge risk betting the Balandra would not rain arrows down in the vicinity of the tarmeuth and distract the being who controlled it.

Of course, the animal would kill them all once Bithzielp loosed it, unless they—Tobin—killed it first. Maybe the Balandra were smart enough to save their arrows for their own defense in case Tobin failed.

Damn Velacy! A third warrior posted to guard his back would have come in handy right now.

But Velacy had served a higher purpose no one could discount. The warlord chose to believe that in the end, the younger Aedec had fought the evil that tried to control him, holding it inside and giving someone—a cursed Balandran, of all things—the opportunity to kill it, and him. A final bold sacrifice for a Geffitz warrior and Seuliac would make sure it was known. Rhynog had been honorably served with his sacrifice.

It would not be well served, however, if he lost focus here. Seuliac dared to flick a glance at the tunnel behind him. An arrow from the darkness could make a clean strike on him and go unnoticed by the tarmeuth.

A handful of leaves strategically scattered would have gone a long way toward his defense.

Cursing his lack of foresight while in the woods, he reached down, fingers scrabbling along the base of the wall. His hand closed on some bits of dirt and debris, possibly freshly flung from Kaphri's surface-cleansing blast. A paltry defense, but better than nothing. He slipped back and dusted it at both corners of the rear opening. He might hear the dry rattle of a footfall in the dead silence.

Or not.

Where was Caspani? As he eased back in position, Seuliac squinted against the blazing light.

There. The other warrior was on the far side of the gate, the glow making him barely visible. Without mental or visual contact, they were at a terrible disadvantage for timing any attack or distraction, forcing them to rely on trust in each other's abilities.

Honestly, in this situation, he could not have hoped for better companions.

Clenching his makeshift spear shaft in one hand, Seuliac slipped a thin stiletto blade free from his boot and tucked it carefully at his waist. Trust your fellow warriors, but always carry multiple backup weapons at the ready.

He watched Tobin inch closer to the back of the cat.

The disturbance grew closer. The crowd separated, people moving hastily aside for a small group of men and women dressed in blue-white robes.

Freya-born.

Of course. With no Arylla-born, Freya must pick up the mantle of Council leadership.

The procession swept up and across their half of the gate, the leader radiating the power of her Birthstar as she stopped four steps from Kaphri to stare at her with cold appraisal.

Kaphri might claim Arylla, but she controlled nothing of its power in comparison to what this woman wielded of Freya. She could crush Kaphri with a simple word if she desired.

If Kaphri penetrated the last membrane of the gate... Which a Freya-born did not have the power to do. Meaning it served for her protection. And possibly an inconvenience to Bithzielp, whatever he was up to.

The Freyan's eyes flicked over her, taking in her white, Wyxan-made shirt and breeches, her wild hair twisted in braids and beads from Uri's handiwork, and the burn of hope in the woman's dark eyes faded. Her shoulders dropped as if she was preparing for a less-than-pleasant encounter. Whatever they hoped for, Kaphri did not appear to represent it.

The Council would have many questions, some private in nature. They would want to communicate telepathically. Was Bithzielp prepared to risk her responding?

She realized she had instinctively raised her mental blocks at the first sight of people who reminded her of her tormented childhood in Kryie Karth. Now she eased her mindshields to a guardedly polite level.

She did not release her wariness behind it.

"Consider carefully what you say," Bithzielp warned.

The woman had noticed the relaxing of her defenses. She nodded stiff respect. "To the lost child of the House of Dolphere. Greetings." She spoke aloud, her voice soft and flexible. Not the creaking, cracked sound of one who constantly relied on telepathy—and a new trigger for Kaphri's mistrust. Those who spoke aloud had their reasons. She should know; she had done it for years in Kryie Karth to block the anger and cruel sendings of the other refugees. And Rath—she hid a shudder—he had spoken to hide Araxis' influence over him. "We are pleased to welcome your return. Where are the others, the elders?" Freyan eyes flicked to the space behind her, searching.

What did they see, Kaphri wondered fleetingly.

"There is no one else."

"A tragic loss, but one we have long suspected." The woman considered Kaphri coolly. "Did you kill them?"

Shocking question. "One. He attacked me."

"Who—?" The woman broke off as heightening sounds of protest rose behind her.

Another group of Ly Kai were pushing their way forward. Their leader strode imperiously, with the two people flanking him shoving aside stragglers too slow to move out of their path.

"What is the pseudo council seeking to do to us today?" The man's voice pierced the low hum of the gathering crowd.

The sight of his white robes sent a jolt of shock through Kaphri until she noticed a slight graying of the fabric down the front of his garment and the borders of his sleeves. He must be a Shade, born almost within Arylla's reign, but not close enough to claim full birthright or to wield the Great Star's true power. Their births would be almost as rare as Arylla-born. Deprived of true legacy, they traditionally became the priests who maintained their higher star's temple.

Six others, robes also highlighted in gray but in varying darker tones, swept in behind him.

The warlord's disdain for what he termed "power-mad priests" flitted through Kaphri's mind. These Shades claimed some pretense of position in the ruling hierarch. Though they could never become members of the governing council, they did wield considerable power, and they were a factor she had not previously considered.

The Shade priest's gaze fell on her, and he twitched, surprised, before he recovered composure. He did not mask the sudden, anticipatory gleam of hungry speculation that fired in his eyes as he stopped beside the Freyan Councilwoman.

"High One." He made a sweeping bow to Kaphri. His companions pressed forward to quickly follow suit.

"She is not High One," the Freyan woman told him sharply.

"She is a Trueborn of the Great Star. You recognize it, the same as I do," the other countered smoothly. "She is meritorious of the title by birth."

"She is only meritorious of the title after due process and ceremony."

The two glared at each other.

Their conflict was not her concern. But—High One? She sensed that this new group of Ly Kai was not as overjoyed by her arrival as the steadily increasing crowd behind them. Then she realized even that joy was beginning to temper, to shift to wariness. Toward her, or toward this new group? There was no reading of emotion from Ly Kai faces to help her gauge their mood in the way she could with a Geffitz warrior. The only way to truly know was to allow them into her mind and she was not ready for that.

"This is the business of Arylla and does not concern the lesser stars," the head Shade declared. He swept out his hand in broad dismissal. "The rest of you, disperse. The Council will be informed of the matters we discuss." Several of the Shades at the rear turned and began to gesture for people to leave.

The people pressing in ignored them.

The Freyan High One's eyes sizzled with outrage despite her lack of expression. "Arrogant priest! You presume too much in your position. What happens on this world is the ultimate concern of the High Council and you will take no action without its approval."

The Shade drew himself up in a haughty stance. "A Freya-born must yield to one born of the Great Star." He looked at Kaphri. "What say you, High One?" The Shades locked their attention on her with hard, anticipatory eyes.

She'd seen the look before in Kryie Karth; she simply had never realized what was behind it until now. They were seeing the potential for tremendous power. But unlike the refugees in Kryie Karth, whose hunger had been tempered by their hatred and fear, these people burned with ambition. They wanted to take her under their "guidance", and they were trying to calculate the best approach to secure her trust. Ironically, it seemed that it had never occurred to them that they should fear her.

They should. They should be terrified of what she was about to do.

Chapter 105
Capturing The Star That Flees the Even' sky

THE SHADES WERE MOVING, forming a perimeter around a group of young, white-robed Ly Kai who were emerging from the crowd. Kaphri's insides gave a jerk when she recognized their robes. She had worn those once, in what seemed ages ago. These were Arylla-born, wearing the robes of candidates for leadership of the Ly Kai Governing Council.

But if the Ly Kai had eligible candidates, why was a Freya-born heading the Council?

Then she realized. They were all younger than her. Less than eighteen years. Likely less than sixteen. Some of the girls had barely begun to grow their red crests.

Neither they, nor she, had the wisdom to lead a world, her mind whispered in protest.

The Shades would not care about that. They only cared that they were ambitiously poised to advise the one who triumphed in whatever power play was taking place here.

All the children gathered inside the crescent were the same starpower as she, so the Warlord must have been correct in his assessment of the Ly Kai holiday of the High Sabbat. Ly Kai leadership—at least the Shades—had unlocked the key to Arylla-born after her and her uncles' births. If the Homeworld had determined that, despite their age, these candidates were eligible for the position of Great One, as signified by their robes, why hadn't they already chosen one to lead the Council?

Because they had not come of age to walk the Paths of Power and remove the safety blocks implanted in their child minds.

Her eyes flicked to the Freyan Councilwoman. A fully acknowledged Freya-born would be more powerful than any of these children or the Shades—at least until the Shades secured control over an Arylla-born who had access to their star's full power. The youths were still empty, innocent shells. Ripe for a stronger force to take them and forge a return, the same way Araxis had planned to do with her.

Of course, Bithzielp didn't want her form! She was not schooled in Arylla's power, and he would consider her contaminated by her life on this world. She would be much less pliant than these young ones. He was going to steal a child's form and use it to walk the Paths of Power, something she had not done.

The self-forged shackles created by her fear of Bithzielp's imminent attack fell away. She was an unknown force he chose not to waste time on beyond utilizing her limited ability.

But he was still a danger to her. Leaving her alive on the Geffitzi world risked letting her gain more power and seek revenge. He would not allow that.

He still needed her right now, however.

She looked at the younger Arylla-born. If she was not Bithzielp's target, then one of them was. Were they aware of the horrendous threat she was bringing to them? Terrifyingly, none of the children inside the half-circle of white and gray looked as if they had enough will to withstand the kind of ambitious pressure the wily Shades surrounding them exuded.

Except one, standing at the back of the group. Her heart slammed hard, the future and the present falling into place when she saw him.

Tobin eased forward, mind locked on one task: kill the tarmeuth at any cost, even if it meant the loss of his brother. He had no choice. If the cat killed the Priestess, everything they had worked for would be undone.

Obviously, this being, Bithzielp, did not want the girl's physical form or he would not put her at such grave risk. He was focused on the gate, whether to leave or to allow another invasion remained the question. Since these damned Ly Kai had proven several times over that they could steal a body, maybe it thought it could secure one on the other side of the gate. Which was fine by Tobin. As long as it didn't come back here.

He edged closer to Frax's back, knowing he had to time his attack perfectly, before the tarmeuth ripped her and Frax, and everyone else here to shreds. If Bithzielp escaped, the rest—closing the gate against his return or to stop a new invasion—was up to Kaphri.

Frax's eyes were locked on the floor before him, the muscles in his back tensed. Blood streamed from his left shoulder. Still, Tobin was sure his brother was prepared to act. Which created a problem. His plan was to use Frax's crouched body as a springboard to launch himself high enough up the tarmeuth's back to drive his blade into the animal's brain through its eye. It was an impossible approach. If Frax twisted and threw him off balance or mentally reacted, the tarmeuth might move and ruin his aim, but he couldn't warn him. The being who possessed the cat wielded a level of telepathy far above any Geffitz, and the slightest brush of communication might reveal his presence.

Still, a bigger problem: when to act? Trapping and slaying Bithzielp inside the cat in the same way the cursed Balandran had killed Araxis was extremely unlikely to succeed, but anticipating when Kaphri would open the gate to rid their world of this threat ranked only one notch below it. Meanwhile, the cursed Grimmen waited, stone silent, in his mind. Tobin's lips tightened. If he died, he hoped the Grimmen would save Uri so he could tell their story, even if he had to tell it across the barrier. Failing that, someone in the distant future would have to interpret their version of events from where their bones lay.

Unless the Balandra ate their flesh and scattered their remains...

Distraction! He tightened his grip on Seuliac's blade, his outrage vanishing as he scanned what little he could see of the balconies above without moving his head. The winged devils were waiting. They had to be. They didn't dare risk distracting Bithzielp any more than he did.

Damned fog! It was beginning to drift down from the heights above. If it reached the floor, it would complicate any fight.

He lifted his body cautiously to survey his path up the cat's back. Damn, the thing was big. But not big enough to stop him from taking it down.

The rainbow colors reflecting off the arena walls abruptly fell to a steady white glow. He froze, his eyes sweeping the area to re-evaluate the situation. The tarmeuth had not flinched, so the shift was a part of the process. He finally spotted his cousin standing in the light at the far edge of the gate, spear gripped in his hand. Not an ideal weapon for a warrior standing out in the open when this situation went down. Regrettable.

Tobin located the Priestess at what must be the center of the gate. Holy Kep! With the falling off of color, things had changed over there. A massive arch of light divided the arena. Bits of buildings and people were visible on its other side.

His anger rippled. None of them would set foot across that break—

The Priestess was speaking to them, and he knew, somehow, that she had not yet opened the final way.

He wished he had a telepathic link to her, to know what she was saying. It might enable him to time his attack better.

Any more delay, however, might close his moment of opportunity. He must act before the tarmeuth killed them all. Before the Balandra rained death down on them. Before the Ly Kai... No. Bithzielp would not set the animal on people entering this world, which meant the bastard did intend to leave and any living thing within the cat's range on this side would die.

Tobin had to keep the Priestess alive for her to seal the gate.

It was over Frax's back, then, to plunge his blade into the tarmeuth's brain.

It was the Ly Kai youth she had seen when she jumped to the edge of the woods for the first time. But instead of mockingly triumphant, now his eyes were cold and calculating. Observing her the way Seuliac did.

Perhaps the warlord had been correct in thinking she might have changed the future by returning to them on the mountainside. Or the time did not match yet. The youth would have no memory of something that had not yet happened or would ever happen if she could prevent it.

He did not intimidate her. Realizing what he was, did. When she broke the final barrier between their worlds, Bithzielp would take this child.

At the same time, she didn't dare ignore the previous warning from her jump forward. This youth might be more of a foe than Bithzielp.

"You," he said, his gaze raking over her. "What trash do you purport to be? You bring shame on the Ly Kai with your appearance."

Her hair. Uri had twisted, braided, and beaded it in Geffitzi fashion. She looked nothing like the carefully coiffed styles she saw across the gate.

"I am allied with people I admire."

His eyes swept the area behind her. "Really?"

Kaphri fought the urge to look back. Did light from the gate hide the lone figure of Uri behind her? She must stand in stark contrast to the mass gathered around and behind the boy.

"Enough of this. Break the veil between the worlds and open the gate!" Bithzielp's demand stabbed her thoughts.

The boy's eyes widened with sudden hunger. "He is here!"

The white-robed children stirred with excitement while the Shades, murmuring anticipation, pressed tighter around them. The Freya-born counsel, in contrast, moved further apart.

She'd seen a similar reaction in the Geffitz warriors when they felt under threat.

"Let the Geffitz warriors go. All of them. Now," Kaphri told Bithzielp.

"Perhaps you need a reminder of who is in charge here."

Do not react, her brain screamed. She closed her eyes. *"Then implant the urge in the tarmeuth for it to leave this place immediately and return to its lair."*

"If you act quickly enough, perhaps you can ensure some of your rabble have a chance at escape."

Grief tried to flood in. If she opened the way to the Homeworld, Frax would die, but his world would be safe—which was the Grimmen's sole purpose in forcing her to this place.

She was meant to die here, too. It was the same as the Wyxa's original purpose in locking Gemma in the Guardian Stone. The Winisp had carried the crystal to the heart of the Black Temple and sacrificed himself and Gemma to lock evil away. Things were coming full circle. When this battle ended, she would shed her blood at the center of the gate and seal it with the Guardian Stone to finish the task.

Unjust! Unfair! Her brain protested. But so was the loss of the warriors' lives around her. The value of it lay in their success at stopping Bithzielp.

Sorrow ripped through her. The vanity! Her previous thoughts of self-sacrifice appeared so shallow and vain. This time it was real and she had no input. We do what we must do: the warrior mantra. Kaphri shrugged away regret. Like her companions, she would accept her fate with eyes open and her back straight as she met her foe.

Focused. For now, she must hide the presence of the crystal. *"Does that child know what you plan to do to him?"* Her fingers went to the knife secured at her waist. Death might be a more merciful fate for the boy, but her blade was not for him...

"I know the honor being bestowed upon me," the boy interrupted. *"And I see you for what you are. An accident of birth. A simple tool to be used and discarded. You are an ignorant savage with no respect for your heritage or the Ly Kai's place in the universe. Do as you are bidden, vermin."*

Vermin!

Her flash of fury vanished under an immense ripple of emotion. A mixture of fear from some and rising triumph from others across the gate swirled over her. It was not difficult to distinguish the sources. The Freyan Council members radiated dread and horror, as if suddenly understanding their precarious situation, while the Shades and their charges burned with hungry exhilaration. The ever-increasing crowd that filled the enclosed space behind them seethed with confusion. The wild emotions, so unlike the control she'd been taught, were disorienting. But one thought cut through the chaos: if she refused to do what he ordered, Bithzielp would remain here to torment the Geffitzi world.

Whichever choice she made, she and Frax would die. She just had to live long enough to close the gate. The warriors were simply the diversion she needed in order to do that.

She clenched her hand to resist taking up the crystal—she and her beloved Gemma would become guardians to Kep's world. It was not the most terrible fate she could imagine, especially if Frax...

"You will pass through the gate immediately and never return," she told him, her sending rigid. In the deeper, private part of her mind rage and sorrow shrieked despair.

"I have no desire to linger here one second longer than necessary," Bithzielp snapped.

Liar, her mind whispered. His essence churned with hatred and the desire for revenge. He might go to the Homeworld to wreak havoc, but he would return here eventually to take his revenge.

She had come here driven by the threat to Frax's life, but she could not save him. He had warned her this might happen, and he had ordered her to act for the greater good of his world...

"Do it, for Kep's sake, Kaphri!" Frax's angry sending ripped her mind.

"It is done." She blasted the mental warning out to Bithzielp, the warriors, the Wyxa, and the Grimmen's forces as she seized the power of Arylla and punched her hand, palm outward, against the invisible membrane dividing their two worlds.

Who had she just condemned to death?

Chapter 106
Gold-clad Star

BITHZIELP BURNED WITH anticipation as he demanded she open the final portal, and Kaphri had reached the end of her delays.

Frax stared at the sweat and blood smearing his thighs and waited. The Priestess was fulfilling her part of their bargain. Not their ideal solution, but one he could rest with. It would have been nice to have more time, to be able to tell his people what he'd learned of their origins. Maybe. Or maybe he would have remained silent about it. Was the shock and horror worth the confusion and curiosity it would create? No matter. He was destined to take it to his grave.

That was only one of his regrets. His heart gave a hard squeeze. He wanted Tobin, Uri, and Seuliac to make it out of here alive. He also wished the situation had allowed him to be gentler with the Priestess. The memory of soft lips and a slim body pressed tightly to his still sent a shot of heat into his loins. But more, respect for her uncomplaining, stalwart companionship filled him with a sense of pride. She would have been a worthy partner with whom to share a future—even Tesla would have to agree on that. He would have liked to tell Kaphri he wanted to try... But she'd made her scorn clear enough.

Bithzielp had made sure that he had experienced Velacy's downfall and the triumph of Araxis' defeat. Frax resented the death of a fellow warrior, but Velacy had made the necessary sacrifice. So, one small triumph for their people.

A quiver ran through his muscles. His body was shutting down from shock. Not an option. He struggled to hold a focus on the pain in his shoulder, to use it to keep his brain clear. He was failing. Failing them all. Bithzielp would kill him if he attempted communication with any of the others. Neither would the damned Ly Kai bastard allow him any relief from his tormented sense of helplessness. The cursed demon kept him in the telepathic loop, forcing him to hear everything in the exchange with the Priestess, exacerbating his sense of being the point on which this all pivoted.

It was time to end this.

"Do it, for Kep's sake, Kaphri!" Frax snarled.

A sudden weight slammed between his shoulders, driving him down as the tarmeuth's body went rigid beside him.

"For Cadarn!" Tobin's mental cry blasted. And *"Roll."* Directed at him as the weight lifted, feet shoving Frax away from the cat with the momentum.

The cat surged upward with a roar, its hind claws slashing Frax's thigh as it sent him rolling in a spray of blood.

Tobin made a swift, silent prayer to the Goddess. The cat was a magnificent animal, and it was not through its desire that it was a threat here. Like him, circumstances sometimes put one in a difficult place. But everything had to die sometime. Today was simply the tarmeuth's day.

"Do it—" The young warrior was already moving before Frax's message to Kaphri blasted in his awareness.

"For Cadarn!" Tobin mentally whooped. And *"Roll,"* as his feet struck Frax's back and he used his brother's body to launch onto the crouching tarmeuth. He hit the giant cat's bony spine hard, the

impact driving the air from his lungs. He slid on its coarse fur, dropping lower, then clamped his knees desperately for traction as bone and muscle bunched and glided beneath him, nearly throwing him off the animal's back as it surged to its feet.

The lithe body twisted, slashing at the thing clinging to its shoulders.

Four-inch claws missed Tobin's kneecap by a hair's breadth as horror at his own audacity shot through him. Too late to second-guess his actions now. He grabbed the cat's left ear and slammed his elbow into the back of the tarmeuth's neck, thrusting himself upward to drive his knife down toward the tarmeuth's eye.

The blade struck bone and skated sideways to lodge at the edge of the socket.

Kep! His mind screamed outrage at his bungled action as the tarmeuth twisted and fell on its side. Pain shrieked through his body as, twisting and grinding, the cat rolled to pin him beneath it. Teeth tore the leather of his pants and grazed his calf.

The tarmeuth roared as if fired by the scent of flesh and blood. Tobin lost his hold on the cat's ear when the animal fell on him, but he still gripped the knife haft, his right arm stretched to its physical limit. Ignoring the pain, Tobin thrust his left forearm beneath the tarmeuth's jowl and levered himself back toward the cat's head. The blade broke free with the shift in his weight, and he swung, plunging it into the side of the animal's neck over and over as the full weight of the animal writhed over him.

Tobin Kitahn was insane.

It was the only way the warlord could describe the scene playing out in the arena beyond him as the tarmeuth surged upward on its hind legs and fell back on the younger warrior. And the whole time, Tobin was crawling up the animal's back. Then the warrior dislodged the blade and began flinging blood in wild, dark arcs across the space.

Seuliac launched two quick arrows into the animal's haunch to add distraction and dived out into the arena.

Damn! The cat's hind claws had flung Frax closer to the gate and further out of his reach. Seuliac lunged out, trying to catch a foot and drag him back into the passage. His fingers grazed the other's ankle. Before he could make a second attempt, a muffled sound forced him to spin about. Two Balandra, arrows trained on him, now occupied the tunnel he'd just left.

They didn't attack.

Realization hit him: the gray men weren't worried about him. They were holding their limited supply of arrows to use on the tarmeuth if Tobin failed to eliminate it. Only if the scout was successful would he come under attack.

How annoying for the warlord of Rhynog to be written off so easily.

Priorities! Kitahn, sprawled lifelessly, was currently the safest of them, and Seuliac had no place to drag him.

He shouldered the bow and pulled his blade.

The cat was biting and slashing, with the younger Kitahn still clinging to it as it mercilessly ground him into the floor beneath its weight. A hot splat of blood sprayed Seuliac's arm as he dived for the animal's exposed belly. A thrashing leg slammed him, throwing him aside, the knife clattering from his hand as the animal's roar tapered to a throaty rattle and the mighty limbs fell to weak jerks.

Tobin Kitahn had done it!

Now the warlord had two Kitahns to rescue. Before the Balandra could react, he squirmed up beside Tobin. The younger warrior's body was firmly pinned beneath the cat's weight.

"Is it dead?"

"Yes. But we have a new battle on our hands." Seuliac fired two quick shots over the mound of the tarmeuth's body and watched the Balandra crumple. Now he had more weapons—if he could get to them. He scurried forward, jerked Tobin's blade free of the cat's neck, and pressed it into the scout's hand. "I can't move this thing off you right now—"

"Leave me." Tobin grasped his forearm. "Get Frax to safety and finish this. Someone has to tell our people what happened here."

"That's Caspani's job." Seuliac looked down. His hand was braced flat in a pool of blood. He brought it up to press, palm down, across Tobin's face, leaving a red handprint. The mark of a true warrior.

Tobin gave a huff of pained amusement.

The tarmeuth's body vanished.

Wyxa? The Wyxa were saving a tarmeuth, but they wouldn't stop what was happening here? Damn them! The swamp dwellers had left them exposed—

A Balandran plummeted out of the creeping fog. Seuliac twisted, drawing his stiletto and throwing himself sideways to shield Tobin. "Kitahn—" His back hit stone floor.

Tobin was gone, too.

The spear plunged toward his belly.

Kep damn it! The warlord raked out with a foot, slamming the creature's ankle and causing it to redirect the weapon to keep from falling forward. The metal tip skittered on the floor, toppling the gray man sideways. Seuliac slashed out, plunging his thin blade beneath the edge of the gray man's ribs.

It shrieked and stumbled away.

Seuliac heaved to his feet, looked about, and swore. Frax Kitahn was stumbling a bloody trail toward Kaphri and the gate.

The weapons or Kitahn?

Seuliac dived for the weapons.

They still had an immense fight on their hands and as long as they were up and moving they might succeed yet.

Chapter 107
Seeking a Path Through Darkness

THE TARMEUTH'S ROAR broke the suffocating silence of the arena, jerking Uri's attention away from the activity on the Ly Kai world. The cat hurled itself backward onto the arena floor, thrashing furiously, teeth snapping as it ground its back against the surface.

Tobin, Uri thought, stunned. Only Tobin Kitahn would dare take on an animal that ferocious in close combat. Was Bithzielp trapped inside the creature? Not likely. But— Uri's attention snapped to the mound of flesh, barely visible in the white glow, lying between the writhing cat and the gate. He saw Seuliac snatch for Frax's foot before being forced to turn and focus on the Balandra peering from the darkness of a portal behind him. The Warlord dived for the tarmeuth.

A pale flicker of movement. An arm, then a leg moved and, to Uri's disbelief, Frax pushed up off the white surface.

An arrow whipped past, barely missing Uri's shoulder, and his flash of relief evaporated. He was under attack. The stars and sky above had been replaced by dense fog and Balandra were plunging through it. He and the other warriors were all out in the arena, fully exposed. A blast of unfamiliar fury rolled out from the direction of the gate, and he saw Kaphri take a step back. Whatever was happening over there, her safety was out of his hands.

The tip of a wing broke the mist above him. Vanished. A clawed foot slashed and was gone.

The Wyxa at work? Perhaps, but now Balandra were pouring through the floor-level openings around the arena.

Kep! His back was placed toward one of those passages.

He spun, makeshift spear readied, to find a stream of Cyrwins charging out of the opening, pouring into the area.

One warrior was not much defense against that surge of muscle and venom stampeding toward him, but he might delay and distract them a bit. Bitter irony, his thoughts flashed, that he would die by the order of a force that should have been an ally.

The smells, the sounds, the mental wave of Ly Kai communication slammed Kaphri.

Had it happened? Her brain screamed. Had Bithzielp crossed between the worlds? Turn now. Save Frax!

If she could scoop up the tarmeuth, Suspend it in the air. Encase it in power. Teleport it out of the temple—!

Despite the ripping desire to turn, she had to focus on the greater task of closing this gate before Bithzielp could stop her. And when she closed it, she would seal it with her blood and with the Guardian Stone, to end the threat.

She must—

"What have you done?" A shriek ripped from the Ly Kai boy's throat. He pitched to his knees and lifted his arms, his hands constricted into claws before him.

"My Lord," the head Shade stammered. "I... We prepared the candidate—"

The boy's head snapped around, eyes fastening on the man. "They were not to walk the Paths of Power. My orders were clear!"

The Shade looked terrified and confused. "It would be such an inconvenience for you when we could have him fully prepared."

"You fools!" The force controlling the youth clambered awkwardly to his feet. "No Arylla-born who walks the Paths can enter the Corridor of the Worlds! It was the final safeguard Hredroth put into place!"

The color blanched from the faces of the white and gray-clad Ly Kai. "But... We thought—"

The boy dropped lifelessly onto the gate.

One of the older candidates, a girl, cried out in terror, then collapsed in the same way, her body quivering. Another of the older boys cried out and fell.

The first boy came back to life, jerking disjointedly to his feet. A faint mental cry for help brushed Kaphri's mind as his face contorted with an expression of fury no Ly Kai should have the facial muscles to form. "All the candidates? What have you done?" he roared.

Reality snapped in around her. Whatever was going on, having walked the Paths of Power appeared fundamental to it. She needed to act now, during this distraction.

"You will wait!" The boy's eyes fastened on her.

Kaphri's muscles locked.

He stumbled around to face the Shades. "You thought you could trap and manipulate me."

"Milord, no! We would never—"

But they had. Kaphri read it in the way they flinched at his accusation.

Memory of the Twenty-Six flashed in her mind. Were all Ly Kai so hungry for power? Did everything their world was based on, with the Hierarch of Power and Birthstars, cultivate that?

"You are unfit to serve Arylla!" Bithzielp threw back his head, his spine rigid, and starpower rolled from him in a massive, invisible wave.

The Shades fell lifelessly to the floor.

The crowd along the rear edge of the gate erupted in panic. People at the rear ran out of the temple opening. But Ly Kai near the front only looked on in terror and confusion while Bithzielp, controlling the boy's body, stared down at the victims of his wrath. The younger candidates whimpered in terror as they huddled together. Their youth and their child-mindblocks had likely saved them from his deadly wrath for the moment. They still might prove useful to him.

The disturbance of telepathy battering the air was almost overwhelming as Bithzielp clumsily lurched the boy's body around to face Kaphri.

She fought to retake control of her movements, but a coil of Arylla's power, dark and hardened with Bithzielp's malice, wrapped around her, squeezing like a serpent's tail. It constricted, burning with his rage as she struggled to break it.

Close the gate! Her thoughts screamed. But neither her body nor her mind responded.

"Surely you did not think I would let you live to stand between me and my revenge for that cursed world behind you?" The words were sharp and hard. "I would slaughter you here and use your blood to hold the gate open, but these fools have robbed me of that pleasure. You are contaminated filth, but, as I have been forced to do for ages, I will make use of what is available until I can create better..."

No! He would use her to destroy the last bits of everything she cared about.

Caring was not too much; it was the only thing.

She mentally writhed, prying at the bonds holding her immobile. They squeezed tighter.

Then, realization flashed. Bithzielp had just confirmed what she had suspected: her blood held the power to affect a gate. She had not stepped forward onto the Homeworld, and her mind and her power still belonged to her. In the reverse of his plan, she could call down the whole might of Arylla, then lose control, letting it burn through her. It would be the last thing she ever did, but she was wearing the Guardian Stone. It, and Gemma, would fall to the gate with whatever remained of her when her star was done, sealing it in the same way the Winisp had in the Black Temple.

Her beloved Gemma would be imprisoned again, and the barrier would never come down on the Geffitzi world, but she and the tiny dragon would end Bithzielp's reign of terror for them.

"Forgive me," she whispered as she dropped all resistance and drew down Arylla's power. She channeled it through her body, driving it into the gate beneath her feet.

Blinding light flared, and a terrible, massive cold struck her.

The horrified screams of the remaining crowd tore at her ears, and her muscles jerked as the bonds holding her body evaporated.

She was not dead. Stunned, Kaphri tried to collect her awareness.

So cold... She had only experienced the deathless, searing sensation twice before—once on the tower heights, when she had stepped from the edge of the abyss into total darkness and found herself floating in a sea of stars. And only moments before, when she had fully claimed her Birthstar.

Now she saw the break between the two gates, a third space somehow impossibly occupying another section of the gate, and the shock of what she had done pushed her mind into churning chaos.

"Impossible!" Bithzielp's disbelief broke through her stunned horror. *"You can access—? All this time, I thought you had walked—"* He slammed against her mental barriers, clawing and tearing at them. Ranting. *"All this time, I could have— You were right before me!"*

Burning pain pierced her brain behind the bone of her forehead as he struck with a rabid force. He was stronger than anything she'd ever encountered, and he would break her mindshields.

"No!" As Bithzielp's control over him shifted, the boy regained control of his body. "I am the chosen one! I am the one destined to serve you!" Hands grasping for Kaphri, he threw himself forward.

One of his fingers tangled in the chain around her neck, ripping it free.

"Gemma!" Kaphri watched in horror as the crystal and chain flew out into a background of stars and night sky.

She snatched out to capture the necklace, but the boy went rigid and toppled against her, knocking her off balance.

"You fool!" Bithzielp roared as she tumbled out behind it.

Idiot! The thought flashed in Frax's mind, but he had no time to devote to his brother. This was the moment to make the most of Tobin's sacrifice.

The sear of tarmeuth claws raking his thigh sent him spiraling into the edge of darkness. It might have been a gift from Kep—an offer of blessed oblivion so he would not feel the killing blow, but he would not take it. He was alive, and there was a battle still to be won.

For a moment, he lay on his belly, fighting for strength, staring through the sheeting light of the gate at a mob of pale people. They were all beautiful. Delicate—like her.

But she was not delicate. She was the fighter who stood beside him at the worst times in their travels without complaint. And he was not ready to lose her.

Scrabbling awkwardly like some half-squashed insect, he crawled toward the lighted surface of the gate. It was not the worst pain he'd ever felt, he told himself. Something caught at his ankle, but he pulled away from it. If the cat seized him in its crushing jaws, he was finished. Other than that, nothing was going to stop him now. His thrusting toes slipped in fluid, sending him sprawling flat on the glowing surface. He pushed up to his hands and knees, unaware of the dark smears shrouding the dazzling light in his wake. Ahead of him, the Priestess stood framed in the arch of the gate. Beyond her lay the Ly Kai world and a mass of people, their eyes locked on her. Closer stood a half-circle of white-robed youths. White robes. She had told him the significance of those things. They were the garb worn by candidates of power.

One of the white-robed figures, taller than her but bald, so, male, was stepping forward to face her. Cold terror seized Frax. Should he risk mental contact with her? Bithzielp was on the attack, and Kaphri had no idea what he was planning to do.

A blast of familiar mental fury ripped the air, and the boy collapsed at Kaphri's feet.

Something in the situation had not suited the Ly Kai monster. Injured and weaponless, Frax could not help Tobin, but he knew what the bodiless being was capable of. If the Geffitzi had truly crossed this gate once, they—he—could cross it again...

Murderous fury and death whipped through his mind, directed at the beings on the other side of the gate, and cries of terror and despair rang out. The smaller, white-robed Ly Kai were dropping limply. The children. The bastard was killing them!

The Priestess seemed to stiffen and the gate blazed with light, blinding Frax. Heat whipped across his skin. She was calling up starpower like she had never done before. He did not have to feel the answering burst of fury to know how Bithzielp was responding. The boy who had confronted her jerked back to life and surged to his feet while screaming in a mental rage. He reached for her. Fell forward.

Kaphri vanished.

The crash of the battle behind him rolled over Frax.

He was useless to that fight. But someone else, the person who had risked everything to come here, who might save their world, still needed him.

Chapter 108
And Warrior of Forest and Blood

INFINITY.

It was the only thing that came to mind. Nothing lay between her and the universe to the left, above, or below. The stars of the Hierarch were lost, mingled with millions of other stars, all their brilliant lights like cold needles piercing her skin. The sense of immenseness was a roar inside her bones. Veils of light wove a glowing lacework of colors through dark and clotted clouds in other areas. All of it moved, but at an ageless pace she would never see.

In terrifying contrast, a row of immense gray slabs, thick-walled and spaced at regular intervals like vertical pages from a book, loomed on her right. They stretched into the distance to both sides of the blazing gap that was the Ly Kai Homeworld. Gates, her stunned brain told her. They were the gates of other worlds. Some blazed with light between their walls. Some flickered feebly, while others sat dark. All ordered and uniform, fading with distance above a path of scattered, glittering crystals, a concentrated strand of star shards, that unfurled past their gaping front edges. The massive, light-absorbing surface of the walls reared to vanish into the void while the dark slabs continued, curving away into infinity.

Kaphri's stomach lurched when she became aware of the stillness that held the space. Then, her hearing adjusted to the rushing whispers, faint taps, pings, and snaps that were the pitched sounds of the universe. Her body seemed to synch with the chorus as it swelled, then faded into the background of her awareness.

Her skin still tingled.

Starpower? She tried to focus on the sensation. Within seconds, it became so intense that it threatened to engulf her.

Mercifully, a bigger issue pulled her attention away. Where was she? And, even more important, how could she stop Bithzielp from triumphing and destroying the Geffitzi world?

Cyrwins swarmed past Uri.

But they didn't attack him.

A distinct, trumpeting cry—one he had only heard imitated around campfires by the oldest Geffitz warriors—pierced his ears. There was no mistaking the battle flute of the Cyrwins, though fireside imitations held no comparison to the real, shrill and terrible sound.

"Tend to what is required of you, Warrior." The harsh order dropped into his mind as the Cyrwins swept forward, their wicked, barbed tails slashing at the sudden horde of gray men plummeting through the swirl of fog above.

Tend to—? Kep! Kaphri and Frax! He twisted back toward the glow of the Ly Kai gate just in time to see the Kitahni commander, streaming blood, pause on the edge of the blazing arch.

His cousin lifted a hand and passed it through the space between worlds, then stumbled forward, across to the Ly Kai Homeworld.

No, no, no... Uri ran into the radiating light, across the glowing star symbols.

The young man lay collapsed on the Ly Kai side of the gate, eyes wide in a death stare.

Bithzielp's work? It certainly hadn't taken him long to begin his rampage.

Over on the Homeworld side, the few straggling Ly Kai disappeared out the far opening into what was obviously a city.

A cluster of people dressed in pale blue robes remained. They stared at him as if immobilized with terror. Did they know the truth of what he was? Did it matter?

Where was Bithzielp?

The more important question: where was Kaphri?

The ancient Ly Kai bastard said the world on the other side of this gate was the actual place of Geffitzi origin. Was it a lie? Frax lifted a hand, feeling a tingle as his flesh passed through the unresisting invisible divide.

He took a staggering step across worlds.

The cluster of people dressed in blue seemed to mentally flounder as they gasped in disbelief.

"Do not interfere," he fired at them. As if he could do anything to them in his current state... But that was not the issue. *"Where is she?"*

The woman who stood at the front lifted a trembling hand and pointed to his left just as his eye caught the impossible corner of the night sky that had not been visible from the Geffitzi side of the gate.

This cannot exist, his brain whispered as he stared into the vast space wedged between the edges of the two worlds. Out there, along one side, a row of massive gray slabs tapered into the distance

The opening seemed to widen as it locked his attention, drawing him in.

Impossible. The Corridor of the Worlds did not exist, his brain screamed.

But it did exist. And Kaphri was out there in the vastness, bathed in its terrible light.

Her terror tore at his sudden awareness. Bithzielp was trying to wrest control of her mind. She was fighting, her struggle mentally blazing as she tried to fend him off. Frax had to help her, but he was a distraction she did not need.

For a moment, everything dimmed as a wave of lightheadedness washed over him. He caught his balance, but not before he saw the red smears on the white surface around his feet.

"You. What are you, and why are you here?" The Ly Kai woman in pale blue robes slammed the question into his brain.

"Don't interfere. I'm here for the girl." The rest of them could rot in hell.

"You have a bond with her?"

"What?" Everything around him wobbled.

Were the Ly Kai attacking...? But no, it was his body that faltered.

"Do you have a mental bond with her?" The woman sent with sharp impatience.

"With her. Not with the rest of you."

"Don't be a fool. You can save both our worlds from a terrible fate by bringing her back. We need her to protect us from them!"

That wasn't right, he thought hazily. But then, she might not know the truth, that Hredroth had closed their Homeworld to any Arylla-born who did not return before his deadline. Bithzielp could not pass back to the Homeworld from the Corridor.

Unless he used Kaphri's form!

The woman stepped in front of Frax and planted her hand on his chest. *"Your pain distracts you. I can block it briefly, but I cannot aid your weakening body."*

He grasped her wrist to wrench it away.

"Don't dismiss my help." Her eyes burned with a fierce intensity as she stared into his. *"We are not all ignorant fools."*

He nearly collapsed as his pain vanished.

"You are dying. Act quickly! Bring her back from the Corridor of Worlds before the retribution he earned catches up with him and destroys us all."

He did not need her words. Bithzielp would never touch his world—or the woman he loved—again.

A poorly timed admission, he thought. He had badgered and tormented her to no end by testing her mental blocks after they had captured her in Omurda. But he had also learned something of the way her defenses worked. Perhaps if he added a reinforcing layer of resistance over them to give her time to physically return to this world...

He reached out, touching her mind, and horror rolled over him.

Kaphri was losing her battle.

A Balandran slammed into the warlord, sending him sprawling to the floor. The creature landed on its feet despite the force of the impact and, with a smirk, angled its spear to skewer him.

A quick roll to one side was not going to save Seuliac at such close range.

Something dark whipped the air above him, striking the gray body across the chest, flinging it to crumple against the wall.

The sound of hooves clacked stone near the warlord's shoulder.

A Cyrwin.

Well, this was a humiliating way to die after all the work they'd put into this whole thing. Still, he refused to fold and die in silence. *"Watch where you put your damned big feet!"* he snapped.

"You cannot win this battle from your backside, Aedec." The thick cord of black tail, flecked with droplets of blood, snaked the air above his belly and hung there, unmoving.

The warlord looked up. *"Really?"* He caught the Cyrwin's tail and let it hoist him back onto his feet. *"Don't tell me this was the plan all along."*

"The plan was to kill you. It has changed. Shall we rejoin this glorious fray as brothers in arms?"

"How long before I have to watch my back again?"

"Your distrust in us is acknowledged as well-merited. This world, however," Demon Tongue's barbed tail lashed out, slicing a Balandran's wing and sending the creature spiraling, *"belongs to both Kep's First and Kep's Second Children."*

"Ha." The warlord caught up a Balandran spear. *"Then let's finish this."*

The Cyrwin did not move. Seuliac looked over to discover it had lifted its rear leg as a mounting boost for a rider.

Gray eyes met red eyes. *"You would carry an Aedec in battle?"*

The Cyrwin gave a mental shrug. *"Carrying the Warlord of Rhynog in this battle will elevate my status."*

Damned right it would! Seuliac gave a short, hard laugh. Without proper trappings, he wouldn't maintain a seat on this creature's slippery back for long during its rigorous battle moves, but, what the hell. He stepped on the proffered leg and launched onto the animal's back.

Chapter 109
Earth And Sky Shall Bind

THE STARS...

The scale he sensed when his eyes raked the space before him tried to blank his thoughts.

But that was not his focus. Frax locked eyes on Kaphri. Interfering mentally or physically would only distract and weaken her resistance. How could he help in her battle?

A glint of light caught his attention.

No! He would not be distracted by— Holy Kep! Recognition shot through him. The Guardian Stone!

The crystal and chain were floating above the glittering path, out beyond the struggling girl.

How had she lost it? No matter. The Guardian Stone had held Bithzielp sealed in exile on another world for over two millennia. That cursed little Guardian was charged with protecting his world and it had left its place in the Black Temple to seek out Kaphri as a part of that charge. She needed Gemma to defeat Bithzielp.

That place beyond the lip of the gate was not the domain of the Geffitzi. But everything that mattered to him was tied up in that fiery little waif and her success.

Frax flung himself into the stars.

"I will have this form!" Bithzielp raged.

Inside her head. He was inside her head. Terror sent her mind nearly spiraling out of control.

Sensing weakness, he struck with renewed animal ferocity.

Her defenses were crumbling as Bithzielp's savagery tore at her mindshields, shredding her mental barriers faster than she could restore them. He did not intend to leave any last bit of her to resist him.

This was her body, her mind, her power! He would not take it! She needed to find reinforcing strength, but Arylla was not an option. Drawing on her star would create the bridge he needed to invade and possess her mind.

Kaphri screamed fear and loss into the vastness around her as invasive fingers of another's awareness plunged deep into her brain, driving surrender and despair into her mind. A last rational thought flashed: retreat. She could flee to the safe spot inside her head, that tightly shielded kernel where she had often sought refuge when Frax mentally stalked her in Omurda.

That would be the same retreat Rath and Ving had taken when they fled Araxis' invasion, and it would not do. Bithzielp would trap her there, a screaming prisoner in her own head, unable to stop his possession of her physical form as he destroyed everything she cared about.

She had never wanted to wield Arylla's true starpower, her mind protested. She would give it up now if she could. But that was not her choice to make. If she gave up—if Bithzielp stole her form—she would suffer endless death while he went on to use it to destroy the things she loved.

He'd already done that, her thoughts whispered. He had sacrificed Frax to the tarmeuth. He had killed all her friends, and he would eventually return to torment the Geffitzi world if she did not stop him here.

She was fighting her Birthstar while a more capable and less worthy user wielded it against her. The realization made her defenses surge. Arylla was her Birthstar. She was here, inside its domain, and she had the physical presence required to command it.

Bithzielp's maniacal laugh of triumph choked off as she seized the force tearing at her mind and wrenched it to a stop.

A heartbeat of much-needed relief flicked through her.

"Getting clever, are we?" The hated voice came back. *"Ignorant child. You think one tiny manipulation of power will save you? You hold the knowledge of an insect in the scale of Arylla's power. Your meager triumph has allowed you the one moment of distraction I needed to slip through your last defense. I am triumphant."* Crushing pain enfolded her as he seized her mental essence and began to peel away the last layers of her resistance.

A last thought: she could still release her control over Arylla and let its power consume her in this place of infinite stars. She dropped control and opened to her Birthstar.

A brilliant light burst in front of her and fire tore through her breastbone.

Geffitzi did not belong in the void of the night sky. But seconds ago, he had stepped onto another world beyond his own, so who knew where the line of impossibility lay? Kaphri needed the Guardian Stone, but it floated beyond her reach. Which made it his duty to bring it to her.

Kep, this place was not meant for living things. The cold was so hard and the silence so deep they nearly immobilized him. He fought to move further into the void, flailing his limbs in swimming motions, fighting the eerie resistance weighing him down. He sank, feet touching the glittering path. Searing cold ripped upward, but it did not lock him to the surface. He thrust up, projecting past the struggling Priestess, his hands reaching for the drifting necklace chain.

It was too far! His cry of desperation caught in his throat as his fingers slashed just short of the glittering links. Despair wrenched him as momentum carried him slowly downward. Too slow. He was sinking to the path again.

But the chain was also drifting down, stirred by the motion of his descending hand. The cold burned higher above his frozen feet, into his calves, when he struck the path again, but his eyes stayed locked on the crystal as he fought to turn and to get his legs beneath him for another leap.

Ruby droplets drifted across his field of vision—his blood, catching the ethereal light.

That was a lot of blood, his mind told him remotely as he bent his knees and launched his body upward again, fingers reaching for the glittering chain. The tips of his numb flesh pawed clumsily. Caught! The necklace tugged against his stiff fingers, and he folded his hand around it.

Now to get the Guardian Stone to Kaphri. He twisted, his body stretching from vertical to horizontal as he fought to change trajectory. This time, he thrashed his arms like wings, working to drive himself up and toward her.

It worked! Not well, but he was making headway.

Kaphri's arms were braced around her head—a defensive action, he was sure—but it made it impossible for him to drop the chain around her neck. And if she should strike out and knock it from his hand...

He twined the links around his fingers, trying to set the crystal against his palm. It clung to the lower outside of his hand against the bone, refusing to move, and he realized the chain was pulled too short for him to adjust it. Dull pain stabbed his wrist as he twisted it to position the crystal against the base of his hand.

Heat and choking gray smoke suddenly enveloped him.

"Warrior of Forest and Blood," The whisper, in a thousand voices, ran through his brain, jolting him with shock as the Guardian Stone contacted his flesh.

Really? He thought with a flash of fury. He and Kaphri were dying among the stars, but the Wyxa were always the manipulators. Still, if it successfully ended this, he would gladly play their game to the end. It remained for him to get the Guardian Stone to the *Star that flees the Even'sky*, in the Winisp's prediction. The crystal was solidly braced now and would make contact, which had to be enough.

He extended his arm, aiming for her breastbone where the thing had sat, snug and safe, from the night she had reclaimed it from the Wyxa, and prayed to Kep as he sluggishly bore in on her. His left arm curved to catch and hold her, so neither she nor Bithzielp could fight him or the crystal away.

With agonizing slowness, his hand moved forward and touched her chest.

Light blazed beneath his palm, and Kaphri went rigid, her mouth opening in a silent scream as he swept her up against him.

Uri's stomach lurched with horror. A trail of blood spatter, black flecks against glowing stone, marked Frax's passage across the gate. Kep, it was a lot of blood.

Yet, his cousin had managed to stumble over the line between the worlds.

On the other side, where a mass of people stood moments ago, now all that were left were the people dressed in pale blue and a cluster of lifeless bodies.

Dread at what else he would find there squeezed his heart as he stepped across the space that separated two worlds.

What he saw was even worse.

The blood pooled in one place a few steps inside where Frax had paused, then became spattered again as he had moved to the left. Into—

Holy Kep...

To his left, Frax and Kaphri were floating in a vast, star-filled void that was somehow placed beyond the bounds of both worlds. Kaphri had her arms clutched tightly about her head, her body contorted in what Uri recognized as a mental battle. And Frax... He was past her, straining to reach something. Their movements were so slow, agonizing seconds seeming to tick by as they hung there, locked in some terrible struggle.

A tiny glint of gold flashed. Before Uri's unbelieving eyes, his cousin caught it and curled back on himself, his body twisting to reverse his trajectory. His other hand was reaching for Kaphri.

The crystal! Of course. How had she lost it? No matter. Uri knew with gut instinct that she needed it to fight off Bithzielp's invasion of her mind and body.

Frax had actually reached her, palm leveled for the center of her chest. His hand, with the crystal, slowly impacted her body.

Blinding light flared.

Chapter 110
A Union Forged

SOMEWHERE FAR AWAY, bone and skin pressed her flesh, and a spark of warmth flickered. Living. Alive. A tiny point lanced deeper.

It thrummed with pent-up vitality like a storm against her skin.

It burst, forcing her backbone to arch backward as familiar strength rolled out, blasting through her body.

Gemma? Gemma had found her? The Guardian Stone—the thing the Wyxa had used to protect their world against Bithzielp's return? The thing she had twice taken and twice lost had returned to her?

Bithzielp screamed outrage and threw his whole force downward, grinding on the last of her mental shields.

Physical and mental agony warred with her heightening awareness. Kaphri loosened an arm and dropped a groping hand to grasp the Guardian Stone before Bithzielp could think to seize her physical movements.

The flesh backing the crystal was not hers, but, despite its chill, warmth flowed from the contact.

A sense of firm will surged to support her fight. *"He will not take you away from me,"* a thought whispered fiercely.

Frax? Impos—

"Listen! He can't return from the Corridor of Worlds without your body. Push him out and come back to me. Hredroth—"

A trick. How would Frax know—?

But he'd been held as Bithzielp's prisoner for three days. Perhaps the monster had revealed something—

"Geffitz scum! How dare you invade this place. You should be dead!" Enraged, Bithzielp slammed into the heart of her telepathy.

Manic claws of fury slashed at the last, thin layer of her mental refuge, focusing to one hard point to break her mindshields.

Kaphri cried out as the last of her mental resistance shredded.

But something else was unfolding inside her head, like a flower bud unfurling. It gently but relentlessly flowed outward over her tattered shields, coating and easing sheared connections and soothing the pain. *"Ask! There are ways we can protect you, but we cannot actively engage."*

The Wyxa. Of course! Ages ago, the Swampdwellers had sealed Gemma in the Guardian Stone and placed it on the gate in the Black Temple with the charge of protecting their world from Bithzielp's return. Then Gemma had abandoned the crystal to seek her out.

Because she was the only one with the power to protect their world from Bithzielp.

The Wyxa were here. And they could block starpower, even in this furnace of stars.

"Intruders?" Bithzielp screamed rage. *"This is the domain of Arylla-born. Of the Stars! Get out!"*

"Help me. Please."

Instantly, Gemma's will surged, shearing Arylla's power away from her.

"No!" Kaphri heaved and groped about, terrified. Arylla was gone, leaving only the evil force who was trying to steal her whole being away. But Bithzielp had also been reduced. Now, he was solely a seething mental presence, deprived of all ability to use his vast power against her. The struggle was reduced to a battle of will and desire. He had nothing but his hunger for power and revenge. Strong

motivations, but she fought for the existence of everyone and everything she loved.

What will you do? Seuliac's question whispered in her memory.

She gathered up every shred of her will. We do what we must do. Her fury blasted as she surged out of the shriveled, battered remnants of her last refuge. Mental forces slammed together, Kaphri pushing and slashing to reduce the intruding force into lesser, more manageable bits, which she ruthlessly continued to break down and discard.

"No!" Bithzielp tried to snatch his fragmented threads and reform them back into a whole. *"You can't— You don't know—"*

Kaphri's body lurched with shock and remote nausea as he tried to seize her mind. But his desperate action focused the last whisps of him into one concentrated place. She gathered the last bits of her mental strength and shoved him out.

Bithzielp shrieked fury as his bodiless, tattered essence burst out into the void. Evil threads of desperation lashed to regain a hold. Through dazed eyes, Kaphri caught the impression of a thin mist forming around an invisible, yet seething, core.

Exhaustion folded over her.

"Finish this, Warrior, before the approaching retribution destroys us all." She heard Gemma order Frax.

Frax caught strands of fiery red hair around stiff fingers and floundered with his free limbs to propel them back to the yawning opening of the Ly Kai. Eerily, the massive, blazing space between the dark, monolithic walls shrank in proportion and leveled with his approach. The last bits of intense cold were stealing away his body heat when his fingers crossed whatever invisible line marked the void from the Ly Kai Homeworld. He awkwardly thrust Kaphri's limp body forward and shoved it onto the white stone of the gate. Someone pulled her deeper in, out of his hands. Heat from the Homeworld tingled over the skin of his fingertips.

But the cold had taken its toll. His limbs, numb and club-like, refused to move anymore. His fingers grated, unfeeling, against the white surface as he drifted back into the Corridor of the Worlds.

A force slammed his failing brain, hot coils whipping inside his skull. *"Geffitz! Touch the girl's flesh."*

If he reached back across the edge of the gate to touch Kaphri, the bastard would use the link to return to the Homeworld.

Ironic, Frax thought, how that sudden frantic blaze of fury inside his head contrasted to the dull cold that gripped his body. He could no longer move his muscles.

"Do it, Geffitz!" Bithzielp shrilled. *"You can live. I'll let you go back to your world. I will never go there again, I swear it. Just touch the girl!"*

The lie didn't even merit a comment as Frax's last finger slipped off the lip of the gate.

A remote sensation tugged at his wrist.

"No." Frax protested. He couldn't—

"The hell you say!" Uri's snarled.

"You must touch her!" Bithzielp shrieked madly. *"Touch her!"*

The ancient Ly Kai's cry peeled out of Frax's head as Uri dragged his cousin out of the Corridor of the Worlds.

Chapter 111
That Will Span All Worlds and Time

THEIR FLESH WAS SO cold. Uri's heart twisted with panic. If either of them had a pulse, it was too faint for him to detect. He wasn't leaving them here, regardless.

For the first time, he noticed the flutter of golden wings on his shoulder. "Damn you!" he swore. "I'll be eating dragon today if this doesn't end well."

Gemma did not reply.

"She must withdraw her starpower from the Corridor Gate! Tell her!" A frantic sending blasted into his mind.

He looked over to discover a cluster of Ly Kai staring at him. Their calm expressions belied the sense of terror in the sending.

Why were they all so damned beautiful?

"Tell her!" The sending rose to a frantic pitch. The female at the front of the group gestured at the slice of night sky from which he had pulled Frax. When Uri looked back into the void he saw a tiny flicker of movement far down the glittering pathway.

A raging ball of chaotic lightning was rushing toward them. It didn't look like something any living thing would survive an encounter with.

How the hell was Kaphri supposed to stop that? She was unconscious.

He'd been sure all his emotions were exhausted, but not so.

The ball of light was drawing nearer.

Well, if he was going to die, it would be on his world. He caught Frax and Kaphri's wrists and, leaving a wide swath of fresh blood smeared over the drying trail of Frax's earlier passage, dragged them back to the gate.

Just another step...

"Uri." Fingers twitched against the inside of his wrist. *"Uri, let me go."* Kaphri twisted weakly.

"No, dammit, we're going home."

"You must," the woman behind him protested. *"If she does not close the Corridor Gate, the vengeance of what is approaching will destroy us all."*

"You. Not us." Uri tried to resecure his grip on Kaphri, but she had slid out of reach and was trying to stand.

"Take Frax home, Uri. I must finish this or Bithzielp will destroy both our worlds with his downfall."

Gemma lifted away from him, fluttering to her old position on Kaphri's shoulder as the girl shakily regained her feet.

Cold reason burned unpleasantly in Uri: if the Guardian was choosing to stay, Kaphri must be correct in her assessment that more had to be done.

"Damn it all to hell. Just come back to us," he growled as he lifted Frax to his shoulder and stumbled beneath the glowing arch back to the Geffitz world.

"You must close the Corridor Gate!" The Freyan High One cried again. *"You can't let them through."*

Them? Kaphri drew a shallow breath and turned her head toward the second gate. A seething ball of light was growing massively as it sped along the glittering way toward them. That was something from outside the Homeworld. The question wafted dully in her mind: how much more damage had the Ly Kai done?

Destroying both their worlds might be Bithzielp's last vengeful act.

She had opened access to the Corridor by driving Arylla's full power into the center of the gate connecting their two worlds. It had been an act of desperation gone terribly awry. But the new opening was still a gate, no matter how horrifically vast. It could be closed.

It would not be simple or random, however. Arylla's power raged around her, unnoticed until that moment. But now...now she became aware of the terrible force she had unleashed. It had not required this blasting, buffeting level of power to activate the gate between their two worlds. This monstrosity was her creation. This was a draw of starpower like nothing she had ever imagined, created by her fear and her desire to break the gate.

Bithzielp had seemed struck beyond delight by her action—enough to shift all his focus onto her. Meaning this fearsome level of power was not an unknown ability to him or the Arylla-born.

But Frax had said Bithzielp could not return across the portal without using her form. The ancient Ly Kai was trapped out there; she could still feel a remote sense of his rage and panic. Now something that terrified both him and the Ly Kai was approaching. She had to dispel Arylla's blasting power and close the gate to the stars. Fast.

Control! Her brain screamed through her swirling thoughts. How many times must she relearn the same lesson? Control!

Kaphri drew a hard breath and exhaled, easing out fear and anger. With it she let Arylla's power flow away from her.

The storm around her increased.

So, simply releasing power outward made things worse. It must be channeled away. Where? She fought to keep her thoughts calm and focused. She had drawn the power from Arylla and driven it down into its starsign at the center of the gate in the hope of destroying the link between the two worlds. Which had unlocked this other place.

Was she able to return power back to its source?

She took a sip, a tiny sip, cautiously returning it to the star. Arylla accepted it.

Of course. The stars took back their power when their starborn died. But so much remained! It would require a massive flow to draw this power away before the glinting ball of fire arrived.

The power that fueled the opening onto the stars did not belong to her. She had summoned it. The battle was done. Bithzielp was locked outside their worlds with, she sensed, a terrible reckoning bearing down on him for things he had done. Frax, Uri, Tobin, and Seuliac were on their world, whether safe or not. If she failed to stop this new approaching force, she did not believe either world would survive.

She must become the conduit for this unrestricted flow, returning what she had summoned back to its source. Then, if she survived that, she would withdraw every flicker of Arylla's power to close the gate between the two worlds.

We do what we must do.

There was still pain and regret. But Frax had come for her. He said she was his.

Tears streaming down her cheeks, Kaphri relaxed control and gathered Arylla's inferno to her. Starpower pummeled every cell in her body as she relaxed all resistance and channeled Arylla out the Corridor gate, back to the source burning so distant in the void.

The gaping maw to the Corridor—the space filled with brilliant points of light and darkness—crackled along its edges as invisible streams of starpower glided outward and upward into infinity. The sides of the horrific portal smudged as if a thin veil settled on them.

The blur thickened as she channeled power—the star's, not hers—back to Arylla.

All the while she could still sense Bithzielp's rage and growing terror, and the warlord's harsh question: can you do it?

We do what we must do.

The space slowly shrank, like ice spreading over a pond, from a huge window down to the size of a clenched fist. Smaller still...

At the last moment, a piercing light blazed from beyond the closing pinhole, and the distant wall of the Homeworld arena shifted back into its original place with a silent yet physical snap.

Whatever happened out there beyond, it was no longer within her control or regret.

Blinking as reality pulled her into focus, Kaphri sagged with exhaustion. Arylla's power still burned fiercely inside her, but her star had not reclaimed her. Yet.

The Ly Kai woman sucked an audible breath. Her posture remained stiff with expectation as she took a tentative step forward toward Kaphri.

"We welcome the High One to her Homeworld," the Freyan Council Head said.

Kaphri stared at her blankly for a moment, then the noise of the battle behind her crashed in.

"I'm not your High One," she said, taking a wobbling step back.

Things on her world required tending.

So many bodies scattered about the arena floor! Kaphri looked around, stunned.

Several Cyrwins stood shivering in the gate's light, blood gleaming stark crimson on black hides. Slashes of pink flesh bulged from tears in their flesh. Others fought Balandra or moved through the unnatural shreds of mist, methodically delivering kill strikes with their barbed tails to the crumpled, fallen bodies. Whichever night sky reigned above the arena, it was hidden by a seething ceiling of fog, the lower layers pearlized by the gate's light.

Where were the warriors? Her mind started to scream.

Then reality jerked her. This scene of death was not her focus. She had to close this gate.

Now that she finally understood, she simply needed to release the flow of Arylla's power in the same way she had released the bindings she had placed on the Cyrwins at the base of the escarpment.

It would take much more, however, to seal the gate.

A deep breath, a silencing of the storm raging inside her... The Homeworld. The arch. The illuminated surface around her...the colors...they all vanished in a horrifyingly simple severing of her power. The blazing circle of the gate went featureless white and the unbroken wall of the arena, now gray in fog-shadow, snapped back into view. Everything plunged into eerie shadows full of moving, thrashing forms.

So much blood smeared the dull white of the gate's surface. She looked down to find herself standing in a dark pool. Its hard edge cut off in a clean line one step forward, where, seconds ago, she had stepped across to the Ly Kai Homeworld.

This was Geffitz blood.

Frax's blood.

A hand caught her upper arm. *"Bithzielp?"* Uri drove the question hard into her mind, digging for a sense of what resided there.

She winced. *"Locked out there..."* Memory of the star-filled vastness sent a shudder running through her. "*Frax said that he cannot return from that place of stars without me.*" Uri had been over there. Seen it, yes? Her heart quickened as she stared up at the blood-spattered warrior. *"Frax? Where is he? Where is the tarmeuth?"*

"The Wyxa took Frax away the minute I stepped back across. Tobin took on the tarmeuth. They're both gone. I don't know what happened—Seuliac..." His eyes raked the seething activity in the arena. *"I don't know. He was over with Tobin. This fog makes it difficult... But we have allies in the fight. The Cyrwins and the Wyxa are fighting the Balandra. You have to go, too. We'll finish this."*

"I have to seal this gate."

"Kep, Willow, you..." he paused, expression agonized. Knowing... *"Do what you must."* He spun away, slashing widely as two Balandra charged him. *"I'll do what I can to give you time."*

Dear Uri. She could not help him return to his beloved Ladrienca now. Arylla's Shades had found the way to restore Arylla-born to the Homeworld and they would eventually try to return to this world. She must prevent that.

Kaphri looked down at the blood that obscured the now-silent symbol of her Birthstar. The Wyxa said the Guardian Stone and the Winisp's blood had kept Bithzielp contained for many years. They had never said the Winisp had survived. Frax's blood... Her heart hurt so badly that she gasped.

She would have to be enough.

To seal a gate? Driving power into Arylla's sign at the center of its gate had opened up something far more massive than her Birthstar. And drawing all the star's power away was impossible. Then what?

She must embrace the source here, become one with it in this place, along with Gemma, as the Guardian of this world.

She locked in mentally, ignoring the agony Bithzielp's destruction had wreaked on her mental barriers and drew Arylla's power from of the symbol. It flowed upward, the sensation dizzying in its strength, beginning to envelop her in its white light.

Unclasping her hand, she let the Guardian stone dangle by its chain and drew the knife at her belt.

"Stop." Gemma's order snapped in her brain as the tiny dragon launched off her shoulder.

"Is there more I should—?"

A sudden impact slammed Kaphri. Arylla's light burst and vanished as she fell to the floor. Somewhere, the crystal and chain clattered against stone.

Uri? She thought, stunned.

"You!" A gray, scarred face, twisted with hatred and fury, filled her vision. Razek's breath blasted hot on her face as his weight pinned her. "You filthy vermin always ruin everything!" Cold metal pressed her skin and the shadow of dark wings loomed over her. "Where is the Master?"

Another knife blade at her throat? This was growing tedious.

"He's gone. Forever. If you stop fighting, perhaps the Wyxa will extend mercy to your people."

"Mercy? This was going to be our world! You have ruined everything. We want nothing from you but your slow death!"

The knife twitched away, his hand lifting to stab the blade into her.

Blazing pain ripped Kaphri's side. But the knife, she thought dazedly, I can see...

Razek's smirk of triumph vanished as scaly black flesh surged over Kaphri, smashing into gray wings. The Cyrwin rammed the Balandran. Its blade clattered to the gate as the two of them disappeared beyond Kaphri's sight.

Blood flowed warm down her side to mix with the cooler crimson pooled beneath her. Well, she thought dazedly, at least the Cyrwin had spared her the agony of self-doubt.

Gold flashed above her. Gemma. Circling. Waiting for her to become the savior of this world that the Guardian had abandoned her post in the Black Temple to protect. Waiting.

"I'm sorry, Gemma," she whispered mentally. In this last, critical moment, she didn't know how to finish the task.

We do what we must do. But dying here was not enough to seal the gate. It was not how starpower worked.

We do...what? Frustration wracked her exhausted body. She would die here, but it wasn't enough. She didn't know how to seal the gate. She didn't know how...

Her breath flowed out slowly as she let Arylla fade...

She heaved in air, her back arching with a sudden cough of laughter. Of course! It was so simple. Struggling to roll over, she pushed up on her side and slapped a hand into the blood. The mixed sensation of warmth and chill, her blood and Frax's, sent a tingle of strength through her as she swept her arm out, smearing crimson across the white stone. Fighting a growing numbness, she forced her arm to make the simple, broad sweeps as she traced the sign of Arylla, reversed, over the center of the gate.

As Kaphri collapsed onto her back, Gemma fluttered down to pick up the fallen Guardian Stone. She carried it over to the heart of the symbol and flicked the crystal into the pooled blood with a clawed foot. Then she slipped over to rest her head on Kaphri's cheek as the girl closed her eyes.

"It is done."

Chaos-Stepper whipped the blood from his tail barb and turned to watch the girl vanish.

The Grimmen must always be perceived as true to its word, and the Wyxa had been very precise in their instructions. The strike, low on her side, though poisoned, should not have damaged any critical organs. Now it was up to the Wyxa to save her.

The Cyrwin slammed its hooves into the mass of mangled gray flesh at its feet one last time before moving to continue its horrific task.

Inside an envelope of thickening fog that obscured his view of the gate, Uri ducked as a cord of barbed tail snaked above his head and smashed the Balandran descending on him.

The Cyrwin's timing was a bit off and the Balandran's ugly black spearhead raked across his arm as the Cyrwin flung the gray warrior back into the heavy swirls.

"Damn, that hurts! Thanks." Uri flicked away the blood that welled to drip off his fingers. He took a wobbly step forward.

"It is time for you to withdraw from the field of battle," the Cyrwin said.

Uri twisted shakily and glared. *"We're not done—"*

"You are poisoned."

The weapon clattered back to the surface as Uri vanished.

Chapter 112
Moving Forward

KLANDAR BAYNE SAID the Wyxa had snatched her from the brink of death. And yet, he added, she had suffered the least actual physical damage of them all. They had returned her to a diffwys bath in what she assumed was the chamber where they had originally held her. But, this time, on the morning she woke, the chamber wall on one side had vanished, giving her access to a small garden. The place was wild and lovely, and its boundaries seemed to expand outward every day, as if the Wyxa were responding to her increasing strength with additional space for her to explore. It was a lovely diversion, but it did nothing to temper her rising apprehension. Every morning when the Swampfather appeared to speak with her, his reply was always the same.

"How is he?' Kaphri shifted on the bench of living wood and tried to mask her stress. After asking the same question for so many days, she was sure it was a waste of effort at this point.

"Recovering." It was the same response every day.

Perhaps it was enough for the Wyxa, but not for her. *"Still in your diffwys bath?"* Waking up to climb out of the fluid was a defining moment in the healing process, giving one the option to linger and heal superficial things like scars, or to get on with life.

"Yes."

But Gemma, sitting quietly on her shoulder, had warned her: the healing green liquid could repair physical injuries. Mental wounds, however, required additional time for recovery. Or might never happen. Because of the need to take air into their lungs, some living beings could not be completely submerged in the diffwys, so it became the task of time and their own effort to heal the mind as well as they could. Sometimes the brain did not recover completely, or sometimes people forgot things they had endured during their traumatic experiences.

If that were true for Frax, she hoped he would forget those horrible moments on the hillside before the Balandra snatched him, when she had said...

No. The thought made her tighten with shame at her selfishness. She had been cruel on that hillside, driven by frustration at her inability to control her fate and their safety. Her actions were inexcusable, and she did not deserve forgiveness.

Still, her heart gave a little lift at another thought; he had come through the gate to the Homeworld and beyond after her.

Duty, her brain whispered. He was bound by duty. Her tiny secret joy plummeted again to anxiety and despair. He had to retrieve her in order for her to finish her sworn task.

A task as yet unfulfilled...

"The others?"

"They begin to move about, regaining strength." The Swampfather had denied her access to the other warriors as well. *"Preparing for the next step in your journey."*

The next step. Her heart lurched. Klandar Bayne had confirmed that after the immense struggle she and the warriors had just gone through, the Wyxa would not resist her effort to remove the barrier.

Should she suggest they go without Frax, to give him more time to heal? Uri, Tobin, and Seuliac—and Gemma—would be enough escort to get her there. That way, she could avoid an encounter with him, saving both of them from deep and painful embarrassment.

Then, with her promise fulfilled, she and Gemma could find a place on this world where they could make their home. She could run away again. A rush of heat ran over her at the recall of her threats in the guard tower of Cadarn. How the Grimmen had used Frax to counter her Wyxan-manipulated urge to use the Guardian Stone with kisses so hot and seductive...

No. She had stopped running away. She had dared to walk into a situation that nearly guaranteed her death. This was so much less. It was only a matter of her heart...

It made her so afraid that she wanted to shrivel and die.

"Please tell me when he wakes," she said. Again.

Today the garden extended down to the edge of the swamp, to a pool covered in water lilies. The pink and white blossoms sat majestically on their spires above the dark water. A new clump of greenery had revealed itself to be an arbor of artfully twisted vines. The back was closed by the natural lattice, offering a private space where she could sit and stare across the water to the blue shadows of the distant woods.

She and Frax had moved in silent, hungry despair and fear through woods like those. Memories of the things they had encountered in the swamp sent a shudder through her.

Gemma flicked and soared over the lilies, catching insects. The little dragon came to her often, spending the night in her room, but she, too, had a need to heal from her encounter beyond the Ly Kai gate, in the Corridor of Time.

"I suppose one always prefers the beauty of one's own world over another." The observation dropped into her mind, unannounced, the way it always did.

Wait! Frax? Kaphri launched to her feet to stare at him.

"I'm sorry if I disturbed you." He stopped walking and ducked his head once in apology. *"I can leave..."*

"No! No." Kaphri drew a deep breath, modifying the strength of her protest—her relief—down. Her eyes ran over him, searching for the marks of his wounds. So thin and pale! The soft white Wyxan clothing he wore covered any remaining scars. *"I simply did not expect to see you. The Swampfather promised he would tell me when you woke."*

The pallor of his skin picked up a little color. A blush? *"It hasn't been very long since I woke. They protested, but I insisted, loudly, on seeing you. And to their dismay, they find they cannot silence me now. Their whole Ankar Mekt heard my demands. I wanted to see you."* He hesitated. *"I can leave if you want me to."*

"Why would I want that?" A wave of suffocating shyness swept over her. *"Come. Please. Sit."*

His movements were slow and stiff, proving he truly had just emerged from the diffwys bath as he settled beside her inside the living stems of the arbor.

For a moment, she could only stare at him. Her heart rushed and she could barely breathe. Then it tightened, fear of what he might say next burning through her. *"The Wyxa are kind, giving me access to this place,"* she said to fill the silence.

"Kinder than our last visit," he said. Gray eyes studied her. *"How are you?"*

"Me?" She gave a short laugh. Hredroth, how brittle and false it sounded. *"I did not suffer much at all. Not like the rest of you."*

"I think you did," he said gravely. *"We came close to losing you."*

"I was not—"

"Kaphri, there is no honor in false bravado between warriors."

Bravado! How dare he compare her injuries to his! *"You were ripped and slashed, bleeding everywhere! Your feet blackened from cold."* Her anger collapsed inside of her. *"You could have died out there."*

Frax smiled slowly. *"And you could have, too. So many times I've watched you put yourself in danger for us, and each time, my heart withered a little more inside of me. Life without you would not be bearable."*

"But I said those terrible things to you." She refused to absolve herself of that guilt.

"You did what you thought was best, given our situation." He gently caught one of her hands in his. *"You were wrong, of course. But you were trying."*

The feel of his warm flesh made her heart race harder. Or was it the tone of correction in his comment, demanding a challenge? *"If I had listened to you—"*

He lifted her hand and placed a light kiss on the back before releasing it. *"There is time to discuss what would and should have happened later, with the others. This time is for us."* His sending took on a fiercer tone. *"Just understand. I do not want to lose you."*

"Nor I, you." His touch had always sent a burning sensation through her. Lying in a pile of grass beside him in the dark swamp had filled her with fear and tingling confusion, but now, simply sitting beside him stoked a deeper fire.

Now she understood desire.

Her hand remained lifted in the space between them. Heart racing with trepidation, she reached forward, her fingers gingerly daring to trace the hard line of his jaw. Moved beneath the heavy silk of his hair to caress the back of his neck.

"I don't sense the Grimmen anywhere about," he said, his sending cautiously amused. Behind it, she could feel the burn of his tight desire.

"We do not need the Grimmen's interference." This was their choice. Their much-delayed choice. Her fingers laced in his dark locks and she pulled his head down for a kiss.

His lips moved over hers. Gentle at first. Cautious. She pressed back with rising need until, with a soft moan, he swept her hard against him. His lips traced down her neck, making her gasp at the ecstatic sensation before returning to catch her mouth, separating her lips against his.

"Give us some privacy, Gemma," Frax ordered as he lifted Kaphri and carried her back to her chamber.

The little dragon happily continued her swooping dives.

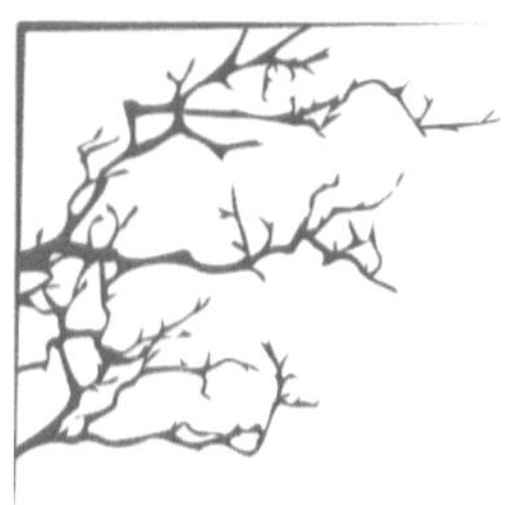

Chapter 113
The Barrier

THEY TALKED. THEY TALKED a lot on their way back to the barrier, deciding their time would be better spent putting everything they had experienced into a cohesive whole rather than accepting the offered quick Wyxan drop at their destination.

One of the first topics, of course, was Velacy. The Wyxa had reclaimed his body with the rest of the warriors and agreed to hold it until the Geffitzi returned to their southern lands. Was he a hero? Seuliac declared it, stating the younger Aedec had held steady to protect their world while knowing he inevitably faced death. The others did not disagree. They conducted their own small, silent memorial ceremony before leaving the swamp.

The Wyxa did insist on setting them down outside the northern edge of the Palenquemas rather than letting them walk across, most likely, Kaphri thought, to protect the swamp's creatures from Tobin. From there they retraced their steps northward on foot.

Frax's revelation of Bithzielp's origins drew shock and fury around their campfire, but it correlated too well with the history they knew for them to contest it. The ancient Ly Kai's claim of Geffitzi origins—that they had been exiled from the Ly Kai Homeworld—was harder to accept. Frax and Uri had both stepped across the gate to the other world without consequence, however, making it difficult to refute. They unanimously agreed that sharing the information beyond their immediate circle was outside their prerogative. They entered a blood pact, something unbreakable in a warrior's mind, to let Frax reveal the information to the Elders of the Inner Circle, who would eventually return to residence in Shada, their sacred center of learning, and let those scholars determine how to use it.

Uri told Kaphri he believed they would put the information into script and secret it away, saying there would always be a few discontents who would want to return to the Ly Kai Homeworld if they knew, and there was no need to create such a problem. At first, she thought his reasoning unfair, until he pointed out the danger it could place her in, then she agreed. The gate must remain sealed with Arylla's reversed starsign, and her and Frax's blood holding the Guardian Stone. Its location forbidden and isolated in Kep's holy domain. "A *union forged, that will span all worlds and time"* Klandar Bayne had pointed out rather smugly to the Ankar Mekt as he declared the fulfillment of the Winisp's prophecy. Kaphri was not pleased when she learned of it, or the simplistic prediction that "if she could, she would; if she couldn't, she wouldn't." Her reaction was to reject both as strongly as Frax had. She understood why he had not shared it with her: he and Uri had feared it might wrongly influence her actions. They had been successful, whether foreseen by the ancient Wyxan or not, and she would not allow it up for debate: she demanded another blood pact, to let those details remain the exclusive lore of the Wyxa.

During another discussion, Seuliac declared Frax an idiot when the commander revealed how he had made his connection with the Wyxa by snatching parts of their memories during Ankar Mekt. At the same time, the warlord had smirked and shaken his head. Tobin declared his brother an idiot, too, but far more harshly.

Gemma remained with Kaphri, the question of whether she still carried the Wyxan charge of protecting their world through their companionship, unasked for now. For Kaphri, it didn't matter. Her beloved companion had returned to her.

Tobin said the Grimmen, a bit humbled yet unapologetic, waited the return of the Kitahn clan to Cadarn, and that the Cyrwins considered certain non-Cadarnian warriors as having been distinctly honored by their cooperation. He declared that the blood chant had been annulled. Seuliac simply gave him an arrogant nod.

They debated returning to Windmer to secure grenies to send north to the holds with messages, if Kaphri would create an opening in the barrier for them to fly through. Again, they were forced to agree that any message they sent, being limited by the birds' content capacity, might endanger Geffitz lives with false hope and confusion more than it would help.

Meanwhile Uri had persuaded the Wyxa to supply them with weapons previously confiscated from past unfortunate Geffitzi invaders into their domain. There remained a threat of an encounter with a roving band of Balandra that Bithzielp might have left about. So, the need for a detour to Windmer was doubly reduced. Instead, they settled on a plan to send Tobin, who radiated eagerness, through the barrier to seek out any clans who were fighting the invaders around the Dark Zone. He would request they send a force to secure the Maugrock, to remove the risk of Balandran invasion into the south when Kaphri took away the barrier.

Afterward, she could find a way to seal the leak in the Black Temple gate.

Tales of the Battle at the White Gate, as they had come to call it, were repeated around the fire, with the warriors proudly displaying the numerous scars left on their bodies as they had hurriedly climbed out of the diffwys before it could erase them. They laughed and joked, but Kaphri recognized their bravado would never erase their memories of the horrors they had seen and experienced. She and Gemma mostly listened, sometimes in dismay, but usually in quiet contentment, happy to simply be a part of the group.

Late at night, however, she gazed at Arylla, and she thought about the barrier: what she knew of it, and what Frax had told her about his conversations with Bithzielp. They could all make plans, but the future of the Geffitzi people, and even these warriors, lay in her success at removing it.

"*What the hell?*" Frax watched as Kaphri picked up a handful of dried grass across the barrier. *"How can you do that?"*

The warriors pressed tighter around her to stare at the debris she pulled back.

"It does not resist me," she murmured in confusion. The barrier was still right in front of them, but if she had not been actively sensing for the building concentration of power, she might have simply walked through. It could explain, however, why she had never found a trace of encountering the barrier's existence in the memories the Ly Kai carried from when they fled north to Kryie Karth—or how Araxis had crossed to invade their tower refuge. *"I don't think I could pass back to the south any more than you or the Balandra without exerting power, though."*

The warriors remained firmly blocked from passing, though they were able to walk up to the invisible wall, unlike the night they had fallen through. That night a force had immobilized Kaphri and refused to let Frax approach the barrier.

Frax gave Gemma a hard, speculative glare. *"Serpent? Did you—?"*

"There are other entities at work on this world," the little dragon responded tartly.

His eyes narrowed with deeper suspicion and Uri's expression brightened with curiosity.

"Not relevant to the situation." Seuliac cut off further pursuit of the topic for now. *"Girl, focus. How are you going to remove this thing?"*

Yes. That.

She placed her hand against the surface and let her mind slip into Arylla's flow while Frax balanced on the steep slope behind her, prepared to snatch her away if anything threatened her.

Surprise rippled from her. *"It flows in one direction. How could I have missed that?"*

"Well, I doubt you could focus on analyzing the thing with your life on the line."

"True." She dropped her hand. *"Something is drawing the power of Arylla and directing the flow."*

"You still think it's...?"

Alexar. *"Yes."* It was the only explanation for how Araxis could walk free of the barrier, unhampered by the massive effort required to maintain its existence on this world. Without a physical form born of Arylla, he could not direct the star's power. The Ly Kai people's shock at Alexar's absence and Bithzielp's comments to Frax had further solidified her belief: Araxis had used his twin to channel Arylla's power and maintain the barrier. It remained her task to undo.

Was the man still alive? Not in the same sense as she and the warriors. Which would explain why Araxis had not stolen his twin's form when the Ly Kai destroyed his physical body.

"Can you locate the source?" Frax asked.

"I can follow the flow, but it might be located anywhere along it." It could take years, a trip around this world! How would they navigate the Great Water, and what if it—he—lay beneath that?

"Easy, Willow." Uri cautioned, acknowledging the intimidation he knew the prospect twisted in her. *"Araxis had ties to this area with the gate beneath the Maugrock. Let's focus around here for now."*

Sound, comforting logic.

"It flows to the east. But I don't know how far, and the terrain is treacherous." They were not fully restored to their pre-Bithzielp-encounter levels yet, though the warriors were gaining strength daily now that Tobin was adding fresh game to their diet.

The thought brought a pang of sorrow; Tobin and Velacy's rivalry for returning to camp with the largest kill had always horrified and fascinated her. Now it made for a ridiculous, bittersweet memory.

"You can't just break it with your newfound control of your Birthstar?" Seuliac asked. He was pushing bits of broken twig through the barrier. They fell to the ground on the other side, but his fingers always stopped against the firm surface.

"I can break it long enough for us to pass through," she said. *"But I can't keep it open."* The short-term solution would not help the Geffitzi clans return to the south. *"I must find the source and sever it from Arylla."*

They settled beside the stream in the cool, damp hollow where Frax had pulled the arrow from Uri's shoulder on the day they had fallen through the barrier.

Tobin slid down the hillside to join them. *"The sun is blazing out on the slope."* He plopped down on the moss and wiped away sweat. *"Two Balandra were moving about on the other side before dawn. Stealthily. Not hunting food."* The gray men had long ago depleted the game along the other side of the barrier, forcing them to range far wider in their search for food.

"Our people must be over there, rooting them out," Uri said.

General grunts of agreement sounded around her.

"We could use this to our advantage if the Balandra noticed our activity," Seuliac suggested.

"Draw the winged devils away from our fighters on the other side? Yes, if they would fall for the distraction," Frax agreed.

"The terrain across these slopes is difficult. It would be helpful if we could move along the other side, using the barrier to help negotiate it. We can't fall through," Seuliac said thoughtfully.

"It's possible," Kaphri said reluctantly. *"But it would also restrict our movement."*

"It won't matter which side we're on for an arrow to strike us, but we would make ourselves more vulnerable to capture over there," Frax cautioned.

"Agreed. We should stay on this side, but we should also contact our forces on the other side," Uri said.

Kaphri could have sworn Tobin actually gave a wiggle of anticipation, but he remained silent as he waited for the order.

Frax nodded. *"Tobin and Seuliac can make contact with our people. You and I will stay with the Priestess."*

"No. I'm seeing this through to the end," Seuliac declared. *"Tobin Kitahn will be fine on his own."*

"He's right." Tobin shrugged. *"I'll be fine."*

"You'll need a password in case you encounter Rhynog first. Take off your colors and discuss what is necessary with the warlord," Frax told his younger brother. *"You can leave around sunset."* The changing light would work against the Balandra's acute night vision.

The threadbare, ragged green and red tabard came off with a swift twist. Tobin shoved it into Uri's hand and leaned over to Seuliac.

More minutes of discussion passed as the warriors carefully crafted messages they wanted the scout to forward to their clans.

"Will he be safe?" Kaphri asked Uri apprehensively.

"No one is better suited for this task than Tobin Kitahn. Our people are down here battling the Balandran invasion. He'll locate a group of fighters, and they'll spread the news to other camps while someone escorts him back to the Circles."

She hoped she would have the way open for their people's return by the time they arrived here.

A few hours later, with a quick grin of triumph and a curt nod, the younger Kitahn vanished into the long shadows of the woods along the northern side of the border. He carried the passcodes for Cadarn, Windmer, and Rhynog, as well as several more holds that Seuliac had given up with a sardonic twist of his fine lips. The others had merely shaken their heads and shrugged silent acknowledgement at the competency of the warlord's spy network.

"Close it quickly, before the rest of us are tempted to follow him through," Seuliac growled. His white lock of hair caught a golden glint off the sunset as the scout disappeared.

Kaphri smiled sadly to herself. How long ago had she grown oblivious to that striking slash of white in his black hair? The shared bonds of their mission were beginning to break apart.

Chapter 114
Seeking the Source

"WHAT DO YOU THINK?" Seuliac asked.

The other three inched forward to peer down the edge of the gray cliff to its base hundreds of feet below. Far off in the distance, and the current point of the warlord's interest, a dark crack split the stone.

The slope they were following had ended abruptly at the top of the bluff. The barrier traced along its upper edge, sitting several feet back from the drop, but looked too unstable to cross, forcing them to their current perch high on the western edge of the rock wall.

"Interesting," Uri replied. *"We've quarried sections of this bluff for ages. Shada and Pen Gerig were built from Charydis' stone. And other structures,"* he added darkly. *"I've never encountered any historical notes about a giant split in the face. But, then again,"* he shrugged, *"we've been locked out of the south for over twenty years. Anything could have happened."*

"The important question is where that crack sits in relation to the barrier," Frax said.

"Impressive, if that's the place," Seuliac observed bitterly. *"We could never reach it from the north."* Now, knowing how the barrier worked, they agreed that if Alexar was the source, he must be located somewhere along its southern border, reasoning Araxis would want access should he ever need it.

"The cliff face projects outward on this side. So, yes. Maybe. If there's a cave or grotto inside the break that extends back deep enough..."

Kaphri sensed out to touch the barrier above them. Over the past days she'd gotten very good at locating its invisible flow without having to physically touch it.

"Great," Frax said flatly as he stared at the field of rubble and massive broken boulders far below. "Too bad we can't just leap over there."

They had learned on exiting the Palenquemas that, despite Gemma's presence, jumping to another location was no longer an option for them. The Guardian Stone lay far beyond their reach, isolated and never to be disturbed again.

It did not mean their tiny companion could not help, however.

"Gemma," Kaphri sent to the Guardian. *"Please find us a way down there."*

It took two days to backtrack and descend the steep, heavily wooded slope, and four more to traverse the rough terrain to the outer edge of rubble bordering the towering cliff.

"Kep, this thing is vast!" Seuliac squinted against the sunlight as he stared at the gray wall. *"I don't see the break now."*

"We were up high, and Charydis extends for many leagues. We just need to keep moving east," Uri told him. *"History says our people were forced to quarry stone in this area when Bithzielp..."* he broke off, drawing a deep breath before continuing. *"Our people have quarried along it many times since, so be careful moving around the big stuff. You could step off into a pit."*

"This place can be seen for miles out over your lands." Kaphri glanced from the clear blue sky to the rolling landscape behind them.

"But would it suit Araxis' purpose?" Frax asked.

"I think so. Arylla would clearly track across this place."

Muttered curses contrasted with a sense of rising hope around her.

"And now?" Frax gave her the expectant look, once so irritating, that she had grown to recognize as respect for the possible contribution of her knowledge.

The sense of the barrier had faded as they moved away, but had risen again as they wound their way through the rubble and massive gray slabs toward the base.

"I can feel the flow faintly from above. It is still moving eastward."

"Then let's find that damn crack."

The crack sat wide and level at the base of the cliff and narrowed as it extended hundreds of feet to a steep, narrow peak against the wall. The edges were darker than the surrounding stone.

"This is it." Fear tightened down on Kaphri so hard she could barely send. After so many days at a distance from the barrier, the power radiating from the break felt like a fierce blast. But there was also something deeper inside. Something that burned almost like the heart of her Birthstar.

"It looks like the stone has been heated to an extreme temperature," Uri murmured. His eyes traveled from the glistening edges to the black shards scattered among the gray rocks and boulders sheered from Charydis' face. *"Did he use starpower to blast the break in the cliff?"*

Gemma gently butted her little golden head along Kaphri's cheekbone, and the girl lifted a hand absently to scratch her scaled jaw as she stared at the dark slivers strewn across the flat terrain. Gray rocks and gray, packed dirt peppered with black bits that were the stone of this world, and yet not. Not even one straggling plant to break the desolation.

"Easy access," Seuliac finally shrugged.

Easy access, yes. A clean path, wide enough for them to walk single file across to the glinting, jagged break. The edge was unadorned. No one other than an Arylla-born would ever sense what a colossal, cruel, and sad monument to the selfish aspirations of one man this place was.

It was time to destroy it.

"I have to go in," Kaphri announced. *"I need to see what he did."*

"Do you sense any seals or guards on it?" Frax asked.

"No."

Seuliac glanced at her. *"Arrogance?"* A warning. The warlord was still teaching.

Araxis' arrogance. Not hers. *"Something like that."*

"When?" Frax asked.

"Now."

"Then we go with you."

It was their right.

The path led up the mild rise to the jagged break. Sunlight glinted off the dark glassine edges.

"Yes." Uri ran a thumb over the ebon edge of the crack. *"Blasted by heat."*

Blasted by star power. Traces of Arylla still lingered in it.

Kaphri mentally shuddered. Had Alexar helped Araxis direct Arylla's massive power into the stone of this world, not knowing he created his own tomb?

Was the man still alive?

"*You said a user required a body. How can that wasted crust maintain starpower to the barrier?"* Seuliac demanded.

The desiccated corpse, its disintegrating robes neatly arranged along its length and its arms crossed on the chest—likely Araxis' last touch—lay on the cold obsidian floor. Sunlight streaming in through the gap they had entered blazed across the dried and stretched skin of the skull.

Uri gave the shorter warrior a scowl.

The warlord ignored him. *"Is he inside it, or is he lurking around us?"*

The three warriors clustered tightly in the narrow opening to the small, circular cavern. Kaphri had slid inside along the wall, being careful not to come into contact with the shriveled body that lay at its center. The barrier ran down the center length of the corpse, slicing the space into two sections. The strength of Arylla's presence singed the edges of her mind.

"Something of Alexar's physical form must remain inside for him to summon Arylla's power," she told them. A haunting, terrible thought, but it must be true.

"Which means you'll have to sever him from that source." A gentle way for Uri to say she must end another life.

The sunlight falling on the corpse dimmed as the big warrior lifted his hand to shield his eyes as he looked upward.

"Wait." Frax caught his cousin's arm, holding it still. "On the stone around the head. Do you see anything?"

In the shadow cast by the warrior's arm, a short line of purple light radiated from the floor beside the skull.

"There are more, all around the head," Uri exclaimed. "Look. They're only visible in the dimmer light."

Frax thrust up his arms to block more light. In front of them, thin veins of purple, intensified by additional gloom, radiated out to a distance of barely half a little finger's length from the stone. *"Priestess, do you see any along the body?"*

"No." Kaphri leaned to her left to study the short, dim lines of purple light radiating along the skull. *"That is not starpower."*

Every muscle in her body abruptly tightened. *"I've seen that before! Araxis tried to use it on me in Kryie Karth. He was trying to bind me to the place, to give him more time to take control of me."* The memory of being pulled along by a sense of evil, the broken purple runes churning around her while she was locked in a drugged sleep, sent chills of terror rippling over her skin. *"I don't know its origin."*

"Perhaps something he picked up from Bithzielp," Frax suggested. "*A remnant of some power stolen from another world."*

"Perhaps." Her fingers brushed the scaley coil of golden tail wrapped lightly about her throat. *"Gemma, what is this thing? What is its purpose?"*

"Frax Kitahn is probably correct. It is a casting of alien power that tethers this being to a powerful stream of this world's lifeforce."

"A ley line?" Uri exclaimed. *"Kep! Of course."*

"I don't understand." Kaphri mentally frowned.

"Kep is a living thing with streams of life energy—we call it ley—flowing through her like blood flows through our bodies. Ley lines." His expression darkened. *"The bastard tapped into her life stream to support his filthy barrier."*

"So, how do we break it?" Seuliac's hard question snapped the shock and fury that gripped them.

"I don't know. In Kryie Karth I escaped by seeking for Gemma, but the signs he cast were not fully formed then."

Uri twisted to put his back against the wall, allowing more sunlight to flood into the chamber. *"Does the position of the body seem peculiar? The sun falls on the head from sunrise until it hits the edge of the bluff directly above, and it's positioned so that rain will not touch it."*

"It's not about the sun," Frax said quietly.

Uri looked at him, puzzled. His eyes widened. *"The Even'star? It follows the same path as our sun, but across the night sky..."*

Kaphri looked up. Sensed out. Gasped. *"Hredroth! Yes! Arylla always follows a path over this break."* Since discovering her Birthstar, she was constantly aware of its placement around this world in regard to herself, but, with all the twists and turns of their journey, she had never realized the star's path remained constant in regard to the world's rotation.

"A perfect nexus of powers. Closing this crack will not affect it." Seuliac summed it up.

"No. And moving him," which she doubted they could do, *"will not weaken it. Arylla's power flows unrestrained in this place."*

Frax squatted to examine the remains of the head. *"Is that a bloodsign similar to the one you had painted on your forehead?*

A flutter of panic ran over her at the memory of Razek slicing her arm and draining her blood into a filthy basin to paint Arylla's reversed starsign on her forehead and lock away all her starpower. She had done something similar on the gate between worlds. But the brown, stained symbols painted on the dried flesh in front of her were far more complex. *"This is something more complicated. This bloodsign is holding the channel controlling his starpower trapped open, directing the flow into the barrier."*

"Didn't you sever its influence by washing the sign away?"

"I had the Winisp's dried blood from the Guardian Stone on my hand, working to counter the sign. I would not attempt to wash this away with only water. I need his blood."

Dismayed realization swept over them all. There was no way she could get that from this dried corpse.

"We could go into the Black Temple and try to get some of that blood," Uri suggested. *"If any remains. It crumbled and vanished when I tried to catch it before."*

"It may have completely disappeared after I removed the Guardian Stone from the gate. And I no longer carry the Guardian Stone, to jump us in." With the possibility of Balandra still holding the Black Tower, invading the temple beneath was very dangerous.

Unless it became a last resort.

"Can you just smash the skull?"

"Really, Warlord?"

Seuliac smirked at Uri's exasperated expression.

Such an abrupt break might prove devastating to them and their world. Or the power might seek to transfer to her.

"Let's consider everything before we settle on trying that," Frax suggested.

Kaphri returned her attention to the bloodsign. The swoop of a line, the loop as it flowed. Her need forced clarity. There! It suddenly stood out from the tangle of dark lines. *"Arylla, painted open. And there's a symbol of binding, too! Araxis bound him to this place."*

"To the ley line," Uri said grimly.

"How do you remove it?" Seuliac asked.

"Do we really want to? We just got rid of one of these madmen. There's no gate around here to shove him through."

"Good point."

She looked up at the others. *"It's meant to keep a part of his mind viable so he can channel power."*

"So, is he still aware inside that crust?"

A valid question. Kaphri looked around the chamber. The area across the barrier from her was empty, but when she twisted to look further to her side, something rustled against the shift of her foot. A small metal bowl lay on its side in the dim light. A matching one lay an arm's length past it.

"Careful," Uri cautioned as she reached to gather them up for inspection.

The refugees in the tower of Kryie Karth had vigorously hoarded their scanty personal possessions. Beyond the books Hyfas had taught from, there were few Ly Kai objects Kaphri had ever seen. As she turned the intricately worked utensils in her hands, the interior of one gleamed dully in the light. But the inside of the other was stained with dark, cracked rivulets along one side and bottom.

"They shared a drink," she told the warriors. But why the difference in the contents?

"Drugged and immobilized?" Seuliac suggested.

Possibly. It was hard to imagine anyone volunteering to lie in a cold tomb with the fire of a star burning through their brain for an eternity.

"Oh, Hredroth." She dropped the stained bowl and sidled toward the warriors. *"He used it to catch the blood!"*

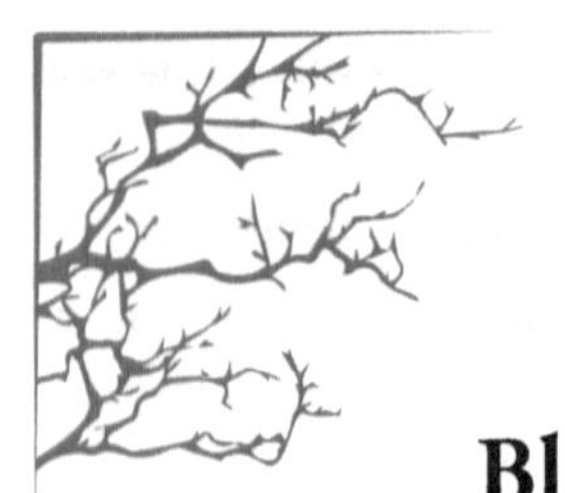

Chapter 115
Blood and Power

A DARKENING HERE, WHERE they crossed. Another there. Kaphri studied the withered skin of the forehead, disentangling the symbol that she traced in the air at the end of her prayers from the rest of the lines.

Trying to stop Arylla's massive flow with her blood would be a dangerous action. "*I have to examine the connection more closely. It's the only way.*" The rest? She didn't know anything about ley lines. Did she need to? The critical issue here was the barrier, not the force holding Alexar's body in place.

"*We can guard you,*" Frax warned, "*but we can't protect you if he mentally attacks and overwhelms you.*"

She looked up at him. "*You must strike me down if you think he's overpowered me.*"

"*That again,*" he muttered.

"*It remains a valid threat,*" Seuliac observed.

"*What if you're merely confused?*" Uri asked.

"*You cannot risk it.*"

"*We need a password,*" Frax said. "*Something with significance to us, but not to Ly Kai. That way we can be sure.*"

"*Perhaps something more intricate,*" Seuliac said. "*An image. Of the tarmeuth's den in the Grimmenwood, salted with our personal reactions.*"

He was right: a word might be grasped by the sense of its significance, without understanding, but an image was far more complex.

A shared image, mingled with their initial reactions at its first sighting, flashed between them. None would ever carry the true level of Velacy's horror, Kaphri thought sadly of their lost companion.

"That will do." Memories only encouraged hesitation at a time when she had to act. She motioned the warriors back and crouched on her knees in the sunlight. Hredroth! Would this work? Her heart raced so hard she thought it might explode.

Mentally edging toward the flow, she dared to touch the faintest edge.

It whipped her up, throwing her forward in a glorious blaze and hurtled her in so she was suddenly a speck in a roaring torrent of power. Power spun in a tightening stream about a massive, heavy center of throbbing darkness. For a fraction of a moment, total immersion with the power of her Birthstar was exhilarating. Before the burn. Before the bits of her that were lifting away. Horror flashed, reality hardened, and she began to fight back. To reclaim herself before she dissolved and scattered. Power whipped her around, drawing her down. Strands of red seethed across her vision, with darker strands following, dragging her toward the core.

"Brother. Brother, end this." The plea vibrated through the fury around her.

Kaphri's terror sent its own wave rippling out. She thrashed as Arylla's power lifted her outward and flung her forward.

For a moment she was stunned, then she realized she was inside Arylla's flow. Speeding along with it. Moving with the power that streamed around this world.

She needed to get out. But her body and mind—where...? The flow was carrying her away!

Panic flashed. Then she caught the edge of reason. Gemma. Always. Gemma was her anchor.

"Gemma!" It came out as a mental scream—she was not so calm as she thought she was. She fought her way to the edge of the flow, trying to stop her forward momentum. Sent out another call.

The answer came, more faintly than when Araxis had snatched her away from the edge of the swamp to the barrier. So much farther away! She sent again. The response came even fainter; the power of the barrier was speeding her away. Which meant there was no more time for hesitation. Focusing harder than she had ever done before, Kaphri launched toward the fading presence of the little golden dragon.

The dull ring of metal. Physical pain of fingers digging into her shoulder. Uri's sharp exclamation. Gemma...

Gemma's presence wrapped around her brain. *"Safe,"* came the whisper before the torrent of Geffitzi concern spilled over it.

Frax relaxed his grip. *"What happened?"*

"Were you attacked?" Seuliac's familiar tone demanded she report immediately and objectively.

"No." She mentally stammered. She could not share the swirling maelstrom with them. *"But that won't work. It must be blood."* Hredroth!

She had to do it now, before fear froze her to inability. She looked around, locating one of the Ly Kai bowls. Picking it up, she blew on the inside to clear it of dust and set it in front of her.

She drew Frax's knife from her belt.

Uri made a low choking sound of protest and she stopped. Not because of him.

Because she knew it would not be enough.

Terrible despair rushed through her. Of course it wouldn't be that simple. *"It has to be his blood."* How was she supposed to do that? A wash of panic chilled her skin.

One of the warriors heaved a sigh. No one stated the obvious.

"Willow, you should take some time to rest." Uri gently lifted the bowl away.

Yes. A wave of exhaustion suddenly slid over her. She put her hands against the floor to push to her feet.

There was a slight, grating ring as her fingers brushed something. The other cup. Its metal rim gleamed dully in the dim light as a sense of revulsion pushed up inside her...

Hredroth—

"Wait!" She snatched it up.

"Willow—"

"No. Wait." A surge of hope pushed weariness away. *"The stains. They are his blood."*

"Stains," Seuliac said in a corrective tone. *"They are over twenty-five years old."*

"They are all I have." Kaphri rotated the cup in her hand, staring at the play of light and dark inside. She set the cup down in the same place as the previous one. *"This is the only way."*

No one protested as she drew the knife again. Battle scars, she thought as she stared at her wrist. If this worked, she would have reason to wear them proudly. She sliced her arm above the previous cut.

Blood flowed, falling to the bottom of the dark stain, rising slowly. She waited, ignored the burning sting, focused on the image in her mind, the reversed image of Arylla. To lock power inside the desiccated form in front of her. To block the torrent that streamed around this world.

Enough. She stirred the blood with a forefinger, scraping it along the interior of the cup to dissolve anything she could pick up from the black stain. The warm crimson of her own blood darkened with tiny flecks.

What would happen to that immense flow of power?

"All of you. Leave this place," she commanded the warriors.

Dismay rippled.

"Leave. Now."

"Do as she says," Uri exclaimed aloud. "Frax! We have to get out of here." He grabbed his cousin's arm and dragged him out of the entrance.

"Gemma—"

"No."

Pointless to argue with a Guardian.

Kaphri waited for the scuff of Geffitzi footsteps to fade before she closed her eyes and refocused on the image to lock it in her mind. Then she leaned forward to paint the sign of Arylla, reversed, on the dry, leathery skin. She stopped at the last moment, finger poised. What would happen to the power fueling the barrier when she broke the link to the star? Would it lash out, seeking another source?

Carefully setting the stained cup aside, she took up the empty one Uri had hurriedly dropped when he dragged Frax away. Frax. She did not want to die. But could she live without power?

"Are you sure?" Gemma asked from her perch on her shoulder as she let more blood drip into the second cup.

"If I can't reverse it, the loss of my starpower will at least make me a less desirable target for any Geffitzi seeking advantage." Kaphri scraped the lip of the cup against her skin to capture the rapidly congealing blood.

Gemma laughed gently. *"You have grown in wisdom. You must add a drop of my blood to yours. To protect you from the ley lines."*

Hredroth! She had forgotten about them!

Gemma glided off Kaphri's shoulder to perch on her thighs. The little dragon extended her tail.

Kaphri stared at the thin whip of gold. Across the scales, the small ridge of a scar drew her eyes. Gemma had told her once that she had been too slow...

"Did you—" But this was no time to discuss it.

The little dragon twitched when Kaphri nicked her tail below the scar. A drop of the Guardian's blood fell to blend with the crimson in the cup.

Heaving a deep breath, Kaphri locked the image of her Birthstar, reversed, in her mind, closed her eyes, dipped her left forefinger, and traced the blood onto her forehead. She could feel Arylla slowly fading as the blood slicked her skin. She stopped once, gasping for breath before she could complete the sign. As before, there was no pain, only a slow, vast sense of loss. Then it was done and this time, for a fleeting moment, she understood what Araxis, maybe even Bithziclp, had experienced with the loss of their physical forms and their connection to their Birthstar. Then she pushed it out of her mind. Ly Kai had done enough to this world in their quest for power.

She picked up the other cup, sent a silent prayer to her Birthstar, and began to trace the same symbol on Alexar.

The sensation was not the same now. The blood began to heat where her finger contacted the dried flesh, burning her skin. The sense of power, its resistance, pushed at her flesh. Tightening the muscles in her body, Kaphri dipped her finger again and ruthlessly continued to work against the direct, open flow of the Great Star. Its resistance pushed, twisting and causing the muscles of her hand to spasm. It tried to lock her joints.

The battle was reduced to the purest physical level, her will against the power she had locked away.

But it was working. The flow of Arylla's power was narrowing with the last few bits of clear flesh. Meanwhile, she could feel power intensifying inside the dried husk in front of her. Tiny cracks broke the surface, letting blazing shafts of Arylla's power, in brilliant white light, lance through.

"That's not good."

Light blazed down the crack in the cliff. As the warriors watched, intense beams began to shoot from breaks in the rock.

"It's breaking the stone of the cliff. It'll all come down," Frax exclaimed. He started back toward the cavern at a run.

"Frax!" Uri started to follow.

A hand caught his arm and whipped him sideways.

"I didn't go through all of this to die unsung," Seuliac shouted as he pushed past Uri and ran after Frax. "Someone has to be alive to tell this story."

White fury burned over her skin. One last bit of the sign remained open, but she could not lift her finger away from the blackened skin to complete it. Awkwardly, she tilted the bowl, letting the remaining, speckled dregs trickle down the side of her hand, down her finger, to flow before her movement.

And with a sudden, immense suck of silence, it was done. Arylla's flow was severed.

But an immense amount of its power was still trapped in Alexar's body, swirling out, feeding the barrier. Somewhere inside the corpse a part of Alexar's mind still lived, controlling his will to channel starpower, despite the death of his flesh.

The star's resistance to her gone, she dropped the cup and snatched up the knife. There was only one way to stop the flow of power...

"Please," came a faint plea.

Please do it? Please don't? Did the plea come from Alexar? The Wyxa? Kep?

The cracks in the body were splitting, Arylla's power pouring out. One chance. She had one chance to find that spark of life and free the man who clung to it. With a choked sob, Kaphri reached out with her mind and plunged down into the raging inferno, seeking for the place that lingered so she could guide the blade into it and set it free.

There! The knife haft gripped with both hands, she drove it down into the skull.

"Arylla blesses you," came the rustle of whisper.

Fingers curled in her hair, dragging her into sunlight as Arylla's unleashed power silently exploded around her.

Kitahn was a sliver of shadow rushing out of the blasting light. Seuliac, snatching blindly, caught one of Kaphri's arms and lifted her as the sound of shattering rock overhead deafened him.

He and Frax ran.

"Here," Gemma slammed a sense of direction into their minds to guide them as a horrendous roar of collapsing stone and a blast of air threw them forward.

"Uhnnh." Seuliac opened his eyes to find Uri dragging him up into the weeds beyond the cliff. "Sorry. It had to be done."

"Shut the hell up," Uri snarled as he dropped him beside Kaphri and Frax's limp forms.

Another earsplitting snap and the crash of more shattered rock brought Seuliac to a sitting position. "Is it gone, Guardian?"

"Is she alive?" Frax struggled upright beside him.

They all understood the order of the two questions: if Kaphri had not survived, it had better be for the success of the thing that had brought them all together.

"It is gone," Gemma fluttered down into the weeds beside Kaphri and gave a quick lick at the scales on her tail. *"You should wash the sign off her forehead now, before she wakes. A Guardian's protection is not infinite."*

And then... (because I would want to know)

"Well," Uri murmured as he, Seuliac, Frax, and Kaphri, with Gemma coiled discreetly about her neck, crested the slight knoll. "It looks like he found some of our people."

Kaphri could see the sky blue of Windmer Hold, the crimson and green of Cadarn, and the gray and white of Rhynog, along with additional clusters of darker green and purple. The Geffitz warriors, grouped by their houses, were a bit bedraggled and sullied by recent fighting, but they stood in proud, formal ranks on the grassy plain beside the Taprock River. Their eyes were all locked southward as they waited. Tobin, obviously having returned from a very recent scouting excursion to track their approach, stood separately, to their fore. Distance could not mask his huge grin as he straightened a bit more to stand at attention. The younger Kitahn had found them three days earlier, as they were making their way back to the slope beneath the Black Tower of the Maugrock. Once he had confirmed that all was well, he had rushed away again to organize this greeting.

"Insufferable," Seuliac observed with dry amusement. "I'm surprised he has not waved."

The silence that hung solemnly over the Geffitzi ranks was breaking, however. Sound rippled. A cheer, faint from somewhere in the back, sounded. Warriors twitched and looked about, unsure.

Tobin whooped, waved wildly, and cheers erupted across Cadarn's warriors.

"Our houses will be claiming us for now." Uri said. *"We owe them some stories."* He turned to Kaphri. *"Besides, I need to make sure you have something safe to eat tonight."* He swept her into a tight embrace, kissed the top of her head, then strolled down the slope toward a knot of warriors wearing sky blue headbands who were stirring with excitement.

Kaphri looked over at Seuliac.

Oh no... This was too soon. She was not ready for them to go.

The warlord smiled at her gently. *"My life has never been dull, but this journey has given me more than I could have ever asked for."* The smile shaded to sadness. *"This is not, however, the ending I wished for."* He had once offered to see her safely ensconced in Shada, the Geffitzi's centralized bastion of knowledge, and Velacy had frequently advocated for them to steal her away to enhance Rhynog's power. His meaning now was different. And more. *"But you know where to find me if you need me."* He stepped back and gave her an elegant, courtly bow. The lock of white in his raven black hair flashed in the sun.

"Let it be for celebration in some bawdy inn, our hair twisted in beads and braids, while we compare new badges of honor. The way warriors should meet," she told him.

"You have learned Cadarn's ways too well," he scolded. *"Until Eryni, then."* With a soft mental brush of sadness he straightened and walked down to the cluster of gray tabards emblazoned with white crosses, their ends scalloped. Unlike Windmer's troops, who were raucously milling around Uri with cheers and upthrust fists, these warriors remained ranked in rigid respect—until, a few yards before reaching them, Seuliac threw his arms wide and gave a bellowing cry. All decorum broke as Rhynog's warriors swarmed forward to engulf him in cheers.

Frax was watching her. *"You kept your word, Priestess."*

Now she was Priestess again. She could feel the unspoken question between them. Was she ready for what came next? Once, in the shadows of Omurda, he had threatened to force her back before the Ruling Circles of the Geffitzi. It would have been one Ly Kai girl against all the Geffitzi on this world.

Things had changed yet remained the same.

She drew a deep breath, the tension in her suddenly easing. She and this warrior had faced down Bithzielp and the Corridor of the Worlds together. As long as he was beside her, she would be fine. *"I am ready. But I don't want to stay there."* They were both aware of the inevitable power plays that would emerge as ambitious Geffitz leaders sought to woo her and her starpower to their side.

"After that?" They had discussed things. But once reality inserted itself, things could quickly change.

There was still only one answer. *"I think I would like to see Azay Rhiad,"* she told him. *"You, me, and Gemma."*

The tiny dragon gave a contented sigh and burrowed deeper into her shoulders.

"Yes. We'll go home." Frax offered his arm to her and they descended the slope to join Tobin and the rest of the Cadarnian warriors.

THE END

ACKNOWLEDGEMENTS

My writing journey began a long time ago, and though there were times when I could not devote time to the process, it was always present at the edge of my mind, like puzzle pieces turning to fit the whole. Being an author is a tough job, and if you choose that path, be prepared for crushing insecurity, impostor syndrome, ripping self-criticism, and disappointment. But there is also the joy of accomplishment, success, and the fellowship of other authors you connect with along the way. Some are people, living or dead, that you admire from afar. But some end up being treasured friends with whom you are privileged to share the agony and celebrate the triumphs. They are the ones who, along with a wonderful, supportive family, keep us moving forward. Endless thanks to my high school friend, Brenda Kirk, and to Joan Summers, who read my earliest, awful work. And, then there are the members, past and present, of our local writing critique group, Noel (Carol) Barton, Gerry Harlan Brown, Kimberly Bartley, and John Bowers—all amazing, published authors whom I admire. I would not have been so bold as to believe I could do this without the inspiration and the help I have drawn from you. I am so grateful.

A special thank you to my loving husband, Sam, who was always there to support me with anything I needed to get the job done. And to my baby sister, Sharon, and my brother, David, for their loving support, I love you both.

I sincerely thank you all.

Don't miss out!

Visit the website below and you can sign up to receive emails whenever Bobbie Falin publishes a new book. There's no charge and no obligation.

https://books2read.com/r/B-A-JJHN-HFVJB

Also by Bobbie Falin

The Starchild Series
Taking the Stars
Taking Control
Taking the World
Taking It All

Standalone
Flashing Dark

Watch for more at https://www.bobbiefalin.com.

About the Author

Bobbie Falin wields magic, thwarts evil forces, pilots sleek ships through space, drinks and carouses with aliens in shabby station bars, and wanders the worlds of other writers with wide-eyed wonder—in her head. Here on Earth, well that's different. Here, she records Kaphri's adventures in the Starchild Series, stows away on the *Thief's Hand*, and complicates Gideon Rhue and Mei's life in Deformation. She still feeds the local stray cats who show up for breakfast and dinner every day, and, yes, it's unreservedly true; if there were a space program to explore the stars, She'd be first in line.

Read more at https://www.bobbiefalin.com.

www.ingramcontent.com/pod-product-compliance
Lightning Source LLC
LaVergne TN
LVHW091021080826
845145LV00002B/316

9781736642221